THE SOLDIER'S CURSE

THE MONSARRAT SERIES

MEG AND TOM KENEALLY

POINT BLANK

A Point Blank Book

First published in Great Britain by Point Blank,
an imprint of Oneworld Publications, 2017
This paperback edition published 2018

ISBN 978-1-78607-382-2 (paperback)
ISBN 978-1-78607-200-9 (eBook)

Printed and bound in Great Britain by Clays Ltd, Elcograf S.p.A.

This is a work of fiction. While, as in all fiction, the literary perceptions
and insights are based on experience, all names, characters, places,
and incidents either are products of the author's imagination
or are used fictitiously.

Oneworld Publications
10 Bloomsbury Street
London WC1B 3SR
United Kingdom

MIX
Paper from
responsible sources
FSC
www.fsc.org   FSC® C018072

'There's a crime at the centre of the story, but it is the detail of early Australian life, the atmosphere and great writing that make the book special.'

Choice

'The evocation of place and time is splendid.'

Mail on Sunday

'Introduces a totally different kind of detective, while at the same time exploring with perception and wit the forces that shaped a nation...the father and daughter duo have hit on a real winner.'

Crime Review

'The Keneallys have produced a murder mystery of admirable depth.'

Sunday Times

About the Authors

Tom Keneally won the 1982 Booker Prize with *Schindler's Ark*, later made into the Academy Award-winning film *Schindler's List*. His novels *The Chant of Jimmie Blacksmith*, *Gossip from the Forest* and *Confederates* were shortlisted for the Booker Prize.

His daughter Meg Keneally has been a journalist and radio producer, and has spent more than ten years working in corporate affairs for listed financial services companies. Both live in Australia.

For Rory and Alex

BOOK ONE

PORT MACQUARIE,
NEW SOUTH WALES,
JUNE 1825

Chapter 1

For someone whose cold hands were wrapped around a cup of excellent tea, Hugh Llewellyn Monsarrat was miserable.

It wasn't the tea's fault. As it was for all the fallen, the liquid was one of his chief consolations. But he could calculate the number of cups he had drunk in servitude not as a gesture of geniality but with a hunger of loss, with his criminality settled on his shoulders. Every colonial child could tell the difference between him and, say, Doctor Gonville, as if the sentence of the court had entered the seams of the face, the fibre of fabric.

'You won't see the future in there, you know, regardless of what that witless article of a washerwoman thinks. Best just put it out of its misery.'

'And it will put me out of mine for a short while longer, I thank you,' said Monsarrat.

The tea's maker smiled. For an English gentleman, Mrs Mulrooney felt, Mr Monsarrat was a decent fellow.

Mrs Mulrooney was generally quick to see decency. While not tolerating any nonsense (and she was the chief arbiter of the behaviour that fell into that category), she rarely took serious umbrage at people. She directed her annoyance instead to objects which refused to do as they ought. She had not discussed much

3

of her history with Monsarrat – not here, where history could be painful and in any case had all the practical relevance of a fairytale – and he had not presumed to ask. But he knew she was a Wexford woman, ticketed and free-standing now.

It didn't surprise him – that trick of misdirected anger, abusing inanimate objects which could not put you on bread and water or lengthen your sentence, was typical of the more successful felons, the ones the system did not kill. Mrs Mulrooney muttered darkly when a tendril of peppery hair had the temerity to escape the confines of her white cloth cap, and glared at the kettle when it committed the sin of boiling over.

The object of her ire at present was the breadknife, which she was using to slice a fresh loaf as part of Mrs Shelborne's futile breakfast. It was letting her down by failing to be sharp enough.

'Would you ever be kind enough to sharpen this cursed thing for me?' she asked Monsarrat.

'Of course. I'll see it's done before you next need it.'

He watched her as she flitted around the room, a finch of a woman in an immaculate white pinafore over discreetly patched black skirts, small and quick with an unexpected wiry strength when called on to heave a log into the grate. The lines evident on other women her age seemed reluctant to settle on her own face in any great number.

She picked up a skillet, examined it to determine whether it was guilty of any crime, and set it to the purpose of cooking the breakfast eggs for Mrs Shelborne, who would not eat them.

'You're casting a pall today with your mood, if I may say so, Mr Monsarrat,' she said. 'And we've enough of a pall as it is.'

This was true. The physical pall of bloodwood smoke hung above her head, denied an exit by the windows closed against the winter, and a nest recently constructed in the chimney by some industrious but unwise birds. Smoke stains were crawling up the distempered brick walls towards the whitewashed ceiling. They would no doubt be admonished and scrubbed away by Mrs Mulrooney in due course.

The smoke wove in and out of an invisible miasma of anxiety, which betrayed itself in the clench of Mrs Mulrooney's jaw.

It was, as far as she was concerned, well beyond nonsense – that her mistress, a young and lively woman, should so quickly have become a prisoner in her own body, stricken by an unknown affliction which had the surgeon puzzled.

She's right, of course, thought Monsarrat. The atmosphere is thick enough without my adding to it. He appreciated, too, her habit of disguising sharpness by delivering any criticisms she felt necessary as simple statements of fact – another prison trick learned by the fortunate.

In fact, Mrs Mulrooney had more patience for Monsarrat than for many – most – others she shared the small settlement with. When he had joined the settlement two years ago, as a convict clerk to Port Macquarie Commandant Major Angus Shelborne, she'd felt pity for a gentleman like him brought low, the pity combined with an Irish delight in finding any gentleman debased.

Now, in her, both pity and delight had given way to warmth for a soul who still seemed interested in the lives of others, despite the privations and injustices of his own. He had also proved entertaining company, and didn't see her lack of letters as an impediment to their friendship. She was gratified that to be her familiar he had crossed the line between the readers who ran the world, and those who could not read and were the earth's beasts of burden, and found a friend in her.

For Monsarrat's part, one of his pleasures was to be able to come across the frost on early mornings like this and into the mothering kitchen, for tea and conversation with someone he suspected had more natural intelligence than him. As a 'Special' – a convict with skills which equipped him for more than hauling timber and breaking rocks – he was tacitly allowed certain indulgences such as visiting the kitchen, as long as he didn't make them too visible.

But now, in the second winter of his friendship with Mrs Mulrooney, the path to the kitchen was well worn, together with the path between his small hut and Major Shelborne's office, in an outbuilding beside Government House.

Coming and going, Monsarrat was aware of time's passage and was unhappy with the lack of movement in his life. He knew that His Majesty's Government intended this; that the real punishment wasn't removal from all that was familiar, but the sense of being caught in a sad timelessness, knowing that nothing was happening, or would or could happen, to interrupt the lethal, even pace of his apparently static, endless penal situation.

'I shall smarten myself up at once,' he said now. 'But I wish I could perform some service to the colony that would jolt things along, other than by opening letters and receiving dictation. I think it's going to take more than my beautiful copperplate hand to *shift* things.'

'You do have a lovely hand,' said Mrs Mulrooney, who could tell aesthetically satisfying handwriting when she saw it, despite being unable to decipher its meaning.

'Yes, I'm exceptionally useful. Is that the problem? I wonder. Am I too useful to be ticketed again?'

'You can make yourself useful for now by taking that kettle off,' she said, pointing to it dangling on its accustomed hook below the stove, flirting with the fire.

Monsarrat fetched a cloth and did as he was told. He moved deliberately, unwilling to risk a stain to his pearl-coloured waistcoat. It was one of two he owned, remnants from his interlude of freedom between penal stretches, which he'd been allowed to keep so as to cut an appropriately administrative, gentlemanly figure. Both waistcoats meant more to him than they should, and were meticulously maintained, even now when their fabric was wearing thin.

'Perhaps I should have asked to go on the expedition with the commandant,' he said.

Major Shelborne had left, very recently, in search of a river, on a rumour from an absconded convict. A man who had evaded punishment by fleeing to the bush had sent a hint of new-found pasturage to the commandant and the commandant had ridden forth, and might give the fellow a reward if the reported valley actually revealed itself. This was what had soured the dutiful Monsarrat.

6

The commandant's departure had immediately preceded the illness of his young wife, who had since progressed with alarming speed from vomiting to coughing to convulsions.

'That journey's not for scholars such as you,' said Mrs Mulrooney. 'And on top of that I should go out of my mind without your company. You have more wit than those others combined, and a ticket will find its way to you. In any case, what would you do on such a trip? They have trackers and cooks and soldiers. They've no need for a man of education.'

'Well, I shall pass the time by assisting you,' said Monsarrat.

A small brass bell near the kitchen door began to move languidly, its clapper barely grazing its sides.

Even Mrs Mulrooney knew this wasn't the bell's fault. She would have liked to be able to blame it on the object but knew its engine, young Honora Shelborne, was losing strength.

Between the kitchen and the back of Government House lay a paved courtyard, to ensure that if the kitchen burned, the house would not. The residence was surrounded on three sides by broad verandahs with sloping roofs. There was a dining room and sitting room at the front with two large bedrooms directly behind them, and wings with smaller rooms extending backwards; the kitchen sat between these arms, like a ball in a cup. But the kitchen was connected to the house by a wire, which enabled Mrs Shelborne to pull a little lever to get Mrs Mulrooney's attention. The bell's peal was getting less vehement with each passing day.

Mrs Mulrooney quickly assembled the breakfast and the pot of tea to take to Mrs Shelborne in her bedroom at the front of the house. Monsarrat knew that Mrs Shelborne lacked appetite and was more likely to ask Mrs Mulrooney to pass her a bowl to be sick in. He opened the door closer to the house to let Mrs Mulrooney through with the tray. There was not room for her *and* the tray side-on, so she had to edge the tray through first to get out into that yard between the kitchen and the house. He dashed ahead and opened the residence door which led into the dimness of the house.

Before she went on up the hallway to the Shelbornes' bedroom, Mrs Mulrooney confided in Monsarrat. 'She used to be up at the table for breakfast by seven o'clock, and always ready to do something – ride or go fishing. But now . . . that spirit's gone out of her.'

'It may yet be mercifully restored,' said Monsarrat. He knew of Mrs Mulrooney's affection for her employer, and wanted to offer what comfort he could.

'Look after the kitchen for me, mind that the fire behaves,' Mrs Mulrooney said as she stepped into the dark house.

~~~

The source of the river sought by Major Shelborne was unknown, but the source of its rumour was an absconded convict called Kiernan.

The penal settlement with its fifteen hundred convicts – all second offenders, who had confirmed the courts' wisdom in removing them from British and Irish society in the first place by now having committed colonial crimes – and the personnel required to keep them both productive and imprisoned was an oddly claustrophobic place for a town on a barely known rim of the world. Claustrophobic, because although it looked vast by some lights, it was hemmed in by three brooding mountains, an unpredictable river, and a sea whose mood, rarely tranquil, seemed to range from tetchy to irate.

These geographic limitations had the advantage, though, of serving as natural gaolers – at least that had been the intention when the penal settlement was founded four years previously by the man it was named after. Governor Macquarie saw a lot of potential in the river, timber and soil of the place, resources which could be exploited by a bonded workforce, who would be kept at their stations by the isolation from the seat of power in Sydney and by an intractable hinterland.

There were always absconders who decided to take to the Tasman Sea. The previous year, eight convicts had stolen the schooner *Isabella*. As they slid past the beaches and the cruel volcanic outcrops, the major had raced up to the signal station, which was also home to two cannon. The balls, though, had not found the ship, instead falling harmlessly into the ocean. The soldiers who had fired had been nervous, and not least about their commander's response – eight convicts and a ship was a loss that would need some explaining. But he had assured them they had done their best.

As for those who had disappeared on the *Isabella*, escape by ocean was far from a safe option, when recurrent southerly storms gave prisoners a regular demonstration of just how rough and wild the coast of New South Wales could be. Monsarrat, who had fractured dreams of escape almost every night, would look out onto the broken, riotous sea and pity anyone anywhere near, in or on it.

It was less lethal to abscond into the bush. But success often depended on the escapee's resemblance to deceased relatives of the Birpai, the tribe of well-formed men and women who had probably been on this land since before Britain could lay claim to being anything close to a civilisation.

Simon Spring, the young Scottish assistant commissary-general who managed the stores, said that the Birpai believed that all whites were ghosts of some tribe or other, and the ones they could not identify were best returned to the settlement. But occasionally the natives would see an escapee plunging through the bush towards them in whose features and markings they recognised a relative or friend returned from the dead. Often a missing tooth helped, as the natives cut out one of the front teeth with stone chisels at the time when young men were initiated.

But other escapees were quickly rounded up and returned by the bush constables, the name used by the soldiers for native men who helped in this way, and who were rewarded with rum and slop clothes, the rough canvas clothing worn by road gangs and convict labourers. Monsarrat sometimes wondered why the Birpai were so obliging, especially for so little reward. They had, after all, been here first and presumably had not invited a band of criminals and soldiers into their home.

When Kiernan escaped, they had obviously seen a dead relative returned in his features; he was also helped by his lack of front teeth. No one was better equipped to avail himself of such good fortune: Kiernan had travelled with a number of expeditions in the colony's south.

The loss of the *Isabella* still stinging, Major Shelborne had spent a lot of effort scouring the wooded foothills and penetrating the deep gullies of the mountains, looking for him amongst tree ferns larger than a house, grass trees, scribbly gum and huge verticals of eucalyptus trees. But it was impossible.

Kiernan had been a particularly troublesome convict, those who had seen him before his escape said. He kept a lurking violence in check most of the time, but unleashed it freely when provoked. On one occasion he had been hit with a stick when making a johnnycake out of meal for his supper at the convict barracks, using an ancient frying pan to cook over the fire. The frying pan was, after years of intemperate use, part sieve, but it was the only weapon he had to hand, so he used it on his assailant's head, breaking the pan rather than the skull, so the other man ended up wearing the pan around his neck, with a secondary necklace of welts quickly springing up. For that, Kiernan got a few dozen lashes on a back which was already scored from at least one other past punishment.

But the fresh cuts in his back seemed to galvanise Kiernan in a way his previous flogging had not. Kiernan had grown up with a code of conduct as strict as any army's, and more brutally enforced. The code of the street said you had a right to strike someone who struck you, and whoever started it was the greater sinner. So when he was not only punished for defending himself, but given the same number of lashes as his attacker, he came to the conclusion that he could not live within such a ridiculous system of right and wrong. This was Monsarrat's assumption, anyhow, for Kiernan had absconded shortly afterwards.

Out of a kind of envy, the other convicts felt rancour towards Kiernan, and a desire to see him caught and flogged again, and sentenced to working in chains or on the lime-burners' gang. But the garrison and the guards had never caught him.

Nevertheless, all contact with Kiernan had not been lost.

Slowly a system had developed by which Kiernan would send messages via one of the handsome and athletic young Birpai men that this or that absconder was hiding in a particular area. Kiernan was protective of his woods and did not want too many other convicts to find a home there. He would also communicate the feelings and attitudes of the Birpai, and these messages went largely ignored, centring as they did on concerns about cedar-cutters tramping through sites of great sanctity and significance to the tribe.

Now, though, Kiernan had sent a message that in his travels with the natives far to the north-west beyond the coastal range, he had found another river valley with what he said were wonderful flood plains and pasture land, and forests full of cedar. In return for this important intelligence, Kiernan sought a conditional pardon.

It was to meet Kiernan at a particular point and visit this river himself that Major Angus Shelborne had started out several days before, led by a local coastal Birpai named Scotty. With the major were Lieutenant Freddy Craddock and six mounted and armed soldiers of the 3rd Regiment, the Buffs as they were called, thanks to the buff facings on their bright red coats.

Also travelling with him were a local ex-convict with some navigational ability and three or four reliable convicts, one of them a cook. It had not been said explicitly, but they all hoped that if they found the river and Major Shelborne came back home happy, he would recommend them to the Colonial Secretary for a reduction of their sentences or even a ticket of leave. A ticket of leave would complete the transformation that their arrival in the colony had begun – at home, on their release, they would have remained condemned, their former felonry a barrier to any decent life. But the opprobrium which rang so loudly at home was more muted here. It tinged the edges of the frame, but did not blot the painting, and its absence created a space in which emancipated convicts could do very well indeed.

Monsarrat knew that, ticketed or not, there were still many traps in a man's way, and many watchers who, out of pure darkness of soul, would love to find a flaw for which a man could be sent back into servitude. Yet he, like those convicts in Major Shelborne's party, desired a ticket so keenly that he would have abandoned the comfortable kitchen and taken to the bush had he thought it would do any good.

⌘

Monsarrat considered making himself a second cup of tea, but knew Mrs Mulrooney would view this as presumptuous. Instead he opened the drawer of a sideboard – one of the few polished surfaces in the room, as it housed the good china – and extracted a whetstone. He sat at a table less substantial than it had been some years ago, thanks to regular and vigorous scrubbing, a penance imposed on it by Mrs Mulrooney, and he started work on her recalcitrant knife.

Just as he had made the edge keen enough to please her, a hammering struck up on the outer door. 'Yes!' called Monsarrat in weary permission. The door opened flat against the wall, its leather hinges complaining. In stepped smiling Private Fergal Slattery, Mrs Mulrooney's pet soldier. His red and buff coat, his plumed hat, rested in the genteel barracks; today he was dressed for work rather than show, in canvas pants, shoes he had woven from straw, and a sheepskin coat over a red shirt.

'God bless all here,' he muttered, as his mother had raised him to say. He closed the door and made sure it was properly in its frame. Then he blew on his hands to warm them and ran one of them through his brown hair. His eyes twinkled as if some fun were about to arise – but it was a futile expectation here.

'Oh, it's the gentleman fookin' convict himself,' he said, twinkling away.

'And it's the worst soldier in His Majesty's whole damned army,' said Monsarrat.

It was an established banter of theirs. Monsarrat would not have taken quietly such a statement from any other private soldier without making a complaint to the commandant. The man was at least ten years younger than him to start with. But there was something endearing about young Slattery.

He never moaned, as some of them did, about how poverty had sent them into the army and now they were no better off

12

themselves than convicts, or how drunkenness had made them take the shilling on a dare at some country fair. The truly amusing aspect of Slattery was the way he recounted serious events, wide-eyed and with unconscious humour. With Mrs Mulrooney he traded the sort of genial whimsical insults at which – Monsarrat had noticed – the Irish were so good. It was the way they expressed affection.

'And how is our Magpie today?' said Slattery, lowering himself into a chair which had never known fine upholstery and brocade, unlike its counterparts in the neighbouring building. Even humble Slattery had the right to sit while Monsarrat stood – Monsarrat might be one of the more trusted and well-treated convicts, but was still beneath all those who were free. Slattery wasn't the only one to call Monsarrat 'the Magpie'. He owed the name to the threadbare but expertly tailored black coat he customarily wore over one of his waistcoats, to his elongated nose, and to his habit of walking with both hands clasped behind his back.

Monsarrat wasn't sure whether offence was intended by those who used the name, but he took none. Magpies were silent watchers, always present but rarely noticed, offering violence only when something precious was threatened.

'The Magpie is as well as he was yesterday, and thanks you for your concern,' he said.

'Where's herself?' asked Slattery.

'She's seeing to Mrs Shelborne.'

'Oh,' said the soldier, tossing his head. 'I could surely appreciate a cup of tea from her dear old hands.'

'There's the pot, on the stove.'

The young man went to the tea chest, which Mrs Mulrooney never bothered to lock even though it contained the most expensive leaves in the kitchen, a delicate infusion flavoured with cinnamon, which was reserved for Mrs Shelborne's sole use. His back to Monsarrat, he made a great show of breathing in the scent of the forbidden leaves, then returned to the table and sat down heavily. 'Sure,' he said, 'although it isn't the same without her pouring it. I'm better off waiting.'

'And you'll be overseeing the men in the sitting room?' asked Monsarrat.

'Oh, I will,' said Slattery, nodding. 'If they know where their true interests are, they should be here in a second. For I am a demon for discipline.' He winked and laughed and Monsarrat shook his head in mock reproach.

Some wallpaper from England had arrived by way of the *Sally*, ordered by Mrs Shelborne when she'd been in better health. It had waited in the storehouse until a party of convict labourers had been put together to plaster the bricks of the sitting room and make all smooth. They would normally have laboured under one of the convict overseers, but in this case Private Slattery had been chosen because he had claimed to the major's second-in-command, the brooding Captain Diamond, that he had once worked as a plasterer and hung paper in a house in Ireland. Mrs Mulrooney behaved as if this was a deception, though her attitude to him was so indulgent that it was evident she did not blame him for the lie.

Overseeing plastering and papering was an easy job. Slattery would sit in the kitchen with Mrs Mulrooney, chatting and drinking tea, and occasionally walk in to make sure that the four convicts were doing the job properly. The four men seemed to work in good order – so Mrs Mulrooney had told Monsarrat – under a pressed-tin ceiling designed to stop the big huntsman spiders, harmless as they were, climbing down to infest the floor.

The plaster the men had put up was now cured and they were onto hanging the paper, a pattern in keeping with Mrs Shelborne's taste for green. Monsarrat had seen this wonderful paper, brought to a settlement devoid until now of such things: vibrant green with bosky white flowers that seemed to grow out of it. There were few shades of such rich colour in the bush, the swamps, the dense forests and the gullies running down the high coastal mountains, and it made Monsarrat think Mrs Shelborne was homesick. She likes green because she comes from green pastures, he thought, and full-bodied flowers because the summer gardens of her childhood were riotous with them.

14

Mrs Mulrooney, her ministrations to Mrs Shelborne at an end for now, re-entered through the kitchen door on the house side. 'It's that Slattery, sitting when he should be standing. How they ever get him upright for parade escapes me entirely,' she said.

'And may the saints smile down upon you, Mrs Mulrooney,' said the soldier, 'and spread their grace upon ye.'

'Surely enough they need to include you in that, and smile on dear Mrs Shelborne too,' said Mrs Mulrooney.

'Dear Mrs Shelborne, with all her family's money, has no need of saints and their grace,' said Slattery.

'You're an awful one for grudges against the rich, especially as a lad who spends his evenings taking money from others across a card table,' said Mrs Mulrooney, making her way to the large teapot on the hob. She got a cup from one of the low wooden shelves beside the stove – the Shelbornes' used china – and re-arranged its shelf-mates before pouring black tea for the soldier and refilling Monsarrat's cup.

'Later than most mornings,' she said. 'This all means a certain boy I know is getting utterly used to his lazy job and taking it for granted. And it means I wish he wasn't.'

'It means a boy was up late last night playing Three Card Brag. Now, I wouldn't call it taking money, Mother Mulrooney. More a redistribution of resources. Making sure everything's balanced.'

'Ah, the devil's work and you're so good at it.'

'Don't you worry. God was on my side and I lost.'

Now there was another knocking on the outside door. Private Slattery rose and opened it to admit the convict labourers, their flat hats on their heads, and their rough canvas clothes painted with broad arrows which indicated their felonious status.

'Come through then, fookin' lags the lot of you,' said Slattery. 'Mrs Mulrooney, would you be kind enough to show us into the sitting room?'

For only she had the authority. She opened the house-facing door and they trooped through the kitchen past Monsarrat, nodding to him because he had a little margin of power compared to them, being the major's clerk, and so they went out the door and into the house to work.

When Mrs Mulrooney came back, Monsarrat stood. 'I must go to the office,' he told her, as if he was some respectable banker or clerk.

'Will you come by in the morning again? I enjoy our talks, though common soldiers and felons might interrupt them.'

'Certainly. But I must go for now – I need to be in the office from half past seven lest Captain Diamond comes by and finds me not there. I'm too old to be an absconder.'

Chapter 2

The port's inhabitants had become accustomed to strangeness.

When they first arrived in New South Wales to face their antipodean punishment, many had been told stories of their new land by more experienced convicts. Stories of kangaroos, which seemed as good a name as any, as there was nothing in the new arrivals' lexicon which would have sufficed. They were said to be capable of disembowelling a man with one downward stroke from their powerful hind legs. Such stories were largely dismissed by those who heard them. Their lives contained enough brutality at the hands of their own species for them to give any credence to tales of mythical beasts with violent tendencies.

There were other oddities to be described too. The body of an otter and the bill of a duck, joined together by some unknown power. Large clumps of grey fur which clung to the trees and ate their leaves. And then cautionary tales about snakes whose venom was, as venom goes, fast as any poison vouchsafed by the devil to the tribe of serpents.

Some of those recently off the boat were more credulous than others. But some things couldn't be dismissed by even the most sceptical. The birds were different, for a start, as anyone who had been woken by their deranged cackling knew. And the seasons, which mocked the calendar months of the civilised parts of the earth by being their opposites.

When their feet struck this land for the first time, most convicts had well and truly lost track of the passage of time. They might have been voyaging for a month or a year. So a warm breeze or a chilly drizzle didn't immediately seem out of place. Until Christmas Day brought ferocious heat, or work crews stepped out into a damp June pre-dawn.

For some, this amalgamation of oddness stood like an unbridgeable barrier between them and the lands of their birth. Any distance which could give rise to such abnormality was distance indeed.

To the miles they had travelled to the colony, some convicts who had racked up a colonial conviction could add the 230 or so between Sydney and Port Macquarie, a sea journey which took between three days and two weeks, depending what mood the winds were in. By that time, the gentle rains, mild summers and familiar livestock of their former homes felt more like myths than the dreary routine which marked their life in the colony.

Still, in Monsarrat's view, one would not have expected the mundanity of a young woman stepping off a cutter to excite such interest, curiosity and speculation.

Honora had married Angus Shelborne two years previously, in a chapel near her family's estate, just before he left to take up his commission. They had met several times during his period in Ireland, as many families considered a well-turned-out officer an essential accessory to any social event. At dances, they made lively conversation. But at hunts, they began chastely to map each other's true boundaries, seeing if these went beyond the official charts, those drawn up for the daughter of a baron and a promising captain (as the major was then). Both were delighted with what they found, their personal geographies sharing many borders.

The major's family had made a tidy amount trading in wheat. People always needed wheat, Angus's father was fond of saying, no matter what other crazes or appetites might come and go. Young Angus's aptitude for all things martial, his instinctive integrity and his ability to lead assisted his advancement, but he had another advantage which was equally important – a family who could afford a commission.

Despite assumptions by those of lower castes that a title and a castle came with a guaranteed fortune, a commission could not have been afforded for Honora had she been born male. A few generations of poor stewardship and her father's ruinous gambling had seen to that. And while the family was in possession of a castle, their capacity to maintain it had been undermined by the collapse of markets after the fall of Napoleon. So while the common Shelbornes were delighted to secure an Irish peer's daughter for their son, the peer was equally delighted by their discreet payment of certain debts.

It was decided that the major (newly minted in advance of his next posting) would precede his wife to the colony, to ensure all was adequate for a highborn bride. A minor lung infection, followed by some temporary financial difficulty caused by Honora's father and his injudicious application of funds to racehorses, had delayed her passage.

Six months previously, when the cutter *Sally* finally sailed past Lady Nelson Beach, traversed the bar without incident and deposited Honora on the dock, Major Shelborne had smiled. It was an awkward smile, rusty from lack of use, too tentative to sit comfortably on the face of a professional soldier and the ruler of this small collection of humanity.

Honora's smile, by contrast, was broad and strong and lacking in self-consciousness, with none of her class of women's tendency to try to hide her teeth with tight lips. They, in any case, required no concealment as all were present and white, the teeth of a woman who had grown up in dairy country. Monsarrat had the opportunity to examine the smile at close quarters when he was presented to the young woman. He, together with the rest of the household staff and a few senior officers, had lined the dock awaiting her inspection. She shook hands with all, even the felons, clearly not sharing the view of some that moral bankruptcy was as contagious as a plague and could pass from one person to another through physical contact.

She spent more time greeting her husband's officers, and Monsarrat noticed that the young captain Michael Diamond, with a broad-shouldered frame which seemed too large for his short legs to carry, bowed particularly low and said he was delighted to see her again. Monsarrat idly wondered where they could have met before.

The major's smile became more assured with use over the next few months, as he discovered he had (as hoped and suspected) married a kindred spirit, a woman at home in the saddle and at ease with a firearm. Honora could expertly and instantly don the mask of a gentlewoman at need. But she was happiest when dragging the major (without much need for force) out for early morning rides in the direction of the new settlement at Rolland's Plains which often turned into races. She also added to the settlement's food stores, proving the equal of any of the men at shooting, felling ducks, and at one point a kangaroo, before handing the gun down to the ancient Quilty, a former convict who had spent his youth reloading guns for aristocrats until he was caught shoplifting silverware on a journey to some English town.

In another place, Honora's spirit would have been viewed as an unladylike amalgam. Here, at the world's edge, she set the boundaries of appropriate behaviour based on her own inclinations and wishes. It was her right as the settlement's ranking female.

The response of the settlement's few other women ranged from admiration to envy. Amongst the convicts, some had seen their youth leak away during the course of their sentence, taking with it any claims they might once have had to an unsoured beauty which the major's wife wore so effortlessly. They felt they could have held onto these assets for far longer had they had the same resources as the young woman, who would never know the need to steal for survival.

The settlement's fascination with Mrs Shelborne was returned, and at her husband's indulgence she was allowed to implement certain measures which she felt would improve the lives of those who lived near her, be they free or felon. She behaved like a normal landlady of some well-run village.

She was equally solicitous to the wives of officers and to the free wives of convicts who had been shipped here to share their spouses' period of sentence and lived with their husbands in huts. It was she whose will prevailed on her husband to allow extra rations for those expecting babies, and she noted the birthdays of all the settlement's children, who attended lessons at the small schoolhouse, given by a man called Wilkins. Occasionally, she would go to the schoolhouse herself and tell the children stories of dragons and princesses, creatures as far removed from their own experience as the kangaroos and platypus had been from that of their parents.

Her first experiment came to Monsarrat's attention during one of his early morning visits to Mrs Mulrooney.

The major had engaged Mrs Mulrooney in Sydney, before departing for Port Macquarie. She had been housekeeper to a family in Camden, who had decided that their antipodean adventure was all very well but it was time to return to the real world on the other side of a long voyage. The major had met the family's father at a dinner at Sydney's Government House (a far grander building than its Port Macquarie counterpart), and on his urging had interviewed the Irishwoman. He had been impressed by her former employer's praise for her efficiency, and even more so by her pleasant but forthright manner.

The housekeeper was quite taken with her new mistress. She had spent the past eighteen months looking after Government House and its sole, male resident, and longed for a little more colour and chaos in the household. This, she felt, was provided amply by Mrs Shelborne.

'She asks after my health every morning when I bring in the breakfast,' Mrs Mulrooney had told Monsarrat in wonder. 'And what's more, she seems interested in the answer.'

It was Mrs Mulrooney's health, in fact, which was the focus of Mrs Shelborne's first venture.

'She asked me to sit, if you can believe it, at the very table where she takes her breakfast. Well, never mind sitting, I nearly fell over, but of course I did as I was bade.'

Monsarrat watched Mrs Mulrooney as she spoke. Her hands, usually so efficient and assured, seemed unable to settle to anything that morning, starting a task and leaving it aside before it was finished.

'What can she have wanted?' he asked.

'Well, she said she wanted my help. In an experiment, to do with the healing powers of the ocean. She's a dote – you know I think very well of her, but at that minute I feared she might have become a little unhinged. And I must confess, I was frightened of anything involving sea water. You know the ocean is only good for drowning in, I've often said it.'

'So you have. But I'm sure Mrs Shelborne is far more trust-worthy, and she certainly wouldn't put you in harm's way. What is she proposing?'

'Has Gonville spoken to you about his … what's the word? Anyway, he said it meant water medicine.'

Gonville, or more fully Doctor Richard Gonville, laboured under the title of surgeon. He was responsible for keeping the settlement's residents alive, as far as possible. He had traded a chance at the oak panelling of Harley Street, to hear him tell it, for an office behind a partition at the end of a long, narrow room which housed the beds of the sick and infirm. He also had a dispensary, and reasonable lodgings near what would be the church. Denied many of the trimmings of a London doctor's life, he had decided to take a creative and experimental approach to maintaining the health of his charges. And he had found a willing ear in Honora.

Monsarrat had been in the major's outer office when Gonville had been summoned, and had heard that conversation as he heard all others, the door to the inner office having been inexpertly fitted to the frame.

'Yes, she's mentioned it,' said the major. 'What d'you say it's called?'

'Hydrotherapy or hydropathy, sir,' said the surgeon. 'It's not fully understood, even by me, but it entails improving one's health through immersion in sea water. My own hypothesis is that sea water contains beneficial minerals which are absorbed through the skin. I also believe the exposure to cold – just briefly, mind – improves the circulation. Makes it work harder, you see, renders it more vigorous.'

'Yes. Well, she is certainly enthusiastic about it. Just for a brief period, as you say, I suppose that can't do harm. There's the issue, though, of decorum. Of modesty. Bathing in the sea, where anyone could walk past.'

'I was intending to ask you for some assistance on that point, actually.'

Monsarrat heard the shuffling of papers, and assumed that Gonville was laying before the major the plans which had entered the inner office under his arm.

'Interesting,' he heard the major say. 'But how will you place it in the ocean?'

'It could be backed in by draught horse, and moved as the tides dictate. Of course it is only for use on the calmer days, but better than nothing.'

'And you want a work crew to build it? Very well. Cowley was a carpenter. You can have him and two others for a week.'

Monsarrat, whose job was to make this promise an administrative reality, found that the project in question was a square wooden framework, covered in canvas and open at the bottom, with wheels which would enable it to be manoeuvred into the sea. And now, it seemed, the structure was complete.

'She wants me to get in the box and go in the ocean with her,' said Mrs Mulrooney, as though trying to convince herself that this was indeed what was being requested.

'I'm sure it would be more enjoyable in there with company,' said Monsarrat.

Each Sunday, before muster and prayers in a building which also served as the schoolhouse for officers' children, Monsarrat was required with the rest of the male convict population of the settlement to take sea baths, and the colonial authorities cared not a whit for his modesty as he did so. He had come to enjoy the practice on warmer days, and had also learned to be vigilant about where he put his feet. Carpet sharks, referred to near Sydney as wobbegongs, didn't appreciate being stepped on, and weren't shy about showing their displeasure.

He decided not to mention the sharks to Mrs Mulrooney, reasoning that the wheels of the contraption would scare them off should any be lurking near the shore. 'Dr Gonville,' he said instead, 'seems to believe immersion in salt water is a powerful tonic.'

'I don't see him doing it,' Mrs Mulrooney muttered.

In fact, Dr Gonville regularly went into the ocean, bare-chested and in breeches, even in the cooler months. Mrs Mulrooney either didn't know or chose not to.

'So, will you accompany Mrs Shelborne?'

'Of course. I can't refuse. I'm to report to her any changes in my health in the days after, so she can see how well the cursed box works.'

'I'm sure it won't be as bad as you fear,' said Monsarrat.

'It will probably be worse. You know how to reach my son, should you need to inform him of my drowning.'

Mrs Mulrooney quite enjoyed the experience in the end, bobbing up and down in a linen shift with a woman for whom she had a great deal of affection. She exhorted the other servants to try it, and reported on her health in detail to Mrs Shelborne.

The settlement's few female convicts had come as rather a surprise to one of the major's predecessors, who had expected to be ruling over a collection of male felons. The women, unlike their male counterparts, did not partake in the regular Sunday bathing ritual for the sake of modesty. Mrs Shelborne had intended to ask her husband to build more boxes, so the female convicts might enjoy the experience without worsening their already degraded condition by bathing in plain sight.

Mrs Shelborne and the doctor had also collaborated on another project.

A Female Factory had been constructed earlier that year at Port Macquarie, intended as a place of both confinement and industry for the convict women. The major had informed the Colonial Secretary that he was now able to accommodate around fifty women, and asked for wool and carding supplies so that they might make themselves useful. The supplies had not been forthcoming, and neither had the women in any great number. So the inmates had been set to picking oakum – extracting fibres from hemp rope – and making nails for the settlement's building projects from nail rod sent from England.

But the settlement's lack of women meant that there was demand for females in positions of domestic service – officers' wives and the like would prefer to have somebody to help them with the daily necessities. So at Honora's urging, the major had allowed some of the better-behaved women to take up posts in the homes of their free sisters.

Those that remained, however, had to contend with the twin enemies of incarceration and boredom. They proved inept at extracting the oakum from the rope, and there were only so many nails a woman could make.

Honora begged her husband's permission to visit the women in the factory, and he allowed it as he allowed most things she asked, realising that she would get her way eventually so time might as well be saved through immediate acquiescence.

Honora told the major after the visit that she was distressed to see these women sitting and doing nothing, without enough outdoor time or exercise, wasting away. One woman, she said, was looking deathly ill, and Gonville, who had visited with her, confirmed to the major that the confinement was doing the women no favours.

Honora had timed her plea well – of those convicts who had managed to escape into the bush, a few had returned, reincarnated as bushrangers who had harried the settlement's outposts, creeping in to steal food late at night, whereupon they had been recaptured. The Female Factory, she argued to her husband, might be better put to use as a place of incarceration for these men, who far outnumbered the handful of women who currently lived there at large expense.

Wedged between Honora's pleadings on behalf of her bonded counterparts, and Dr Gonville's professional view as to the medical repercussions of such confinement, the major agreed to close the factory, the remaining women to be found situations of employment with families of good character.

Shortly afterwards, Monsarrat himself was called on to help Mrs Shelborne with another experiment.

She came into the kitchen early one morning, dressed for hunting. Mrs Mulrooney, who had been preparing breakfast, jumped back from the stove. Monsarrat, on his accustomed morning visit, stood and bowed and moved into a corner.

'Good morning, Mrs Mulrooney,' Mrs Shelborne said, smiling at the housekeeper. 'I thought I would take breakfast in here this morning, as it's on my way.'

Mrs Mulrooney began efficiently assembling a table setting to go with the breakfast, inspecting each item more closely than usual in case it had decided to become blunt, dull or cracked overnight.

Mrs Shelborne sat in the chair Monsarrat had just vacated. 'Mr Monsarrat,' she said. 'Please, sit down.'

Monsarrat was paralysed, both by the sound of the 'Mr' attached to his name, usually used by itself when uttered by the upper echelons, and by the offer to sit.

'Please,' she said. 'I have an enterprise in which I require your assistance, and I would rather not strain my neck looking up while we discuss it.'

The kindness wasn't lost on Monsarrat, who recovered some of his composure. He took the seat opposite her, remaining stiffly straight. 'I will certainly assist you in whatever way I can, madam,' he said.

'I am pleased you are willing. Tell me, Mr Monsarrat, what do you think of the prospects for rehabilitation for the convicts under our care?'

'I imagine it depends on the character of the individual,' he said.

Mrs Shelborne clapped her hands. 'Exactly so! I knew you would understand. And how, do you think, we can improve that character?'

Monsarrat, who had long abandoned the task of improving his own character, because it brought so little reward, had no concern for anyone else's, and no answer for her. Nor was one needed, it turned out. Mrs Shelborne had decided on her beneficial project and presumed everyone else would see its merits.

'I propose,' continued Mrs Shelborne, 'that character may be improved through education. The more one knows of the world, and one's place within it, the more one appreciates the necessity to uphold order. And education can raise a person's eyes, don't you think? Let them know there is more than crime and degradation. Do you agree?'

'Absolutely,' said Monsarrat, who had never thought about it in those terms. He had met many men with educations who lacked the wit to dress themselves.

'I'm so glad. So, I wish to give a series of lectures, for the convicts and anyone else who cares to come. We will start with the classics. The Greeks and Romans have given us so much, after all, including the very system of order these wretches have run foul of. I have a notion that some of our audience may need to be eased into learning, so I thought mythology might be a good place to start. All the lessons of a homily, and interesting besides. It will expose them to a system of morality without the need for preaching, which they wouldn't listen to.'

'It sounds a noble enterprise,' said Monsarrat.

Mrs Shelborne laughed. 'Nobility doesn't enter into it. You mustn't think me some sort of paragon. No, I have a personal interest. My children, when God blesses me with them, will grow up amongst free people who may be the children of these very convicts, or others like them. I wish for them a society where survival or the accumulation of wealth are not the only concerns, where people take the time to think deeply and well. It strikes me that I might play a part in creating such a society, if only in a modest way. And I would like you to help me do it.'

'I am at your disposal, Mrs Shelborne, assuming of course that the major can spare me.'

'Oh, I've spoken to him and he is very much in favour. He says you may dedicate one hour a day to the project. He tells me you can accomplish more in one hour than others do in a day. Apparently you are the best clerk he has had, and he dreads your freedom as much as you no doubt yearn for it.'

'How kind,' said Monsarrat. 'And how would you like me to assist you, in this one hour a day?'

'You, Mr Monsarrat, are going to write the lectures. Now, do you think we should start with Sisyphus, or no? They may listen more keenly as they probably feel they have their own endless burdens, or it might make them melancholy. What do you think?'

Monsarrat had not, of course, seen Honora Shelborne since she took to her bed. He found it difficult to reconcile the frail, ill and sad woman Mrs Mulrooney described, with the girl who had seemingly entranced the settlement with her inaugural lecture.

All convicts were compelled to attend, with the Buffs keeping an eye on proceedings, at the major's order rather than Honora's, since he foresaw the risk that she might be ridiculed by the lags.

She and Monsarrat had decided, in the end, to start with Hercules, in the hope that his labours and their successful conclusion might provide a model of perseverance and industry to the audience.

The lecture, as Monsarrat had written it, was somewhat dry, as befitting a clerk enumerating a collection of facts. Indeed, he knew there were punishments attached to being flamboyant.

In Honora's deft hands, it was transformed into a story with the immediacy of events which had happened yesterday, as she leaned in and related tales of Nemean lions and Erymanthian boars as though she were gossiping over a fence. She did, it must be said, avoid mention of Hercules' murder of Augeas, after the demigod had cleaned the king's infamously filthy stables and then been bilked on the promise of one-tenth of the livestock. Promoting murder as a solution to a contractual squabble was not one of her objectives.

When she summoned him to discuss their second lecture (on the cautionary tales embodied by Icarus and Prometheus), he told her the convict who cleaned the stables was now referred to as Hercules, due to the stables' frequently Augean nature. He was rewarded with an unrestrained and abandoned laugh of the kind he had only ever heard in alehouses, and only from men.

28

But she had not given that lecture, being overtaken by her illness soon after. Mrs Mulrooney had brought her tea on the broad verandah of Government House one sunny winter afternoon, so she could read and look out through the passionfruit vines over the sparkling water.

On occasions such as this, she enjoyed having Mrs Mulrooney sit with her for company. Sometimes they chatted, and sometimes Honora seemed to prefer to read her book, so Mrs Mulrooney brought some sewing so she could sit with her employer and not feel like a 'pimple on a pumpkin', as she put it to Monsarrat.

Honora tended to keep several books by her on the small round table on the verandah. Some were books designed for educated ladies, fit for her station. But she had a secret passion for rollicking adventures, which she could hide amongst the more sedate volumes from Shakespeare, Goldsmith (Fielding was considered a little too racy for the genteel) and Wordsworth. On the day her illness made its presence felt, she was engrossed in the adventures of Sir Walter Scott's *Ivanhoe*.

After a time, when most of the tea she had been absently sipping at was gone, she looked up towards the river. 'Do you know, Mrs Mulrooney, when I was little I would squint at the water and see thousands and thousands of diamonds. I wanted to get a fishing net and scoop them all up.'

Mrs Mulrooney looked up from her stitching and smiled at Honora, who returned the smile. Then her expression changed – to confusion, then alarm. She stood, dashed into the house and to her bedroom. Mrs Mulrooney ran after her, and found her hunched over her chamber pot, vomiting violently and slick with sweat.

She looked up apologetically and gave a weak smile. 'I might rest now,' she said.

Mrs Mulrooney fetched some water and gently cleaned her – a process she would need to repeat, as the vomiting was soon joined by more noxious emissions – and helped her into her nightclothes and into bed, before running to fetch Dr Gonville.

This was where Honora would stay, with Mrs Mulrooney bringing her endless quantities of tea, and food which went largely uneaten. For the first few days, though exhausted and racked by fits of coughing, she was conscious and alert. Then, as her breathing became more laboured, the convulsions started, and brought with them a delirium which had her begging her father not to commit some unknown atrocity, and asking an unknown spectre why it had followed her here. The outbursts were punctuated with increasing periods of unconsciousness.

Dr Gonville could determine whether a wound was infected by smelling it. He was far more experienced with dysentery than he had any wish to be. And he had made the regular acquaintance of smallpox, consumption and cholera, amongst a great many others. Mrs Shelborne's symptoms, however, left him perplexed. He had considered cholera but her emissions lacked the characteristic rice-water texture (knowledge of which could not be forgotten, once acquired), and there were no other cases in the settlement.

While he worried at the problem, he prescribed the only treatment he could – boiled and cooled water, as much food as Mrs Shelborne could take, and rest.

Monsarrat feared that Mrs Shelborne might never leave her bedroom, with the settlement poorer for having glimpsed a world beyond everyday survival, only to have it snatched away. With her incapacity, the settlement's small diet of grace had vanished.

Chapter 3

'Those keening banshees are driving me out of my wits!'

Slattery's outburst was accompanied by the sound of the door hitting the wall with enough force to make Monsarrat worry about the structural integrity of the hinges.

'What wits you haven't already lost to poteen,' he said, hoping to restore a sense of normalcy through reversion to their accustomed banter, and aware that the potato-based spirit, pronounced 'pocheen', was a feature of the card games Slattery attended. He was rewarded with a glare from the young man, who threw himself into a seat as though he was trying to punish it.

Monsarrat had to sympathise – the sound was beautiful, to his ears. But, entering its second hour, it was beginning to interfere with his ability to concentrate.

Mrs Mulrooney seemed likewise affected. The indulgent tutting with which she would normally have greeted Slattery's petulance was not in evidence today. 'Stop hurling yourself about – you'll have the timbers down around our ears,' she said, swatting him on the head with her cleaning cloth. 'And while the strong young soldier sits there squalling like a babe, at least the old woman and the convict are doing something.'

'Drinking tea until they grow old and die?' said Slattery. But his genial nature, which sometimes ran away like a young child trying to make a point, usually returned just as quickly. 'At least your tea, Mother Mulrooney, is a suitable drink, along with some others I could name, to eke out the course of a lifetime.'

Mrs Mulrooney succumbed to his twinkling, giving him a distracted smile and pouring him a cup of wonderfully bitter black liquid. She was right, though. So far, she was the only person making the vaguest attempt to take the situation in hand.

Mrs Mulrooney had fetched Monsarrat that morning. He was using the grey time before the sun was fully aloft to scrub his teeth with a eucalyptus twig, ensure his cravat was properly tied and his waistcoat unmarked. Monsarrat had always been particular about his personal appearance. Now it had risen to the level of obsession. His dress was as important as any soldier's uniform, distinguishing him as it did from his fellow prisoners in their slop clothing. His presentation was also one of the very few things over which he had any control.

Monsarrat was able to complete his daily preparations in the privacy of his own timber hut – a relative luxury afforded to him along with other trusted convicts, or those with wives and families at the penal station – rather than in the less congenial atmosphere of the convict barracks. He knew barracks living, and hoped never to know it again. In a pack, personal grooming could easily be seen as pretension, an attempt to separate oneself from the group. The responses ranged from derision to violence.

It was possible that the convicts who had built the one-room hut had guessed it was for one of their number who thought himself above them, a toff, as culpable as they, but with access to comforts and privileges they would never know. If they were aware, they had clearly taken their revenge in the shoddiness of the construction – surely it must have required effort and planning to engineer gaps in the woodwork which would admit chilly winds but not gentle summer breezes, and a door that fitted so poorly it would blow open at the merest waft. Like many buildings here, the floor was made of river pebbles, but these had not been packed so tightly with dirt as they had in other structures, making their surface uneven and prone to damp. And Monsarrat feared that the red earth of this place – so unlike the polite brown English soil – had designs on his waistcoats, and might yet achieve them due to its looseness amongst the pebbles.

Mrs Mulrooney had never knocked on Monsarrat's door, so she wasn't aware of its frailty. When she had knocked this morning, the door had flown open as if hit by a battering ram. It was the first time Monsarrat had ever seen her blush. 'I'm sorry, Mr Monsarrat, I intended to wait until you answered.'

'Of course, please don't worry, it's the door's fault. And as you see, I am ready. In fact, I was about to make my way to you.'

'I couldn't wait for you to get around to the kitchen this morning, Mr Monsarrat. There is a situation on which I need your most urgent advice.'

'I am in your debt to the tune of gallons of tea. How can I assist?'

'It's best if I show you. I wouldn't know where to begin to describe it.'

Together they made their way to Government House, Monsarrat struggling to adjust his loping gait to Mrs Mulrooney's small, quick steps as they climbed the hill towards the construction site which would ultimately produce the church, surrounded by the medical holy trinity of hospital, dispensary and surgeon's quarters. From there, Mrs Mulrooney fastidiously lifting her skirts to avoid the kind of mud only a building site can produce, they crossed to Government House.

Mrs Mulrooney led Monsarrat to the front of the house. As he approached, he became aware of a low, thrumming sound, felt in the gut as well as heard by the ears. The sound of human voices – female voices – singing, or at least making the same noises at the same time. Their song had none of the baroque flourish of European music, and was the more fascinating for it. It seemed to rise and fall to match the mountains and the tides of the river, rather than by any human intervention. The closest thing Monsarrat had heard was Gregorian chant, but even that was a poor approximation for the hypnotic music he was listening to now, and he began to understand why some convicts believed native women could sing spells.

Rounding the corner to the front of Government House, the entrance reserved for the free and important, Monsarrat saw perhaps fifty Birpai women, old and young, their bodies streaked with white and red, sitting on the grass in front of the house and its empty verandah. Somewhere behind the verandah's sloping roof, Monsarrat knew, lay Honora Shelborne, entering the second week of her sickness in an uncertain state of consciousness.

A few of the singers looked distracted, like women in a parish church reciting familiar prayers. They seemed to Monsarrat earnest as a company, their eyes taking in either the house or the sky, seriously concerted in what sounded like prayers. A few of them looked up, half-seeing him before their eyes flicked back to their immediate environs.

'Now, tell me,' said Mrs Mulrooney, 'what does this mean? For what purpose are they disturbing the poor woman's rest?'

Monsarrat thought. He could hear or see no meaning. 'Perhaps we should ask Mr Spring,' he said.

Simon Spring had a Birpai lover, and the Birpai seemed to like him, rather than merely adjust to his presence as they had done with white settlers in general.

'I must be back to the kitchen in case the bell rings,' Mrs Mulrooney said. 'Mrs Shelborne may have more need of me this morning, with this disturbance. Can I ask you, Mr Monsarrat, to talk to young Spring? I don't like this, but there is nothing I can do to prevent it. They don't seem to mean harm, so I don't want to get the soldiers. If Spring can tell us their intentions, we can decide what to do, hopefully before Captain Diamond notices.'

Fortunately, Monsarrat thought, the captain would be busy that morning. Major Shelborne had mandated frequent drilling for the troops – Monsarrat had transcribed the order himself – to prevent boredom. Diamond would be marching his soldiers up and down this morning, with a sense of urgency which would make you think a French invasion was imminent, and no doubt thinking himself very gallant while doing so. Only soldiers with specific assignments, like Private Slattery and his plastering job, were exempted. The military barracks and its parade ground were close to Government House – too close for Monsarrat's liking. But perhaps the sound of boots striking the ground, muskets being shouldered and unshouldered, and the captain's love of his own voice as it barked commands would allow the song to escape his attention.

'Come to the kitchen for a cup of tea first.'

So back they went, Monsarrat avoiding the accusing gaze of the blank office window as he passed. It was as he was finishing the fortifying cup that Slattery had made his abrupt entrance.

Now, having heard the plan, Slattery looked into his own nearly empty cup. 'I'll come with you,' he said. 'Spring might be more forthcoming to a soldier than a convict.'

'Ah, you have your own work to do,' said Mrs Mulrooney. 'Mrs Shelborne will need the solace of a papered sitting room as she recovers.'

And indeed, Slattery's work crew were gently knocking at the outer door, as if to atone for their overseer's roughness. They waited while Mrs Mulrooney let them in, led them through the kitchen and then across the intervening yard to the main house. 'You'd best be off,' she said to Monsarrat as she left. 'Parade won't last all day.'

As he made towards the commissariat stores, Monsarrat heard Slattery's voice from the verandah. 'Off with you, you heathen bitches,' he was yelling. 'We've a sick woman here who doesn't need your fookin' pagan screeching!'

His words failed to cause a ripple in the ocean of chanting voices.

❧

Simon Spring was a vigorous young man, despite his myopic eyes, for which he wore thick-lensed glasses. He shared Monsarrat's interest in history, and with his wages had built up a small library. It was rumoured he intended to marry his native woman, which offended some (and very possibly the offence was shared by the Birpai, if they were aware of his wish).

Like many a man taken with a native woman, Spring's chief purpose in life was to make a Birpai–English dictionary. His work was routine, and probably always would be, and this dictionary was his chance of intellectual glory.

'Mr Monsarrat,' he said, not standing. He did not share the common view of convicts as irredeemable, spoiled goods whose humanity had vanished with their offence. Nevertheless, he felt no impulse to rise as Monsarrat entered. 'I enjoyed our discussion on Celtic barrow graves,' he said, removing his glasses and absently polishing them on his shirt. 'Made me wonder how many of my own people lie in them.'

'My ancestors are more likely to be in mass graves,' said Monsarrat. 'My father's Huguenot forebears courtesy of the French, and my mother's Welsh thanks to the English.'

Monsarrat would never have made this statement to an Englishman. But he knew Spring had a rebellious streak which he kept carefully concealed. The arrangement with his native paramour, and the occasional use of the word 'sassenach' when drink had been taken, had alerted Monsarrat to its existence. He hoped to awaken it now, in hopes it might incline the man to help.

'Yes, well,' said Spring. 'Our graves, yours and mine, will be in a land which has never known our kind. I wonder whether it will revolt as it consumes us? It's not used to consuming people, you know – the Birpai leave their dead in sacred trees in the hinterland.'

'Well, they may be in a state of mild revolution as we speak,' said Monsarrat.

'Surely not! Hard to imagine a more peaceable people than the Birpai, when they have been given cause not to be, as well. What can be happening?'

Monsarrat described the scene outside Government House. 'Mrs Mulrooney is chiefly concerned with Mrs Shelborne's rest,' he said.

'As well she might be,' said Spring. 'I understand the dear lady is very ill.'

'Indeed she is, but there are other concerns. Parade will finish before noon. If Captain Diamond comes upon the scene at Government House, he may act rashly. He's been playing at soldiers all morning, you see, and he might decide he's finished with playing.'

Monsarrat knew Spring had little liking for Diamond with his clipped vowels, moustache and manner. In the major's absence, Diamond had been feeling his way through the command, and had ordered an audit of the stores, offending Spring with both extra work and the implication of thievery.

'We thought,' he said, 'if you could help us divine their intention, we might be able to convince them to disperse before any harm is done.'

'Of course,' said Spring, laying aside his ledger and standing. 'It sounds like a matter of utmost urgency.'

~~~

Spring tried to share his fascination with the Birpai and their ways with those willing to listen. Monsarrat had cause to see Spring on a regular basis, as with the rest of the settlement he lined up weekly at the commissariat stores for his rations – bread, salt beef, and vegetables, which he was encouraged to supplement with whatever he was able to grow in the small garden attached to his hut.

The patch of red dirt was, in his view, unworthy of the name garden, producing the occasional anaemic carrot or runtish bean, and despite his coaxing utterly failing to give him a pumpkin. He refused to believe this was down to his own gardening skills, adopting an attitude of which Mrs Mulrooney would have approved – it was the garden's fault.

So his visits to the store were necessary for his continued survival. On occasion he had seen Spring there in conversation with a particularly tall and strong Birpai man called Bangar, one of the bush constables, in unmarked canvas. Monsarrat was under the impression he was the brother of Spring's lover, and the pair certainly seemed friendly whenever Monsarrat saw them together, conversing in the Birpai tongue, although Bangar was an intelligent man, and also spoke English.

Bangar faded in and out of Monsarrat's daily life. In his free time (of which he had more than another, more disciplinarian commandant would have allowed), Monsarrat frequently walked down to the river, along its southern bank, turning as it emptied into the ocean, until he reached the blackened tongue of rock which jutted out from Lady Nelson Beach, pointing into oblivion. He preferred to stand at an angle to it, facing south towards the hundreds of miles separating him from Sydney. Sometimes he would take a few symbolic steps, and tell himself he had begun his journey back.

Occasionally on these walks he would find Bangar in step beside him, the man's movements quick and quiet. Sometimes they talked, sometimes they walked in silence. But Bangar noticed everything. Recently, they had seen the corpse of a pademelon – which looked like a small kangaroo – rolling backwards and forwards at the edge of the ocean. An odd place for it, as pademelons preferred the forest. Bangar frowned at this. The pademelon was his totem, he told Monsarrat. All life had its meaning and purpose.

When he had seen Monsarrat looking towards the Three Brothers, Bangar had told him the story of these mountain triplets.

The land around here, he told Monsarrat, had once been flat, and amongst its people had been three brothers whose mother was the spirit of the lake. When the brothers grew old enough to be initiated into their tribe, they were sent to other Birpai clans. The oldest, Dooragan, went to the stingray people to the north (no, Bangar smiled when Monsarrat asked, they didn't look like stingrays – the animals were their totem). The middle brother, Mooragan, went to the crab people near the sea. And the youngest, Booragan, he went south to the shark people.

Mooragan was jealous of the youngest, and tried to engage Dooragan in a plot to kill Booragan, so there would be more maternal love to go around. Dooragan refused, but Mooragan was not to be dissuaded. He pursued Booragan as the youngest walked south to meet his destiny. That destiny, unfortunately, ended with his death at the hands of his brother.

But the murder did not take place unobserved. A watchful bird, known as a willie wagtail, saw everything, and flew to the boys' mother with the news. The lake spirit was enraged, and immediately exacted her revenge on both of her surviving sons, discovering too late that only one of them was guilty.

In punishing her boys, she angered the Gamal, the head of the Birpai people and the one who had the power to dispense justice. His justice, on this occasion, was to turn the three boys into mountains – Dooragan in the north, Mooragan in the middle and Booragan in the south. He took care to position Dooragan so that the boy-mountain split the lake in two, sundering his mother's spirit.

Monsarrat was fascinated by this tale. He knew the mountains had also been named the Three Brothers by his own people, although Captain James Cook had a far more prosaic reason for giving them the name – when he saw them from the deck of his ship, he simply felt they looked alike. The fact that they had been given the same name by the Birpai countless generations ago made them seem to Monsarrat to have an independent consciousness. After that, and despite himself, he often looked warily at the looming, murderous Mooragan.

'Why do you put up with us?' Monsarrat asked on one of these walks.

'You're here, aren't you?' Bangar said.

But of course, it was a little more complicated than that. When the Birpai had first seen a party of whitefellas stumbling their way through the bush, they were somewhat amused at the newcomers' incompetence. We'll keep an eye on these ones, they thought, but they don't seem up to much.

But then more came, and more. And the rougher ones, the cedar-cutters and the like, would just as soon go through a Birpai home as around it.

The Birpai people realised that these men did not share their connection with the land. They didn't know how to use spider webs to pack a wound, how to light a fire in a canoe when fishing at night, using the right wood to keep the mosquitoes away, or how to make fishhooks from thorn trees. They didn't know how to cut a shield from a tree in a way which wouldn't kill the tree itself. They took what they wanted and more – timber, fish and, it was rumoured, sometimes women. And they seemed to believe the land would always provide more, no matter how much they abused it.

There had been skirmishes – Birpai tribesmen, protecting their land, had raided parties working upriver. From then on these parties were heavily guarded, and the Birpai spears, lethal as they were, did not have the range of the muskets which took many of their lives.

'If we'd known the nature of you, we might have speared you before there were so many,' Bangar had once told Monsarrat genially. Monsarrat smiled as though Bangar was joking, but he knew he wasn't.

'There's a lot of land, though,' said Monsarrat. 'Why not just move on a bit?'

Bangar's face tightened. 'So what if I come in and take that kitchen,' he said, 'and I say, eh Monsarrat, it's a big house up here on the hill – which used to be ours. Why don't you just go and make your tea in the bedroom? But there's no stove in the bedroom, you say. Well, this place is *our* house. We have places for hunting, places for ceremonies. Every place has a use. We can't just move on.'

'We share that, at least,' said Monsarrat. 'Neither can I.'

⟲⟳

'Oh dear,' said Spring, as they approached Government House. The verandah was again empty, Slattery clearly having given up on his haranguing. Of today's strange events, the young soldier's reaction had been amongst the strangest. Slattery, too, was on good terms with Bangar and some of the other Birpai men. On one occasion, Monsarrat had come upon a group of them on the beach, being taught Three Card Brag by Slattery, using twigs for their stakes.

'Are you doing them any favours, introducing them to the scourge of gambling?' Monsarrat had asked him later.

'Probably not, but I may be doing myself some, if the lads in the barracks get sick of losing to me,' Slattery had said.

While Monsarrat had heard the natives spoken to in the most vile manner, he had never thought to hear such verbal violence from Slattery, and wondered if the soldier's friendship with Bangar would survive the report of it from the women.

Spring seemed to be searching for the face of his own woman amongst the mass there. When he'd found her his eyes flew back to Monsarrat. 'Oh dear. I shall get them moving,' he said.

'Could you tell me, Mr Spring, what they are doing?'

Spring did not answer him; instead, he began to speak loudly in their language. Some of the older women made dismissive gestures at him. One even laughed. The laugh spread amongst them, but then they became solemn again.

Spring spoke up again. An old woman answered him in the language which sounded to Monsarrat like a cross between the cries of birds and the thud of earth – a voice in fact *from* this earth, which was not his, but to which he was condemned.

The women began to concede, rise to their feet, shake themselves and move off. A beautiful young open-faced native in a kangaroo skin and a string around her waist acknowledged Spring as she left. Spring's mistress. He seemed quite consumed with adoration. If he were a dishonest man, he could probably siphon off enough from the stores to enable him to start farming up here – not an inexpensive matter with all the goods needing to come from Sydney and at a high price. Monsarrat could see that the man would need either to fall out of love or he would live here forever, condemned for his choice of wife by the world. There were probably worse destinies. Indeed, Monsarrat knew there were.

'Sir?' said Monsarrat, not having had his original question answered.

'Oh,' said Spring, collecting himself. 'Tell Mrs Mulrooney – and Diamond if he finds out about it – that it was a prayer for Mrs Shelborne.'

'A prayer?'

Spring leaned in towards Monsarrat, although they were the only two people on the lawn able to speak English. It occurred to

Monsarrat that Spring, and the accursed Kiernan, might be the only two whites able to speak the Birpai's tongue.

'They were easing her spirit away from the earth. They are sure she will die. But that means nothing. *They*, I emphasise, believe she will die. Fortunately Mrs Shelborne does not know it.'

'Well, she is certainly gravely ill, but how would they be aware of her condition, much less care?'

'As for the caring, I told you, they are peaceable. They acknowledge things, these people. Without rancour, without barracking, without condemnation. They were acknowledging ... well – and say nothing of this – they were acknowledging her departure. There is more to it, though. They don't see themselves as owning the land, not the way we do; they believe they belong to it. That all life belongs to it. That includes us, by the way. They resent our hunting their animals and catching their fish. Resources are not so plentiful that our presence hasn't affected their own ability to eat well. But they reason that if the land will tolerate us, it must have a use for us which they cannot perceive. And therefore our lives and deaths have a relevance for them, even if they don't understand why.'

'But how do they know of her condition?'

Spring removed his glasses to polish their now spotless lenses, and Monsarrat wondered whether word of Mrs Shelborne's illness had reached the Birpai via the Scot. In fact, now he thought of it, he could see no other means for the news to travel, Kiernan being no longer part of the settlement.

'Well, at the height of her powers, Mrs Shelborne ... but I'm saying too much, Monsarrat.'

'You can depend on my discretion, sir.'

'Very well. She hunted widely. And fished. And she was indiscriminate – she took totem animals too.'

'And that made them angry?'

'Not angry, no. But there is a balance, you see. The land can only support them – and us – if no one takes more than they need. She may have taken too much. And I'm speculating now, but it may be they feel the balance is being redressed.'

He cleaned his glasses yet again. 'I suggest you tell Mrs Mulrooney they were praying for Mrs Shelborne. That is, actually, what they were doing. Praying for a peaceful passing. And so her soul does not inhabit the trees and river and blight them.'

'A peaceful passing?'

'Well, that is their view of what is happening.'

After Spring took his leave, Monsarrat decided he had enough time to quickly report to Mrs Mulrooney before Diamond came to Government House to ensure all was as it should be, and perhaps to imagine the changes he would make when he became commandant, which he saw as probable, given the major's eminent talents and the likelihood of a higher post for him.

He found her in the kitchen, cooking a broth.

'She loses all her food now,' she said as Monsarrat walked in. 'I thought maybe a broth would stay more easily where it is supposed to.'

Slattery was at the table too. A morning of yelling at women and labourers had earned him a cup of tea, he no doubt felt. Monsarrat would have preferred to talk to Mrs Mulrooney privately, but lacked the time to wait for Slattery to return to his work. In any case, Slattery was a member of their kitchen commonwealth. Not the most judicious member, but Monsarrat felt he owed Mrs Mulrooney an explanation.

As he had agreed with Spring, he told Mrs Mulrooney the women had been praying for Mrs Shelborne.

'My God,' said Mrs Mulrooney. 'And the major away chasing pastures somewhere.'

'I would not be distressed, Mrs Mulrooney. As Spring sees it, they might believe she is dying for having taken too much game, that there is some sort of cosmic set of scales at work. But she is not aware of it and nor do any of us believe that. So she has no duty to die.'

'Something has certainly befallen her,' said Mrs Mulrooney. 'It is so sudden to go from full health one day into a total decline the next, and to stay in that decline without getting better or ... well, I'll say it ... without dying. It is a strange, strange business, and if in the country in Ireland such a thing happened, people would certainly believe that curses and the fairies were at work. But this is a girl who would laugh off a curse.'

'Did Mrs Shelborne hear them singing?' Monsarrat asked.

'I think so. Her eyes were open. But who can tell? Just the same, I sat by her, at the start, holding her hand, until I came to you for help.'

'Well, neither you nor she need concern yourselves further. The matter is dealt with.'

Slattery, who had been silent, stood and handed his teacup to Mrs Mulrooney. 'You are a queen amongst housekeepers,' he said, bowing. 'But now I must return to make sure those dullards haven't made any mistakes with the papering.'

'Off with you then, you spalpeen,' said Mrs Mulrooney, smiling.

Monsarrat also said his goodbyes, feeling an urgency to be at his desk and obviously well into the day's industry by the time Diamond arrived, if indeed he did.

But the notion of an overhanging curse continued to oppress the settlement. In the days following, he heard rumours of a curse from certain of the junior soldiers and convicts, particularly those from the countryside, and he noticed as well that some, when passing the forests, which to them represented Birpai lands, made signs that seemed an attempt to ward off curses hunkered in the shadows of the trees.

Chapter 4

Monsarrat was, perhaps, alone amongst his convict brethren in liking his daily work. His status as a Special exempted him from the gangs cutting wood or hauling timber; the worst-behaved convicts had to perform this work in double irons. He avoided the attentions of the more brutal overseers, so was also able to escape the seeping ankle wounds the men of the chain gangs suffered, and the sloughing skin of those sent to work as lime-burners.

But his enjoyment went beyond relief at worse fates avoided. He liked the fact that here, as far from the world's administrative centres as you could possibly get, there was a tiny scrap of perfect organisation, and copperplate to rival any found in Lincoln's Inn, where some of his own work no doubt still resided.

This morning he walked to Government House, to the outbuilding from which Major Shelborne ruled the settlement and reported to the Colonial Secretary in Sydney. The building was divided into two rooms, the larger one serving as a study for the major, with a window looking over the ocean. Monsarrat's smaller workroom also had a window, the first he had had any claim to since his transportation.

On the shelves in his office, catalogued in huge envelopes tied with black ribbon and thick enough to have their spines inscribed, were some of the older communications between Sydney and Port Macquarie. Others, perhaps more recent and more sensitive, were kept in Major Shelborne's office, which was locked with a key but one Monsarrat was permitted to wear around his neck.

He unlocked the inner office door now and went into Major Shelborne's study. He preferred it here to his other place of work, the police house in the Government House garden. There the major, who was also the magistrate and justice of the peace, heard and adjudicated minor offences, with Monsarrat making notes on the squabbles or skirmishes or petty theft or neglect of work which made up the majority of the transgressions. The work was no more repetitive than the monthly reports and returns Monsarrat transcribed in the office next to Government House, but he would take the latter any day, and had much more liking for writing about thriving crops than about black eyes or stolen chickens.

Monsarrat picked up a number of rough written drafts of letters to Sydney which he was to transcribe in his own good hand for signature by Major Shelborne on his return.

But for this copying work, Monsarrat was a free man, or as free as was possible in his current circumstances. Port Macquarie had been intended to be a place of unremitting labour – its inmates proving themselves resilient to all but the bluntest of punishments, by virtue of their second offences. The governor's instructions to the settlement's first commandant still hid amongst the ribboned documents on Monsarrat's shelves. The governor had told him to keep the convicts' 'minds constantly employed and their bodies inured to hard labour ... they are always to be kept at work from sunrise to sunset, the whole of the weekdays, allowing only a reasonable time for their meals'.

Monsarrat had read these instructions as he had read most documents in the office, aware of the irony that the leisure time which enabled him to read them contravened the governor's instructions. The reality was that some of the convicts had far more free time than Sydney would have been comfortable with.

Diamond had now put his own stamp on the settlement by imposing extra work on a great many functionaries, like Spring in the stores and Dr Gonville, who had been asked to compile a list of all the dead for the past year, together with the cause of their death.

Monsarrat saw little point to this busy work, as such events were covered anyway in the reports to Sydney, and was grateful that Diamond had not yet got around to him, probably thanks to his relative unimportance. So once his copying was done, he availed himself of another aspect of the major's room, a collection of histories and biographies of great men, arranged in two bookcases either side of the sea-looking window and designed in their grand leather to intimidate visiting officials, soldiers and convicts.

Under Major Shelborne, tasks were only assigned which could be completed by mid-afternoon, leaving convicts with some free hours before night descended, even in winter. So once three o'clock came Monsarrat would stop for a meal, his rations cooked by one of the women and eaten off a tin plate in a mess reserved for those Specials who had proved themselves trustworthy – the convict overseers, Spring's assistant storekeeper, the coxswain, the surgeon's assistant.

Then he'd be back, read a little Roman and Greek history again, or alternate the gossipy Seneca with the fact-obsessed Tacitus (the man would have made a good clerk), or some Catullus, the Roman poet he loved. The only version in the study was in Latin, which was just as well, as some of the Roman's work made even Monsarrat blush. But he would have dearly loved to see how Catullus would have fared as a clerk – the man's habit of issuing insults, invitations and even recalls of debts in verse would have made for some interesting dispatches.

On this morning, Monsarrat took the proposed dispatches to the Colonial Secretary which were written in the major's fast hand before his departure. He went to the outer office, locked the major's door again, and sat down at his own desk, in front of his brown earthenware inkwell and the selection of pens which sat beside the great sheet of leather-bound blotting paper.

Monsarrat had also picked up reports which were to go with the major's dispatches to Sydney, standard monthly documents: receipts and issues, labour performed, infractions and punishments, convicts received and discharged.

The most notable case of the month was a man who had absconded unsuccessfully southwards, trying to walk to Sydney, but had returned himself after ten days, looking skeletal. Why do it in winter? Monsarrat thought. Surely better to wait for October, with its milder temperatures. The man deserved punishment for idiocy if nothing else. He copied the major's sentence – thirty days in the gaol on bread and water, along with the thirty lashes he had already been given.

The first commandant of the settlement had been urged by Governor Macquarie to use the lash only as a last resort, and then only up to a total of fifty lashes. He had been instructed to err on the side of mercy where a crime was uncertain. The current governor, Brisbane, had done nothing to countermand this, and in any case the major was an efficient but not a cruel man. In Port Macquarie, he had found an expression for both attributes together, as humane treatment tended to lead to better returns from the plantations and the timber parties.

He was even-handed in his punishments and knew that his future career, in this place, in this colony or in some other far-flung wing of the British world, depended exactly on that, on his calm reports and his willingness to obey the precedents of colonial punishment. But an absconder was an absconder, and there were far too many of them for a place which had been touted as providing excellent natural security. Examples must be made.

Spring's report had been compiled in haste that month, to clear some time for the audit. It noted quantities of beef, pork, flour, rice, butter, maize, wheat, tea, sugar, wine and spirits, these last two kept in a locked room at the back of the stores, and reserved for the use of the officers. Alcohol was forbidden to convicts (there was humanity, and then there was stupidity), in spite of which a great many of them seemed able to get drunk. Spring gave an account of the amounts of fish brought in by the coxswain and his crew on the days they went trawling, and rum produced from the locally grown sugar cane lived with its imported cousins in the locked room.

Gonville reported on sicknesses in the settlement – catarrh, now that winter was here, one case of pneumonia, a doomed case of consumption amongst the women. This was all nicely tabulated according to the practice of the British Civil Service, lists of illnesses, records of pregnancies and deliveries – a child had been born to an unmarried woman named Lawson – and deaths, of which there had been a balancing one, as though to keep the scales of both worlds equal.

The dead man was an old lag who had been allowed for some years to sit by the hospital in a wicker chair whenever the weather was good. He was quite mad and would have thick-accented conversations with passers-by in the belief that he was still living in a village outside Manchester and had much to report about it – men smashing weaving shuttle machines and such. After he related the tale he always said, 'And more force to their arms. Those boys know the way the world is going.' Now Port Macquarie had been relieved of this one demented voice, and it was replaced by an infant yelling for the milk of its bonded mama.

The superintendent of convicts had left a note for the major's perusal on his return. The treadmill installed at the granary was working well, he said. This contraption served as a punishment in place of lashes, having the advantage of grinding grain using the power of the legs of those sentenced to a few hours' service upon it. The superintendent reported on the number of men in chained and unchained gangs, those in cedar parties, those making bricks from the red earth, those employed at Settlement Farm and Rolland's Plains, and those on the lime-burners' gang.

This last was the worst job in the settlement, Monsarrat felt, and was only given to those not fit for other work. The lime-burners collected oyster shells and burned them to extract the lime, which was used to hold together the settlement's bricks. With the construction of the first church underway, and ships from Sydney under instructions to backload with as much lime as possible, their services were in demand, but the lime exacted a terrible toll. It was caustic and bestowed red eyes on those who worked with it, often eating away at their flesh into the bargain.

Now Monsarrat began copying the major's dispatches. They generally reported tranquillity and progress. The sugar cane growing on the allocated area near the river was flourishing (and being used to produce decent rum), as were the crops at Rolland's Plains nearby. The dairy cattle were fat from the fertile mud plain pastures and were giving good quantities of milk. The major (or Monsarrat in his stead) then briefly summarised the details of the reports of the surgeon, the storekeeper and the superintendent.

And then Monsarrat came to the section of the report which he felt did not deserve his penmanship.

The unreturned absconder Kiernan has been of some service through the intelligence he has on occasion sent us. He has reported a considerable river beyond the mountains to the north of our settlement. This could be the river that debouches into the sea near Smoky Cape. I am about to depart with an appropriate party to look for this river with the intention of following it both some distance into the hills and downriver to the sea.

We have asked Kiernan to meet on June the sixteenth. He may not have a Christian calendar, so we have also given him the number of moonrises between the date of our dispatch and the proposed meeting.

Making allowances for such a person! thought Monsarrat. Kiernan is playing you for a fool, my dear major, and you are conspiring in it. I would bet one of my pearl waistcoats that the river does not exist.

The report continued, 'Should we find the river, and the pastures which Kiernan says surround it, I propose Kiernan be given a conditional pardon for his services in guiding us there.'

So, absconding was not the sin. Doing it unsuccessfully got you bread and water, not to mention a back with thirty-times-nine scars. But if you eschewed society and managed to survive in the forest like a wild animal, and insisted on evading capture in a most embarrassing way, freedom would be yours for the price of a fictional river.

And what if you possessed one of the finest hands to cross

the seas between England and the colony? What if you could transcribe, order and organise faster than any other man on this outcrop? Then you must work for a man who sees your freedom as his sentence to a substandard clerk, a man who depends on your continued imprisonment. Then the days stretch out before you without even the courtesy of having a number, uncountable as they slither past the horizon, until they deposit an older version of you on an unknown shore.

Usefulness, as Monsarrat saw it, was a curse. He was incapable of allowing himself to do work which he viewed as below standard. But that very work kept him bound to a life he did not want. And it had, he felt, been responsible for his first crime.

As a young man, skilled in penmanship and Latin but with no particular aptitude or enthusiasm for any specific trade, he had got a job clerking for a group of young and middle-aged barristers at Lincoln's Inn. He had been terrified on his first day, seeing lawyers as enhanced specimens of humanity, with wit, intelligence and drive which had been denied him. Pleased to be of service to such greater beings, he had applied himself to taking dictation, transcribing, and organising the lawyers' affairs in a manner which earned him high regard from his gentlemen, if not a rise in salary to go with it.

Knowing he would function better if he understood the lawyers' affairs, Monsarrat took to reading any document he could. By the time he was able to identify which lawyer was about to enter by the sound his heels made on the stones outside, Monsarrat felt he had a working understanding of the legal system. And by the time he was able to identify the calibre of an approaching client by their footfall (the wealthier the person, the better the shoe leather), he had a working understanding of his employers.

But as his understanding grew, his respect diminished. The senior lawyer in the group, by dint of years lived, was industrious enough, if unimaginative and lacking in drive. The younger ones, however, in Monsarrat's opinion, knew nothing of the law or scholarship. They had merely attended the necessary number of dinners at their Inn of Court and had been able to afford to buy a £500 legal library.

His regard for the profession and those who practised it disappeared altogether the day one of the younger lawyers, worse for wear after a night of carousing, asked Monsarrat to write a brief in his stead: 'There's a good fellow.' And it turned into something altogether darker when he heard the young man accept praise on the brief from Mr Fairburn, the taciturn senior barrister who viewed praise as a finite resource which needed to be used sparingly.

Monsarrat earned enough to live in the normal London squalor for men without a fortune in a one-room lodging in Cursitor Street. The walls were discoloured by damp, but they were the only walls he saw save for the mahogany panelling of the law offices. By then he was thoroughly sick of the sight of both sets of walls.

If he left London for a provincial town, he thought, he might be able to live better and more cheaply. He had a notion of becoming a schoolmaster, and believed he could churn out better minds than those which currently inhabited the legal chambers. He had Exeter in his sights because, though it was a long way from London, he had relatives around on his mother's side and had lived there as a boy. He knew that if he stayed in the law office, he would be a clerk for life, or until his health failed.

So he sought an appointment with Mr Fairburn, knocking gently on the older lawyer's door the following week.

'Come,' said Fairburn, who was sitting at his desk with papers spread in front of him. He didn't look up as Monsarrat entered, deeming the papers of more importance. Nor did he offer Monsarrat a seat.

'Mr Fairburn, thank you for seeing me,' said Monsarrat. He noticed that the crystal decanter which sat on the older man's desk was relatively empty today. He often tried to gauge the lawyer's mood by the amount of liquid in the vessel. Empty, or close to it, was either very good or very bad, as old Fairburn had either been celebrating or commiserating the night before.

Fairburn didn't respond to Monsarrat now, knowing the young man would state his business and seeing no point wasting breath asking.

'Mr Fairburn, I would like to inform you that I have decided to leave London, and my employment with you. I am grateful for your generosity over the past two years, and I would like to respectfully ask for a letter of reference.'

'Mr Monsarrat,' said Fairburn, finally looking up. 'Be so kind as to locate the contract of employment you signed when you commenced here.'

Monsarrat went to fetch it, but he could have told Fairburn what it said: he had two years left to work for the lawyers. He had nourished a faint hope that Fairburn would overlook it, but knew Fairburn overlooked very little.

When Monsarrat laid the contract in front of the lawyer, he examined it only briefly. He too, Monsarrat realised, already knew what it said.

'Ah, yes,' he said. 'You see, you have two years left to serve here. You could of course depart without our permission, but you would have no letter of reference, and I would make it my business to ensure any prospective employer knew of your tendency to break your word.'

'I am sorry, sir, but I was hoping you would forgive the additional two years.'

'Out of the question. You are far too good a clerk. We would not be able to find one of similar quality for the same wages. That will be all for now. But see you bring the Harkness documentation to me by the end of the day.'

So Monsarrat worked on. He decided that if his usefulness was not to be reflected in his wages, he would make sure he was compensated in other ways.

His intelligence and discretion were relied on by the lawyers, even Fairburn, and if he was found in possession of a file which wasn't directly relevant to the task at hand, it was assumed it was being used in the service of one of the other lawyers, and Monsarrat's silence on the matter was seen as completely appropriate.

But outside of the daily fourteen hours Monsarrat gave to his employers, he turned his penmanship in a new direction. On the walls of the offices hung many documents saying that this or that of the barristers had been called to the British Bar and had the right of audience in the higher courts – the House of Lords, the Court of Appeal, the High Court, Crown Court and county courts. In between other work, Monsarrat took rough notes of some of these 'call to the bar' documents. He also took notes when he could of the seal and wax and red ribbon with which the documents were encrusted. At night and on Sundays, he forged a wooden seal to make the right impression, and experimented with melted wax.

He left the law offices on the day his contract expired. He took with him no financial consideration in gratitude for his years of service, nor any verbal thanks. But he did take a document, perfect in every respect except for its authenticity, admitting Hugh Llewellyn Monsarrat to the Bar at Lincoln's Inn.

Chapter 5

Monsarrat felt he had been virtuous in applying his best penmanship even to the sections of the major's report regarding Kiernan.
He collected the papers and took them into the major's study, anticipating a pleasant half-hour with the *Edinburgh Review*. It was
more liberal-minded than *Blackwood*'s, so he read the *Edinburgh
Review* to confirm his opinions and the Tory *Blackwood's Magazine*
chiefly to give himself the thrill of disagreeing. He took care to
surround himself with the signs of business, so he might lay the
magazine aside and look plausibly industrious should Captain
Diamond come by.

The captain and Major Shelborne had served together in
India and Ireland, and the major seemed to trust Diamond. It
was a trust for which Monsarrat could see no foundation, and
he could only assume it had been built from extremity, forged at
the borders of human tolerance which could generally only be
reached through war or captivity. That and the fact that the limited
number and unpredictable flaws of regimental officers available in
the colony meant that any request for a replacement would be
considered frivolous and precious by the authorities in Sydney.
The personnel of the garrison did not increase in the same way
as the ever-enlarging numbers of convicts. So the major was left

to work with Diamond, who had none of Shelborne's humanity, nor his appreciation for the nuances of life here, the understanding that accommodations and adaptations must be made to build a functioning settlement.

To the captain, anyone wearing a red coat was fully human, others less so. There were degrees, of course. Free men and women were better than convicts and natives, for example. But jumped-up convicts with a pretension bestowed on them by the ability to write a pretty letter and translate Latin were at the bottom of Diamond's heap. So for Monsarrat, the ability to look busy was as much of a shield as the well-shaped ovals the Birpai excised from trees.

He would never have thought himself to be interested in Scottish kelp farming, but found the most recent *Review* had an article on the matter, and was toying with the idea of mentioning it to Spring when he heard footsteps crossing the courtyard. They weren't strident enough to belong to Diamond; nevertheless, he calmly laid the magazine aside and picked up his pen.

The man who entered, Edward Donald, was Dr Gonville's convict orderly, an uncomplicated northerner who neither sought nor encouraged a fight, but who was quite happy to use his stout frame as a weapon if a fight couldn't be avoided. Monsarrat liked him – he spoke only when needed and didn't waste words on trivialities.

'Mr Monsarrat,' he said, 'the surgeon has asked me to leave this report for the major on his return.'

'Thank you, Donald. I'll see it reaches him when he gets back.'

'Mind, he stressed it was for the major only.'

'Of course. The seal will be intact when I put it in the major's hands.'

By the way the light was slanting onto his desk through the windows, Monsarrat thought it must be nearly time for the afternoon meal. 'Are you returning to the hospital, Donald, or going to eat?'

'To eat. The bell has gone – did you not hear it?'

'No, I didn't. May I walk with you?'

Donald made a guttural sound which could have meant anything. Monsarrat decided to interpret it as 'if you must'.

He was grateful for Donald's silence on the way to the mess. He knew that once he entered, it would be impossible to avoid over-hearing convict constables' talk of drink and women. They would be lucky to get a whiff of either, but their imaginary conquests would have been enough to fill a few lifetimes, and no one called them out on the fallacy of their tales, chiefly because those who would do so wanted to be next at spinning a yarn.

Monsarrat ate near the coxswain, Farrier, a former wool smuggler from Essex. They'd been smuggling wool out of the country to avoid excise for centuries, and when he was caught Farrier had cracked an exciseman's skull. He and Mr Neave, the harbourmaster, shared a passion for things Monsarrat failed to understand, talk of lee shores and gunwales far more impenetrable to him than ancient Greek. They could tie bowlines or splice rope without looking, their practised hands remembering the moves, in a process which was the closest thing Monsarrat had seen to a dark art.

Farrier did not talk about the years when he took wool to the Low Countries or to Dieppe. One didn't. After a time the prisoner realised there was no profit in reimagining the life that had brought him to transportation and all its indignities. In this mess, and in the other eating places around the settlement, conversation was so much about the here and now that it was as if the there and then simply didn't exist.

'Did you see the whale went north this morning?' Farrier asked Monsarrat.

'No,' said Monsarrat, 'I didn't.' He wanted to say, I'd only be interested if I could travel on its back.

'Yes, there was a whale went past this morning. Blowing. Out maybe a mile. A big one. You know what you can find, Mr Monsarrat? Off Point Plomer, there be still lots of the Spanish mackerel. Never known them late as this in the season. It's very late for the Spanish and spotted mackerel. They're generally gone by June. Lots of nice bream though. I love bream for eating. What is your estimation of the bream, Mr Monsarrat?'

'Oh,' said Monsarrat, 'oh, it's . . . it's very succulent.'

'Yes,' said Coxswain Farrier laboriously. 'That's the word there I would have used. Succulent is what they are. This be a good time of year here. We took one of the cutters right in behind the breakers and took a netful of mullet and bream. And I had the other boat fishing at the same time in the river at the Lemon Tree Hole, hauling in blackfish. This is a wonderful time of year for blackfish. I always says we are fortunate to be in a place where there are not so many human beings but armies of fish, in numbers greater than the heathen. Yes, this is a good season.'

'When is the low tide this evening?' asked Monsarrat, an idea forming.

'Now, a good question,' said Farrier. 'You get down there to that beach about four in the afternoon, and if you don't have whiting and flathead by half past four then I'd be most surprised, most surprised indeed. In fact, I would stake my soul upon it. You'll have bream out of the waves and flathead off the bottom within half an hour. Just with the handline. Whiting. And flathead. You complain to me later if it ain't so.'

The convict constables and their overseer Nathaniel Conder, a creature of small but ruthless authority over people who had none at all, were actually comparing the private capacities of a number of women of the settlement. One of them mentioned Daisy Mactier, a woman who accommodated men in return for payments in cash and kind – kind being more important here than cash was. It threw Monsarrat into a depression to think that he had visited Daisy in the same way, with the same need, as these loud men.

The settlement bell rang and everyone went promptly on their way. It was a habit they had learned. If they dallied, they would not enjoy the status they had, and would be eating with the work crews.

Monsarrat returned to his room to restore himself again with reading, but couldn't settle to it. The talk of the damnable constables had stirred him despite his abhorrence for anything they did, said or represented. His mind visited Sophia Stark, for whom he had lost his freedom a second time. But he knew his body would shortly have to visit Daisy Mactier (or more accurately call her to him), who was in his view as far removed from Sophia as clay was from marble, but who had the advantage of being present, and available for the right consideration. Monsarrat hoped a fresh fish would act as sufficient inducement.

He put away his books, locked up and went back to his hut to fetch his fishing line, and change into drill trousers, for he was sure to get wet to the knees, and made his way to Lady Nelson Beach. It was soothing to have wavelets running over his feet and to hurl the line out and feel the sinker take it into the air and deposit it, if he threw well, just beyond the breakers.

If Farrier spoke for the fish, he spoke accurately. After a few minutes he felt that electric tug at the end of the line, and quite a weight – although fish were never as heavy as they seemed at the time of the first strike.

Hauling in a bream, he killed the fish briskly with a knife, since he didn't like to see them gasp. As he was struggling to gut it in the failing light, a horseman appeared on the track that came down from the inland corner of the headland onto the beach.

Monsarrat didn't recognise him at first – an unfamiliar sensation in a place such as this, where he knew every man with sufficient liberty and means to ride a horse. But when the man stood in the stirrups to ride into the shallows, Monsarrat saw it was Captain Diamond, in a civilian suit – or mufti, as soldiers called it these days. Captain Diamond rode his grey horse along until he reached Monsarrat, and rode out of the water. He looked down at the fish, lying half-beheaded on the hessian bag.

'Not bad, Monsarrat. Not bad for a man of intellect like yourself. Perhaps we are applying your talents in the wrong place.'

'Thank you, sir,' said Monsarrat. There was nothing else to say. Strictly, he wasn't allowed to be here, or indeed in the kitchen with Mrs Mulrooney. His Majesty's Government intended Monsarrat's universe to be bounded by his workroom and his hut, regardless of what the major turned a blind eye to. Diamond did not deal in nods, winks or implied permissions. If it wasn't codified in triplicate, for Diamond it didn't exist.

But for a man who was superior to Monsarrat in every conceivable way – young, free, commissioned and mounted – Diamond seemed agitated this evening. He looked out to sea for a while and gathered inspiration for what was to be next said.

'Wouldn't you say, Monsarrat, that it is a sadness to think that Mrs Shelborne in her indisposition is locked away from such a tonic evening as this?'

'It is a sadness,' Monsarrat agreed. He knew it was important to act as though his presence on the beach with a freshly caught fish was sanctioned. If he behaved as though culpable, Diamond would not doubt his culpability for a heartbeat.

'Believe me, I have served in Madras, where there are no evenings as fine as this,' the officer said.

'I'm sure not,' said Monsarrat, drawing on the practised convict skill of neutral agreement.

Diamond looked down at Monsarrat. But his face didn't look like that of a man with the power to snuff out any lingering hopes Monsarrat had of freedom; he looked in need himself, this young man. 'You are very trusted by the major,' he observed.

'I try to earn that honour, sir,' said Monsarrat, hauling in his line. All the pleasure had gone out of the evening and only the dark lust was left. That and the necessity to talk like a white slave.

'An honour indeed, and one with which I am familiar. The major looks after his most useful tools, particularly those who perform certain tasks with which he would rather not be bothered. Messages need to be sent on occasion, you know. Sometimes to the Colonial Secretary in Sydney. But sometimes, also, more than a copper-plate hand is required. When we were stationed in Madras, I needed to convey a message on the major's behalf to a Madras nabob whose sons believe beating an English soldier to death is an activity which can be undertaken with impunity. In both cases, the major would prefer not to have his hands stained with . . . with ink.'

Monsarrat did not think Diamond was drawing the parallel out of a sense of fellowship. Possibly, instead, it was a warning. People sometimes used one tool to destroy another which had outlived its usefulness.

'It's a funny thing about servants,' Diamond said. 'They will sniff a liberty they are permitted to take even before the master has thought of it.'

Monsarrat kept focusing on his line, whipping it up and down as he hauled to dislodge imaginary kelp. He could think of no safe response.

'I could, of course, report you. But then under the current circumstances, I'd be reporting to myself. Still, what say you? D'you feel like transcribing a recommendation to the Colonial Secretary that you be sent to the work gangs? Although, you are unused to physical labour – perhaps the lime gang would better suit your capabilities.'

Monsarrat kept his eyes lowered. The panic he believed would flash from them would no doubt make things worse. 'I apologise if I've caused any offence, sir.'

'Well, apologies are fine things when they're offered freely by someone who hasn't just been caught in a transgression. Still, perhaps His Majesty could spare you one bream.'

Monsarrat thought that given the untold multitudes of fish off all the coasts of the Empire, His Majesty might not be too alarmed by the loss of a Port Macquarie bream. Nevertheless, he felt his next utterance could prove fatal. If he thanked Diamond for the indulgence, it would be tantamount to an admission of guilt. He would be saying he knew he wasn't permitted to fish for his own purposes, but had done so anyway. But failing to show gratitude might inflame the protocol-driven officer.

Fortunately, though, Diamond hadn't finished. 'Of course, I would expect a service from you.'

'Naturally, sir, it is your right to ask of me any service you wish.'

'Any service which goes towards the running of the settlement, yes. But this service is of a more personal nature. You are friendly with the major's housekeeper, the Irishwoman, yes?'

'We are on amicable terms, yes. I see her sometimes when I need to pass the kitchen on an errand for the major.'

'Hmph. And you have a great many errands for the major which take you to the kitchen, I understand. And this housekeeper is currently functioning as a nurse to Mrs Shelborne.'

'She does what she can – under the surgeon's direction.'

'Mrs Shelborne's condition is of significant interest to me. I wish to stay apprised of it so I can alert the major should he need to return. And Gonville, charming and qualified as he is, may not provide sufficient . . . texture.'

But surely you could ask Gonville for as much texture as you want, and he would be obliged to comply, thought Monsarrat. You are, after all, acting potentate. But then, he might be too busy with the Book of the Dead you have set him to writing.

Speaking that thought would have seen him back on a work crew by morning, the small privacy of his hut afforded to some other trustee, and Catullus and the *Edinburgh Review* left to their own devices.

'Housekeepers,' continued Diamond, 'know everything. This one probably more than most. Find out what you can. I am most interested in the kind of information Dr Gonville is unlikely to note. Mrs Shelborne's spirits, for example. The tenor of her speech. Any prognosis the surgeon gives in the housekeeper's hearing.'

Kiernan manages to survive in the wild, thought Monsarrat, but he might have trouble negotiating this forest. There was no way Monsarrat could refuse the captain's request. He had no doubt the young man had every intention of following through on his threats.

It was less clear, though, why the captain wanted such information. A simple inquiry as to Mrs Shelborne's condition would be enough to satisfy propriety, to show concern, and in any case could be directed to Dr Gonville. But an interest in the state of her mind, even in the way she spoke, seemed disturbingly intimate to Monsarrat, especially as he had no indication that Mrs Shelborne would welcome such interest, were she in full command of her senses.

If he were caught by the major, implicated in some sort of sordid plot to spy on his wife, he would be lucky to get the work crew. That said, Diamond might have some questions to answer himself. But if Diamond denied all knowledge, claimed that Monsarrat had a twisted fascination with Mrs Shelborne, Monsarrat wasn't sure whom the major would believe, or which tool he would view as having the greatest long-term utility. And even if Diamond was ejected from the regiment, that didn't help Monsarrat.

The worst of it, though, was that he now had to conceal information from the only person he trusted. She would think his inquiries sprang from a shared concern for the dwindling life in the settlement's best bedroom. He would extract information from her and put it to a use of which she wouldn't approve, she who had never extracted anything from him but admiration and the occasional chuckle. And he would need to make sure she never found out, as in his mind her disapproval stood alongside the lime gang, equal in both severity and permanence.

~⁓⁓~

Monsarrat washed the fish and himself in a bucket of sea water, before wrapping the bream in a cloth and trudging back to the hut to change back into his clerical garb.

Half an hour later he was walking through the settlement, the fish under his arm as though it were a copy of the *Edinburgh Review*.

The few female convicts here were mostly in service, and could not often be found wandering around the settlement waiting to be propositioned. Daisy had her own hut, but could not afford to be indiscreet. The phrase 'improper association' had the potential to bring with it an extension of her sentence. Monsarrat had to try to catch her at home, rapping quietly on the door. She would see him and nod, and he would walk away and wait for her to arrive at his own hut, assess the compensation on offer, and decide whether it was adequate.

He didn't want to be doing this. He nearly turned back several times on the way to Daisy's, as he usually did on this journey. He was driven on not by passion alone, but by the knowledge that something dark had begun to grow and gain strength inside him, and needed to be exorcised.

He knocked on the crude bark door of Daisy's hut, which opened slightly to reveal her face. There was no stab of affection when he saw her features. In the dim light she looked both agelessly young and agelessly aged.

63

She nodded, and he went to his hut to await her. I am doing this, he thought, so I'll have even better reason to dislike myself.

She walked in without knocking, and he handed her the cloth-wrapped fish. 'I caught this today.'

She opened the cloth and looked at the bream. 'Well done, Mr Monsarrat. I can't be long, so let's make it sharp.'

The transaction complete, Monsarrat was setting his cravat to rights with more than his usual haste, and less than his usual precision, anxious to have the draughty safety of his hut to himself.

'Will she educate us again, do you think, her ladyship?' said Daisy, rearranging her clothes. She, too, was anxious to be getting along, so she could cook and glut herself on the bream.

It was hard to tell in the dark if Daisy was speaking sarcastically. But her tone did not have the avidity of someone looking forward to another treat.

In some ways, Daisy was better than Monsarrat. She, like he, had been transported on professional matters, and they both still practised the professions they had in London. But Daisy, at least, had not pretended to be something she wasn't. Still, Monsarrat couldn't help feeling supercilious, if only for a moment. Perhaps even mythology, he thought, is too challenging for some.

Then he caught himself. My God, he thought, is this how Diamond views me? If so, I'm doomed.

To Daisy, he said, 'Did you like it? The lecture?'

'I might have, had I the time and liberty to like anything. As it was, the whole thing made me sick. We need food, and she gives us stories.'

'It is what she is able to give, and it is quite a gift,' said Monsarrat stiffly.

'I might come for the next one. Those Greeks were dirty buggers, so it could be good for business. One of my gents in London was a schoolmaster. Told me stories about Zeus that'd, well, make a whore blush. I wouldn't go with a swan like that Leda, I tell you, not for nothing. I have my standards.'

Monsarrat stared at her, his cravat forgotten. His hands went behind his back.

'Of course,' chuckled Daisy, 'it sounds like she'll be visiting the gods herself any day now. So I will be saved from having a rich woman preach at me to make herself feel better.'

Monsarrat stalked over to the door and opened it pointedly. His outrage at Daisy's ingratitude was compounded by the fact that when he knocked at her door, it stayed in the frame rather than flying back out again as his did.

Never again, he told himself. Of course, he told himself that every time, but now, oddly, he felt that a visit to Daisy would be a betrayal of Mrs Shelborne, who would neither know nor care.

Risking a further run-in with Diamond, or with one of the fanged denizens of the night-time ocean, once Daisy had gone Monsarrat went down to the river and, as he usually did, turned the corner to the beach, stomped down the sand towards the water, stripped, and washed himself clean. He took care to stay near the northern end – those vicious black rocks towards the south could not be seen at night, but were no less hard than they were during daylight.

He stood on the shore naked for a short while, punishing himself with the cold, before slowly and deliberately dressing and heading back to his hut, to spend a sleepless night trying to justify using one of the colony's two best women to spy on the other.

Chapter 6

The scrubbed table played host, the next morning, to two sets of forearms, hands clasped, the heads above them bent in prayer.

Monsarrat paused in the doorway. He was unwilling to interrupt even the observance of a religion which he considered to be the corpse of paganism with a thin cloth draped over it, the features of the deceased still clearly discernible through the shroud.

He considered leaving, had started to angle one shoulder away from the kitchen, when the man sitting opposite Mrs Mulrooney looked up. 'Mr Monsarrat. An unexpected delight. Please, sit down.'

It was neither Father Hanley's table, nor his right to offer Monsarrat a seat at it. And he certainly was not allowed in the house frequently enough to know whether Monsarrat's presence was expected or not.

The settlement's only church was little more than a large square footprint on top of the hill, slotted into the same space as the hospital and dispensary. Much of the port's convict muscle was concentrated on raising it from the ground. In any case, it was to be Anglican, and therefore no church at all to the likes of Mrs Mulrooney. Father Hanley no longer had a parish or a congregation, not officially. But his constituency far outnumbered those whose faith would allow them to darken the door of the church when it was constructed. He was a frequent visitor to Port Macquarie, arriving unannounced with the permission of the major to minister to the settlement's Catholics. He went where he was needed, or where he thought there might be a welcome, and he tried never to leave unfed.

The priest's mission today seemed to have been a success, as Mrs Mulrooney was now placing a large bowl of porridge in front of him, anointed with a dab of honey. There was none forthcoming for Monsarrat, nor did he expect it. Tea was one thing – everyone drank it, with the leaves sometimes boiled again and again. Some drank sweet tea made with native leaves, thought to ward off scurvy; however, Monsarrat found it too astringent and preferred the robust black leaves from China, so cheap they resided in a jar rather than in the tea chest beside their more refined cousins. But Mrs Mulrooney risked sanctions if caught feeding a convict – no one was to receive more than their allocated ration – and Monsarrat would never have allowed her to do so in front of an outsider to their small kitchen colony.

'Good morning, Mrs Mulrooney. Father.' Monsarrat nodded to the man as he scraped a chair along the ground with slightly more than necessary force, catching an edge of Father Hanley's cassock as he did so. Not that it would make much difference, he thought. Like the clothes of most of the settlement's inhabitants, the black fabric showed signs of repair, but repair effected without finesse or any attempt at concealment.

'Tea?' asked Mrs Mulrooney, she who was usually incapable of asking such a question in less than five words.

She turned away to the hob, Monsarrat observing her face during its transit. The eyes displayed signs of a night uncomfortably spent. And strands of hair were escaping her cap with impunity. She placed her plain, worn wooden rosary beads on their customary shelf.

'How is Mrs Shelborne this morning?' he asked, unable to do so with any equanimity since his acceptance of Diamond's secret commission. The presence of a priest did not make matters any better, even one whose claims to sanctity were as spurious as they were impossible to confirm. Father Hanley made the room feel stifling, even though its air was now clear of smoke thanks to the recent removal of the chimney's bird population.

Mrs Mulrooney didn't turn away from her tea things and Monsarrat noticed there were four cups out, perhaps in expectation of Slattery's usual morning visit.

'You might say she's no worse. The rackings of the disease come no more frequently than they have been. And they're no more severe. You might point all of that out, if you were Dr Gonville.'

'And is that in fact what Dr Gonville points out?'

'Yes. Like a man saying there was no more rain today than yesterday, while he stands on the broken banks of a river.'

'You disagree.'

'I agree as far as it goes. But she's so weak now. Sometimes, during the worst of it, I think she's going to break in two, or smash like a poorly made jug.'

'How did it start?' Hanley said. 'Vomiting? Difficulty breathing?'

'Perhaps you're best advised to keep your probings for ills of a spiritual nature, Father,' said Monsarrat quietly. He was irritated, not just at the question, but at the fact that Hanley was taking more space than his rough wooden chair was able to give. It seemed to Monsarrat the height of rudeness to presume a kitchen chair was capable of supporting a rear much larger than those belonging to the kitchen's regular inhabitants, those without access to favours from every Irish cook in the Hunter Valley and the wild country between there and Port Macquarie.

Hanley seemed willing to turn a fleshy and red-veined cheek to this. 'Indeed, sir,' he said, pronouncing it 'sore' in the same way as Mrs Mulrooney. 'And so I shall, but I have another reason for asking, which I'll tell you about should the answer be relevant.'

'She asked for honeyed tea a lot in the beginning, yes,' said Mrs Mulrooney. 'And there was some coughing, but nothing unusual for a wet winter, not at first. The damp, it does these things. And the parlour smells like mice, which wouldn't have helped. Mr Monsarrat, while I think of it, would you ask Spring for some more of that white powder for me? I've used it all since I started smelling them, and there'll be a ship in soon.' As she spoke, she handed him a pottery jar, empty but for a few white grains clinging to its sides, to be refilled at the stores. She always made sure she had plenty of poison stored up for the arrival of a ship, as most of them disgorged rats as well as convicts.

'And have you seen any?' asked Monsarrat, who was usually asked to dispose of the corpses, his friend having an aversion to touching her victims.

'Not a one. I expect Slattery's lummoxes have scared them off.'

'Slattery has one less lummox,' said Hanley.

Boots on the other side of the door were having the mud stamped off them. And here, thought Monsarrat, is the lummox-in-chief.

'God bless all here,' said Slattery automatically as he and his sheepskin coat entered.

'And you as well, dear Fergal,' Father Hanley said expansively, rising to clasp the young man's shoulder. 'What a burden and a sorrow today must be for you.'

Monsarrat rose as well, a sign of conditioned respect for a clergy which had done nothing, in his view, to earn it. One must observe the niceties, even if one was a twice-criminalised agnostic. Especially then, in fact.

'Good morning, Father. Hello, Magpie,' said Slattery, dispensing with the more profane aspects of his usual greeting. Like Monsarrat, he did so out of respect for the office rather than the man. Recently, as his crew had smoothed plaster on the wall next door, Slattery had told Monsarrat he didn't approve of Father Hanley. There was, for a start, the nature of the transgression that had brought him from Kildare to Port Macquarie.

The adored horse of a landowner of Father Hanley's parish in Ireland had gone missing, to be eventually located under the priest's buttocks. Hanley claimed to have found it wandering, that he was intending to return it after using the stroke of luck to do God's work by visiting a sick parishioner. The invalid, as it happened, lived quite close to the local racetrack, where a horse of the same description was listed to run that afternoon (fourteen hands, roan, highly favoured). On investigation, the constabulary found evidence of two minor miracles. The invalid was seen vigorously chopping a tree in the copse near his home. And the horse listed in the afternoon's race vanished, scratched for non-appearance.

Father Hanley was saved from a criminal stain by his priestly status, accepting an amnesty. But this salvation only went so far. He was informed that he could live as a free man in the colony, provided he remained a priest, and provided he never returned to Ireland. No one was certain whether Hanley remained a priest in the eyes of the Holy Catholic and Apostolic Church. No one was inclined to check, least of all Hanley.

His crime outraged Slattery. Not that it was the worst of those committed by the men under Slattery's stewardship – although the purloined item was larger in both size and value than many others which had sent people to the port. 'I've no quarrel with a priest running foul of the constables,' he'd told Monsarrat. 'But horse theft! Any theft. If you're a man of the cloth, and you want trouble, you should at least have the decency to do it for someone else.'

'Stealing food for the poor, that sort of thing?' asked Monsarrat.

'No! You're being slow today, for a man of fookin' letters, even if you forged half of them. No stealing. Not needed – plenty to do that. No, give me a priest sent here for standing between a bailiff and a tenant. For interceding with his lordship – any lordship – on behalf of a poor family. For preventing an innocent man from being gaoled. Or – here's one – for speaking against the greed of the landholder, trying to make sure they leave the tenants with enough to get by. Natural justice, that's their job. Or should be.'

'Why should that be up to the priests?'

'Why shouldn't it? It has to be up to someone. And barely an inconvenience to them if they're slain in the process, with guaranteed passage into heaven and all.'

'Unless they steal horses. Then it's guaranteed passage to the colony,' said Monsarrat.

'Exactly so. And then they're no good to man or beast, and shouldn't be able to hide behind the Holy Father's skirts.'

'But then what would you do for weddings, baptisms, last rites? Surely you wouldn't submit to Reverend Ainslie?'

Monsarrat knew that Fergal Slattery's relationship with his own religion was problematic at best. The settlement's most redeemed regular resident, the Reverend John Ainslie, had been appointed chaplain last year, and the thought of being part of his flock had drawn an Irish curse from Slattery. Frail though they were, priests like Hanley were at least able to make allowances for frailty in others, while Ainslie and his like condemned even the thought of a sin. Certain Anglicans referred to their spiritual leaders in New South Wales as 'almost Methodist'. It was not intended as a compliment.

'There is that, I suppose,' Slattery had said. 'A priest is a priest, even if he doesn't deserve it, and he has his uses.'

The major might have agreed with Slattery on the general usefulness of the clergy, Monsarrat thought. Before Ainslie's appointment, religious observances had amounted to the chief engineer reading prayers each Sunday in the schoolhouse. Now Ainslie conducted Sunday services in the same location, or sometimes, in fine weather, on the hill where the church was slowly rising. The major felt that the Reverend should restrict himself to these activities, together with attempts to increase the moral rectitude of his crime-stained flock. But that wasn't how Ainslie did things. All roads led to God, he was fond of saying. What he didn't say was that this meant everything which went on in the settlement was his business.

Monsarrat was party to a great many administrative secrets, of which he would never speak in case he lost the major's trust and the privileges it brought. One of these secrets was the number of meetings Ainslie had with Shelborne, arriving unannounced and closeting himself in the inner office for at least half an hour, lecturing him on everything from convict drunkenness to gambling amongst the ranks (he had his eye on Slattery and others). Ainslie's sermonising leaked out around the edges of the inexpertly fitted door, giving Monsarrat a free but unintended insight into Ainslie's views on a range of moral perils. The major was unfailingly polite and patient, thanking him for his concern and showing him out, sometimes unable to resist a raised eyebrow in Monsarrat's direction on the way back in.

In public, the major and his wife treated the Reverend with the greatest respect – or had until the Female Factory closed. Anticipating objections about increased opportunities for loose behaviour, the major had invited the Reverend to his office and laid out his plans and the reasons for them – the expense of keeping just three women in such a large building; the alternative uses it could be put to; and Dr Gonville's concerns about the health of the women detained there. The Reverend had nodded thoughtfully, and informed Major Shelborne that he intended to visit Sydney in the near future to attend to some personal matters.

Those matters, it turned out, included a visit to the Colonial Secretary with tales of women prisoners at large in the settlement, roaming amongst the male population in a most disgraceful manner.

Monsarrat knew the major had already written to Sydney about his intentions for the Factory – he'd transcribed the letter himself. When the Colonial Secretary responded with the concerns Ainslie had brought to him, Shelborne asked Monsarrat to read the letter aloud. He was undeniably angry, but controlled. Until Monsarrat read one of the closing paragraphs.

The Reverend has expressed a concern that you have been unduly influenced in this matter by your wife, who has commendably taken an interest in the welfare of the females, but perhaps lacks the necessary appreciation for the moral dangers these women may face abroad in the settlement, being no doubt innocent of such matters herself.

At this, the major's control temporarily slipped. He grabbed the letter from Monsarrat's hands and read it for himself.

'That sanctimonious bastard,' he said. 'I hope he stays in Sydney – we're well shot of him. Monsarrat, draft a reply to the

Colonial Secretary reiterating my reasons for closing the Factory. Don't address that ridiculous reference to Honora. Then I want you to draft another letter, to Ainslie. Use your best hand, please, and as many pleasantries as you can muster without making yourself sick. Tell him that I hope he is enjoying his time in Sydney, and that in his absence we have reintroduced the practice of reading prayers in the schoolhouse – yes, yes, I know, but I will, this very week. We shall revert to the situation in place before his arrival, whereby I conduct any necessary marriages, funerals and so forth. This in hand, he should feel no immediate pressure to return, but should take all the time that he needs to conclude his affairs in Sydney. Please make sure to add Mrs Shelborne's regards.'

So for the present, Hanley was God's only representative in Port Macquarie, standing and gripping Slattery's arm in commiseration.

Slattery shrugged off Hanley's grasp. 'As you say, Father, very sad. Young he was, too. Did you get to him in time?'

'Yes, barely. I was able to absolve him. He died in a state of grace – assuming no unclean thoughts traversed his mind in the minute or two between amen and his final breath.'

'He has no further need of you, so,' said Slattery. 'Very good, you lot, at opening the door to the next world. Only God can say how good a job you're doing there. But I have my own thoughts on the job you're doing here. You should be making sure the door doesn't open too soon, and that passing through it isn't the only hope.'

'Ah, Fergal. I do what I can. A powerless priest in a cradle of the heathens. Don't think, lad, that all of the work of Our Lord and his Blessed Mother needs to take place in the glare.'

Mrs Mulrooney, having now distributed tea, reflexively crossed herself.

'Who's died?' asked Monsarrat.

'One of my plastering crew. Fellow called Jeremiah. He was taken ill a few weeks ago but kept working. Well, in honesty I didn't give him a choice. Not until he wasn't able for it. You'd not believe the ruses they pull sometimes.'

'And taken, from what I understand, by the same malady that torments Mrs Shelborne, or something very like it,' said Hanley.

Mrs Mulrooney's eyes made brief contact with Monsarrat's, then directed themselves towards the floor.

Monsarrat sought to salve his own rising sense of unease by burying it in administrative activity. He stood, placed both hands on the table and leaned forward on them. 'Private, are any others amongst your plastering crew ill?'

'Not deathly so. One of them has a cough, not looking his best. But that's not unusual. He's still able to work.'

'Anyone else of whom you've heard?'

'No, not like that anyway.'

'Father, have you ministered to anyone with a similar sickness?'

'No, Mr Monsarrat, nor have I heard any rumours.'

'Mrs Mulrooney . . . are you feeling well?'

Mrs Mulrooney drew herself up, offended by the implication that something as trivial as a wasting sickness could render her incapable. 'Apart from a certain lack of sleep, my health is excellent,' she said.

'I am pleased to hear it. Private, may I suggest that you confine your crew to the sitting room for the morning?'

Slattery, for all his regard for Monsarrat, did not appreciate receiving orders from a convict. But he was not unintelligent and saw sense in what Monsarrat was suggesting. 'I suppose so,' he said. 'Until when?'

'Until I have had a chance to deliver a report.'

Chapter 7

Monsarrat meant to make two reports, in fact. With two purposes. To the same man.

He found Captain Diamond by the river, gazing at a work crew and their overseer working on the breakwater. After the rains, the frogs were competing with the sound of the convicts' tools, although Monsarrat didn't approve of their song. They didn't croak like any self-respecting frog. They tapped, in mimicry of the sticks the natives used to accompany their strange crooning. For Monsarrat, the sound was unsettling, being not far removed from the tap on the door at his Exeter lodgings, the tap which had ended his liberty and sent him here.

Diamond observed the worksite from horseback, on a sturdier and less refined beast than someone of the officer class would be used to. Nor was he self-evidently anymore an officer. For this dirty work, he had replaced his beloved parade ground reds with duller clothes, making him look from a distance like a reasonably prosperous farmer.

With the commandant away on the hunt for the fabled river, the works which had been approved before his departure were being undertaken with more than the usual haste, to clear the building schedule for his return so he might look with favour on more important projects. A report on the poor state of the barracks roof, for example, sat amongst the increasing sheaves of paper Monsarrat had laid by for the major.

Diamond looked at Monsarrat sharply when he stopped beside the horse. 'You have a report for me?'

'There is no change in Mrs Shelborne's condition. Or at least in the way it manifests itself.'

Diamond spat. 'The major should have a soldier for a secretary. Not someone who spends words like a drunk. Is she any worse, or is she not?'

'The digestive disturbances, the bouts of coughing and the convulsions are no more frequent than they were yesterday or last week. No more severe, either. But she weakens. She takes no food, and her only sustenance is tea fed to her on a spoon. She is less able to withstand the onslaught.'

'You don't mean to say she is closer to death?'

'That I don't know, sir. You would need Dr Gonville's opinion.'

'Which is precisely what I can't avail myself of, which is precisely why I have given you the opportunity to be of service,' said Diamond.

'I think I may be of service to both you and the common good in one stroke today,' said Monsarrat. He told Diamond of Jeremiah's death, and the precaution Slattery had taken in confining his men to the parlour.

'You fear contagion,' said Diamond.

'I don't know, sir,' said Monsarrat. 'But I do believe that two illnesses following the same course should be brought to the surgeon's attention. In so doing, it would be natural to discuss the condition of the surviving victim.'

Diamond looked at the men, hauling rock on top of rock in a probably vain attempt to protect the landing place from the worst of the nearby ocean's moods. The bottoms of their canvas pants would now be permanently stained brown by the river mud, which was silky to the touch and crafty at worming its way into the gap between threads. It had managed to climb, in patches, to the workers' shirts, and had also taken up residence on most of their faces.

Monsarrat wondered whether his news was causing more internal turmoil than was apparent on Diamond's features. He knew Diamond would consider it bad form to show any strong emotion in front of a convict clerk.

'I can't go,' the captain said. 'You must. You are right: Gonville should be informed. So inform him.'

'And then? What if he should recommend some restriction of movement?'

'If he does, return at once. I'll take the necessary action. Otherwise, gather what information you can on the other matter between us, and return here tomorrow. And be aware that I require more than second-hand generalities if you're to settle your debt.'

Gonville, as it turned out, did not feel a general quarantine was necessary. 'Too disruptive to the function of the place, without any evidence of plague,' he said.

Monsarrat was aware that a plea for a larger dispensary rubbed against the to-be-approved request for the repair of the barracks roof, and that too much disruption would jeopardise both.

This knowledge sat beside a galloping fear of what a plague could do to the settlement. Monsarrat's imagination had been scurrying into dangerous and dark places during his short walk from the river up the hill towards the hospital, and he chastised himself for it. Best not to allow one's mind to create terrors, when enough of them existed in reality. One of those real terrors wore a red coat, and had handed out a secret commission which had unsettled Monsarrat more than he liked to admit. But when his thoughts were all he could control, it was crucial not to let them off their leash.

As he passed the convict barracks, the scent of the river eucalypts gave way to murkier, more human odours, which did not help. If plague was allowed to take hold, he suspected, those barracks would putrefy so much that a forest of gums wouldn't be able to compete. Its slow pace would gradually quicken – another case tomorrow, perhaps. Two next week. And then, suddenly, twenty.

Thirty. The barracks roof would no longer matter, and the need for the larger dispensary would be acute.

His mood lightened slightly as he neared the hospital. He didn't see, as he had half-expected, corpses being removed for burial, or the afflicted lying on canvas stretchers outside, their number having overwhelmed the small hospital's capacity. And now, in the doctor's office – or more accurately at his desk behind a partition at the end of the long hospital – the threat seemed even less likely. A sideboard stood next to a window, which admitted a smell of lye so strong that it would surely make any contagion impossible. The sideboard was a twin of that in which Mrs Mulrooney kept the best china and cutlery. Here, though, its surface was draped with a white runner, on which were displayed implements of unknown purpose (and Monsarrat wished their purpose to remain unknown, at least as far as he was concerned). The shelves held more books than Monsarrat had seen anywhere in the colony save the major's study.

'What is it, then,' Monsarrat asked, 'to strike down two people with the same symptoms? Both young, too.'

'Mrs Shelborne has not been struck down,' said Dr Gonville sharply. 'In any case, there is no fever. And I remain standing, as does Mrs Mulrooney. We would surely be amongst the first to fall, if the disease were liable to jump from one person to another.'

The doctor, in fact, did not remain standing, and occupied one of the office's two chairs. It would never have occurred to him to offer the other to a convict.

'Have you seen Daisy Mactier recently?' he asked now.

Monsarrat had never regarded Gonville as particularly prudish. His employment as a colony doctor told against squeamishness, both moral and otherwise. Nevertheless, he made it a rule not to answer a question unless he was sure of the intentions of the questioner.

'I believe she's been about, yes,' he said. He smothered his own puerile speculation on whether he and Gonville had trod the same path. He preferred to relegate such awkward likelihoods to the mists at the edge of his consciousness, where they had less chance of coalescing into facts and thus demanding attention.

'And she's well?'

'I've no reason to believe otherwise.'

Gonville slapped his desk. 'There you are, then. Harlots are a bellwether of plague. They're at the crossroads, so to speak, and they can infect a great many others before being outwardly stricken themselves. No, if Daisy's well, so is the colony. Not that contagion from that source would be a concern for you, of course, Monsarrat.'

'I hope to avoid contagion from any source, doctor. Is there nothing we can do to lessen the risk?'

'Keep yourself as hale and well fed as possible, I suppose. Not difficult for someone with fishing privileges.'

I must be more careful on my next trip to the river, Monsarrat thought.

'Beyond that,' said the doctor, 'in order to advise you I would need to know which disease we are dealing with. And in all honesty I don't. The humours of this place are different. The seasons are reversed. It's not impossible that some bodies would react badly to the change in natural order, while others would be unaffected. Perhaps the air or water here is more acidic, and it's an excess of acid in the lymph glands that causes it. I have to admit, I thought of cholera for a short time. Or gastric fever. And yes, I did fear the very event you have come to discuss. But there would be more, far more by now. If we were at home, and if the circumstances were right, I might suspect arsenic poisoning. But Spring keeps the arsenic under lock and key, and makes a note of everyone who wants some for the rats. And there's no one with a wish to do in a kind gentlewoman and a harmless young felon.'

'Your advice, then, is to watch, wait, eat and hope,' said Monsarrat.

'It's the best I have for you right now. And you may like to take a fatalistic approach – if you are marked for it, no art of mine, and no precautions of yours, will save you.'

Monsarrat worried at the conversation as his feet pushed the path away behind him and his hands kept each other company behind his back. He had had more than enough of professional men who seemed to lack necessary knowledge, or the shrewdness to apply it properly. He supposed that if Gonville had been a truly talented doctor, he might now be taking his ease on Harley Street.

Monsarrat's pace gradually slowed and then stopped, his feet no longer pushing the path but holding it in place.

After a few moments they quickened in a far less gradual and seemly fashion, closing the distance between their owner and the bookshelf in the study of Major Angus Augustus Shelborne.

⌒⌒⌒

When Hannah Mulrooney was a child, the worst insult that could be hurled at you was that you were useless.

In her family you needed to justify not only the food you ate, but the chair you occupied at the table and the air you displaced as you sat down. Now, however distant and dead he might be, she feared her father would level the dreaded accusation at her. What good was brewing tea – doing it the proper way, the only way – when you were serving it to a near-corpse, dull-eyed and slack-skinned and unrecognisable as the young woman who had captivated the major, and much of the rest of the port.

But still she brewed, delicate infusions for Mrs Shelborne and strong, black concoctions for those amongst the regular visitors to the house whom she liked well enough. Monsarrat was one of the chief consumers, and had labelled her kitchen 'a temple of tea and counsel', earning himself a swat with a damp cloth and a reminder that he might be lettered but he was still a convict and must therefore avoid acting above his station, even verbally.

Yet secretly, Hannah Mulrooney hugged the name to herself, for Monsarrat did seek her counsel on a range of matters. How should he phrase a letter to the Colonial Secretary warning of the port's overcrowding, so that it sounded reasoned and not wheedling (for Major Shelborne often left the composition of the first drafts of such letters to Monsarrat, and Mrs Mulrooney had a gift for manipulating a language she could not read)? How much salt pork should be put by for Christmas, and should there be a Christmas pudding in the cursed summer heat? And, chiefly, how was Monsarrat to secure another ticket of leave, this one without conditions, and be as good as free in the whole vast colony of New South Wales? She gave such answers as she could, and Monsarrat often seemed pleased, sometimes even conveying her advice to Major Shelborne (without mentioning its source).

'You know, you're shrewder than me,' Monsarrat had said to her once.

'Of course I am,' she said. 'For all the good it will do me, with no letters.'

'Maybe one day I'll teach you some letters,' said Monsarrat.

'Well, don't think I'll find the time to take them on board me.'

In the meantime, he took to writing letters on her behalf to her son, Padraig, who was droving in the plains beyond the hazy mountains. He would also read her the replies, for Padraig had enough of an education to pen them himself – Mrs Mulrooney had made certain of that, would have sold her very shoes to win for Padraig the induction into what seemed to her a mystical art.

Padraig had travelled to the colony while still in his first year of life, transported as a satellite of his butter-thief mother. When he was eight, she had earned her ticket of leave, and since that day she had been putting money aside in the hopes of eventually helping Padraig into ownership of a public house, installing herself as the power behind the alehouse throne.

For a time, Mrs Mulrooney had considered inviting Fergal Slattery to join them in the enterprise, whenever that might happen. Padraig had breathed Ireland's air for less than a year, and she believed the venture needed someone with a working memory of the place, to ensure things were done properly.

Now, though, she was beginning to think she would need to look elsewhere, perhaps even to herself.

She had just returned from delivering tea to Slattery's plastering crew during their confinement to the parlour. Even if they were contagious, she believed the disease had enough sense to leave her alone. Indeed, it clearly had more sense than the plasterers themselves, as she'd had to admonish them for damaging the paper, which showed white in some small sections where the green colouring had been scraped off.

Slattery was waiting in the kitchen, his feet up, whittling a stick.

'Get your dirty great hooves off my table.'

Slattery obliged without looking up. 'Not yours though, is it?' he said.

'Of course it is, as good as.'

'Try making off with it and see if the Shelbornes agree.'

'I've no patience for this today, Fergal,' said Mrs Mulrooney. 'There's a long night ahead, if last night was anything to go by, and I can't be doing with talk of stealing tables.'

'Hopefully not too many more sleepless nights for you; I imagine she'll be dead soon.'

Mrs Mulrooney was shocked by the baldness of the statement – even in a settlement where barely a week passed without a funeral, talk of death was couched in euphemisms, as though by referring to it obliquely people could avoid attracting its attention. 'You be careful, young Slattery. Ears everywhere.'

'Including two on my head, to keep my eyes company. Those eyes which saw her ladyship stepping off the *Sally*, followed by trunk upon trunk – when the rest of us arrived with so little. What does one person do with so many possessions? And why do they feel the need to haul them about?'

He was unfolding himself from his chair when Monsarrat came in. 'Private, you can do as you will with your men. Gonville says there's no threat of contagion.'

'Why, thank you very fooking much,' said Slattery, bowing with no trace of his usual good humour. He flung his much-whittled stick towards the grate and marched out – without thanking Mrs Mulrooney, an omission of which his mother would have been ashamed – and could be heard a short time later barking at his unfortunate charges.

Monsarrat took his place, spread a publication out on the table, and began to read. Though she couldn't string the letters together, Mrs Mulrooney recognised his beloved *Edinburgh Review*, which he had just retrieved from the major's study. Monsarrat sometimes liked to read in the kitchen, comforted by the sounds of domesticity. He also liked, from time to time, to seek Mrs Mulrooney's view on what he had read.

'Mrs Mulrooney,' he said now, looking up from his reading, 'what colour is the wallpaper in Mrs Shelborne's bedroom?'

Mrs Mulrooney had spent too long, recently, staring at that wallpaper, a restful blue and white stripe. It was the inanity of the question, rather than its personal nature, which bothered her the most. 'Do you think I've the time to be discussing wall decorations?' she said, casting him into the outer darkness by removing his half-drunk tea.

'Please, it may be important. I'll explain when I understand more. Is it green, as in the parlour?'

'No, blue and white. The blue may have a nodding acquaintance with green in certain lights, but that's as far as it goes.'

'I see.' Monsarrat, disappointed, returned to his reading.

Mrs Mulrooney had heard other men talk as Slattery just had. The dispossessed often did, even those who took the imperial shilling. It was a symptom of a spreading malaise which dug trenches in their minds, diverting their original natures down courses that ended in black and stagnant ponds. Here, they bloated into new and terrible shapes. She still had hopes that the lightsome Slattery would resist taking these paths, find a way to avoid the swamp. So she decided, for now, not to mention the scraped wallpaper, or the green flecks she had noticed on the knife Slattery was whittling with. A few of these had transferred themselves to the stick he had flung aside, an object which now found its way into Mrs Mulrooney's pocket.

Chapter 8

Slattery's good humour was restored the next morning.

He entered the kitchen shortly after Monsarrat, with his usual assault to the door, loped over to Mrs Mulrooney and sank into an exaggerated courtly bow. 'Mother Mulrooney, queen amongst housekeepers, would you ever forgive me for yesterday? It was worry about Mrs Shelborne's condition that took hold of my spirits. I'm myself again and I beg your kind pardon.'

Mrs Mulrooney had been intending to give Slattery the kind of dressing-down she usually reserved for household tools and cooking utensils. She turned her back on him now, but Monsarrat saw she was smiling. 'Go on with you then, Fergal,' she said. 'I'll forgive you so your poor dear mother's soul can rest, as it would certainly have been roused by your carrying on yesterday. And the same worry is disturbing my own rest. In penance you can fetch me some firewood.'

Slattery left, and returned with an armful of quartered logs, whistling as he laid some on the fire and the rest on the scuttle. He then guided her to the chair he would have occupied and turned to fiddle with the tea chest, scooping some leaves into the fine china pot reserved for Honora.

'You're too cheerful to be suffering from a night soaked in poteen, or any other kind of the swill you boys like to drink,' said Monsarrat, as Slattery sat down opposite him and awaited his tea.

'Ah, not a drop of poteen has passed my lips since I left Ireland, water of life though it is,' said Slattery. 'It's my virtuous living that has lifted my mood.'

Monsarrat said nothing, his challenge to the claim evident in his stare.

'And I won a decent amount at Three Card Brag,' said Slattery.

'Better. Next time you lie to me, please have the courtesy to make it convincing.'

'Oh, he's convincing,' said Mrs Mulrooney. 'Last week he begged me for a piece of the shortbread I'd made to try to tempt Mrs Shelborne's appetite. Said it was for someone who was ill. Don't think I didn't see the crumbs on your whiskers, Fergal.'

Slattery smiled and winked at Monsarrat. He wasn't, as Mrs Mulrooney no doubt assumed, sharing boyish glee at having misappropriated shortbread. He was urging Monsarrat to silence.

Monsarrat would have had no trouble believing Slattery guilty of obtaining shortbread by deception. But in this case, he knew, the Irishman had been moved by purer motives.

Of the three surviving members of Slattery's plastering crew, two were subject to regular tongue lashings by the young soldier. Frogett and Daines were Cockneys and had occasionally worked decorating houses in London. The fourth member of the crew, Jeremiah Cassidy, lay freshly in his grave, but in life had looked as if he had never decorated anything except maybe a pigpen with swill.

Frogett (who had assaulted a bailiff and then a fellow prisoner in Sydney) and Daines (who had robbed a man at knifepoint and was then found drunk in Windsor) looked unreliable, and Slattery blamed them for looking like that. But Monsarrat knew it had been bred into them – the powerful had proved to them that surface reliability got you nowhere in the end. They were not characterised so much by sullenness, a quality often attributed to convicts, but by great wariness; their eyes were foxy because they believed they needed to be foxes to negotiate the system.

But the last man in the crew, William Dory, still had some sensibility left in his features. Dory, originally a country boy from somewhere in the west of England – or maybe he was Cornish, Monsarrat had forgotten – had grown from a boy to a man as a convict, but at eighteen was still only a sapling and had hopes that the other two had lost.

Those hopes, as it turned out, were fed by Slattery. So, occasionally, was Dory himself.

Monsarrat had become aware of the unlikely connection one morning when, passing the sitting room on the way to the office, he'd heard Slattery's dancing laughter, which often graced the kitchen but had never, as far as Monsarrat knew, reverberated off the wallpaper.

Dory had been telling Slattery about his first attempt at riding a horse, during which he had hoisted himself up at the wrong angle and found himself facing the wrong end of the nag. While Slattery laughed, the other members of the plastering crew worked quietly, if resentfully, occasionally glancing in their over-seer's direction. When Slattery noticed, he barked at them to stop wasting time and get on with it and then, spotting Monsarrat in the doorway, gave him a mock salute.

The next time he saw Slattery, Monsarrat said, 'Playing favou-rites, aren't you?'

Slattery grinned, his first response to any situation. 'Ah, he's a good lad,' he said. 'And I don't think he deserves to be here, not really. He didn't hurt anyone, not like those other two lags, crim-inals to the bone. His family lost their farm when the rent went up, you see. They moved to London, and it didn't agree with his mother's health. His father couldn't get work, so Dory took some bread – stale, mind – off a cart for his mother. Unfortunately, a peeler was watching. Then in Sydney he met another boy his age – he can't have been more than fourteen – and the overseer of their work gang used to single them out for special attention, them being the youngest and weakest. The overseer had Dory's friend flogged for neglecting work, and was going to flog him again the next day for the same offence – poor bastard could barely walk after the first flogging – when Dory flattened him. So here he is.'

'He seems reasonably cheerful for a convict,' said Monsarrat. More cheerful than me, certainly, he thought, when he has even less reason to be cheerful than I do.

'He's a bright boy, and he has letters,' said Slattery. 'I've told him a decent fellow such as himself could do well in Sydney, once he gets his ticket. He's making plans, wants to apply for a baker's licence when he's free.'

But Dory, like Jeremiah, had started coughing, and then vomiting. Slattery had insisted Dory take regular rests, and sent him outside, between the kitchen and the main house, to do so. Monsarrat was unsure about the wisdom of sending an ill boy outside in winter to rest, but presumed Slattery was trying to avoid a mutiny by sending Dory off on invented errands.

And Monsarrat had seen Slattery take the shortbread outside and offer it to Dory. Dory took it, broke it in half, and handed a piece back to Slattery, who raised it as though it was a cup of ale, before they both ate.

Monsarrat was more than willing to comply with Slattery's winked request for silence, although the need for secrecy was beyond him. In any case, it was not the only winked request between them. The other one held a far greater peril, both for Slattery and for the friendship between the two men.

Just after Major Shelborne's departure into the hinterland, Monsarrat, with his customary efficiency, had finished the morning's transcribing in good order. It was unnaturally sunny, so he decided to leave Catullus and the *Edinburgh Review* to themselves for the afternoon. He adored, when the mood was upon him, climbing up to a headland several beaches away – this was particularly the case if the wind was forcing the waves to stand to attention for an instant before hurtling against the sandstone cliffs, as though they harboured the same self-hatred as Monsarrat did.

The route he chose would take him three headlands to the south. He was reasonably assured of not meeting anyone on the way, as this was the territory of Goliath – an unusually large snake the rumour of which had reached the settlement, although the serpent itself hadn't.

Goliath was known to reside in the south, along with many more of his kind – Slattery had been headed that way some time previously and, seeing several snakes imitating sticks as if to deceive the unwary, had later warned Captain Diamond of the danger. Neither Goliath nor any other snake had been known to pierce regimental skin, but they were to be presumed venomous until proved otherwise.

To replace a soldier fallen to a snake, Diamond would have had to negotiate a lengthy administrative labyrinth, as well as wait for a replacement to arrive from Sydney. He preferred to avoid the trouble, and therefore forbade all soldiers from going to the place that Slattery had described. Convicts, presumably, were more expendable, and he had not placed a similar prohibition on them. And while conditions were nowhere near as harsh as even the progressive Governor Macquarie had envisioned, most convicts did not have sufficient liberty (or inclination) for long rambles, especially under Diamond's command. So the snakes and the distance and the need to scramble up loose diagonals of sandstone meant that few people, free or felon, visited the area.

But Monsarrat, who had called for Daisy the night before and felt in need of scourging himself, decided that the exertion, and the likelihood of a run-in with the dread Goliath, would serve well as a punishment.

Monsarrat crossed a headland, a tiny escape. It was hard work getting up it, but the view from the top of it, of the ocean and the coastline, was sublime. No man who stood atop it on such an afternoon could be considered entirely a slave.

Another headland. This was further than he'd walked before; below him stood a beach into which a creek flowed, fringed by low swampy country and those paperbarks which, had the Egyptians begun their civilisation on this river instead of the Nile, would have provided them with papyrus.

Scrambling up the headlands had taken him longer than he had anticipated – his physique was not as able as it had been the day he was discovered in Exeter. He noticed now that the horizon was beginning to reel in the sun, to submit it to its nightly drowning.

Monsarrat knew that if he continued, he would be back after curfew. This was before Diamond had caught him fishing, but he was already cautious of the captain, and did not care to be caught in a transgression, not least because it might affect his trusted status with the major.

Besides, if he turned around now, there might just be time for a cup of tea from the hands of Mrs Mulrooney before the curfew bell rang. But now a point of light snared the corner of his eye, dragging his face around to the direction of its source. He looked away from the beach, down into a swampy valley, saw a yellow lick in the middle of a stand of paperbarks. It could have been a native fire, but was a strange place for one, given the mosquitoes which bedevilled the more watery parts of the landscape.

He knew that if he investigated and found evidence of illegal activity on behalf of a soldier, or better yet a convict, this information might offer him some level of protection when he brought it to Diamond, whose autocracy was beginning to worry him.

Fortunately, Monsarrat was able to find a sand dune to half-slide, half-walk down, as sliding down a sandstone scree slope would have announced his approach as effectively as any trumpet blast. Walking cautiously up to the stand of trees, he passed some of their wilder brethren. The strangling figs, growing down as well as up over other trees after birds had deposited their seed in the unwary branches, looked as though they had been poured molten over their hosts, and here and there grew trees with oval incisions where the Birpai had excised shields with the help of wooden wedges, before sanding them with rough leaves.

Peering between the scrofulous trunks of the paperbarks, Monsarrat saw that the source of the light was deeper in. The rain had made the ground wet, so again luck was on his side and he was able to approach without the crunching which would have announced him after a long dry spell.

Monsarrat could now see amongst the trees ahead. On a fireplace constructed of small lumps of sandstone a large pot sat above the fire. And stoking the fire with fallen eucalypt and paperbark branches which hadn't got too sodden in this fenny area was Private Slattery. Even though the muddy ground had given Monsarrat a quiet approach, Slattery looked up, and then stood, his face alert before it took on its customary Irish grin, a smile honest enough in Mrs Mulrooney's kitchen, but which now had an edge to it, the edge of learned subservience, which welcomed the visitor while at the same time wishing God would strike him dead.

'Well now, Mr Monsarrat, you'd have the soul out of me, sneaking up on a man like that. Not trying to abscond, are we?'

Clever, thought Monsarrat, to turn the blame back on the discoverer of his illegal still, for that's what it undoubtedly was. The liquor distilled from potatoes and other organic substances was prohibited in the settlement, the consumption of a bad batch enough to send a man blind or insane, so it was said. But the prohibition had had no effect on the plentiful supply of the moonshine. And the moonshine had to come from somewhere.

Monsarrat had been under the impression that its manufacture required more equipment than a copper pot, but reminded himself that the making of Irish grog was not one of his areas of expertise. He had also heard Slattery say, on a great many occasions, that he never touched the stuff. Monsarrat didn't quite believe him, but it was irrelevant – whether he touched it or not, he must be responsible for supplying it.

But then, if Slattery was careful, and didn't make the kind of poison which could sometimes do such damage to the unwary drinker, why not? Monsarrat was certainly no supporter of Diamond's pedantic rules, and would not begrudge his friend the opportunity to make a few extra coins, especially in a place where the scope for profit was so limited.

'Of course I'm not, you fool,' he said, smiling to telegraph the fact that the words were meant in the way of playful banter. Usually no such signal was needed. But in this fraught situation, Monsarrat didn't want to take any chances.

'Just as well – I would hate to have to take you in.' Slattery stood and walked around the pot, rubbing his hands together over it to extract such warmth as he could. 'Well now, how shall I express myself? You've stumbled upon my secret brew. Surely not the greatest of sins, nothing like the one that sent you here, but still ... Just as well you're a felon. You have your secrets, and I have mine. Could we respect each other's secrets, do you think?'

'Slattery, I don't know who you think you're talking to. I have no intention of revealing the existence of this place. And if you want to brew poteen, good luck to you. I'm no great respecter of the laws, as you point out.'

Slattery smiled again, and Monsarrat wondered whether it was just his recent thoughts of snakes which made the smile look reptilian.

'Grand then,' said Slattery, clapping his hands. 'It would break Mrs Mulrooney's heart to see you flogged for absconding.'

'And her heart would be equally broken were you to be killed by one of those snakes,' said Monsarrat. 'I don't suppose Goliath has been about today?'

'Goliath?' said Slattery, looking momentarily distracted. 'No, no, I seem to be the only living thing here.'

'I suppose the snakes don't like the smell of poteen,' Monsarrat said.

'No,' said Slattery. 'I don't suppose they do.'

Next morning Slattery was already at the kitchen table, drinking tea, when Monsarrat arrived. A knowing nod and smile passed between them.

⤙⤚

'So these winnings of yours,' Monsarrat said now by way of distraction from accusations of shortbread theft. 'What would you classify as a decent amount?'

'Thirteen shillings. And easy to earn. None of them can keep still, none of them can clear their faces. They always twitch or turn or fiddle. Dray, he twitches the corner of his mouth if he thinks he has a good hand. Cooper rubs his thumb and finger if he thinks he has a bad one. Not one of them can stop things seeping through.'

'But you can?'

'Better than they can, yes. It's why I don't play cards as often as I'd like – they're leery of playing with me because I generally win. The angels could be smiling on my cards and you'd never know it from my face.'

The gentle knocking which announced the arrival of the plastering crew always surprised Monsarrat, as he knew the soft tapping came from knuckles which had once connected with the face of a bailiff.

'In with you,' Slattery yelled. 'Down to three now – they'll all have to work harder,' he told Monsarrat.

But only two figures – those of Frogett and Daines – entered the kitchen.

'Where's Dory?' asked Slattery, getting shrugs in reply.

'The eejit,' Slattery muttered. 'I'll have to go and fetch him. He's lucky it's me and not Diamond. You two! We'll get you back to the barracks, can't leave you here. But you'll be working twice as hard when you get back.'

Monsarrat took his leave at the same time as Slattery, treading the well-worn path to the office, grateful for once to be leaving the kitchen and Slattery's problems for the quiet order of the workroom.

As he sat at his desk, his eye caught on the red wax sealing Dr Gonville's report on Mrs Shelborne. This, he thought, could satisfy Diamond, could make him free Monsarrat from further obligation. And it would remove the need to extract information from Mrs Mulrooney. He felt exceptionally uncomfortable when she praised him for being kind enough to ask after the young woman's health.

He also remembered his promise to Edward Donald – that the report would find its way into the major's hands with the seal unbroken. Well, he thought, I can read the letter and still keep that promise. I have the conviction to prove it.

Thankfully, the wax imprint was that of a cross – easy enough for Monsarrat to whittle a forgery that night, and have the paper sealed again well before the major's return. And as a clerk, access to wax would not be an impediment.

Breaking open the seal, he saw that the document was headed 'Port Macquarie Penal Station Medical Department', and addressed to Major Shelborne, Commandant.

'Sir,' wrote Gonville (or more accurately Donald, in what Monsarrat felt was a serviceable but unimaginative hand):

Shortly after your departure on what one hopes will be a significant survey of a region adjacent to the location of the settlement and to the valley in which it is located, your wife fell ill with an unknown sickness.

It is my fervent hope that by the time you read this report, it will no longer be relevant and the lady will have recovered. However, so that you may have a continuous record of her state of health, I have taken it upon myself to describe her condition as it stands, for your perusal on your return.

I must confess, I bear grave concerns for her current condition. Her illness progressed from nausea, vomiting and coughing, with a little dizziness, to her present situation, which sees her racked with convulsions and unable to take sustenance. She has suffered gastrointestinal disturbances. And her maid and housekeeper has told me that the lady confessed to pains in the urinary organs.

Your wife barely uses cosmetic substances but I have taken the liberty of examining what she does possess, in the hope that I could find some egregious agent therein which is contributing to her state. It has been speculated that certain compounds used by women of fashion can adversely affect the health, and give rise to the same symptoms exhibited by your wife.

What she possesses has been made up by reputable chemists in Sydney but chiefly in London. Her facial powder is entirely zinc oxide, which is quite harmless. She does not possess any lip-reddeners of mercuric sulphide, as many fashionable women do but which a lady of her youth, refinement and beauty would not need. Nor does she possess any belladonna for the eyes. Obviously she has not foreseen any circumstance in which she would need these more questionable preparations. Her only perfume is rosewater – again quite innocuous.

One can conclude therefore that her disease has an entirely natural cause and yet one which eludes our current medical understanding. It shares characteristics with gastric fever and cholera; however, it would be unusual for her to be the only one stricken in either case. Though an outsider might argue that some depression of spirit is at work upon her, anyone who beheld her until recently can tell from her presence that she is not subject to such things, at least not to the degree which has now afflicted and disabled her. If we are to be thankful for anything, it is that she has no fever, enabling me to rule out some of the deadlier afflictions, including particular types of plague.

I have bled the lady with leeches, plentiful along the river-bank, and have cupped her in an attempt to draw out any dark humours which might be causing her condition. Here we have met with some limited success, as her symptoms have not worsened over the last few days.

Sir, I also wish to bring to your attention a certain rumour, which I have had from several sources. It is said the Birpai people have cursed your wife, due to her hunting. As educated men, we know this cannot be possible. Yet the simple minds which outnumber us in this place have latched onto the speculation; indeed, many have accepted it as fact. I mention this only to warn you of its potential to cause conflict with the Birpai, as I am sure this is not your desire, given the resources it would require, including medical resources we do not have.

I shall continue to report on Mrs Shelborne's condition, so as to build a medical history.

Until then I remain your humble and obedient servant,
Richard Gonville

So more reports will be arriving via Edward Donald, thought Monsarrat. He decided to refasten the ribbon around the document and lay it facedown, so the tampering with the seal wouldn't be immediately obvious should Donald come by that day. He might even seek Donald out, under the guise of saving the orderly a trip to Government House.

While the letter was still in his hand, the door was shoved open. In the rarified atmosphere, it was unused to such rough treatment, and complained loudly.

Slattery stood in the doorway, which had rarely framed so large a specimen. The young soldier's pupils were dilated, and sweat gave him a gleam which, in winter, usually spoke of a fever.

Monsarrat forced himself to lay the document aside slowly, as though he had been perusing it with a legitimate objective.

'He's a fool, he's a fooking simpleton,' said Slattery. 'You know what he's done, Monsarrat? Dory? He's only gone and absconded. He was seen crossing the bridge at Shoal Arm Creek. Only one reason to do that, Monsarrat. He's heading to Sydney. By land.'

Monsarrat felt a stab of vicarious panic. Dory's chances of a successful escape were slim. And if he were to make it to Sydney, he'd have to subsist as an anonymous labourer, with no hope of a baker's licence and the respectability it conferred.

Slattery let loose a torrent of Irish invective. Monsarrat didn't understand the tortured syllables, but their delivery left no doubt as to their general meaning.

'What will you do?' asked Monsarrat.

'Well, I'll have to go after the bastard, won't I? With any luck I can get him back before Diamond is made aware of his absence. Although . . .'

Monsarrat shared Slattery's doubt. Word of Dory's escape was likely already filtering through the convicts. It was a matter of time – and not much of it – before the news reached Captain Diamond. 'You had best go then, and quickly.'

'Yes. Say nothing of this to Diamond, when he comes by. We'll need the smiles of all Mother Mulrooney's saints if we're to spare the eejit a flogging.'

Chapter 9

Monsarrat had always thought Major Shelborne was an even-handed fellow. Given the distance from his immediate superior, and the time it would take for an order to reach him, the major realised he was, effectively, the absolute ruler of the settlement, rather than simply a custodian or administrator. There were some, in Monsarrat's opinion, who would have let this authority run away with them – Captain Diamond, of course, came to mind. But the major seemed to understand that life on the margins required certain adjustments, that the rule-bound way of operating he had learned in the army might not, in some circumstances, be the best way to run the settlement.

Monsarrat also felt, oddly, that while his own life had stagnated, his assignment allowed him a role in ensuring the life of the settlement moved forward. The major would dictate his wishes on punishment and mercy, on the allocation of resources, on the building of this structure or the tearing down of that one, and Monsarrat's pen stroke would make those abstract thoughts a reality. Far better than scribing for a flint-hard old man and his frivolous colleagues.

But Monsarrat, like Dory, was not at liberty to cross Shoal Arm Creek, and the knowledge of this blighted his internal landscape.

Contentment, at any rate, counted for little with Monsarrat. He had a high opinion of his own intellect, and wanted a stage on which he could show it off. So his months as a counterfeit barrister had been amongst the happiest of his life.

Finally free of Lincoln's Inn, and with his forged call to the bar, Monsarrat had known that practising in London would be impossible. The chances of detection would be unacceptably high. In fact, it was fairly likely he'd be eventually found out anywhere, and one part of his mind knew this. But the compulsion to prove he was better than the Inns of Court gadflies ('Write a brief for me, Monsarrat, there's a good chap'), and the impulse to correct what he saw as a grave injustice, that which prevented him from coming by a call through honest means, overrode this knowledge.

In the early stages, when Monsarrat would try to honestly assess his chances of exposure, he would look at the likelihood out of the corner of his eye, quickly turning away from the unpalatable truth which stared back. After a while, he stopped looking. And from the darkness behind his closed eyes there rose another Monsarrat, a shadow who convinced him, almost, that if he found a provincial town and served his clients honestly and well, giving them no reason to discuss his failings with others, he could continue his ruse indefinitely.

By the time of his capture, the shadow had just about convinced him it was no ruse at all. He had settled upon Exeter. His father had been a clerk there, to one of the many wool merchants operating in the city, and Monsarrat had attended a small grammar school. He felt the combination of his childhood knowledge of the place, its mercantile air and its distance from London would protect him.

He had saved as much as possible over the past few years, and now put the funds towards a law library – a tenth of the cost of the libraries of the young carousers at Lincoln's Inn, but adequate – and leasing chambers and rooms, from which he called upon a carefully constructed list of solicitors who dealt chiefly in civil matters, as these attracted less attention than their counterparts in the more lurid criminal courts.

'Yes, it was a wrench to leave London,' he'd say to their inevitable inquiry as to why a Lincoln's Inn lawyer should be paddling in Exeter's shallow pond. 'But my father doesn't have a peerage, you see, so Oxford and Cambridge were out of reach. And I do find the people of Exeter more . . . practical.'

This appealed to many of the solicitors he visited, coming as they did from a merchant town which valued industry, and resented those with wealth and status who hadn't had to earn them. Many had yearned for years to sweep assuredly into their own chambers at one of the Inns of Court, equal in law with the sons of baronets. The fact that someone who had achieved this happy state had chosen to eschew it in favour of their own town made them feel their situation was perhaps not so mean as they had supposed.

Slowly, the solicitors started to send work to him. They already had barristers they liked dealing with, of course – some of whom paid a healthy commission for referred work, which Monsarrat couldn't afford to match. But when those barristers weren't available to act on minor matters, they decided to give the young man from London a chance.

So Monsarrat represented clients in matters to do with small debts or wills. He did his job well enough to widen the channel of referred work, and larger cases began to trickle through – breach-of-promise suits, contractual issues.

In one case, Monsarrat successfully defended one of the town's most wealthy wool merchants against a breach-of-contract allegation. Johnathan Ham had met a man claiming to be a London cloth merchant at the New Inn, near Ham's own premises on the Exeter high street. The man, Dodds, was unable to attend the weekly wool market, so Ham arranged to show him some broadcloth and serge. They agreed on a price per bale, as long as Dodds liked what he saw. Dodds didn't, saying he had expected better from someone of Ham's reputation, and leaving Ham's premises with a sniff.

Ham didn't think much of the man's judgement, given that his wares were universally acknowledged to be amongst the finest in Exeter. But Dodds, a small and aggressive man, returned the next week, saying he would do Ham a favour by taking the defective (in his view) cloth off Ham's hands for a reduced rate.

Ham took a great deal of delight in telling Dodds the cloth had been sold, to the East India Company at the wool market just gone, for slightly more than Dodds had agreed to pay (he may, he told Monsarrat later, have added to the price in the retelling).

Dodds became furious, saying the pair had a contract which Ham had breached, and for a while Ham regretted his insistence on writing down the terms of their agreement, as a successful action against him would deal a possibly fatal blow both to his finances and reputation. A fifth-generation wool merchant, Ham couldn't begin to imagine what he would do if he had to leave the trade.

He was spared from having to do so by Monsarrat, who successfully argued that as the agreement included the price, any variation voided it. It was an easy argument to make, as Dodds's position was weak, and Monsarrat could have taken the fee and been done with it.

But the flimsiness of Dodds's argument made him wonder why the man bothered, and in the Sundays leading up to his appearance, he made several trips to nearby towns. He spoke to those who were willing, and in Dawlish discovered a merchant who had had a similar experience with Dodds. But the Dawlish merchant had lacked the stomach, or the resources, to meet Dodds in court, instead paying him compensation of half his revised offer for the goods he claimed were substandard.

Monsarrat continued his travels and found similar cases – all involving Dodds – in Seaton and Exmouth. As he laid this information before the court during the contract hearing, Monsarrat had the pleasure of seeing Dodds's vicious smile falter, then die. Dodds, as it turned out, was no merchant at all, and relied on his targets' desire to avoid a potentially damaging legal action by paying him to go away. He had been seriously concerned when Ham let the matter progress to court. He was later charged with fraud, convicted and transported to the colony.

In the weeks afterwards, Monsarrat found himself on the receiving end of an increasing number of briefs, many of them revolving around thorny contractual matters. He was viewed by many merchants as something of a hero, saving them from Dodds and others like him, who would likely be deterred by the man's forced journey south.

He even received permission to walk in Rougemont Gardens with Ham's daughter Lucinda, under the supervision of her nanny, but a walk was as far as things went – she had no interest in Roman poets, and he was unable to converse on the doings of London society.

The increase in his work was matched by an increase in his status in the Exeter legal community. He was invited to and attended legal dinners, but did not make himself conspicuous by standing on benches and singing songs, or by getting notably drunk. He attended both the cathedral for evensong and the Quaker meeting house, since many Exeter merchants were Quakers. They were very decent people, the Quakers, Monsarrat found. Hard-nosed in business but not murderous, unlike some of the self-regarding bankers and merchants one saw at the cathedral.

He relished that gentler, less frantic city, over which clouds of soot did not hang, a city which looked like an English city should, not like the reports of dismal Manchester or Birmingham. In the meantime, he read his Blackstone's *Commentaries* as strenuously as any barrister in Britain, and more so than a whole lot of them.

He prospered perhaps modestly by the standards of some, but bountifully by comparison with the income of a clerk, and he was able to take two rooms and a little boxroom. His life was not that of a monk, although he would not have objected if people thought so. He had enough money left over for an occasional wilder evening in the inns along the River Exe, and would sometimes invite a few of the younger, more sociable solicitors out with him.

One of these was Samuel Smythe, who, like Monsarrat, was approaching his quarter-century. Smythe, the younger son of a merchant who had served as Exeter's mayor, was well established, and already one of the town's busier solicitors, with friends of his father's sending him business to 'help the young fellow along'. This business was increasingly finding its way to Monsarrat.

Monsarrat liked Smythe. He honed his legal knowledge as though it was an implement, was single-minded in his business, and operated honestly, if a little bloodlessly. His only drawback, as far as Monsarrat was concerned, was a tendency to be overly impressed with London lawyers. He frequently boasted to people of his friend's Lincoln's Inn pedigree, which made Monsarrat profoundly uncomfortable.

Still, as their birthdays were only a few weeks apart, Monsarrat agreed with Smythe that they should celebrate together. Arriving at the alehouse Smythe had nominated, Monsarrat saw his friend was not alone.

'Hugh, this is James Dawkins. His father does business with mine, and he's here for his sister's wedding, and a few gulps of fresh air. You probably know each other, both having been at Lincoln's Inn. Hugh, you were there until almost a year ago, weren't you? So you must have crossed paths.'

Monsarrat, of course, had never seen Dawkins. He hoped, desperately, that Dawkins might have seen him on some errand and remembered Monsarrat's face but not the context.

There was an odd frown on Dawkins's face as he examined Monsarrat's features. He's looking at my nose, thought Monsarrat, and thinking, Surely I'd remember that.

Monsarrat's lips began to tingle. His intestines liquefied, solidified again, and knitted themselves into a physiologically impossible pattern – perhaps a noose.

'A funny thing,' said Dawkins. 'I thought I was on speaking terms with everyone at the Inn. You do look familiar though. We have met?'

'I'm sure we must have,' said Monsarrat. To his relief, he sounded casual.

'Who were you in chambers with?' asked Dawkins.

Monsarrat knew his next words would be likely to prove fatal. But it was a likelihood balanced against a certainty of discovery if he did not utter them. 'Oh, with old Fairburn – you know him? Bit of a tartar but very thorough. You could always gauge his mood by how much was in his decanter.'

'Yes, you still can. I know Fairburn and the rest. How odd that we never met.'

'Well, I wasn't there that long,' said Monsarrat.

Smythe was perplexed, as they drank their ale, at the subdued mood which had descended on the table. Dawkins excused himself after a cup or two, glancing at Monsarrat over his shoulder as he left.

Monsarrat was desperate to leave himself, but he and Smythe had both been looking forward to the evening; it would look very strange indeed to suddenly plead a headache. And while a small but spreading corner of his mind knew he was done for, he forced himself to believe he might just have saved it, that Dawkins might just think, Well, he did look familiar, I must have just forgotten him. It would be a shame to escape revelation, only to bring it on by acting out of character.

He resolved, though, that a period of absence from Exeter might be wise. He would depart first thing in the morning, send word to Smythe and his other instructing solicitors that he had to deal with a family emergency. He would fail to say what family member, or where they lived. In the meantime, the safest course was to act as though nothing was amiss, which meant drinking ale with Smythe. The ale, he thought, might do him good.

In fact, his nerves made him consume rather more ale than he was used to, being only an occasional drinker. By the time he had tottered home to his lodgings, he reasoned that he could start the preparations for his departure at first light. Dawkins, after all, was unlikely to be certain of Monsarrat's real background, and it would take some time for him to return to London, check with Fairburn and alert the authorities, if that's what he meant to do.

But Monsarrat had miscalculated. Dawkins did think he'd seen Monsarrat before, and in connection with Fairburn. But he was equally certain he knew every lawyer at the Inn. Perhaps he was doing the familiar-looking stranger a disservice, he thought, but as it was still early when he left the inn, he called on Mr Justice Allen, whom he knew, to raise his concerns. If the fellow really was what he claimed to be, the matter could be quickly laid to rest. If not – well, the more swiftly the rot was excised, the better.

The dawn found Monsarrat still asleep. He was woken by a tap on his door, polite but insistent. On the other side, a beadle and two constables told him he was required before Mr Justice Allen. Yesterday, he was angelically clever. Today, he was being called upon to explain what could not be explained.

Ten years later another Monsarrat, a different man in the same body, relived that experience when he heard of Dory's apprehension, as he had whenever anyone was apprehended for any reason.

Slattery had indeed lost no time in going after Dory, taking a horse from the stables and riding it hard, praying he was not passing the young man hiding in the trees.

When he came upon Dory, who had stopped for a rest, the young man had looked up at him with deadened eyes, and had not tried to escape. Slattery told Dory he would take him back to the settlement. If they returned before his escape had been reported, he might be able to pass it off, he said. If word of the escape had made its way to the higher-ups, Slattery would have to take Dory in.

'I asked him why he did it; of course I did,' Slattery told Monsarrat later. 'He had five years left, but it's not forever. He said he looked at Frogett and Daines every day and saw nothing. They've both been here a few years, were amongst the first, in fact, and in the colony for five, six years before that. Dory said he didn't want to be hollowed out like them, but he could feel his soul beginning to bleed through his feet.'

'So why did he stop?' asked Monsarrat.

'He realised, as he walked, that his chances of making Sydney were slim. He also realised he would never make it back to the settlement in time. He knew then, he said, that he was doomed either way. There was nothing to be done. He might as well sit and wait. Breathe air that wasn't putrid, probably for the last time. And let me and his fate take him.'

Slattery's fear that Diamond would find out about the escape became a reality when he approached the Shoal Arm bridge, Dory on the horse behind him, to see Diamond crossing it.

Slattery said that when Diamond saw him, he gave a smile which 'turned me to river water'. 'He looked at me and he shook his head, and that smile didn't flicker,' said Slattery. 'He just said, "Private, how unwise of you to go after an absconder without taking irons."'

Diamond had not made the same mistake. He had brought shackles. He had Dory dismount, and ordered Slattery to apply them. Then the young man was marched to the prison to await whatever punishment Diamond decided to bestow.

Chapter 10

Dory was a foolish boy, Monsarrat thought, not only to escape, but to do so while the settlement was under the control of Captain Diamond.

Monsarrat himself bypassed the kitchen the next morning, the solace of a cup of tea and Mrs Mulrooney's comforting presence. He felt certain that Diamond would be by sooner rather than later, and knew it was important, particularly now, to demonstrate rectitude by being at his desk and well into the day's work when the captain got there.

His instincts were proved right when Diamond swept into his workroom mid-morning. Ignoring Monsarrat for the moment, he went directly to the major's study, and sat himself behind Shelborne's desk – a place no one but the commandant had sat before – only then showing he was aware of Monsarrat's existence by calling him in.

'I shall require your services, Monsarrat, when it comes to dealing with yesterday's absconder. First, though, there is another matter between us.'

Monsarrat related the contents of Gonville's report, with Diamond unaware that the source of the information lay near his elbow, resealed in a way which would withstand all but the most thorough of examinations.

The captain's face was impassive as he listened. 'Well,' he said when Monsarrat finished, 'things seem to be moving with a frustrating sluggishness.'

Monsarrat assumed, or wanted to assume, that Diamond was referring to Honora Shelborne's failure to rally. If he let his imagination run away with him, he could almost believe that Diamond was referring to the young woman's failure to die with efficiency.

'I shall be expecting another report tomorrow. See that your information is fresh.'

'Yes, sir,' said Monsarrat. He would redouble his efforts, from here on in, to be scrupulously correct in his dealings with Diamond. There were a handful of genuine monsters sprinkled amongst the settlement's mostly petty criminals, and Diamond, to Monsarrat's mind, was fast assuming the mantle of one of them.

'Now,' said the soldier, 'you and I are going to the police house to sentence the absconder William Dory. I will give you the sentence so you can make a start on the administrative necessities.'

Monsarrat presumed that Diamond wished him to transcribe a report to the Colonial Secretary. It would be telling, he thought, whether he left it with Monsarrat for the major's signature, or signed and sent it himself.

'You may inform the Colonial Secretary that given the number of recent escapes and the generally refractory nature of the prisoners here, I feel the convict population would be edified by witnessing a more severe punishment than usual,' said Diamond.

Monsarrat felt a sudden wrench of fear for Dory.

'Please inform him that I am sentencing the absconder to one hundred lashes,' said Diamond.

'One hundred!' Monsarrat was unable to stop himself. 'Sir, prior to his departure Governor Macquarie left instructions that no punishment was to exceed fifty lashes, and the major has never ordered more than thirty-five.'

Diamond slowly rose from behind the desk and leaned forward. His eyes narrowed, and Monsarrat fancied he saw a spark there which had not been present as he listened to the report on Mrs Shelborne's condition.

'Now listen, Monsarrat, with your ridiculous intellectual pretensions. I don't care if you can recite the Psalms backwards in Latin. You're a convict like the rest of them. Worse than the rest, actually, as you're educated and should have known better. Clearly beyond redemption, criminal to the bone, and no amount of Roman poetry will change it. This settlement has been left in my care, and I will do what I think best to ensure its integrity.'

He sat back down. 'The governor who gave that order is taking his ease in Scotland. He and I never even stood on this landmass at the same time. One hundred lashes is the maximum allowable by law, so one hundred it shall be.'

Monsarrat was certain Diamond would have ordered more, had the law allowed it. One hundred lashes, he knew, was a discount on the brutality of previous years, which had seen several hundred administered. Sometimes, by the end, the scourger had been flogging a corpse.

But one hundred lashes could kill a man too. Sometimes the heart gave out, simply stopped beating in protest at the pain. Or it stopped beating due to lack of work, too much blood having been drawn off by the knotted cords of the flail. Or if it struggled on with its work, the wounds could absorb the noxious atmosphere around them, turning blood into poison.

But he was sure any further protest would see him on a work gang, or worse, by that afternoon. He confined himself to a small bow.

'The sentence will be administered tomorrow,' said Diamond, rolling his shoulders as though to entice the robe of a ruler to settle there. 'Dory will then endure solitary confinement on bread and water for one month. Please draft a report to this effect, and be sure to emphasise that past punishments have failed to prevent further escape attempts.'

Monsarrat swiftly withdrew to his workroom to begin writing up the loathsome report, until Diamond told him to make for the police house for the sentencing. He hoped Dory got the right scourger. One of the convict constables was usually appointed to do the job. Two of them usually had to be urged to strike harder.

But a third, an ill-favoured man with scrawls of black hair around a bald crown, like a demented parody of a monk's tonsure, needed no such urging. He enjoyed inflicting the punishment, smiled while doing so. Quietly, Major Shelborne had decided not to appoint him to the task in future. Monsarrat doubted Diamond would have the same reluctance.

The business at the police house was a quick affair. Dory was brought in, and Diamond had Monsarrat read the charge. Diamond then pronounced the sentence. Monsarrat looked at Dory in a way which he hoped conveyed support. Dory didn't see him, though. His eyes lost focus when he heard the sentence, and it seemed he was channelling all his concentration into maintaining a neutral expression. In his short life, he would have learned the dangers of showing fear to wolves.

Monsarrat had hoped Diamond would make for the parade ground on their return, but he seemed to like the commandant's office. As Monsarrat forced himself to calmly compose the report, he heard papers being moved. He's playing at commandant, Monsarrat thought. Trying it on for size.

After a few minutes, Diamond stalked into the workroom. 'Oh, Monsarrat,' he said as he pushed open the door. 'Please also make a note that we will not be using a trustee to carry out the sentence. Clearly they are not doing a proper job, if thirty lashes is not putting people off. Slattery, now there's an interesting soldier. You're acquainted with him, I believe. Do you know, he went after the absconder with no means of restraining him? He brought him back without so much as a belt or a rope around his wrists. I applaud his initiative, but he really needs to be more careful. He will give the prisoner his hundred lashes. It will teach him not to be sloppy in future.'

~♦~

He knew it was cowardly, but Monsarrat would have liked to avoid seeing his young friend scourge a fellow he had some regard for. The choice, however, wasn't his. All convicts were required to watch floggings. In a society where many viewed convicts as

108

irredeemable, born criminals who could not change their nature, Monsarrat found it odd that observing a flogging was thought to prevent further, similar misbehaviour. If transportation and its attendant miseries hadn't forced a man to change, what difference was watching someone else suffer going to make?

So he stood in the yard near the convict barracks that afternoon, with a great number of other felons, staring at the triangular frame, slightly taller than a man, which had been set up there. The wood of the frame was light but festooned with darker blotches, which Monsarrat knew to be blood stains.

Dory was brought in, his eyes down. He was made to face the frame, his wrists tied to its apex. Then Slattery entered, both arms straight, trailing the scourge, its nine cords knotted to increase their capacity to sunder flesh. His jaw was set, whether in determination or horror was not immediately clear. But as he approached the frame, his eyes moved over the crowd, settling on Monsarrat.

The older man had to stop himself from stepping backwards, shrinking from the alarming change in his friend. The laughing rogue he had faced across yesterday's kitchen table was gone. Slattery's eyes seemed to have sunk deeper into his skull, as though he had balled up his fists and pushed them in with the considerable force of which he was capable. Leaping out of them, in almost visible arcs, was a ferocious anger. This is not our dancing boy, Monsarrat thought. This is not our bluffer, our teller of tales. He has been scooped out and replaced with refined hatred.

Slattery gave Monsarrat the briefest of nods, and approached the frame. He put one hand on Dory's shoulder, placed his head next to the boy's, and whispered something. He saluted Diamond, who was watching impassively. Then he stepped back, and struck.

Monsarrat had seen coachmen use whips on horses in England. At the first flogging he attended (and there had been dozens since), he had expected the flail to emit a similar crack. But the sound he heard was duller and all the more horrifying for it, and became more muted as the flesh of the back opened up, the blood and tissues absorbing the noise.

Slattery's first blow was far weaker than it could have been. He did not turn his body and extend his arm backwards. He simply held up the flail, and propelled it towards Dory. Even so, the first lash left large welts, as did the next three. The fourth left a line of blood. Slattery, Monsarrat noticed, was taking care to strike in different places each time, to put off the inevitable moment when the flesh would shred beyond repair.

Diamond, though, was getting impatient. 'Use more force, private,' he called. 'If you are incapable of carrying out a task we usually give to the convicts, we may have to reconsider your position.'

For a moment, Slattery showed no sign that he had heard. Then he did reach backwards, and the lash connected with Dory with enough force to open a wound from one shoulderblade to the other. Dory, who until now had been impressively silent, grunted but did not cry out. Convict etiquette dictated that punishments be endured with as little evidence of pain as possible, and younger felons were told by gaolyard elders with scarred backs that crying out only made it hurt more anyway.

The next few blows were just as strong. Then, Monsarrat noticed, Slattery began to decrease the force of each blow, almost imperceptibly, no doubt hoping Diamond wouldn't notice.

Diamond did. 'If it's too much for you, private, we can get one of the ladies to do it,' he said, earning a snicker from some of the more sadistic or toadying soldiers.

The next thirty or forty lashes continued in the same vein, with Slattery gradually decreasing the force until Diamond noticed and urged him to greater brutality.

By fifty lashes, when Dory's back was more welt and wound than skin, he was grunting with every blow, but still managing to resist the urge to cry out.

Diamond had clearly decided he wanted more noise, and was sick of Slattery's game. He stepped forward. 'Private, I find myself forced to give you some guidance in administering punishment. Hand me the flail.'

Slattery looked momentarily alarmed, before the instincts which served him in Three Card Brag enabled him to rearrange his features into a study in neutrality. He gave Diamond the flail, and stepped away.

Diamond turned his torso side on to the frame, stretching his arm as far back as he possibly could. He paused for a moment, uncoiled, arcing the flail upwards and then down towards Dory. When it connected, it made a sound which was as close to a whip crack as Monsarrat had ever heard at a flogging.

And he kept doing it. Turning, stretching, uncoiling and lashing with inhuman detachment. Each movement was precise, coordinated and perfectly timed. It was calibrated to cause maximum damage.

Everyone watching, including Slattery, had expected Diamond to make his point and then hand back the flail. But he didn't. He seemed to become lost in the dance, seeing nothing except the flail, caring about nothing except its trajectory and velocity. He did not stop. He did not seem to tire from the effort. He became an extension of the flail, merely its power source, a river to its mill.

After Diamond's first few lashes, Dory was unable to stop a cry escaping him. After the next ten, he was no longer trying to stay silent. After twenty, the cords on the scourge began to excavate glimpses of bone, which became larger as Diamond continued with the same force, the same gap between strikes, and the same vacant look. By now, Dory was screaming.

'Captain!' shouted the doctor. 'Let me examine the boy!'

But Diamond ignored him. At around eighty lashes, Dory's legs stopped supporting his weight, and he fell silent. Monsarrat couldn't see his face, but hoped he had only lost consciousness. He was now held up solely by the ropes tethering him to the frame, his toes the only part of him making contact with the ground, as though he had been frozen in the act of kneeling. His back was a gelatinous, glistening red field, dotted with snowflakes of exposed rib, and streaked with a few – a very few – yellow smears of fat, a commodity he didn't possess in any great quantity.

Monsarrat wondered what Dory was experiencing, wherever his mind had taken him. Was he still dimly aware he was being flogged, or was he lost in a dark wasteland, the sky illuminated by red flashes of pain?

Monsarrat had been counting every stroke, partly because of his natural clerk's thoroughness, and partly as a distraction. On the hundredth, he exhaled. Whatever was to come, Dory's suffering was at an end for now.

And then Diamond coiled, released and struck again. And again, hard enough to make the frame scrape backwards, taking Dory with it. Diamond did not seem to notice. There was a vacancy to him, and the lashes seemed to be powered more by momentum than by any will of the captain's.

Dr Gonville stepped forward. 'Captain,' he said, 'the sentence has been carried out. You are exceeding the maximum allowable number of lashes, and I am officially informing you that further punishment may jeopardise the prisoner's life. Please, stand down.'

Diamond stopped, looked at him, smiled as if in a daze, and then struck again, and again.

'Stand down, captain!' Gonville shouted again. 'By God I will report you!'

He started towards Diamond. The captain gave no sign he noticed Gonville's approach, but as the distance closed, he suddenly shoved out a hand and sent the doctor staggering backwards.

Monsarrat had by now counted one hundred and twenty lashes. Gonville was gathering himself for another approach, but Slattery, who had been watching in shock, suddenly darted forward and grabbed Diamond's wrist as he drew back to strike.

'Let him alone, you mad bastard!' he yelled. 'You've punished him enough.'

Diamond did stop, then, looking at Slattery's hand on his wrist, and then into the young man's face. 'Those additional lashes were not to punish the felon, private,' he said. 'They were to punish you.'

He dropped the lash at Slattery's feet, and ordered Dory taken down from the frame. Then he gave orders for Private Slattery to be taken to the guardhouse, there to spend the night as punishment for insubordination.

Dory was being handled by another private, who had hold of him under each arm, dragging him facedown towards the gate. Major Shelborne always had convicts taken to the hospital after a flogging. He claimed it was to ensure the convict returned to a productive state as soon as possible, but Monsarrat suspected him of more humane motives. He fervently hoped Diamond would leave this practice in place.

He did. But as the prisoner was being dragged past him, he held up a hand to stop the private. He bent over, examining Dory's back. Then, with the deliberateness he might have applied to loading a musket, he spat into the wound.

Chapter 11

Slattery did not come by the kitchen the next morning, being possibly still incarcerated, and nor did his diminished crew. Monsarrat himself had only intended to make a brief appearance, perhaps even denying himself a cup of tea. But when he arrived, he found Mrs Mulrooney standing at the stove, quietly weeping. Her tears were not interfering with her work. Some of them splashed, fizzled and died in the skillet in which she was frying the breakfast eggs she knew would not be eaten.

In two years, these were the first tears which had been allowed to escape Mrs Mulrooney in Monsarrat's presence, and they alarmed him. Without words, he took her by the shoulders and guided her to a kitchen chair. He took the skillet off the stove and tried to ignore the small splash of grease which hopped from it onto his pearl waistcoat. He poured her a cup of tea – the first in their acquaintance, balanced against the hundreds she had poured for him – and sat down opposite her, waiting in silence.

Mrs Mulrooney was breathing deeply now, regaining her composure and dabbing at her eyes with the edge of her pinafore. 'I'm a foolish old woman,' she said.

'That is the most extreme falsehood I've heard since leaving England, and I've heard hundreds, some quite imaginative.'

One side of Mrs Mulrooney's mouth quirked up in a distracted half-smile, before her despondency quashed it. 'I don't think it's long, Mr Monsarrat. I held her hand all night. Her fingers are so thin, her wedding ring slipped off her hand into mine – I've put it in the drawer of her dresser, by the way, should the major be looking for it. No point putting it back on her finger, not until . . . well, the major might wish it to make the last journey with her.'

'Is there no hope? I thought the bleeding and cupping had curtailed some of the worst of her symptoms.'

Mrs Mulrooney looked at Monsarrat strangely. 'Had I told you about the bleeding and cupping, then? I can't recall it.'

Monsarrat was tempted, sorely tempted, to confide in her regarding Diamond's interest in Mrs Shelborne's condition, and the task he had been set. But her distress worried him, manifesting as it was in someone not prone to histrionics. 'You must have mentioned it, I suppose.'

'Hm. Well, the wedding ring, those fingers made of sticks, they're not the worst of it. If she's sleeping fitfully, I give her hand a squeeze. It calms her. She knows someone's there, then, watching over her, I know she does because she squeezes back. So last night, she began moaning. She does that a lot now, and I gave her hand a little squeeze. Her finger twitched. That was all. There was no squeeze. If she's too weak to squeeze my hand, Mr Monsarrat, she might be too weak to keep breathing.'

'You should mention it to Dr Gonville – he surely should be told of such a change in her condition.'

'I can't leave here though, Mr Monsarrat. I don't know what time that awful man is going to let Fergal free. He's friendly with some of the other young soldiers, told one of them he would return the stake the man had lost at the last card game if he would come to me with the news of Fergal's whereabouts. He brought the news of the flogging for free. I want to be here when Fergal comes by, if he does. After a night in the guardhouse he'll need tea. May I ask you as a favour to me, would you go and see the doctor?'

'Of course,' said Monsarrat, 'though I'll need to wait for Diamond. Nevertheless, I'm sure his interest will prompt him to allow me to make the errand.'

Mrs Mulrooney looked up sharply. 'His interest, you say. And you have sparked mine, for I must confess, I have long suspected Diamond's chief interest is taking everything that belongs to the major.'

'You mean his job,' said Monsarrat, in a futile attempt to dodge the question.

'His job, yes, that's part of it,' said Mrs Mulrooney. 'You know what they're all like, Monsarrat; they're interested in advancement, in glory. And there's precious little of either out here. They could commit the most outrageous act of valour here, but without anyone to record it, without a general there to witness it, what's the point? That's what they think, anyway. Some of their eyes are as dead as those of the felons. I suppose it's a kind of sentence for them as well. That's why young Slattery is such a tonic. That boy could find fun in hell.'

'Well, if our captain wants advancement to the lofty rank of major, he's going the wrong way about it,' said Monsarrat. 'I would not be at all surprised if the doctor reported his conduct yesterday.'

'Oh, advancement's only part of it for Diamond. If you were to ask me, I would say that there's something else of the major's he wants. Do you remember when Mrs Shelborne let me come with her in that sea box?'

'Let you? To hear you talk at the time, she nearly had to compel you at the point of a musket.'

From the look Mrs Mulrooney gave him, Monsarrat considered himself fortunate he was not in swatting range.

'A most delightful afternoon it was, and I won't hear you talking ill of it, Mr Monsarrat. But while we were there, we heard someone passing. Just as well, thought I, for the canvas sheet protecting the young woman's modesty. It was a bright day, and whoever it was passing by outside cast their shadow on the canvas. It was no woman.'

'You know who it was?'

'Indeed I do, for he spoke. I recognised the voice as Diamond's, right enough, but I'd only ever heard it barking orders before. It sounded different that day, though. Oily, like someone trying to convince you they'd found a way to weave gold out of straw. He must've thought that that was what Mrs Shelborne was used to hearing, or that it would please her. But his presence didn't please her, anything but. I saw her draw her shift more tightly about herself, even though he wouldn't have seen more than her outline through the canvas.'

'And what did he say, in this oily voice?' asked Monsarrat.

'That he hoped she was well and enjoying her time in the ocean. That one of the great benefits of this place was that imaginative individuals such as herself could start undertakings which would have been impossible in the old world. Then he just stood there for a while. Well, Mr Monsarrat, she is the soul of courtesy, that girl; she thanked him, and wished him a good day. It's a funny thing with those who are born to it – they can let you know you're dismissed without actually dismissing you. But he didn't seem to realise he was being sent on his way. He stayed there for what must've been a full five minutes. I think he was facing us, because I couldn't see the outline of his nose. She glanced towards him every now and then, and kept giving me little smiles, as though she was concerned I might be discomfited by his presence. She was right about that, I can tell you. After a while, he moved off. Without another word. She turned to me, all smiles, and said how wonderful it was that even here, one could still find a familiar face from home. Then she asked me how I was finding the water, whether I was becoming chilled or would like to stay in the box for longer. Well, I didn't want to get out right then, didn't know whether Diamond would be lurking nearby. Although to be honest I was becoming a bit cold. We stayed in for another little while after that, and she didn't mention the captain again.'

'I must admit,' said Monsarrat, 'that I did get the impression when we were presented to her that she and Diamond already knew each other.'

'I'm certain of it,' said Mrs Mulrooney. 'But how or when, and what the nature of their acquaintance was, is not something I can shed any light on. And judging by his performance yesterday, the captain seems to be a bit deranged. It frightens me.'

'Yesterday was certainly amongst the more disturbing things I have witnessed,' said Monsarrat. 'He was always a martinet, but he seems to be straying into a level of brutality I haven't seen since my time on the road gang.'

'Then you should be on your guard, Mr Monsarrat, for he is the authority here now. And he seems to believe you have too lofty an idea of yourself. It's to be hoped he doesn't decide to teach you your place.'

'That very eventuality is one of my chief concerns at the moment,' said Monsarrat.

Mrs Mulrooney got up then, and traced with her feet the well-trodden but invisible lines that marked her daily path around the kitchen. The eggs had congealed in the skillet, earning it a glare from her, and a few muttered words of Irish which may or may not have been entirely appropriate from the mouth of a woman her age.

As she restored the skillet to the stove, her eyes on it all the while, she said, 'Mr Monsarrat, you're to tell me at once, what do you know of the captain's interest in Mrs Shelborne? And of the cupping and bleeding, for that matter?'

Monsarrat had known it was foolish to hope Mrs Mulrooney hadn't noticed his slips. Really, he was surprised at himself – he believed in using words with surgical precision, and took a great deal of care in how he employed them. Having one word out of place, he believed, could make an entire structure collapse, leaving him standing in a verbal rubble from which nothing useful could be constructed.

And that being the case, thought Monsarrat, was I really being careless when I mentioned the cupping and bleeding and Diamond? Or is my conscience still alive somewhere? Is it trying to position me so that confiding in Mrs Mulrooney is my only choice?

'I will tell you, but I fear you'll despise me afterwards,' he said. He was surprised by how despondent the prospect of her disapproval made him.

'I'll not despise you, Mr Monsarrat,' said Mrs Mulrooney. 'Of course, I may be wrathful, and for some time, and I may not consider you worthy of tea, but I shall never hate you. You've shown yourself too decent a man for that, even though I suspect what I'm going to hear from you today won't be an act of decency.'

Monsarrat noticed that the speed of her movements had increased as she was talking, her hands carrying out their accustomed tasks without, it seemed, any conscious direction from their mistress. She dreads the moment, he thought, when there is no longer a need for a tray of eggs and tea to be brought to the house.

'An act of desperation, perhaps,' he said, 'but I don't offer that as an excuse.'

He told her about his conversation with Diamond on the beach, and all of their conversations since. 'I must say, I am becoming increasingly unsettled by the change in the man. He has always been far from soft, but, as you say, his behaviour is beginning to verge on the unhinged. And there was a point, while he was flogging Dory, when I believed he had lost all sense of who or where he was. This is not a man I felt I could refuse. My brief period on the work gangs nearly killed me, Mrs Mulrooney, and as poor a motivation as it is, I did not want to go back there. Please forgive me.'

'For a smart man,' she said, 'you can be a bit of an eejit sometimes.'

Monsarrat felt, a little unjustifiably, annoyed. 'What would you have me do?' he said. 'Who would it serve if I was building a road, with a few years of miserable life left in me before my health failed? I know I have behaved in a way which is less than honourable – and believe me, I chastise myself for it daily – but if you could have thought of another way out of the situation, I would be very interested in hearing about it, for none presented itself to me.'

'You really are making me doubt your intelligence, Mr Monsarrat,' Mrs Mulrooney said. 'I wasn't talking about your agreement with Diamond. Of course you had to do as he said, we are all of us under his rule at the moment, and the only person who can overrule him is several days' ride away. Don't get too hopeful – I am very angry at you, and will exact my revenge in due course. But for the moment, does this knowledge not make you want to ask any particular question?'

'You mean, why would Diamond want such information? Of course. However, I had thought that I asked and answered that question in the same moment. He's clearly in love with Mrs Shelborne, or at the least has a kind of obsession with her. It wasn't just details of her medical condition he wanted, but of her spirits and so forth. Why would he want to know that unless he did have some tender feelings for her?'

'But you're a student of human nature, Mr Monsarrat. You must realise that love, even the twisted kind that the captain seems to have for Mrs Shelborne, can provoke one of two responses. Tenderness, or something a bit darker.'

'Yes, I suppose . . . But what are you suggesting?'

'Only that Diamond, with his leanings towards brutality, might have decided his chances of ever getting either the major's job or his wife were slim. We know he's a violent man, and after yesterday we know his violence is out of its cage. So, what does a man with those inclinations do when he realises the object of his adoration will never be his?'

A sickly unease unfolded itself in Monsarrat's belly. 'He might,' he said, 'decide that destiny meant her to be his, or no one's. Therefore, he will make her no one's. But you're not suggesting that Diamond is responsible for Mrs Shelborne's condition? How on earth? It beggars belief.'

'Her entire condition beggars belief, Mr Monsarrat. Dr Gonville confesses himself perplexed. And if the doctor hasn't seen anything like it in nature, perhaps there is nothing like it in nature.'

'What, then? Are you suggesting some sort of poison? How would Diamond administer it? Especially as Mrs Shelborne has now been cloistered for nearly a fortnight. If poison were involved, wouldn't the poisoner need continuous access to the victim? Even now, with Diamond in a position of unalloyed power, that's a stretch, if I may say so.'

'You may say so,' said Mrs Mulrooney. 'But I tell you, Mr Monsarrat, I feel sure there is a human agency involved here – either that or the native curse is indeed at work. But I've never been a believer in fairies and curses, and nothing I've seen in this strange place has changed that.'

As the notion stretched out to fill the corners of his mind, Monsarrat realised it had an awful elegance. He remembered that the doctor had mentioned arsenic. 'Very well. I think we must at least entertain the idea, Mrs Mulrooney. You have one of the sharpest intellects I have ever had the pleasure to encounter. You would leave those dullards at Lincoln's Inn standing in the dust. So if the facts are suggesting to you such a terrible explanation, we must at least do what we can to prove you right or wrong. What do you suggest?'

Mrs Mulrooney had left the stove unattended for as long as she ever had in Monsarrat's presence. Now she removed her cleaning cloth from its hook and went to a great deal of trouble to slowly circle the table until she reached the empty space behind his chair. She very deliberately pulled back on the cloth and then released it so that it connected with as much force as possible with the back of his head. It would never have occurred to him to object. If Mrs Mulrooney believed he deserved a thrashing with the cleaning cloth, he had no doubt it was true.

'If I didn't know you, Mr Monsarrat, I'd think you'd been at Slattery's poteen, so dull are your wits today. Why, are we not in the ideal situation to look into this? Are you not on your way to the workroom, in anticipation of a visit from the very man we're discussing? And will he not be expecting a report from you on the woman whose life he may be in the process of ending?'

'As always, what you say is true,' said Monsarrat.

'So do as our captain has asked you. Make sure to emphasise that Mrs Shelborne's condition is unlikely to give her much more time on this earth. Observe his reaction. And then, report everything to me.'

So Monsarrat made his way to the workroom, now with two commissions to fulfil, for two different but equally formidable taskmasters. He was ashamed, given the mortal peril in which Honora Shelborne lay, to feel a stirring of excitement, of the kind he had last felt when he realised what Dodds was up to in forcing payments from wool merchants.

He had barely settled himself at his desk when a solid, even tread announced the captain's approach. The man pushed open the door with more force than even Slattery would have used. Why do these soldiers feel the need to abuse timber so? thought Monsarrat.

Mrs Mulrooney had been right when she said he was a student of human nature. Monsarrat made it a habit to look people in the face while conversing, believing their expressions could tell him as much as their words, if not more. But recently, with the dark turn in Diamond's character, more often than not he had observed his boots while in conversation with the officer. Today, he realised, that would have to change.

Diamond had made immediately for the study, where he was going through the dispatches, shuffling the sealed papers like a deck of cards. Setting them aside in frustration, he called Monsarrat in.

Monsarrat entered and stood respectfully in front of the major's desk – it was still the major's desk, he told himself, despite the usurper currently sitting behind it. 'Good morning, sir,' he said, with what he hoped was the right level of obsequiousness. Overdoing it might scare the horses.

'Monsarrat,' said Diamond. 'I trust you have a report for me.'

'A troubling one. Mrs Shelborne appears to be unresponsive. It is not known whether she is still able to hear speech, but she is incapable of it herself. Breathing is becoming more difficult for her. I have not yet had a prognosis, but it is hard to see how she can survive much longer.'

Monsarrat forced himself to look at the officer while delivering the report. Diamond kept his eyes down on the dispatches. He did not betray any emotion; however, Monsarrat fancied he saw a flicker at the corner of the man's right eye.

'Well, that's of limited use to me. The suppositions of a housekeeper are hardly likely to give us an accurate picture of the lady's condition. What do you propose to do about it, Monsarrat? And I do hope, for your sake, that you have a proposal.'

'Indeed, sir. It would be a very natural thing for you to send me to report the housekeeper's observations to the surgeon. With your permission, I will tell him that you have requested his urgent attendance on the lady, and accompany him back to Government House. During the journey I may learn something.'

'You had best be off then, Monsarrat. And deliver another report this afternoon. My arm is tired from my exertions yesterday, but I fancy it may have a few more lashes left in it. Or Slattery might enjoy some company.'

Chapter 12

Monsarrat tried to dismiss Diamond's throwaway threat of imprisonment. He was, after all, the settlement's best clerk, and nothing here moved forward unless the orders for it to do so were transcribed by his pen. Still, Monsarrat was only an inch away from imprisonment at any time, and had experienced several gaols now. Some were better than others, but he had no wish to revisit them or any of their relatives. He also hoped Slattery wasn't suffering too greatly in the guardhouse – the man was not made to be confined.

Monsarrat's first night as a prisoner in Exeter County Gaol was more comfortable than it could have been. The gaoler did not particularly care that Monsarrat's funds were the proceeds of crime, and was more than happy to take some of the tainted money in exchange for a private cell. He drove a hard bargain on the matter of fetching Monsarrat some dinner from the Wool Sack Inn, but eventually they agreed on the price for that service too.

As he finished the meal, Monsarrat wondered whether he had wasted his money – although he was outwardly calm, every cell in his body had gone into revolt at the thought of his exposure, and the dread of what was to come. It seemed that his ability to taste food had shut down so that his body could direct its resources into more useful areas. What these areas might be was lost on Monsarrat for now, for unless he was able to grow wings, he could not see a way out of his present situation.

His generosity to the gaoler also meant that, in theory, he could receive visitors. But Monsarrat did not believe he would get any. He was proved wrong when Samuel Smythe appeared at the door of his cell. His friend was smiling, though Monsarrat could not for a moment think why.

'Well, of all the adventures, this takes it, Monsarrat,' said Smythe, clapping his hands with enthusiasm. 'We will be able to dine and drink on this one for months. Our first port of call will be that fool Dawkins. We will make him buy us the most lavish dinner ever seen in Exeter in exchange for his putting you to this inconvenience. Have you sent to London yet? When will the letters attesting to your good character start to flow in?'

Since leaving London, Monsarrat had become skilled in convincing himself he was who and what he pretended to be. He now realised this conviction had been crucial to his ability to convince others of his credentials. He thought, for a moment, of going along with Smythe's interpretation, of pretending that he had been unfairly accused by Dawkins, but he knew this would only delay the inevitable moment when Smythe would learn that his friendship with the London lawyer was grounded in fiction.

'Smythe, I beg your forgiveness,' he said. 'It's true. I should be here. I have never been called to the bar, although I know a good deal of the law, as you've seen yourself. Still, I have appeared in court when I have no right to do so, and my next appearance will be on the wrong side of the dock.'

Smythe continued to smile, perhaps believing that Monsarrat was extending the joke. But when he realised the look on Monsarrat's face was anything but mirthful, his own glee began to fade, and in its place rose the first stirrings of anger.

Smythe's mouth began to work, but for a few moments no sound came out. He took a deep breath, collected his thoughts, and in an even voice said, 'You're serious. I can see that. But how? I've seen you in court, Monsarrat. You have the same knowledge as any other man who appears before the bar, more than some. Why would you go to the trouble of acquiring that knowledge without acquiring a genuine call to the bar to go with it?'

'Calls to the bar are beyond the means of the likes of me. I lacked the connections to be accepted to any Inn of Court, to attend those dinners which the gentlemen I served complained were so tedious. To me it would have been like an invitation onto Mount Olympus. But to them it was a chore. As to the knowledge, I worked for several learned barristers, conversed with them on the same level of intellect, read their briefs and sometimes saw in them overlooked but crucial points bearing on the outcome of cases. I read everything which went through my hands, and every law volume I could find. My competence owes everything to diligence and nothing to privilege.'

Smythe was glaring now. 'I trusted you. I funnelled work to you which could have gone to other barristers, real barristers, those with families. You made a fool of me, you made a fool of the whole damned court. Did you think there would be no reckoning? How could you possibly have expected to evade detection indefinitely?'

'I hoped my success in court would reduce any chance of discovery, and for a short while I deluded myself that I lived in a world where skill could excuse my presumption,' said Monsarrat. 'Still, I became very used to living from one day to the next, and evading detection by sundown seemed a good enough result for me. I did not know how many sundowns I had, but I'd convinced myself there would be more than in fact there have been. Smythe, I am sorry. I didn't do this to make a fool of you, and if you feel that that's been the result, I regret it more than I can say. Our friendship has been one of the delights of my time in Exeter.'

'Our friendship was no such thing, based as it was on a falsehood,' said Smythe. He was silent for a minute or so. 'But I will do one thing for you, Monsarrat, criminal though you be. You know I deal in criminal matters as well as civil ones. There's another young man I've been dealing with lately, who is proving himself very able at criminal cases. Now, I don't for a moment believe that you will be acquitted – you've confirmed your guilt to me, and those letters I expected to flood in from London may yet still flood in, but with rather different information. You are doomed. But you deserve representation. I'll ask this man – Telford is his name – if he is willing to represent you. But do not be surprised if he declines. You've made a mockery of his profession as you have of mine. You and I will not be meeting again.'

When Smythe left, Monsarrat realised he was probably on his way to a legal dinner which Monsarrat himself had been going to attend, and at which he would now be the chief topic of conversation.

◦━◦◦━◦

Monsarrat's only other visitor, during the long wait for charges to be laid, was Matthew Telford, the lawyer sent by Smythe. It turned out that Telford was willing to assist Monsarrat out of conviction that even the meanest criminal deserved representation. He was one of the young Exeter radicals who belonged to the Reform Society and who understood the frustrations of young men of intellect who were faced with the phenomenon of unworthy wealth and rank in other men. Nonetheless, he made no secret of his disapproval of Monsarrat's actions, or of his dim assessment of Monsarrat's prospects. Monsarrat and Telford expected the charges, when laid, to be serious.

Both men were right. Monsarrat was charged with forgery and fraud. The statement of facts said Monsarrat had wilfully passed himself off as an officer of the court, had knowingly received fees under false pretences, had been guilty of forging a document. With all the fees he had falsely claimed, he had exceeded by far the amount required for a capital sentence. Combined with the forgery, they meant that he could be found hangable on two counts.

Monsarrat was put down to be judged at the summer assizes. He could just manage until then to rent a modest room from the warder.

The assizes, as Monsarrat knew, were presided over by two judges of the High Court. These were men of eminence from the outside world, who were met at the borders of the county by the best people in their carriages and by the sheriff and his bailiffs, and the mayor and his liverymen.

As the assizes judges neared Exeter city, the church bells tolled, and trumpeters began to accompany the procession. Monsarrat could hear all this as the judges' carriage approached the Crown Court. He knew that these men would be appalled when a fraudulent barrister appeared before them. He anticipated the sentence they would hand down would be all the harsher for the fact of Monsarrat's education. A man of his intellect and knowledge, they would say, would be fully aware of the laws he was breaking, making his crime one of moral depravity. He was in a different universe, they would say, from the uneducated man who stole to survive. Monsarrat knew, however, that when such an uneducated man inevitably appeared before them at the same assizes, they would not let his lack of learning ameliorate the sentence they handed down.

Monsarrat lay on his bed the night before the trial was to start, in a room comfortable only by the standards of Exeter County Gaol. He looked at the stone walls. From the damp walls of my London lodgings to the mahogany panelling of the lawyers' chambers at Lincoln's Inn, and now to this, he thought. These will be the last walls I have the opportunity to stare at. And stare at them he did, through the night, training his ear on the smaller sounds, particularly natural ones – the call of an owl, hoof beats in the yard. The sounds he had taken for granted, but feared he might never hear again. In the early hours, he began howling and crying into the cell's stones with no one to hear, or care. The next morning when constables escorted him across a yard into the court itself, he believed he was no longer breathing, and if he'd expired in the dock, that would have suited him greatly.

A large part of the day had been taken up with choosing members of a grand jury, made up of mayors and other officials and county worthies.

Monsarrat had pleaded not guilty, as all those accused of capital crimes were advised to do – entering a guilty plea would mean the certainty, rather than the probability, of execution.

When he stood in the dock he saw that the public gallery was full of nearly every lawyer in the town, except the one acting as Crown prosecutor, his own barrister, and Samuel Smythe, who was no doubt still feeling humiliated. There too was Johnathan Ham, the wool merchant. The eyes which had once looked on Monsarrat as an ally now blazed at him with impotent fury.

The prosecution had an easy time making Monsarrat look abominable, a man who had undermined the dignity of the court, a man who had used a forgery to deny his clients their right to genuine legal representation. Many of those clients had received excellent representation anyway, better in fact than that provided by real lawyers. But none of them came forward on Monsarrat's behalf. They, like Smythe, felt embarrassed to have been duped, and the sting of it overrode any impulse they may have had to support the young man who had worked so hard on their behalf – and, it must be said, taken a handsome fee for doing so.

Matthew Telford, in opening remarks, argued that his client was a man who had found himself in the position of many well-educated but unprivileged men now. They saw men of inferior sensibility raised to eminences of which they could be considered unworthy – it was money and time that the poor lacked, and in society as it now existed, money and time were given too much value. None of Mr Monsarrat's clients, though fraudulently represented, had suffered before the courts as a result. Though he was not a barrister, and nothing could make him a barrister, he had been in his way a competent advocate. And not only that, he had been able to discourse with fellow lawyers in social and indeed in trial conditions without their feeling that in any way were they speaking to a man of inferior intelligence, and without in any way suspecting he was guilty of deception.

'While we can deplore the crime,' said Telford, 'we must feel some sympathy for this young man of notable talent whose limited resources condemned him to clerkhood, but whose intellect made him desire a profession. Surely we are poorer, as a society, when men like Mr Monsarrat have no legitimate way of pursuing careers for which their intelligence fits them.'

Monsarrat could see that these arguments were not resonating well with the judge, who was probably not an enthusiast for reform and French-style equality. He started to wonder whether Telford was in fact undermining him.

But Telford was not in the business of securing an acquittal, not today. The lawyer's aim, and his only realistic prospect, was to save Monsarrat from the death sentence.

Various of his clients were called – they were embarrassed to have been fooled, but the judge would lean forward like a kindly uncle and tell them not to be because this man before the court was obviously the deepest-dyed and most skilful imposter. In the judge's eyes, the fact that he had done well by the clients made his crime graver. For he had thereby stood in the place of better men, men who had earned the right honestly to wear the gown and the wig.

When the trial was nearly concluded, Telford turned to Monsarrat with eyes full of pity and gave a little shrug in which the whole tragedy of Monsarrat's human existence was summed up. There was nothing that could be done. Iron-bound laws were about to descend like an axe.

By now Monsarrat felt surprisingly little. He saw the judge put a black patch of cloth over his wig and he felt as though he was watching a play which he had seen several times in dress rehearsal. He knew, of course, what the black cloth signified. In it, he saw a future measured in days.

As the judge was pronouncing a sentence of death by hanging, Monsarrat's thoughts turned to how he could make a respectable end. He had expended his emotion in his private cell the night before. Now he approached the business of his death as though it were a legal problem. How to make sure he didn't mewl or snivel when mounting the gallows. Perhaps he would need one more purging, one more hour raging at fate, weeping for the years lost to him, and shuddering with fear. Other felons would see him, of course, as he was unlikely to get a private cell again. But he didn't care for their good opinion. He would be remembered for the wrong reasons by his friends, colleagues and clients. But when they gave future accounts of him, he wanted them to say, 'He made a good end, though, I'll give him that.' If it wasn't too much to hope for, he might wish them to add: 'And he was a good advocate, if a false one.'

Planning one's death tends to absorb a man, so Monsarrat almost missed the judge removing the black cloth and recommending him to the King's mercy.

He knew what that meant. If mercy were indeed to be granted by the King, he would be following Dodds to a place no man here had seen, a place wreathed in misty tales of murderous natives and rampaging monsters. A place which, if half the tales were true, might make him wish the black square had stayed resting on the judge's wig.

His initial, reflexive relief at not dying soon fell away to dread of a land as unmapped as the one which lay beyond this life.

❦

As Monsarrat had expected, there was now no possibility of a private cell. He was put into the condemned cell, which gradually filled up that day with half-a-dozen other men. There, he awaited word on whether the King would follow the recommendation of one of his subjects, and spare the life of another.

He was in there for two months, until the sheriff appeared at the grille one breathless summer day and informed those within that the King had extended his mercy to five of the prisoners, and that their sentence had been commuted to transportation for life.

Monsarrat's spirit until then had not been too dismal. One of his few negotiable assets was his ability to convey a sense of threat and a certain dignity, despite the mockery of common criminals who declared him a fantailer and a nob. So he was left alone by the others in his cell. He had found himself moping very little and was entertained by the frequent fashionable visitors who came to look at the condemned men as some people would go to an art gallery to look at paintings, paying the gaoler for the privilege. Young men would bring pretty women, who would exclaim over the evil aspect and obvious moral degradation of the men there, and move closer to their escorts for protection (this making the place one of the chief attractions for young couples). Monsarrat, though, was a particular favourite. He had the advantage of being able to converse with gentlemen who visited the prison as a spectator sport. His accent, his sensibilities, so like their own, leavened their visit with a delicious tickle of fear that they could easily, if rash, become him. Some of his regular visitors had kept him well primed with liquor, passing tankards from the inn through the bars. And since the warder was running such an interesting zoo, he protected his own reputation by ensuring his charges had fresh straw weekly and clean blankets on which to lie.

But sometimes the full weight of knowing he must endure a lifetime of penal suffering descended on Monsarrat and sank him into a deep despair. There were times when the noose seemed to him a lost opportunity for escape. The warder could see this and made sure that all sharp tools and implements were kept far from Monsarrat – even a spoon could be honed on stone to make a blade with which a man might cut his veins.

The next day, chained at wrist and ankle to each other, the transportees rode by cart into Plymouth, where people hooted at them in the streets, and at last down to the dock, where they were rowed out to the prison hulks moored in the Tamar River, and given suits of wool and canvas marked with black arrows.

The hulk in which Monsarrat and the others were placed to await their transportation to Australia was a dismasted asylum of a place. Its prisoners, most of whom would work building docks and harbour fortifications while they waited for their ship to leave for the south, were locked down at night into a Hades where young boys were taught every criminal skill known to the combined faculty of felonry that presided over the dimness. The new men were threatened and pawed, and Monsarrat was driven to think only of his own flesh and its integrity.

Each morning he was taken ashore in a rowboat and guarded heavily at his work, although he was not chained. He was of course unused to the work with stone. He wished he'd bent his skill to being a mason, because they toiled much less harshly than the mere haulage animals he and most of his fraternity now became.

But a few weeks later, someone on the hospital ship scanned the record for a clerk, and he was called out of the work gang and, grateful once again for his education, he became a clerk on a hospital ship, the *Charon*.

Relieved to be spared the work gang, Monsarrat did such a good job that he was held back and missed the next ship sailing for Australia, into which were absorbed his four former cellmates from the Exeter assizes. Instead, he found himself taken aboard the *Morley*, a small ship barely more than four hundred tons, but fast sailing, and not badly run, with a good surgeon who had made a number of journeys to Australia and knew how to deal with prisoners in the early stormy days through the Channel, the Bay of Biscay, and into the Atlantic past the Azores, the terrible belt of heat and slack winds off West Africa, and the roaring gales then encountered to the south.

The ship itself, as Monsarrat would discover, had already made the journey to Australia, either to Port Jackson or to Hobart, a number of times. Whether the caulking between the planks of decking turned liquid in the tropical sun or collected a gloss of ice much further south, the ship's timbers seemed to Monsarrat to be accustomed to those stresses, and to be able to accommodate them. With time Monsarrat could not help thinking of the ship not perhaps as an alma mater, a sweet motherly floating institution, but at least as a mater, the mother who gave birth to his Australian existence.

The journey into the penal netherworld was made less painful for him by the fact that the surgeon, after a suitable period of probation, had him up to the ship's hospital to write his correspondence and the details of his medical log.

In calmer weather he copied out sections of a book the surgeon was writing on the motions of the earth and heavenly bodies as explainable by electromagnetic attraction and repulsion, and on the impact of this magnetism on the health, growth and decay of man. The surgeon also had various notes for a tract on irrigation of land, based on what he had seen of Egypt, Syria and South America.

It was from offhand remarks by the surgeon that Monsarrat got a picture of New South Wales, this colony now half-free and half-convict; of its systems of discipline and the various steps a man or woman could take towards freedom: an absolute pardon, which would enable a person to return to Britain if he had the means to do so, or a conditional one, which made him an Australian for life, and the steps in between – the ticket of leave and so on. From the surgeon he learned that at the end of seven years, a life-serving convict could get his ticket of leave, which allowed him to work for himself, and at the end of fourteen, a condition of freedom within the colony.

More than a decade later, thanks to Monsarrat's second, colonial conviction, that condition now appeared almost unreachable, receding further with every passing day, and seemingly quickening its retreat under the glare of Captain Diamond.

Chapter 13

Monsarrat needed to walk through the long room of the hospital, with the beds on either side of one central alley, to get to Dr Gonville's office behind its partition at the back. And so he could hardly have missed Dory's prone frame.

Dory was lying on his stomach. Now that most of the blood had been sopped up, the wound that took up the entirety of his back looked far more gruesome, more jagged, the exposed bone more visible. Some parts of it had also taken on a disturbing purple or grey puffiness at the edges. Most of it had been smeared with hog's fat, in a bid to provide a barrier between the wound and the outside world and thus prevent infection. But Monsarrat feared this measure might have sealed the infection in, especially if Diamond's saliva was as poisonous as his character.

Dory had his head to the side. His eyes were slightly open, only small white slivers visible. His lips were parted, and his breathing ragged. Despite the cold – not a cold any self-respecting winter in England would have produced, but cold just the same – Dory's forehead had a slick of sweat on it. This was being mopped up, at intervals, by the rotund Father Hanley.

Dory didn't respond as Monsarrat neared his bed, save for a grunt which told of the pain he felt even as his mind struggled to protect him from it by shutting down. He was beyond response, perhaps permanently. Hanley, however, looked up. His face was drawn in a way that Monsarrat wouldn't have thought possible for a corpulent man, and his greeting lacked the self-conscious formality to which he had subjected Monsarrat in the kitchen the other day.

'Good morning, Mr Monsarrat,' he said. 'I understand you witnessed these wounds being inflicted.'

'I did, Father. And I hope never to witness anything like it again.' Not wanting to be reported for gossiping about the captain, Monsarrat lowered his voice. 'You've heard, Father, of the captain's unusual intervention?'

'I have. May God forgive him. An excess in brutality when delivering a punishment is a sure sign of a compromised soul. I'd go to the man now offering spiritual guidance, but he wouldn't take it, and I might find myself here in a similar situation.'

'How long have you been here?' asked Monsarrat.

'All night. I heard of Fergal's incarceration, came to find him. The soldier on guard is a good son of the church, now, and he let me in. I know Fergal doesn't like me. He wants a warrior priest, not a corpulent cleric. But he told me about this young fellow, what he had been through. Asked me to be with him, in case the fellow passed away and needed shriving. I have no idea whether he is a follower of the one true faith, but the Reverend is in Sydney, and surely even a Protestant would take a Catholic rite over no rite at all.'

Monsarrat, having heard Diamond and many others rail against Catholicism, wasn't certain.

Father Hanley reached over again towards Dory, and Monsarrat noticed the sweat on the boy's forehead had been replenished. Gently, and with a small smile as though Dory could see him, the priest dabbed at the boy's face. It's just possible I might have misjudged Hanley, thought Monsarrat.

'Has he been in this condition the whole time?'

'Much like it, although his fever seems to be getting worse. Dr Gonville, not a bad man when all's said and done, has looked in a few times. But apart from the hog's fat he hasn't done much. He says we must allow the healing to take its course, although I can see precious little evidence of healing on this bed in front of me.

'The soldiers pride themselves on having seen more death than anyone else, as though it were a matter for boasting. But I tell you, Mr Monsarrat, a priest sees death too, and in all its forms, not just the glorious blood of the battlefield. And there's an air to them all, man or woman, when they're about to leave, when their heart is counting out its last beats. To my mind Dory has that air to him now. I don't believe he will be with us for long.'

'Do you think, Father, that Dr Gonville might be persuaded to give him something to help with the pain? Or I could try to find some poteen – a few drops on the lips might do some good.'

'Poteen can take away pain in all its forms, surely. And I must confess, I have found myself in need of it. But there's been not a drop of it recently. That other absconder, the one last month, used to be able to get some for me, but now he's confined I wouldn't have the first clue where to lay my hands on the stuff.'

'But does Slattery not distil it?' asked Monsarrat. He stopped short of saying that he'd come upon the young soldier's still – a bargain was a bargain. 'Perhaps you could visit him again, although he's probably been released by now. Ask him where he keeps it. He'd not begrudge some for young Dory, of that I'm certain.'

'Ah, now, if Slattery was indeed a purveyor of the remarkable stuff, I'd not have a second's hesitation in procuring some. But he never touches it – he told me himself – much less brews it. A man in his village was sent out of his wits when he drank some which hadn't been made properly, and made blind besides. He told me he swore off it then and there. He made no such pledge in regard to other liquor, but he thinks poteen is the devil's work, devilish though he is himself at times.'

Monsarrat frowned. He didn't necessarily see a dislike for poteen as a disincentive to brewing and profiting from it. He resolved to ask Slattery himself, when they next found themselves facing each other over Mrs Mulrooney's scrubbed table.

He said goodbye to the priest, and as he moved between the beds towards the surgeon's partition, he heard Hanley humming an

air which he presumed to be Irish. A little jaunty for the circumstances, perhaps, but who knew what would ease the boy's pain, in
whatever state his mind currently rested.

'Monsarrat,' said Gonville, as Monsarrat moved around the
partition to stand in front of his desk. 'You're here to inquire about
the boy. I must confess, I feel partly responsible for his present
condition – I should have intervened sooner, and more forcefully.'

'You did what you could, doctor. I'm certainly concerned for
him. But I'm here on a matter of greater concern. Mrs Mulrooney
reports Mrs Shelborne is not responding even to a squeeze of
the hand. Her breathing has become laboured, and she does not
seem to have been in a state of anything resembling consciousness
for some time. I alerted Captain Diamond to this change in the
lady's circumstance, and he begs you to come at once.'

'I'm sure he does,' said the doctor. Then, standing and rounding
the table: 'Very well, Monsarrat, let's go and see what can be done.'

On the walk to Government House, Monsarrat decided to risk
a small gambit. If Mrs Shelborne was truly lying under a poisonous
cloud, it was worth the danger.

'It's kind of the captain to be concerned for the lady's
predicament,' he said.

'Yes, and from a man not especially known for his kindness.
I understand he and Mrs Shelborne had an acquaintance in
Ireland. You know Diamond has been with the major for some
years: in Madras, Ireland, and now here.'

'Yes. They do seem to have different views on how to run the
settlement, though,' said Monsarrat.

'Very different men. Most people here have been into the hospital
at least once, and you hear rumours. Of actions which someone
of the major's nature would consider ... unpalatable. Things that
needed to be attended to nonetheless. By someone with fewer
scruples. Anyway, I've heard Diamond claim he has a particular
friendship with the lady, although nothing untoward, I'm sure.'

'Forbid the thought,' said Monsarrat.

On arriving at the kitchen, they found Mrs Mulrooney cleaning
skillets that she had already cleaned twice that morning. Her

hands were raw from scrubbing the kitchen table, which must now have lost at least half an inch to her brush.

'Please conduct me to the bedroom, Mrs Mulrooney,' said the doctor. 'Monsarrat, do you know where the captain is to be found?'

'In the major's study, sir. At least that's where he was when I came to you.'

Gonville's eyebrow quirked up slightly. 'Please inform him I'm here.'

'Will you come by the study to make a report, doctor?' said Monsarrat.

'Make a report? Diamond has no right to a report. Mrs Shelborne's condition concerns her husband and no one else. I will recommend urgent action, if I feel it necessary. If not, I will return directly to the hospital, where there is a young man with a wound beginning to look infected. Saliva is a filthy substance.'

Monsarrat returned to the workroom. The door was hanging open, as was the door to the major's study, with no sign of the captain. Evidently, Monsarrat thought, he did not apply the same force to closing doors as he did to opening them.

In the major's study, he was confronted with the kind of disorder which offended his clerk's sensibilities. The dispatches which had been laid aside, the reports to the Colonial Secretary awaiting the major's signature, all correspondence he had organised so neatly to await the major on his return, lay in a jumbled mess on the desk. Some of the document seals were broken. Rifling through the chaos, Monsarrat noticed that one of those belonged to Dr Gonville's report.

What had he been at? thought Monsarrat. Was he simply a man unused to dealing in papers, who had decided to leave the clerk to clean up the mess? Or had he been looking for something?

Monsarrat started the task of setting the desk to rights. Resealing those seals that had been broken, checking the documents to make sure their contents were not sensitive, placing them back where he believed they should live. The work soothed him. He always enjoyed creating order where there had been none. It gave him an illusion of control, which he knew his reality did not match.

When she was well, Honora Shelborne had been in and out of the major's study. He allowed her to keep some of her own documents in there, and to use his desk when he had no need of it. As he sorted through the papers, Monsarrat noticed that while most of them were jumbled in no particular order, papers concerning Honora were set slightly to one side. There were letters, notes on speeches she might now never give, recipes, jotted observations on how life in the settlement could be improved for its inhabitants. There were even notes on the success of the experiment with the hydrotherapy tent, which she proclaimed had returned colour to the cheeks of the ageing housekeeper.

Monsarrat had never dealt with Mrs Shelborne's papers, as she preferred to completely manage her own affairs. So he had no way of knowing whether anything was missing. He did notice that some of the letters bore a family crest, a rampant stag on a background of crimson and white. These declared themselves to be from Castle Henry, Wicklow, Ireland. Monsarrat presumed these were from her family. He knew he could have confirmed his suspicion by reading them, with very little risk of a consequence. Even had the captain re-entered at that moment, he could simply busy himself with reorganising the place. But despite the fact Mrs Shelborne would never know or care, he felt he had spied on her quite enough as it was.

He was on the verge of completing the task of restoring the study to its former state of glorious organisation when the main door opened. It wasn't flung open by Slattery's shoulder, or by Diamond's fist, but nor was it tentatively nudged, in the manner of Edward Donald.

Walking into the outer room, Monsarrat found Dr Gonville. The surgeon stood as still as always, but a red tinge climbing his neck betrayed a state of agitation. 'Not here then, eh? Do you know where he is?'

'I'm sorry, doctor, I'm not sure where he's gone, but I imagine you may find him near the barracks. Is there anything I can do to assist?'

'As a matter of fact, Monsarrat, there is, I very much fear Mrs Shelborne has little time left. I intend to entreat the captain to lead a party in search of the major, so he may have a chance of returning before his wife departs. I would be very grateful if you would come to the hospital, as soon as your duties allow, to assist me in transcribing a letter to the major laying out the case for his return, and urging him to make haste.'

'Of course, doctor. And will you seek out the captain now?'

'I must get back to the hospital, Monsarrat, to see to the man the captain put there, amongst others. May I ask you to search him out, and have him come to me at his earliest convenience? If a party sets out at first light tomorrow, there may yet be time.'

After the doctor left, Monsarrat fought down an impulse to visit the kitchen. Given Mrs Mulrooney's state recently, he could only imagine the distress she must be in. But that distress would be compounded if any time was lost on her account.

Captain Diamond had, it transpired, merely laid aside temporarily his work of rifling through the documents on the major's desk, intending to return after the day's main meal. Monsarrat found him in the mess. He would gladly have endured a week without Mrs Mulrooney's tea to avoid disturbing the captain at his dinner – bream caught by the coxswain, who had clearly taken his own advice on the tides.

Monsarrat attracted several sideways glances from the officers sustaining themselves there, and even a nod from Lieutenant Thomas Carleton, who was a soldier in the vein of Major Shelborne – efficient, ruthless when necessary, but not inhumane.

The captain didn't look up as he approached, but as he drew in front of Diamond, the officer laid down his knife and fork.

'Monsarrat,' he said, taking a swig from his cup.

'Captain, I beg your pardon for disturbing you. I have been sent on a most urgent errand.'

'State it then, and leave as soon as you can.'

'Captain, I fear it is a matter of delicacy. You may wish to hear my report in a more private setting.'

Diamond put down his drinking cup with more force than necessary, and walked towards the door of the mess, Monsarrat following.

'Captain, the doctor has examined Mrs Shelborne, and fears her time may be drawing to a close. He begs you to mount an expedition to find the major, so he might return before his wife . . . departs.'

Again Monsarrat forced himself to look into the captain's face, trying to keep his gaze as neutral as possible lest Diamond read some imaginary insult into it. And again Diamond failed to reward him with much obvious outward sign of distress. Monsarrat did, however, fancy he noticed the captain's lips compressing slightly, and perhaps an increasing pallor.

The two stood for what seemed like some time. Monsarrat feared to break his gaze. The captain seemed to be searching his features for any sign of delusion or deceit.

Finally, he said, 'Go to Dr Gonville and tell him I'll do as he suggests. Then return to the study. Please make sure it is in a state of organisation when I meet you there,' he added, as though Monsarrat had been responsible for strewing papers about, perhaps in a fit of childish pique.

Diamond went back into the mess, took young Carleton's drinking cup away from him when it was halfway to his lips, beckoned, and the pair stalked off through a grey drizzle which had just started up.

Chapter 14

Monsarrat hurried through the delicate curtains of rain towards the hospital. The water left glittering beads on the wool of his coat, before slowly being consumed by the fibres. He thought of the sweat on Dory's brow, and wondered if the boy's body was still in a condition to produce it.

Hanley was gone, but otherwise there was little change at Dory's small bed. The man remained on his stomach, eyes half-open, unconscious, sweating and moaning. Dory's wounds seemed more pustular, the rot more pronounced.

Monsarrat reported Diamond's response to the surgeon, and begged leave to return to the major's office to fetch paper and ink to take dictation. He concealed the writing supplies in a canvas sack which he had made for this very purpose – occasionally he was required to ply his trade in various parts of the settlement, and the rain of winter (not to mention the torrents of summer) was frequent enough to threaten the parchment, considered far more valuable and rare than the convicts.

On his way back to the hospital, he passed a work gang trudging in the other direction. Their shoes, woven straw or cobbled together from canvas, would be no protection against the puddles which had quickly formed in the ruts on the road. After a few days, he knew from experience, the skin on the feet of these men would soften and crack, admitting any foul substance they came into contact with.

By the end of Monsarrat's own time in a work gang, a great many of his fellow convicts were hobbling. Some had lost toes, and one man his entire foot, to gangrene. Monsarrat had heard the screams as the offending extremities were removed. He understood the men would die if the infected portions remained part of them, but he thought such an extreme of pain must change a man, and wondered if the bestial screaming announced the arrival of a being less human than the one who had limped into the surgeon's tent. But alive, at least, as the decay had affected an area which could be easily removed, unlike Dory's back.

When he had first arrived in the colony, Monsarrat had held hopes of a clerkship, particularly given his experience on the *Morley*. But either his paperwork hadn't been read properly or there was no need of a clerk in the vicinity of the convict barracks at Hyde Park, where Monsarrat slept in a long room, his own small hammock dangling from wooden beams along with scores of others. So he went to a work gang, dressed in canvas pants and a shirt emblazoned with arrows which declared him to be untrustworthy, felonious, and fit only for manual work. Wearing his arrows, he spent a miserable three months on an unchained gang on the road between Sydney and Parramatta. It was the hardest his body had ever been worked.

Monsarrat found himself in company with another educated convict, a man named Cathcart who had forged a contract for the delivery of sugar in order to get a bank loan. The overseer on their road gang, a terrible bristle-headed and jowled monster and former smuggler named Jevins, had loved having two gents on his gang. He singled out Cathcart with a special barbarity, hitting him regularly throughout the day, making him stand forward at assembly in the mornings, and delaying him on his march, often of two miles or more, back to the feeding station at the dinner hour, so that the poor fellow would just arrive when it was time for him to turn around and go back to work digging drainage and pounding stone.

Cathcart absorbed most of Jevins's malice, a fact for which Monsarrat was guiltily grateful. But sometimes Jevins would remember that he had not one but two jumped-up convicts to deal with, two men who thought themselves better than him.

One morning, the beast cracked Monsarrat over the ear for daring to wipe his nose at assembly. 'Who said you could wipe your fucking nose?' he said, drawing back to strike again but checking himself at the last moment, perhaps not wanting to disable Monsarrat for the day's digging.

As Monsarrat and Cathcart shared a similar background, both in education and forgery, Monsarrat attempted to engage the man; he had a kernel of hope that perhaps Cathcart, too, was a lover of Catullus, and that they might lose themselves in discussion – quietly of course, as there was no telling what Jevins would do if he overheard them discussing poetry. But there was something not quite right about Cathcart. Monsarrat wondered if he was being a little harsh in this judgement, yet Cathcart's eyes always slid sideways in an unsettling way, looking for a chance to filch some food from under the nose of another convict, or the opportunity to call someone else out on an infraction, thus drawing Jevins's gaze off himself, at least for a short time.

In the end, Cathcart made a diabolical bargain with Jevins – he would run away from the gang, so that he could be quickly retrieved by Jevins himself, who would receive a reward of two pounds. Cathcart would be subjected to twenty lashes, but then fed and left without molestation. It was a questionable contract, lining up behind the equally questionable contracts which had got Cathcart to this point.

At first Monsarrat had thought less of Cathcart for making the bargain. But after several weeks, with Jevins beginning to share his attention more evenly between the two felons, he considered asking for a similar deal.

He was saved from this necessity by the death of one of the clerks at the courthouse in Parramatta. Again the records were scanned for a clerk and again Monsarrat's name came up. It was

145

of course an unpaid position, but Monsarrat knew he would likely be dead had he been left on the road gang.

The Port Macquarie road gangs, chained and unchained, were certainly not pleasant. But neither were they as brutal as the one Monsarrat had had the misfortune of serving on – Major Shelborne saw to that. With his usual strategy of cloaking humanity (which he possibly feared some would see as weakness) in a drive for maximum efficiency, the major ensured the gangs were fed and left relatively unmolested. But not even the major's beneficence extended to their feet, and Monsarrat still occasionally heard the shrieks from the hospital as a putrefying growth which used to be a toe was removed.

If the rain lasted, the surgeon might have more such procedures to perform, Monsarrat thought. But for now, Dory remained the hospital's main patient, wedged between life and death, in a condition that was possibly worse than either.

'My dear major,' dictated the doctor, when Monsarrat had settled opposite him and laid out his writing equipment, 'I write to advise you that your wife is suffering from a grave illness. We had hoped to restore her to full health before your return from the important expedition you are currently engaged on. But in recent days, her condition has deteriorated to the point where I fear no human agency can assist her.

'Enclosed is a report I compiled on her condition two days ago, set aside for your perusal on your return – please put that report in the packet, Monsarrat – so you may see how her condition has progressed.

'Since this report was written, her periods of consciousness have dwindled to nonexistence. She does not respond to stimuli in the way she did as recently as yesterday, and lack of nourishment has sapped her strength.

'She will continue to receive the best treatment to be found anywhere in the colony, in the hopes she may yet rally. However, I beseech you to return with all haste. Your humble servant, et cetera, et cetera.

'Now, Monsarrat, see that this goes directly to the captain as soon as it is transcribed. I wish the major to have the news from me, and none other.'

Monsarrat returned to the workroom to put all in order for when Diamond came by. The captain was busy arranging matters so that a party could leave in search of the major at first light the following morning. He himself would lead the party, and Lieutenant Carleton would manage the settlement in what was envisaged to be a short absence – it was hoped that the major had reached his objective, and was already returning.

Monsarrat wondered how Diamond could possibly hope to locate the major. The pathways such as the natives used were no pathways at all to the eyes of men on horseback who didn't know the country. The natives seemed to navigate using a system of songs and stories, which somehow infallibly got them to their destination. The songs and stories of the paler-faced inhabitants belonged in a world which might as well no longer exist. They were certainly of no use in negotiating the uncertain terrain in the unexplored north. Nor would they help in choosing a path which would not see a man eventually having to squeeze a large horse through close-standing eucalypts. The vegetation here refused to behave like its English counterparts, not stopping a polite distance before precipices but crowding in a rabble all the way up to the edges of cliffs, so man and horse could ride out of a stand of trees and into oblivion.

So Spring, the Scots commissary, had been invaluable to the captain. Perhaps relishing the idea of having the man out of the way for a time, he had interceded with the Birpai to procure the services of a tracker, who had visited the area for which the major was heading and knew where the fresh water, as well as the dangers, lay. The tracker, as Spring later told Monsarrat, was Bangar, brother to Spring's love and Monsarrat's occasional walking companion. Monsarrat knew Bangar was well capable of looking after himself, but feared for him under Diamond's intolerant rule.

Had it not been for Major Shelborne himself, this bargain might not have been possible. A scant four or five years ago, relations between the Birpai and the strange ghosts who had usurped their territory were seemingly impossibly strained. The cedar-cutters, who were often the harbingers of the coming invasion, were rough and hardened men, and did not have the incentive or ability to deal diplomatically with the natives. Having no other experience of the foreigners, some natives must've concluded that all of the ghost people were brutish, violent and not to be trusted, and the resemblance of some of them to dead ancestors was a cruel trick. This may have been the motivation for some of the attacks on cedar parties, as well as a raid on a vegetable garden which had resulted in the death of a convict.

Some raged over the insult, and insisted it be avenged. But Major Shelborne, who had been appointed commandant shortly afterwards, quickly recognised that the landscape did not care who was in the right. It was chiefly concerned with keeping all humanity in the same place, guarded by mountains and thwarted by sea. Not everyone in the settlement was a convict, but everyone was equally imprisoned in practical terms. So, to Major Shelborne's mind, the need to develop a working relationship with the Birpai was acute.

The young man was arrested. The major later told Monsarrat that when he first saw the fellow, he had a moment's regret that natives could not be enlisted in the British Army, so well formed was he. Kiernan was still an ornament to the settlement at that stage, but his natural talent as a linguist, which had never been called upon before, was already enabling him to converse in passable Birpai. He was used as an intermediary, and it was agreed the man would be returned to his tribe, and punished under native law, not British.

The rapprochement continued, over the next few years, with each tribe punishing their own for infringements on the other. Monsarrat remembered Diamond becoming indignant when the major punished a soldier for attempting – and failing – to take a Birpai woman. Surely, Diamond and others said, a sin against the

British was a far greater one than infractions against the natives. But this act, and others like it, had helped to build a relationship from which Diamond was even now benefiting.

The captain stomped in and out of the workroom and study throughout the day. After the second time, Monsarrat no longer bothered to close the door behind him as he left; clearly closing the door himself was the furthest thing from Diamond's mind.

He lolloped in, shouted some commands to go to the store and requisition some salt beef, write a report on the second expedition to the Colonial Secretary, and then go to the barracks to check the water skins were being filled, because one couldn't trust some of the more junior soldiers.

The soldier and the clerk worked well into the night, and the early hours of the following morning. As Diamond wished to be off at first light, Monsarrat saw no point in trying to ignore the cold and capture sleep in his little hut. Instead, the rain having blessedly stopped, he walked down to the ocean to confront the cold head-on. He stood looking at the white crests as they loomed out of the darkness and destroyed themselves on the sand below. To the south, a few headlands away, he could see the light of a fire. It was in an area where natives were known to dwell. Had they, too, some presentiment of what was to happen, without the need for modern medical arts to tell them so?

After a time he felt the cold tightening its grip on his fingers and immobilising them. That would never do – he would need them in working order, particularly over the next few days.

A barely perceptible lightening of the sky betrayed the sun, as it attempted to hide behind the clouds. Normally he did not appear at the door of the kitchen before six, but this being winter it must be nearly that hour now. In any case, he doubted Mrs Mulrooney had got any sleep either.

He was right, and the kitchen together with its uncooperative utensils were being driven by Mrs Mulrooney far more ruthlessly than Jevins had ever driven him in the work gang. She always seemed to believe a frenzy of activity was the best way to ward off disaster. As she flitted around filling this, pouring that, chastising anything that looked like it was even thinking about not working, Slattery sat at the table, a full cup of tea sending steam towards the ceiling.

'Have some more tea,' Mrs Mulrooney was saying. 'You'll need some warmth inside you for the journey. The rain will be back, I guarantee it.'

So accustomed a presence was Monsarrat in the kitchen that neither of them so much as glanced at him as he pulled back the chair opposite Slattery, and sat down tentatively, unsure whether he was facing the old laughing rogue, or something newer and darker. Monsarrat had heard many people say taking a flogging changed a man. And he feared it might have changed this one in the giving.

'A journey, private?' he said.

Slattery raised a brow and gave Monsarrat a half-smile, in a way which made it look as if the corner of his eye was dragging up the corner of his mouth. 'Yes, Monsarrat, I thought I'd take in a little of the seaside to the north – does a man good, you know. And His Majesty is paying for the excursion, God bless and save him.'

'You're going with Diamond, then.'

'For my sins, which are legion, yes. He said he'd rather have me under his watch. He thinks Carleton is a bit too soft and might let me get away with things. I've always found Carleton a decent man myself, but I suppose there is no secret between the three of us as to what I think of Diamond's decency.'

Monsarrat didn't know how to frame his next observation. The two men had traded insults only – insults which were intended to mask affection while at the same time communicating it, but insults nonetheless. It was their conversational currency, and they had never used any other. 'Slattery . . . You know you did your best. It was a brave thing to go up against him like that.'

The smile disappeared, and the arcing anger threatened to return. 'There's nothing to be done, Monsarrat,' Slattery said flatly.

'The captain is the authority here. And there's none to overrule him in the godless waste between here and Sydney. So he might as well be the ruler of the world.'

He stood up, slowly, as though his frame had suddenly become heavier. He went to stand beside Mrs Mulrooney, his back to Monsarrat, and began helping her in assembling the tea things.

'You're kind to do that, Fergal, but there's no need. You've a big journey ahead, please, sit down.'

'Not a bit of it, Mother Mulrooney, I might as well, while I can.'

Mrs Mulrooney smiled. She turned to Monsarrat. 'He's a good boy for all his many faults, isn't he, Mr Monsarrat? He saw me struggling with the tea tray a few weeks ago, and ever since then he's put it together for me and carried it across to the main house whenever he's been here when it's time to take it. It's a weight off my mind as well as my arms – I often fear I'll drop the thing.'

With the tea things laid out to his satisfaction, Slattery turned, picked up the tray. He wormed the tip of his boot between the house-side door and the frame, opening it with his leg and standing against it to let Mrs Mulrooney through. They both trudged across the avenue to the house, Slattery handing the tray to Mrs Mulrooney and opening the door for her, and bowing with a flourish.

'A good boy indeed,' said Monsarrat when the soldier returned. 'Private, you mind you stay good on the road. If Diamond is willing to act like a brute in front of the whole settlement, there's no knowing what he'll do when the only witnesses are a native tracker and some trees. And keep an eye on Bangar, won't you? He's a fine lad – I'd as soon not see him abused by Diamond.'

'Ah, never you mind, Mr Monsarrat. I like Bangar – I'll make sure no harm comes to him. Apart from that I have no intention of causing the slightest trouble. Not on this trip.'

'Not on this trip? And on your return?'

Slattery's half-smile reasserted itself. 'Ah well, then I will revert to my troublesome self, of course.' He muttered something in the impenetrable Irish tongue.

'What was that?'

Slattery said it again. God alone knew how the words were spelled, Irish spelling being one of the universe's great imponderables as far as Monsarrat was concerned. But it sounded like *chockie-o-lah*.

'Just a little thing I say to bring myself luck from time to time, Mr Monsarrat. Now, you stay good yourself too. And look in on Dory for me now and again, won't you?'

And the soldier stepped out into the dawn.

Chapter 15

It was an hour yet before Monsarrat was due to be in his workroom. He decided to spend that hour in the kitchen, as in the normal run of things he'd be here at this time anyway. He got the whetstone and took to sharpening some of the blunter-looking knives while waiting for Mrs Mulrooncy to return.

When he heard footsteps, he sprang up to open the door. He was a little shamed, to be honest, by the assistance which Slattery had so willingly given the older woman. He chided himself for not doing likewise more frequently. Leaning against the door to hold it open for Mrs Mulrooney, he immediately took the tray from her hands and set it on the table. It seemed unnaturally heavy for a tray bearing an empty teapot.

Mrs Mulrooney looked approvingly at the array of sharp knives before him. 'Thank you, Mr Monsarrat,' she said. 'If I were a superstitious woman, I'd think the fairies came in at night and blunted them all. They can't be trusted to retain their sharpness, so you've given me easier work.'

'You're most welcome. And I'm happy to see you in a more cheerful frame of mind than yesterday. With Slattery going, I must confess I feared you'd sink further into despondency, but the reverse seems to be the case.'

'I'll miss the young devil. But I hope his journey won't be a long one. They may yet come upon the major not far from here, if he has completed his mission and is indeed returning. Those Birpai trackers, now, they are a marvel. But my spirits owe more to Mrs Shelborne this morning.'

Monsarrat, who'd been arranging the knives as she spoke, looked up. 'You don't mean to say there's been an improvement?'

Mrs Mulrooney surprised Monsarrat with a girlish laugh, she who had a great impatience with girlishness. Frivolity didn't get the tea made. 'Yes, there has, Mr Monsarrat. Christ and his saints be praised. Particularly his saints, to whom I've been praying these past few weeks.'

Monsarrat had only a vague acquaintance with the basic tenets of his own Protestant faith, which he had left behind in childhood, so the mechanisms of the Catholic religion went over his head. He tended to view Catholic saints like ministers of the Crown – each responsible for their own area, and vying for the attention of the prime minister so they could progress their portfolios.

'And who have you been dealing with?' he asked.

'Well now,' said Mrs Mulrooney, 'I went to Father Hanley, you see, and asked him who would be most likely to help Mrs Shelborne. Her ailment has so many manifestations; I thought they might be too many for one saint to handle. So we agreed, he and I, that we'd asked St Pio to direct the efforts of the other saints, him being a general healing saint.'

'Ah. And which troops have you asked St Pio to marshal?'

'Well, there's quite a list. I asked Father Hanley to repeat it to me several times so I could make sure to remember them all. We have St Bernardino of Siena for the lungs, St Pancrus, St Teresa of Avila and St Crescentius for her headache, St Elmo for her digestive disturbances, St Quinton for her cough, St Vitus for those awful wrackings, and St Deodatus of Nevers for plague. I know Gonville's ruled it out, Mr Monsarrat, but I'm praying to so many as it is, it's hardly a trouble to add one more. Even if it's not plague, it might sway him, in case he's been considering blighting us for our lawlessness anyway. Yesterday I put them all aside and started praying to St Joseph for her peaceful death. But I may have done so too soon, because it seems they are in the midst of answering my prayers. Ah, would you ever put that pot back on the counter for me, before we forget?'

Monsarrat did as he was asked. The pot he took from the tray was most definitely still full. 'Well, it must've been the saints, as clearly it wasn't your tea, as reviving as it is – it seems she didn't drink any.'

'No indeed, Mr Monsarrat, we've no time for thoughts of tea. I went in there as I do every morning. I put the tray on at the table near the window – she keeps a small table and chair near the window, so she can read in the light. Or she could, when she was still in a position to. So I put the tray on that, as I do every morning, and went over to smooth out her covers. I haven't needed to do that much lately. When she first got sick she would be thrashing around all night and I would come in to find the covers on the floor, or tied in knots by her legs. Now, unless she's having convulsions, they stay perfectly still. But it's a habit. So I went over and did it. And do you know what happened, Mr Monsarrat?'

'I'm sure I don't.'

'She opened her eyes – praise be to the Blessed Virgin, she actually opened her eyes. It was the first time I'd seen them in some days. Even a week ago, her eyes were usually only half open, and there was no spark behind them – they could have belonged to anyone. But this morning, she opened them properly, and I saw her in them. You have no idea, Mr Monsarrat, how many times over the past few days I have had the awful feeling that I was tending to a breathing corpse. There seemed to be nothing left of the dear woman, and I wasn't sure what was keeping her body going. I thought maybe she was like a carriage wheel which had been lifted off the ground – they keep turning, you know, for a little while, even after the carriage is no longer moving.

'But when she opened her eyes – not half an hour ago! – I saw immediately that it was her. And I just stood there like an eejit, gasping and gaping, unable to believe it myself.

'And then she smiled – the most beautiful smile I've ever seen. I don't want to tempt them, but none of those saints I've been praying to could match it. Her poor lips are very dry; it's been two days since I was even able to get much moisture between them. So when she smiled, gaps opened within them, and I saw that they would soon start to bleed. Still, it was her, her smile, and therefore lovely.

'Thank the Lord I managed to remember to bring water with me – I haven't been bringing much on those trays recently, to be honest. There's been very little point. But I like to bring something every morning, as you never know what will be needed. While she draws breath I'll not stop doing it.' She sounded annoyed now, as though Monsarrat had suggested she should desist from bringing sustenance to the invalid's room.

Monsarrat himself was listening to her recount in astonishment. Everything he'd heard had led him to believe that Mrs Shelborne would die, and soon. The doctor had believed so, and more importantly Mrs Mulrooney had agreed with him. But this sudden reversal had him considering the possibility that Mrs Mulrooney's saints had indeed had a hand in things. If he were a saint, he would most certainly respond to her entreaties with the greatest speed.

'So I brought the water over to her and dribbled little teaspoons of the stuff in between the lips, just to moisten them to start with. She smiled again, and this time one of the cracks started oozing blood, which I mopped up. I've been washing her face every day, and now I went over it with a cloth soaked in cool water. It seemed to soothe her. Then she spoke – actually spoke, and here was I thinking she'd uttered her last words. The voice sounded like dried leaves in the wind, I had trouble at first hearing what she was saying. Then when I leaned in I realised she was thanking me.

'She's still so weak, though, Mr Monsarrat. Even that small effort exhausted her. I made her as comfortable as I could, smoothed down the coverlet, and held her hand. I gave it a squeeze, and I got the strongest squeeze in return than I'd felt for many days. Then she drifted off again, and sleep will be her doctor for the next little while.'

'I have no doubt this sudden improvement is due in large part to your determined nursing,' Monsarrat said. He realised that he was grinning, and made no attempt to stop himself, despite the fact that it went against the usual gravitas he tried to project. 'I must confess, it has been so long since I received good news that I had stopped looking for it in any form.'

'Ah, you must never do that, Mr Monsarrat,' said Mrs Mulrooney. 'I'm afraid I do have some bad news for you, however. She took no tea, and that which is in the pot is the last of the chamomile infusion she favours. I'd as soon keep it, and warm it on the stove before I go up again. So I'm afraid your own tea will have to wait, perhaps all day. I am sorry.'

'While life is made bearable by your tea, I am more than happy to sacrifice a day's worth for the continuing health of Mrs Shelborne. Congratulations, Mrs Mulrooney. Don't give too much credit to the saints – you had more than a little hand in this. I won't forget it, and if I have any claim to know Mrs Shelborne at all, neither will she. Would you like me to fetch Dr Gonville?'

'Would you be kind enough, Mr Monsarrat? Have you time before you're due at your desk? I'd like to have her examined as quickly as possible by him. He might have some idea what has caused her recovery, so that whatever it is, we may get more of it!'

Monsarrat assured her he had sufficient time to visit the doctor. His main incentive for being at his desk on the very dot of seven had just ridden out of the settlement. In any case, it should not take the half-hour remaining between now and the official start of his workday to fetch Gonville.

He left a delighted Mrs Mulrooney in the kitchen, humming and neglecting to chastise a single pot, spoon or knife.

~᠅~

There had been times in Monsarrat's life when he had resented the weather for failing to conform to his moods. The day he was transferred to the prison hulk was quite pleasant, for England.

Surely it should have had the decency to rain, and to clothe its sky in a mournful grey.

The opposite phenomenon was apparent on the day Monsarrat received his ticket of leave. He had been, by now, in Parramatta for some years. There, he was sometimes called on to fill out tickets of leave for local convicts. The tickets would come to him up the river from the Attorney-General's office in Sydney with the names already inscribed by another clerk, and he would write in the sentence, the date, the ship the felon arrived on, and various other minutiae. They would then go back to the Colonial Secretary for signature, before being delivered into the trembling hands of the new emancipee.

The slips of paper were practical documents, with none of the flourish Monsarrat felt they should have, given their importance. They listed the prisoner's name, what they'd done to get here, where they came from, where and when they were tried, what their trade or calling was, and what they looked like. They entitled the felon, or now former felon, to employ him or herself in any lawful occupation in a particular district. They didn't warn the newly freed convict that leaving this district would send them back into servitude. They didn't need to.

Monsarrat was doing this work one day, with his eyes half closed so that he wouldn't have to be continually reminded he was writing freedom for someone else while he remained enslaved. He completed a ticket of leave, blotted it, and put it to one side. He glanced down at the next one. It informed him that His Excellency the Governor had pleasure in dispensing with the attendance at government work of Hugh Llewellyn Monsarrat, who was hereon restricted to Windsor.

With a shaking hand he filled in his own details. Tried at the Exeter assizes in 1815. Sentenced to life. Arrived per the *Morley*. Native place, London. Trade or calling, clerk. Five feet and eleven inches tall. Pale complexion. Dark brown hair. Blue eyes.

He put the paper – inscribed with a little less finesse than the others – in the stack to await signature. Within a week it was back in his hand. He needed to take several deep breaths to stop that hand shaking so much it risked damaging the paper, and then he stepped out into the kind of rain England was too restrained to produce, great gouts of water pouring from some celestial amphora. Through the grey sheets, he made his way to the Prancing Stag boarding house, where a certain party would have an interest in both his freedom and its restriction. Then he would try to find a visiting stockman or merchant willing to give him a ride to the area to which he was now confined. Beyond this limitation, however, he now had as much liberty as anyone else.

Monsarrat longed to see that document again, with a fresh date on it. He tortured himself with its image. For a moment he wondered whether Major Shelborne, out of relief at his wife's recovery, might distribute a few extra tickets of leave or conditional pardons. But the thought made him suddenly a little sick with himself. Mrs Shelborne's life should not be used as a bargaining chip for Monsarrat's freedom.

Still, he walked to the hospital with more lightness than he had managed in quite some months. But once he entered the long narrow room his step slowed and faltered.

Edward Donald, the orderly, was moving slowly and methodically around the room, washing bandages and cleaning equipment. He looked up, gave an almost imperceptible nod as Monsarrat came in.

Dory was still there. At least, Monsarrat assumed it was Dory. The shape that was now entirely concealed under a white sheet looked to be the lad's height and breadth. And blood, now browning and congealing, made a large part of the sheet adhere to whatever was underneath it.

The poor boy spent his last days on his stomach, thought Monsarrat. He was looking down from the moment he was tied to the frame. Monsarrat found that thought profoundly depressing – to be laid down facing the earth, never to face the sky again.

Perhaps it's a balancing of the ledger, he told himself. The strange earth would devour Dory, and spare Honora. He chided himself for thinking like a superstitious Irish peasant, before remembering that the best thinker he knew was an Irish peasant who, while claiming not to be superstitious, still threw spilled salt over her left shoulder to thwart the demon who habitually sat there, urging her to wickedness.

Gonville had heard Monsarrat enter, and came around the partition to see who it was. He saw Monsarrat looking at the figure underneath the sheet.

'Very unfortunate,' he said. 'But an infection entered through the wound on his back, and took hold of his system quite quickly. I have my own views as to the source, as I'm sure do you. He went shortly after I returned from examining Mrs Shelborne. I noticed that he was breathing very rapidly, and went over. I mopped his head, which was boiling hot. He took a few more quick breaths, then he seemed to settle down. I went back to my desk, and when I returned to check on him half an hour later he had gone. You know, when you first start as a doctor, Monsarrat, you expect death to announce itself somehow. You almost expect a small tremor of the earth, or the dimming of the candle, to signal someone's departure. But most of the time people just slip off. No fanfare, no farewells – they just go. That's what this fellow did. At some point I'll send for Father Hanley. He should be told.'

Monsarrat was for a moment disabled by a spasm of grief for such a barbarously inflicted death. He feared, too, that the news would put an edge on Slattery's darkness. But expressions of sadness from a convict were almost as dangerous as expressions of anger.

'I can organise that for you in due course, doctor,' he said. 'At least when Lieutenant Carleton gives me leave.'

'Your third master in a month,' Gonville observed dryly.

'Naturally I try to serve all masters to the best of my ability, doctor. But it's on a far more promising errand that I've come to you. Mrs Mulrooney reports Mrs Shelborne's eyes are open, that she is uttering words, and taking water. It is a most unlooked for and most welcome development, and she begs you to come at your earliest convenience, so that the lady's recovery can be safeguarded.'

'Truly? This is wonderful.' The doctor looked thoughtful. 'I must confess, I don't know what could have improved the lady's condition, as I didn't know what was causing it in the first place. It may become apparent, with time and study, that it's a new disease which is limited to this place, so that we've not seen it before. You know, of course, that many of the natives were felled by a cold which to us would be a minor inconvenience, because their systems had not encountered it before. That may yet prove to be the case with Mrs Shelborne – an unheard-of disease, encountered by a person with no resistance ... But now perhaps she is building up that resistance, and beginning to prevail.'

He smiled. 'Donald!' he called. 'Please have some fresh paper and writing things on my desk by the time I return.'

Turning to Monsarrat, he said, 'Gonville's arsenosis, I believe I'll call it. After its mimicry of arsenic poisoning. Let's be on our way now, Monsarrat – quickly, man. The more we understand of the defences Mrs Shelborne is developing, the more we can help her shore them up.'

Chapter 16

Monsarrat delivered the doctor into the hands of Mrs Mulrooney, and then made his way to the workroom. Thomas Carleton was standing at the major's window. He had not had the presumption, unlike Diamond, to settle himself behind the major's desk. But like Diamond, he was shuffling through papers as though about to sit down to a game of cards with Slattery.

He looked up when Monsarrat entered. The clerk feared for a moment that he would be chastised for his tardiness, but Carleton gave him a smile – a distracted smile, to be sure, for Carleton was known to be a distracted man – and looked back down at the papers.

'Monsarrat, can I speak freely and in confidence?'

'Of course, sir. Without discretion I would be on a road gang.'

'Well, to be honest with you, I'm not entirely sure what I'm supposed to be doing. Is there anything that I need to drive forward? Anything I need to tidy up? Or am I just here to make sure the place doesn't burn down in the absence of the major and the captain?'

'More the latter, sir, if you don't mind my saying. And to make sure that there is no breach of the peace, no riots. I shouldn't imagine they'll be away long – perhaps a week? Hard to know for certain, but in any case no significant works can be progressed without the major's signature. I will assist you in any way I can. For example, reports to the Colonial Secretary – should we even need to make one in the absence of the major – you needn't write those, I can draft them and you can look them over.'

'Stout fellow, Monsarrat. Very good, then. If you could provide me with a list of all works currently underway, I'll ride around and have a look today. And I'll keep up the parades for the rabble who like to call themselves soldiers.'

The lieutenant left, earning Monsarrat's undying gratitude by closing the door behind him. Monsarrat sat down at his desk and began to sketch out a report on Mrs Shelborne's recovery – he imagined he would be asked to do so by Dr Gonville anyway, and he had by now long finished the transcribing the major had left for him.

He noted what he knew of Mrs Shelborne's case to this point. He put the document aside for the moment, under his own desk – until he was officially asked to compile a report; it wouldn't do to be seen to be taking an unhealthy interest – particularly if word got back to he whose own interest had reached unnatural levels.

He went into the major's study and scanned the shelves for his old friend Catullus. Diamond had clearly decided to rearrange them so the distracting frivolities of poetry were further out of reach from the desk. As he was taking down the book, he heard something he had never expected to hear from the direction of Government House – a full-throated female roar, anguished, only part-human, and stretched out longer than he would have believed breath would allow.

He raced to the door and listened. It started up again, a little shorter this time, as though the breath behind it was running out. It was coming, he realised, from the direction of the bedroom where Honora lay, on the side of the house which abutted his office and barely ten feet distant.

He sat down at the desk, his head in his hands. He wasn't sure what the noise meant, but its animal nature left him with the kind of foreboding not even Catullus could dispel. He debated whether to go to the kitchen, in case Mrs Mulrooney had need of him there. But he reasoned that this office was where they would expect to find him, and should he be wanted, this was where they would come.

And come they did, in the form of Dr Gonville. His face was immobile, as though he was putting a significant amount of effort into ensuring it didn't betray his feelings. But his eyes had a sheen to them which Monsarrat had never seen on the man. 'Monsarrat, you'd best come to the kitchen. Mrs Mulrooney requires assistance. As, I must say, do I.'

Monsarrat didn't remember the journey across the courtyard, but he must've bounded, as he was in the kitchen in a moment.

Mrs Mulrooney was sitting at the table, her forehead on its scrubbed surface, taking in huge gulps of air with each breath. Her white cloth cap lay on the floor beside her – the first time in their friendship that Monsarrat had ever seen her without it. He fancied that, underneath the fabric, the hair was usually groomed with precision, but now it stuck out at odd angles, and she made no attempt to bring it under control. The tray, her long-term companion on the walk to Mrs Shelborne's bedroom, lay askew on the table, the pot on its side, its lid off, surrounded by liquid.

Monsarrat looked at Mrs Mulrooney and then back at the doctor, raising his eyebrows to indicate concern at her state.

Dr Gonville nodded. He sat down next to the housekeeper, placed his hand on her shoulder. 'I'll leave you here in Monsarrat's care while I return to the hospital to mix you a sleeping draught. You've had a shock which would fell stronger constitutions than yours, and I believe a period of rest is essential.'

Mrs Mulrooney looked up, eyeing the doctor. Her face was blotched red, and if Monsarrat didn't know she had been crying he might have thought that she too was the victim of an unknown malady. 'I'll not be taking any sleeping draught, doctor, so you can save yourself the trouble of the trip. There're still things to be done for the poor darling, and I won't rest until all of them have been attended to.' She drew her shoulders back, challenging him to contradict her.

The doctor knew better than to do so. 'As you wish,' he said, 'but do send Monsarrat or somebody else to me, at any hour, should you require assistance.'

He turned to Monsarrat. 'I know I don't need to exhort you to provide Mrs Mulrooney with any assistance she requires. I will leave her to describe to you what has transpired, if she feels able for it.'

Mrs Mulrooney gave him another glare, for suggesting that any force would prevent her from doing so.

'I'll locate Lieutenant Carleton, and let him know what has occurred,' Gonville continued. 'I'll also ask him to release you to me for the next day. I am going to want a clerk with a fast hand. Donald does his best, but he's not up to your standard.'

On another day Monsarrat would have taken great delight in the compliment, would have repeated it to himself over and over. Under the circumstances – or what he suspected were the circumstances – he could take no pleasure in anything.

Before leaving, the doctor took a teacup from the tray, and checked it to make sure there was liquid inside. Monsarrat noticed he held it within a cloth he had borrowed, rather than with his bare hands.

Monsarrat went over to Mrs Mulrooney, awkwardly putting his hand on her shoulder. She shrugged him off with a vehemence which surprised him. 'I'm sorry, Mr Monsarrat,' she said. 'I'm undone just at the moment.' She groped around on the floor for her cloth cap and, finding it and replacing it, she jammed her hair into its folds with some violence.

Monsarrat moved to sit down opposite her. 'The doctor beseeches me to look after you, and I need no such urging, because I would consider myself a poor excuse for a friend if I didn't. But sometimes the best way to look after someone is to leave them alone. I have a great fear of what you are about to tell me, and I suspect I know already, but the details can wait if you would like some time to yourself. I'm at your disposal; I'll go or stay at your word.'

'Stay, please,' Mrs Mulrooney whispered. She took a deep breath, and in a stronger voice said, 'You look at the sky every day, and you know you'll see the same thing, more or less. The sun will be there, the moon will be there at night, and you might be lucky enough to see a shooting star. Now the sun has winked off, and my young star has shot away into the bush. I've only the moon now. Don't leave me in complete darkness.'

So Monsarrat sat, while Mrs Mulrooney gradually reconstructed herself. She regained enough composure to realise that some strands of hair were still peeking out from beneath her cap, and dealt ruthlessly with them. Thinking to help, Monsarrat went to take the tray, sop up the spilled tea and set the teapot to rights, but Mrs Mulrooney shot out her hand and grabbed his wrist with a strength he would have more likely expected from Captain Diamond.

'I wouldn't be touching that, Mr Monsarrat. Look at it sitting there, all innocence. But it's the devil's work, there on that tray, spilling out of that pot. I'm going to leave it where it sits until Dr Gonville advises me what best to do with it.'

Monsarrat looked at the liquid, trying to discern any diabolical intent within it. It looked to him like spilled tea, and nothing more. But he knew better than to defy Mrs Mulrooney, particularly in her domain, the place from which she drew strength. So he sat, and waited for her to speak.

Eventually, she did. 'She's gone, you know. God rest her.'

'But she was improving. Bad enough if she were to go when she was on death's door anyway, but for it to happen when she'd been showing signs of improvement is too cruel.'

'You're right, Mr Monsarrat. It is cruel. And the cruellest part of it is, I killed her.'

'Now, don't be ridiculous. You've often told me that for an intelligent man I can be an idiot. Well, for an intelligent woman, you're heading down the same path. Of course you didn't kill her. You probably kept her alive longer than she would have survived otherwise, truth be known.'

'But I did, Mr Monsarrat. I did kill her. I didn't mean to, naturally I didn't. But it was by my hand that she died, and now I feel like cutting it off, were any of the knives in this place sharp enough.'

'What on earth makes you believe that? And there will be no cutting off of limbs, by the way. I'll physically restrain you even if Diamond flogs me for it. Tell me what happened, please, so I can show you you're not culpable.'

'Well, when Gonville arrived, we went into her room. Her eyes were open, and she was looking at the sunlight coming through the window. She turned and smiled when she saw us, and it looked as though her lips were a little less cracked, although she did have a nasty rash all over her. That's been there for a while though, and wasn't getting any worse. She even attempted to sit up as we got closer, but Gonville told her to rest where she was. He began to examine her; he took her pulse, felt her forehead, felt her stomach, asked her never-ending questions about how she was feeling.

'After you'd gone to fetch him, I put her favourite tea back over the fire. I got it just hot enough so she could have it off a spoon without burning her poor lips. So while he was examining her, I fed her some. After the first spoonful she smiled at me again. It was the third smile that day, after a long time without, and I was gladdened by it. I gave her another spoonful, thinking the tea was doing her the power of good, if it was producing such a smile.

'So I filled a cup and held it to her lips and she drank it down, so quickly I was worried she might make herself vomit. But she seemed all right, so I settled her back on the pillows and sat with her, held her hand, told her stories of the fairies from my own childhood – only the nice ones; some fairies are anything but nice.

'After a while, though, I began to worry. She stopped focusing on me, she seemed to be looking at the ceiling, at something I couldn't see. Then she opened her mouth and drew in a breath which shuddered her whole body, so strong and ragged was it. She glanced at me then, and I could tell she was afraid. I held her hand and squeezed it, but she didn't squeeze back. She breathed again, and this time she juddered the whole bed while doing it. By now she looked on the verge of panic. And then there was a third breath. It stopped and started as it was going in. Then she released it. It just slowly leaked out of her; she wasn't making any effort to expel it. And after that, she didn't take any more breaths.'

Mrs Mulrooney had already purged the screaming, panicked, wild-eyed aspect of her grief. It had exhausted her in its passing, and now that she had told Monsarrat, she seemed to see no more use for herself. Her shoulders sank, and her head lowered to the table. Not in despondency this time, but in exhaustion.

'God rest her soul,' said Monsarrat. He felt a loss, probably more than many other losses the small settlement had endured, but he said the words in the same manner that Slattery said 'God bless all here'.

Mrs Mulrooney had sprawled her arms out across the table. Had he not known it was the gesture of someone who was spent, he would have thought she was trying to claim the table as her own and prevent someone else taking it.

He put one hand over hers, and squeezed her small hand as she had squeezed Honora's smaller one. 'I still don't see,' he said, 'how any of this supports the notion that you killed her.'

She put her chin up then, resting it on the table so that only her upper lip was visible above the forearm which screened her mouth. She looked like the elder boy in Monsarrat's classes in Windor during his brief period of freedom: unable to concentrate, knowing it, resenting it, and masking it by pretending not to care.

'Of course you do, Mr Monsarrat. You're just far too polite to say it. Haven't we been discussing the very same thing between us? Poison. And now what happens? She dies from poisoning. And it was my hand which tipped the poison down her throat.'

'Surely Dr Gonville can't for one second believe you responsible.'

'He certainly didn't give any indication of it, no, unless by asking you to look after me, he meant to ask you to detain me. But that would be an odd request to make of someone who is themselves detained, if you don't mind my saying, Mr Monsarrat. What worries me, though, is what others may make of it. Particularly those who may themselves have had a hand in the business, and would be only too happy for the blame to float around and then attach itself to a former convict.'

'Then we shall ensure that the major's aware of the extremities to which certain individuals have gone in his absence, and of their interest in his wife. Please, try not to worry. I will make sure that the major knows of the captain's behaviour, before the captain himself can pour lies into his ear.'

'I know you'll do your best, Mr Monsarrat. And I hope you'll succeed. Because if you don't, you know as well as I do that I'll hang.'

BOOK TWO

Chapter 17

Dr Gonville, as it turned out, had made straight for the barracks, to request the use of Monsarrat for the next day or two. Lieutenant Carleton readily agreed. He was genuinely appalled at the death of his commander's young wife, as well as regretful that it had happened before the major's return, and on his watch.

And so Monsarrat packed his canvas bag with more than the usual complement of writing gear, anticipating a lengthy period in the hospital.

Dory was gone. Most of the other beds were empty, and Gonville evidently didn't have a very busy day ahead of him. An elderly lady lay in one bed, the wetness of her cough announcing some kind of lung complaint.

Rounding the partition, Monsarrat noticed that the doctor's usual energy had been replaced by what looked like a kind of thoughtful torpor. The man sat at his desk, his fingertips touching each other so that his arms formed a triangle, on the apex of which his chin rested. His eyes were focused on nothing at all, or at least nothing which was visible to Monsarrat.

'Ah,' he said, 'good, we can get started. Please ready yourself.'

Monsarrat had sat in the doctor's presence only once before, when he had recently taken some dictation from the man. He did so again now, emptying his bag and laying out all the requisites. Gonville continued to examine an invisible object in the middle distance. Without looking at Monsarrat, he suddenly said, 'You're concerned for the housekeeper.'

He had unknowingly just resolved a dilemma which had been troubling Monsarrat. He desperately wanted to ascertain the doctor's view on Mrs Mulrooney's culpability or otherwise, while at the same time not wanting to suggest it to the man if the thought hadn't already occurred to him. But of course the thought had.

'I must confess, I am. And she herself is distressed. She believes that as the poison was unwittingly administered by her hand, she will be accused of the crime, if a crime there was.'

'Oh, there most certainly was,' said the doctor. He went over to his sideboard, and picked up something which Monsarrat hadn't noticed before – the corpse of a chicken.

'I took some of the tea that was given to Mrs Shelborne. A fellow called Metzger has invented a most ingenious test for detecting the presence of arsenic; however, I don't have either the knowledge or the equipment to carry it out, so I had to resort to a blunt instrument. I poured the tea on some grain, and fed the grain to this chicken, not half an hour ago. You can see for yourself the results.'

Monsarrat had known it was a reasonably futile hope that the tea had not been the agent of death. But he was still very worried to have it confirmed. He decided to dispense with caution. The danger Mrs Mulrooney was in was too real for him to worry about causing a slight to someone with power over him. 'Dr Gonville, Mrs Mulrooney did not do this. She has been holding the lady's hand through the night for many days now, racking her brains for recipes which might tempt Mrs Shelborne's appetite, weeping and praying over her. She is not a murderer, particularly not of this person.'

Gonville exhaled sharply in frustration. 'I know that, man. 'Course I do. Why do you think I have you here?'

'I understood, sir, that I was to take dictation of your report on Mrs Shelborne's death.'

'You're going to do a little more than that, Monsarrat. You and I are going to construct things so they allay any concerns the major might have on the point of Mrs Mulrooney's culpability, without raising the idea for him in the first place. The man has a deep fondness for his wife, and is likely to be somewhat undone by her death and looking to apportion blame.'

So Monsarrat laid out his paper and immersed his pen in the ink, and he and the doctor started the collaborative work of drafting a report which acknowledged that Mrs Mulrooney had fed Mrs Shelborne the poison, while at the same time exculpating her.

Dr Gonville first went through the bare factual details of Honora's death. He outlined the chicken's response when fed the tea-soaked grain. He also noted that there was a quantity of arsenic available in the stores, for the purpose of killing rats. He would take the liberty, he said, of sending the major's Special to ask the storekeeper whether anyone had procured some.

To produce the state that Honora had been in leading up to her death, she would have needed regular doses of the poison, Monsarrat wrote at Gonville's prompting. Yet the poisoner would be unlikely to want to get too close to his ('Make sure you use the word "his", Monsarrat') weapon – there was some possibility of arsenic being absorbed through the skin, or inhaled, making the poisoner as sick as his victim. So he would have needed to choose a method of administration which did not put him into close contact with the stuff.

With the contents of the doctor's report agreed to, Monsarrat set about making a fair copy. But Gonville stopped him. 'I wonder, Monsarrat, if I may ask you for another service.'

'Of course, doctor,' said Monsarrat, secretly gratified at Gonville's pretense that he had an option to refuse.

'I know you're friendly with Spring. Go to the stores, if you will, and find out whether anyone has recently picked up some arsenic.'

'Doctor, I must tell you, I myself procured some recently at Mrs Mulrooney's urging – she had smelled some mice, you see.' He knew the declaration might make Gonville look on him with suspicion, given his own frequent presence in the kitchen. But if Gonville chose to examine the store records himself, he would in any case see that Monsarrat had procured the poison.

'And I dare say you're not the only one, Monsarrat. Let's find out who else, eh?'

Monsarrat did as he was told and found the storeman at his desk, polishing his lenses. It was one of Spring's idiosyncrasies – a sure sign of some upset – that he worked particularly hard to remove spots which only he could see.

'I've been sent by the doctor,' said Monsarrat, 'to discuss the matter of arsenic with you.'

'Was that the cause? The Birpai don't know what it was. They weren't overjoyed about her hunting, but they didn't seek any retribution. There were a number of them up last night, singing a song for her, even though she couldn't hear.'

Monsarrat didn't want to start rumours of murder in the camp, and had reason to doubt Spring's discretion, given the speed with which information made its way to the Birpai. 'Yes, Gonville thinks it was possibly arsenic. How it got into her system remains a mystery at this stage. But he's asked me to come and see whether anybody has procured any of the stuff recently.'

Spring finished rubbing his glasses and put them on, jamming them onto the bridge of his nose as if he didn't trust them to stay in place. He went over to a ledger, opened it and ran his finger down a column, muttering to himself as he did so.

'Well, there was yourself the other day, of course . . . and Private Cooper requisitioned some. Apparently the rats over at the barracks are getting big enough to carry off some of the soldiers. Filthy habits they all have, no wonder.'

'Thank you,' said Monsarrat. He had no doubt that the young Private Cooper had been sent on his mission by the captain.

When he re-entered the hospital, he saw the doctor was busy applying a salve of some kind to the hands and arms of a man.

Gonville glanced up as Monsarrat entered. 'Come here, Monsarrat. I sent Donald off on an errand, as I have the use of you for the next day, so you'll have to be orderly as well as clerk.' He handed Monsarrat an earthenware jar in which the salve rested, and dipped into it to spread liberal amounts over the man's wounds.

The man's eyes had a raw red tinge, as though they had been scrubbed by sandpaper, and his arms and hands were covered in blisters and pustules, with very little unbroken flesh. He winced and occasionally let out a small sound as Gonville rubbed the ointment in.

His condition marked him, to Monsarrat and anyone else who lived in the settlement, as a lime-burner. It was a common jest – though a grim one – in the settlement to say that if you did well on a lime-burning gang, you might get a promotion to a chain gang.

'This is what we do to our weakest, Monsarrat,' Gonville said, without looking away from the irreparable skin. 'This is how we treat our lame. If they can't cut stone or haul lumber, we sentence them to death by slow burning.' For only the weakest needed fear a stint as a lime-burner – those who were more robust went to the chained or unchained gangs, depending on their level of criminality. Or they went to the crew which was even now building the settlement's first church, creating a greater demand for a substance which was slowly devouring their comrades.

Monsarrat was surprised at the doctor's candour. Gonville was, after all, part of the establishment, and apart from Spring when in his cups, Monsarrat had never heard such an admission from a member of the ruling class.

He wasn't sure how to respond. Privately, he quite agreed with the doctor. But what if it was a trick, something to draw him out, something to make him reveal a hidden revolutionary seam in his character? He confined himself to a neutral, 'As you say, doctor.'

The doctor finished attending to the burned man, and sent him back to the convict barracks.

'I find myself in need of some air, Monsarrat,' he said. 'Would you please accompany me down to the river?'

Monsarrat could hardly refuse, and didn't want to.

The pair walked down Allman Street towards the river and, reaching the banks, went along towards Shoal Arm Creek, which took them past the lime shed, eliciting a grunt from the doctor.

At the mouth of the creek, the doctor paused. 'Monsarrat, as irregular as this is, I feel I should make you aware of an incident which might yet have some relevance to our current situation. I did not report this event at the time, as there are delicacies involved, and I didn't know the absolute truth of it. I feel, though, that the time has come for some record to be kept of what transpired. I'd like you to record what I tell you in secrecy for now, and lay it by should you or I need to show it to the major at some future time.'

'It concerns Captain Diamond?' Monsarrat asked.

'Oh, it most certainly does. This happened a year ago, when the major was visiting Rolland's Plains, overlooking the plantations there. He was gone for a night, perhaps two; you probably recall better than I. And at that time, too, he left Captain Diamond in charge.'

Monsarrat did recall the major's trip, but had not seen Diamond during the few days he was away.

'I now wonder whether I should have reported this at the time,' continued the doctor. 'But Diamond was silent on the story. I didn't have the pleasure of knowing him quite so well then as I do now. I reasoned that the major would be back soon, and it was best not to cause upheaval in such a small place. In any case, Diamond is very good at earning the trust of those whom he deems important. And he has the major's trust. Best, I thought, to leave it alone.'

The doctor paused, allowing Monsarrat to absorb a justification for actions he didn't yet understand.

'So,' continued the doctor, 'the incident centred around the family of a convict called Mercer, an older fellow. His first sentence was for receiving stolen goods, and his second was for public drunkenness. But he was harmless, and he'd shown application while he was here.'

Monsarrat remembered the man. Quiet and industrious.

'He had two daughters. The older one, I think she was about sixteen, was a well-favoured girl. In fact, she looked a little like Mrs Shelborne. Her father was very sensible to the need to protect his daughter's virtue. The girls' mother had died, so they were living with him here, and because he'd behaved well since his arrival he was allowed a small house to live with them in.

'One night, Diamond sneaked into the girl's house. He had been courtly to her up to that point, when they met at prayers and so on, more so than you'd expect from an officer to the daughter of a convict. I'd noticed it, but just put it down to the strangeness this place works on people. I would never have dreamed that he would go as far as he did – walking into the house while all were asleep, and lying down in the girl's bed with her.

'She woke up and started screaming. Her father came into the room. It was dark, and I don't think he would have been cognisant of who was lying in his daughter's bed, but I doubt it would have mattered in any event. He grabbed Diamond by the collar, held him against a wall and then dragged him to the door and gave him a shove, sending him stumbling into the doorframe. It was only when Diamond turned around that Mercer saw who had intruded. I think he must've been a little frightened then, but any fear would have been secondary to the outrage he felt. He yelled at Diamond to leave his daughter alone, that he didn't care who he was, he would report him to the major on his return.'

'The major would most assuredly not have approved,' said Monsarrat. 'But as you say, Diamond has his trust. Perhaps he would have put it down to a tale spun by a convict trying to cause trouble.'

'Perhaps,' said the doctor, 'but the young lady woke half the settlement with her screams. You must have heard it yourself, Monsarrat. The man lived near the Specials' cottages.'

Monsarrat did recall the disturbance, but next day Slattery had told him that Goliath had sneaked into one of the cottages, to be driven out with a broom, and he thought no more of it. Diamond had mentioned the incident at breakfast, Slattery said.

'The next morning, Diamond ordered Mercer to receive fifty lashes for his insubordination. Now, you're aware, Monsarrat, that he is not allowed to administer that punishment without me being present. I couldn't have prevented Dory's flogging by absenting myself – the man was an absconder, and what Diamond did was legal until he took things too far. But in this case, for a man to be flogged for safeguarding the chastity of his daughter seemed to me unconscionable. If I attended, I might as well be swinging the flail myself.'

'You refused the captain?' said Monsarrat, trying not to betray his surprise. Gonville had always struck him as a time-server, every bit as much as the convicts, here to get much-needed experience which would have been unavailable to him in Britain's overcrowded medical profession. At some point he would return to England, attempt to ascend to the heady heights of Harley Street, and regale dinner parties with tales of his time in the colony, with its exotic natives and lascivious felons.

'Yes,' said the doctor. 'He came into the hospital to notify me and I told him I wouldn't attend. He went into quite a terrifying rage, then. Upended one of the beds, if you can believe it. Fortunately there was no one in it at the time. But do you know Margaret McGreevy? She's the one who got into an argument with one of the younger females over some sort of accusation that she'd been supplying rum to the gaoler. Anyway, her gout was acting up so she was in the hospital, in one of the beds facing Diamond. She looked absolutely terrified, as well she might, because he turned to her and said, "Avert your eyes, you raddled old bitch. If I hear a whisper from you, it'll be bread and water for a month."'

'If I may say so, doctor, I respect your fortitude in refusing him.'

'I'd had my doubts about him for a while. I'd treated a few wounds which were inflicted by him, for infractions that were relatively minor. Normally they might have earned a day on bread and water, or eighteen hours in the cells, but what they got was a crop across the face or some such. But if he hoped to sway me, he'd done just the opposite.'

'And what became of Mercer and his girls?' asked Monsarrat. He'd noted that the older man and his daughters were no longer around. But arrivals and departures were frequent here, and he had not given the matter a lot of thought at the time.

'Diamond sent him to Rolland's Plains. He muttered about putting him in the lime-burners' gang, didn't want him around making accusations. The man took his girls with him, and I've heard nothing of them since.'

'And what do you intend to do now?' asked Monsarrat.

'Well, I'm hoping you will assist me in a delicate balancing act. An official report on the major's return, when he is obviously coming back to such awful tidings, would not get the recognition I believe it deserves. But I wish to be in a position to quickly make an official complaint when the time is right. When that time comes – given Diamond's current mood, God knows what will happen to anyone – I feel the information should not reside only with me. If you'd be kind enough, Monsarrat, I'd like you to draft a report based on what I've told you, and hold it until such a time as I deem fit to share the information with the major. Or, if for any reason I am no longer present, use your own judgement. But it is a story I believe must ultimately be heard.'

The two men now turned around, and when they reached Allman Street again, the doctor said, 'I'll continue from here, Monsarrat. You may prefer to go back to Government House by way of the riverfront.'

Monsarrat walked on alone, past the commissariat stores where Spring was no doubt scratching in some ledger or another, and leaving the river when he reached the lumberyard. He knew the doctor had insisted they part ways for the sake of discretion, and felt it could do no harm to vary his route, so he doglegged halfway up the hill, passing the five huts which belonged to the overseers.

Young Billy Branch was sitting outside one of the huts. He was named after his father, one of the overseers, and was more properly referred to as William (or Master Branch, to Monsarrat). Branch the Younger attended the schoolhouse with the children of the officers. He had the liveliness of all young boys, but had always seemed to Monsarrat to be a decent lad.

There was no trace of that liveliness now, though. Billy sat on the ground in front of the hut, toying introspectively with some marbles in his hand, the ground being too soggy to roll them on.

'Master Branch,' said Monsarrat as he approached the hut, 'you seem a little downcast. Where's that monstrous hound in whose company I always see you?'

181

The monstrous hound was in fact a middling-sized dog of indeterminate breed, which young Branch had adopted and persuaded his father to let him keep. The pair always seemed quite content in each other's company.

Billy Branch, who could not have been more than six, looked up with unusually sad eyes. 'He gone and died, sir. Didn't come for breakfast, so I went to look for him. He was laid down in the yard and his face was all snarly. He never snarled at me. We would jump in puddles today if he was here. Do you think he's snarling in heaven?'

The boy's eyes had started to fill. Monsarrat assured him there was a special place in heaven for loyal hounds and promised to bring him some of Mrs Mulrooney's shortbread when he was next by.

Before resettling in his office, he went to the barracks to see Lieutenant Carleton. He intended to keep the mask of mundane clerical activity in place, by reporting to the lieutenant and removing the need for the lieutenant to come and find him.

The lieutenant was parading his soldiers up and down the yard behind the barracks, his face arranged as though he was in the midst of some act of great importance and necessity. When Monsarrat approached he looked down from his horse. 'Have you need of me, Monsarrat?' he said, half-hopefully.

'Sir, I simply wish to report that Dr Gonville still requires my services, and has given me dictation to transcribe. With your permission I will return to my workroom and carry out his requests.'

'Very well then. I know I can trust you to do just that,' said the lieutenant, turning back to watch the soldiers march across the ground for the umpteenth time.

Chapter 18

There had been no hound, monstrous or otherwise, in Monsarrat's youth. His boyhood companions had been an irascible widower and a dead Roman.

He had fractured memories of the scent of his mother, her smile, and the almost suffocating nature of her hugs. She had been a large-bosomed woman, and had been able to almost completely envelop him when he was small. But on a grey winter morning, on the outer fringe of London, consumption had dismissed her from this life not long before her son attained his eighth year.

His father, also a clerk, was affectionate when he remembered to be. He would have liked to have more children, young Monsarrat heard him telling an aunt, but the way things had turned out it was probably a blessing that there was only Hugh, for he did not know how, on a clerk's salary, he could have supported a bigger family, when he couldn't even afford the governess who was now needed for his son.

The solution to the problem of his son's education came in the form of a friend, a Mr Collins, who offered for a modest stipend to put the boy up in his house. Mr Collins was a schoolmaster near Exeter, and for a further fee he agreed to teach Hugh.

Mr Collins, a widower with no children, ran a small grammar school, and he and Hugh would walk there together each morning, although Mr Collins insisted the boy stay a few steps behind, so that one of Monsarrat's clearest childhood memories was the sight of Mr Collins's hands clasped behind his back as they made their way to the schoolhouse.

Monsarrat had been told by Mr Collins that he must never let on that he knew the master outside of the walls of the school. Monsarrat understood that this was a serious exhortation, and that he would disobey it at his peril.

So the silent boy lived with the silent man, the former occupying a cramped room to the rear of the house, well away from the living quarters, which Mr Collins reserved for his sole use.

It was one of the boy's greatest fears that Mr Collins would find disfavour with him and send him away to who knew where. There might be a poorhouse in his future if he didn't tread carefully, and he knew that once people went in there, they rarely came out, and when they did, they were shadows.

So as he grew tall and lean, and his voice shattered and re-formed itself into a sound with a deep, pleasant timbre, Monsarrat studied and studied, hoping to please Mr Collins, or at least to avoid displeasing him.

There were very few things which seemed to excite any kind of emotion in Mr Collins, but one was poetry, in particular the Roman poet Catullus. On Saturdays, when Monsarrat was allowed into the main living areas of the house to clean them, he would often find volumes scattered about, poetry from ancient times as well as more recent volumes from the likes of Wordsworth and Blake. But Catullus was, in Mr Collins's view, the pinnacle.

Mr Collins used some of Catullus's tamer verses – and Monsarrat had heard it implied that there were many which were less appropriate for young ears – to teach Latin in the grammar school. Monsarrat had never seen one of the Roman's poems in English. As far as Mr Collins was concerned, if you couldn't read the work in Latin, you shouldn't read it at all.

So while it took him many months, the boy eventually found the courage to ask his master, teacher and gaoler if he might peruse one of the volumes that lived in the front parlour of the house. 'I would very much like the opportunity to improve my Latin, sir,' he said.

Mr Collins narrowed his eyes. 'Latin can always be improved, particularly yours,' he said. 'Very well then, you may look at the volumes for one hour each Saturday, after you have finished your other work. I need not remind you that there will be a severe penalty should any harm come to them.'

Young Hugh certainly needed no such reminder, and if he'd had gloves of sufficient suppleness, he would have used them in handling the books. His reading was restricted to the volumes which contained material Mr Collins considered appropriate – this disappointed him somewhat, as he'd been looking forward to finding out exactly what wickedness lurked in some of the other verses. But he was grateful for the indulgence, and quickly came to look forward to that hour on a Saturday as the highlight of his week.

One morning, as he walked to school several paces behind his teacher, he found himself reciting one of Catullus's poems under his breath, in time with his steps. The poem appealed to him: it was about a boat – and what boy does not love boats – but written as though the boat were alive. The idea intrigued him. So that he could squeeze every drop of meaning out of the poetry, he had taken to translating the verses in his head from Latin to English, and back again. He was, without thinking, reciting in English now.

> This boat you see, friends, will tell you
> that she was the fastest of craft,
> not to be challenged for speed
> by any vessel afloat, whether
> driven by sail or the labour of oars.

Collins stopped in his tracks, and turned around. 'Stop muttering, boy! What is that you're saying?'

Young Hugh was too flustered to think of a convenient fiction; in any case Mr Collins was skilled at spotting fabrications and dealt with them harshly. So he repeated the first few lines of the poem, in English.

'And where did you come by the translation?' Mr Collins demanded.

'I translated it myself, sir,' said Hugh.

'Did you indeed?' said Mr Collins thoughtfully. 'Well now, if that is the case, you will not mind giving me the verses in Latin.'

Hugh swallowed, and began to recite:

'Phaselus ille, quem videtis, hospites,
ait fuisse navium celerrimus
neque ullius natantis impetum trabis
nequisse praeterire, sive palmulis
opus foret volare sive linteo . . .'

It transpired that Mr Collins had been working on translations of Catullus and other Roman classics. Despite his aversion to teaching the works in the vernacular, he had been giving some thought recently to the benefit of allowing the boys under his tutelage to compare the more easily read English verses to their Latin originals.

So it was that Hugh came to be Mr Collins's tacit assistant. In the evenings, he was permitted to eat in the parlour with his teacher, rather than retiring to his room with a plate as had been his habit. After supper, they would work together on the translations, with Hugh transcribing a first version, which would be polished by Mr Collins, whose Latin was, after all, far and away the best in Exeter.

The man noticed, too, the neatness and precision with which the boy wrote. He had no way of knowing that the young fellow, anxious to please the man who represented his only security, had practised on the back of stray scraps of paper, in the dirt, even sometimes on his own arms when writing paper wasn't available, in a bid to please his teacher. Mr Collins was indeed pleased, and quickly got into the habit of dictating his correspondence to the boy.

Before his mother's death, Hugh had been an affectionate child, and had not been wanting for affection in return. He constantly found himself fighting the urge to embrace Mr Collins, but knew this would be an indulgence too far. Nevertheless, a kind of guarded amity developed between them, so that by the time Monsarrat was ready to leave Mr Collins and his school, the man found himself uncharacteristically distressed. This only betrayed itself to Monsarrat via certain quirks in the face, more frequent rubbing of the eyes, Mr Collins staring at him just a fraction of a second longer than usual after finishing a sentence. But Hugh knew that face well by now, and could read some degree of genteel desolation in it.

He toyed, for a while, with asking Mr Collins whether he could stay and assist him in the school. Had Mr Collins made such an offer, he would have accepted immediately. But no offer was forthcoming, and Hugh had dreams of legal greatness, entering that world in the only way open to him, as a clerk. On the day of his departure, the old man gave Hugh a handsome glass inkwell, and his favourite volume of Catullus.

Monsarrat didn't know, now, what had become of those items. The book had been in his Exeter lodgings, and the inkwell on the desk in his fraudulent barrister's chambers. They had probably been seized by the constables, and sold at auction. He vaguely hoped they had brought the new owners more luck than he had had.

❧

Monsarrat returned to his workroom to carry out the doctor's orders. Sometimes the information he was given to transcribe was so dull that he wished for something of interest to happen in the settlement just so that he could distinguish one day from the next. He cursed himself now for that wish. He tried to concentrate on rendering each word as though it was a picture, rather than something with a set meaning. Hearing the story once was enough; he didn't want it ingrained on his soul.

He finished the doctor's report on Mrs Shelborne's death first, and laid it aside to dry, thinking to take it to the hospital later for Gonville's signature.

Then he wrote down the particulars of Diamond's treatment of Mercer. He did not attribute the tale, nor did he give the paper a heading or inscribe a title for signature. His penmanship alone, far above that of which anyone else in the area was capable, would identify him as the author of the report. But its source should remain mysterious to any reader until the time was right.

He made to put this last document under the blotter on his own desk, then thought better of it and slid it into the pocket of his black coat, thinking to secrete it in such a hiding space as he could find in his small hut.

Throughout the day he had been quietly fretting about Mrs Mulrooney. Her sentence, long ago served, was harsh enough for a woman stealing to feed a boy who was now a large and lolloping man droving cattle somewhere to the west. That she might hang for no greater crime than lavishing attention on a sick woman was an unthinkable prospect. But so were lashes or banishment for a man guilty only of protecting his daughter, and in Monsarrat's mind the shadow over Mrs Mulrooney was beginning to grow larger and close around her.

He made sure his workroom and the major's study were in order, as he had no way of knowing when the major would return, and did not wish to add to his coming grief by leaving him with an administrative mess to unpick.

As he made his way across the courtyard to the kitchen, he noticed that very little smoke was trickling out of the chimney.

He entered to find Mrs Mulrooney staring into a dying fire. She was sitting down, a rarity in itself, but particularly so when the fire or anything else was not behaving. She had her hand over a small stack of papers. Their thickness spoke of quality, someone with enough means to afford fine writing paper rather than directing the funds towards food. But they looked quite comprehensively crumpled, as though their recipient had meant to inflict significant damage while still preserving their contents.

She glanced up as Monsarrat entered, and then returned her gaze to the flames.

'You should know,' he said, 'that Gonville has dictated to me a report which comes as close as he possibly can to clearing you of involvement in Mrs Shelborne's death. I have left it as the first packet of paper the major will see on his desk when he returns.'

'Kind of him, and of you,' she said.

'I don't believe that description can be applied to either of us, at least not all the time. You are far more worthy of it. Please, try to lift your spirits.'

'Is there any need to, though? The major's still away, and I've no one to make breakfast for now.'

'You realise, I hope, how important your care of her was. It doesn't seem that anyone could have saved her, which I regret greatly. But no one did more than you.'

'Still, it wasn't enough, of course.'

Monsarrat had an uneasy feeling her listlessness would grow and consume her, if something wasn't done. 'I wonder,' he said, 'if you would show me how you make your tea. I've tried, but I can never achieve the depth of flavour which I find in your cups.'

Mrs Mulrooney gave a wan smile, perhaps recognising the question as an attempt to divert her. But the temptation to hold forth on the proper handling of domestic objects (which would get up to all kinds of mischief otherwise) proved too great. And, it must be said, she wholeheartedly agreed with Monsarrat's assessment of her tea.

She stood, pocketing the crumpled papers, and got down a pumpkin-shaped teapot, painted simply with tiny flowers. The more elaborate, taller pot in which she had brought Honora her tea was nowhere to be seen.

'I would venture, Mr Monsarrat, that you fail to warm the teapot first.'

'Ah, when I've had occasion to make tea I've poured the water directly from the kettle into the pot, over the leaves.'

Mrs Mulrooney gave a small, derisive 'Tch'. How, said her expression, have you survived to manhood knowing so little?

The fire needed stoking so as to bring the kettle to the boil. This done (by Monsarrat, under Mrs Mulrooney's direction on the precise placement of each quartered log), Mrs Mulrooney poured hot water into the teapot, leaving it for a few minutes to warm the china before pouring it out. As she went to refill the pot, Monsarrat asked, 'Won't you need to boil the water again?'

Mrs Mulrooney gave him a look of pure pity. 'If you scald the poor little leaves, they can't give you all their flavour, can they? The water needs to be hot, yes, but not boiling. Honestly, Mr Monsarrat, did they not teach you anything at that fancy grammar school?'

'Clearly not,' said Monsarrat, 'at least nothing of any practical value.'

Mrs Mulrooney said the tea needed to be given a decent amount of time to steep. 'I usually leave it for two Hail Marys and an Our Father, but as you're not of the one true faith you wouldn't know how to time it properly. Recite one of those Roman poems you like so much in your head twice, and that should do it.'

Mrs Mulrooney strained the tea through a cloth, and they both sat down to drink the product of their collaboration. She pronounced the results adequate, 'although you'd never have been able to do it without me'. Monsarrat readily agreed.

When he was able to see the bottom of the cup through the brown liquid, he said, 'Are you going to tell me what those crumpled papers are?'

Mrs Mulrooney exhaled loudly. 'I would, if I knew what they were myself. And I am glad you reminded me, because I wanted to show them to you. But you led me down the path of tea making, and I forgot them for a while, and all of the nastiness and grief which probably surrounds them.'

She drew the papers out of the pocket, and smoothed them out on the table. Monsarrat could see that the writing was cramped and inconsistent, with odd gaps between sentences and then none at all, and lots of dripped ink like crushed flies.

She handed them to him. 'I'll need those back, now. I was tidying Mrs Shelborne's room, you see, after ... well, after she stopped being her and became that object which lies in her bed. I went to make sure that her wedding ring was still in place in its drawer – which it was – when I noticed a piece of paper crammed right into the back of it. When I drew it out, it turned out to be several pieces of paper. Now, I know she is – was – particular about her things, she used the major's study from what I understand. So these wouldn't have been put there accidentally, or treated as they have been unless there was a reason to do so.'

'Would you like me to read them to you now?' said Monsarrat.

'No, I most certainly would not. I've no wish to go prying into her affairs. But I feel somebody should read them, as they may have something to say which bears on our current situation. May I ask you, Mr Monsarrat, to take them to the major's study with you, go over them while you're doing your other work? I'd then be very grateful if you would return them to me, so I can replace them where I found them.'

Monsarrat was about to say he would be delighted to help her, but delight didn't really enter into it. He had a sense of foreboding about the contents of the letters, which wasn't helped by the fact that he had immediately recognised the handwriting – being a student of such things – as belonging to Captain Diamond.

<hr />

Not knowing when the major would return, or when he might be interrupted, Monsarrat set straight to going over the mysterious correspondence.

The letters were unsigned. Nor did the salutations mention a name. The earlier ones started with 'my darling' or 'my love' or 'my heart's desire'. There was no date on the letters, so it was impossible to know in which order they had been written, save for the order in which they had been placed before being crumpled together into a ball. But Monsarrat was nevertheless able to detect a progression.

The earlier letters, in which Diamond had clearly been attempting to use his best penmanship, were unblotched and relatively neat. They were nothing more than descriptions of the lady's beauty, the radiance of her smile, the grace of her movement, and her amiable disposition.

After a few of these, however, Diamond must've decided that Honora was not sufficiently galvanised to action by his protestations of love, and made so bold as to suggest courses of action to her – that she should meet him for a walk in the woods near her family's home, or that she should grace him with her presence at tea in one of the finer hotels in Dublin when she was next there.

He clearly did not receive the response he had hoped for. The later letters began without endearments, and chided her for ignoring his most appropriate and earnest suit.

The last letter was the most cramped and blotched, and the words had taken on a jagged appearance which hadn't been apparent in the earlier missives. The letter informed Honora that the captain had learned of her engagement to his commanding officer. He would have hoped, he wrote peevishly, to have heard of such an arrangement from her own lips, given that they had what he termed 'a particular friendship'. He intimated that she had been holding out for the highest rank she could get, given that her family's nobility wasn't matched by appropriate funds. The letter ended with an ominous statement: 'Those who spurn the honest regard of an upright man may find themselves reaping a response which is equally strong as his former love, but nowhere near as benign.'

Underneath the last letter there was a note. This was on a less fine type of paper, the kind that Monsarrat himself used for reports to the Colonial Secretary. It was also, he knew, the type of writing paper used by the settlement's military and civil officers. This letter was brief and correct. Diamond welcomed Mrs Shelborne to the settlement, and said he hoped they could resume their former good relations from some years past. It was the only letter which was addressed to Honora by name, and signed by Diamond.

Monsarrat had smoothed each of the letters as he read them, and assembled them into his best guess at the order in which they were written. He now folded them – as neatly as their former ill treatment would allow – into one packet, enveloping this in a blank sheet of paper and sealing it with a ribbon and some wax. He felt it should join the doctor's report on the convict Mercer's daughter in a safe hiding place in his hut.

He knew he should acquaint Mrs Mulrooney with the contents of the letters, but equally knew they would distress her greatly. She had had little peace recently, and if he was right, there was less still in her immediate future. He decided to delay the evil moment when he would have to lay out the letters, and the story they told, in front of her.

He longed to dive into the cool, calm waters of Catullus, but looking at the bookshelf, he found his eye instead snagged by a copy of the *Edinburgh Review*, the same volume he had taken into Mrs Mulrooney's kitchen to read the other week. It contained the article which had prompted him to ask about the colour of the wallpaper in Honora's bedroom.

He had dismissed it, after feeling an initial thrill of incipient discovery. The doctor had at the time, after all, ruled out poisoning. And surely any poisoner, of humans or rats, would have to go to the stores for their weapon, risking discovery. Now, though, he began to see the information in a new light, and decided that it was timely to reread the article.

In keeping with the *Edinburgh Review*'s anti-Tory leanings, the article started by decrying the government for not taking in hand the manufacturers of wallpapers, cloth, and other dyed materials. The article's author wanted such regulation because a particular dye used in wallpaper, cheap and therefore commonplace from the most sumptuous drawing rooms to the meanest of huts, had been implicated in a number of deaths.

There were reports of a family of children in Limehouse dying after developing coughs, respiratory complaints and other problems. Their deaths were said to have been caused by diphtheria; however, mysteriously, other children in the area failed to fall to the disease.

Then there was the physician who was overcome by nausea every time he sat behind his desk in his recently papered study, only to find the symptoms dissipate when he retired to bed. The same physician noted the case of a couple he had treated, who after redecorating their home were overcome by sore throats, nausea, dizziness, headaches, and an odd, raindrop-shaped discolouration on their extremities. Their beloved parrot was similarly overcome – listless and off his food – although the physician couldn't attest to whether the raindrop rash had appeared beneath his feathers. The couple and their avian friend retired to the seaside, where they regained full health almost immediately.

There were also a great many cases of ladies wearing cloth coloured with the suspect dye fainting and becoming ill.

In the author's eyes, though, the most damning evidence came from a German chemist who noted a mouse-like smell emanating from the damp walls of houses papered in a particular colour, and, after taking scrapings, confirmed this to be the result of an acid produced by the pigment. He found that a lethal dose was present in each of the samples he took, and theorised that small particles had broken free of the paper and been inhaled.

This looming public health scandal, the author said, was threatening to kill – was, indeed, already killing – people in their homes, in their place of greatest refuge. But because the government profited from the mining of the substance used in the pigment, and because paper manufacturers were good taxpayers and influential lobbyists, nothing had been done to ban this insidious evil.

The pigment in question was known as Scheele's Green. And the substance which gave it its brilliant emerald hue was copper arsenite, a derivative of arsenic.

⌖

It was dark by the time Monsarrat walked across the Government House courtyard towards the kitchen, wondering for a second time whether he should share the information about the wallpaper with Mrs Mulrooney. The question turned out to be moot – the kitchen was dark, the fire out. Mrs Mulrooney had clearly retired to bed in Government House's smallest room, at the tip of one of the arms of the U.

In a way, he was glad of the reprieve. Today's information was curdling in his mind, refusing to mix and mesh happily. He decided to retrace the route he had taken this morning after talking with the doctor, walking past the now quiet lumberyard to the water's edge.

The Hastings River looked relatively calm tonight, despite the muttering he could hear from the sea a few hundred feet away at the river's mouth. As that mouth was wide, this waterway wasn't always so peaceful. Men drowned unloading cargo in heavy weather, underestimating the fury which spilled in from the Tasman Sea.

But on this occasion, the river did not appear to be in a drowning mood. It lapped and murmured, making its presence felt, but did not seem to be howlingly angry at Monsarrat or anyone else.

The river was calm enough, in fact, for the Birpai to supplement the food stores which, Monsarrat felt, had to have been affected by the presence of so many ghosts, as the natives thought of the new arrivals. They were, unfortunately, not ghostly enough to forgo the fish which jumped so willingly out of the surf or swam tantalisingly close to the surface of the Hastings.

The natives were ingenious when it came to fishing. Monsarrat knew they made use of a particular kind of tree sap to put fish in a watering hole to sleep, enabling them to scoop up as many as they wished.

But the Hastings was obviously a little larger and more unpredictable than a watering hole, and here they took advantage of the nocturnal habits of the fish. They used hooks made from particularly vicious thorns which grew here, and paddled canoes. Their path along the river, and their work in the canoe, was illuminated by small fires they lit inside their vessels, using melaleuca or paperbarks to dispel mosquitoes.

Tonight, a flotilla of Birpai canoes was engaged in this activity. Monsarrat couldn't see them, or the men who paddled them, but jewels of fire shone from various points in what Monsarrat knew to be the middle of the river, lining up to make a necklace around the estuary's throat.

From the opposite shore, also invisible in the dark, he heard faint singing. It was low and thrumming, and seemed informed by natural rhythms rather than any design of man, much like the singing Monsarrat had heard at Government House. Perhaps they were singing Mrs Shelborne to sleep, he thought.

Perhaps they were lighting her way out to the ocean with their canoes.

～∽∝∾～

A day's hard ride away, a group of soldiers, a few trusted convicts, an absconder who was about to be freed, and a Birpai tracker lay sleeping under the forest canopy. The major, who had indeed been on his way back when he was discovered by Diamond and Slattery, wanted to make all haste to ensure his quick return to his ailing wife. But travelling at night, in this country, was an impossibility, so they had made camp as the daylight faded, with the major appointing a sentry and warning him to wake the camp well before dawn, so they could be away on the sun's first rays.

One of the soldiers slept fitfully. He was too far away to hear the Birpai song, but the rendition from the other day still haunted him. It wove in and out of his dreams, showing up incongruously in places half-remembered, as well as in places wholly imagined.

He was a little boy now, drawing pictures with his forefinger in the dust. His mother was very insistent that he learn his letters, so he was practising, while turning the letters into something a bit more interesting – the 'c' was given pointy ears and whiskers and made into a cat, while the 'd' had the body of a duck appended to it, his bill raised in the air.

It was unusually warm, but not unpleasantly so – in this barely remembered place, warmth was welcome, not searing and punishing. Indeed, it was only to be had a few weeks of the year, when the gentle rain left off and the green all around could be appreciated on its own terms, rather than through a window.

Close by, his older sister Mary was with her friend. They tended to ignore him as they played, drawing pictures of elaborate dresses and playing with jacks made out of boiled-down pigs' knuckles.

Mary's friend didn't go to the hedgerow schoolmasters who were teaching him to read. She was from the big house up the road. And she was so important that the teachers came to her, and had to call her 'my lady', or some such nonsense.

196

But she didn't like the house, she said, although it seemed to the boy to be a miraculous place, one room for each person with more left over, rather than one room for eight, as was the case in his family.

The girl was probably about two years older than him – perhaps eight or nine – but a few years younger than his twelve-year-old sister. He didn't play with the girl himself – if she had been willing to tolerate him, he was still a little scared to. She was a creature of fascination, her hair always smooth, her clothes bright and crisp – at least until she and Mary had scrambled through a few bushes.

He didn't know why she came down here to play. The children from the big house rarely gave the time of day to his sort. But he had heard her tell his sister that she was the youngest, that there wasn't as much money as people supposed, and that her governess had left after an argument with Father. She was nominally in the care of the cook, who had enough to do making what money there was stretch to the large family without entertaining a little girl. So as long as she was back by nightfall, present and correct and clean, no one seemed to worry what she did. And she did seem to adore Mary, who told her stories and braided her hair and followed her on whatever adventure she wanted to have that day, making sure she didn't end up in a mud puddle.

The day his sister's life changed, the girl had brought down some shiny marbles she had been given as a gift. She and Mary were holding them up to the light, giggling as it caught them, half-closing their eyes and imagining that they were jewels in a dragon's treasure hoard.

The sound of hoofbeats was common enough, but rarely were they heard hitting the ground with such velocity and force. The horses around here weren't capable of it. The only horse the young boy knew of which could go at that speed lived in the stables up at the big house.

And then that very horse hove into view in front of their house. The man on it owned all of the land around here, including the land that the boy's family farmed, or tried to farm amid the plentiful rocks.

The passage of years had given the man's face a monstrous quality in the soldier's memory. Red and contorted, snarling, purple lips pulled back over yellow teeth.

The reality may have been a little less frightening. But it may not.

The man stalked over to the girl, and grabbed her roughly by the arm. 'You have been told, I believe, that you are not to associate with these people. They're peasants and papists. How are we to get you a decent dowry if you talk and smell like them?'

He hoisted the girl up onto the horse, and made to mount himself. The girl started wailing and reaching for Mary. Mary hated to see her young friend distressed. She put up her arms in case the girl's flailing caused her to lose her seat. The snarling man mounted then, and his foot caught Mary in the stomach. She just resisted the urge to double over, as she wanted to keep a hand up to catch the girl should she fall.

The kick may have been an accident. But what happened next was certainly not.

After he mounted, the man drew back the hand in which he held his riding crop, and slashed it with full force across Mary's face. Mary fell backwards into the dirt, howling and holding the bleeding gash in her cheek, as the man rode off with his daughter, her face looking back, an anguished mask.

The incident probably didn't have a bearing on the man's subsequent decision to raise the family's rent to unpayable levels, some time later. Certainly, they were not the only ones in the area to face such an impost, but their increase was the largest. Without a hope of paying, they packed up their belongings and headed towards the nearest city.

Mary's face was permanently disfigured by the blow. She could probably still have made a marriage, but felt she wasn't in a fit state to do so, and never would be. Surely the only man she could attract with such a horrific wound, which pitted her cheek almost to the corner of her mouth, would be a man not worth having, she said. So she hunted for work. She told her brother she wanted to be a nursemaid, but no one would hire a disfigured woman with threadbare clothes and no references. Neither would any of the shops take her on. She tried to sell flowers for a short while, but as she picked her ragged stock from the roadside, there wasn't much interest.

The city wasn't kind to the family. They found a space in a squalid tenement, for a little more than they had paid for the farm, but there they had at least had fresh air and access to the running water of the nearby stream. Here, neither of those things existed.

The boy's mother sickened and died. His father took to drink, and eventually lost his wits and his sight to it. Mary found enough work to keep them fed. When he was thirteen, a friend, whose father was one of his sister's customers, enlightened him on what kind of work she did, in the slightly jeering tone of one whose sire had enough money to pay for such visits. The men she let inside her didn't care about a marred face.

In fact, they weren't above marring it further. One night the back of a hand against her one smooth cheek sent the side of her head into a wall, with enough force to sever the connection between her brain and the rest of her body.

It was as well that the boy was resourceful, and that the petty thievery with which he fed himself went undetected. One by one the boy's brothers and sisters drifted away, until he drifted himself, and kept drifting until he found himself sleeping at the foot of a strangling fig and its host, the one slowly enclosing the other until no trace of the original was left.

Chapter 19

Monsarrat was greatly troubled by the tone in Diamond's letters. Not just the escalation from endearments to admonishments, although that was concerning enough. But there was a frantic depth of feeling there, a well of need, which Monsarrat had never personally experienced and did not understand. He wondered whether it was Honora, and only Honora, who had been capable of stoking such feeling in the captain, or whether the grasping desire was floating like a cloud around him, latching onto the first likely prospect.

Monsarrat had never come close to being married. He had his pretensions, and a great number of them, and they would not have been satisfied by the kind of woman who would have been happy to settle for a clerk's salary. There had been that walk with Lucinda Ham in Exeter, and a few others with various young ladies of good family. He might have pressed his suit with one of them, were it not for the fact that even shadow Monsarrat knew it would lead to certain discovery.

And then, of course, there was his trial, conviction, and transportation, none of which were conducive to meeting the right kind of woman or, for a while, any woman.

For many years after he left Mr Collins's residence, there was no one for whom Monsarrat felt genuine affection. Samuel Smythe probably came close, but that friendship was built on deceitful sands, which had of course ultimately opened and swallowed Monsarrat whole.

There had certainly been women. Many of them found Monsarrat's dark, brooding appearance compelling, and sought to rescue him from whatever turmoil sometimes appeared so plainly on his features. And occasionally, after a wild night in Exeter with some of the rowdier solicitors, he would find himself following the group to a house of ill repute, thankful that his barrister's fees stretched far enough to allow such indulgences.

Apart from these fleeting encounters, female companionship had not been easy to come by, nor did he desire it once his circumstances changed. But when reversals occurred in Monsarrat's life, they tended to occur swiftly and completely. And one such reversal bore the name of Sophia Stark.

Before his ticket of leave, Monsarrat's diligence and fine work at the Parramatta court had earned him some small freedoms. In his own time in the late afternoons and evenings, before he returned to his hut on the floodplain beneath Parramatta's version of Government House, he was permitted to sit in a small parlour in the Caledonia Inn in Church Street and rent himself out as a scribe to the considerable number of convicts and former convicts – called 'emancipists' – who wanted letters written for posting to other parts of the colony or to relatives in Britain.

As he seldom spoke without purpose, and maintained a neutral expression, some of his customers came to view him as a vessel into which they could pour their distress. Barely coherent ramblings of wives and families left behind, wise fathers and gentle mothers who might well now be dead, paramours who had probably married somebody who had not committed a crime, or at least not been caught in that commission.

He drew what meaning he could from these emotional purgings, put them into finer and more measured language, and wove them through the words dictated by his customers.

It became known that you could go to the tall dark-haired man at the Caledonia with only a vague idea of what you wanted to say, and emerge with a letter written in the finest script, and with the finest sentiment. Gradually, demand for his services grew, so that he had to turn people away in order to return by curfew to his hut. He had no intention of jeopardising the ticket of leave which he hoped was coming by being found away from his quarters after the allotted time.

He even, to his chagrin, had to turn away a pretty, trim dark-haired woman, with a slightly foxy face which stirred him.

She was back the next afternoon, however, and had evidently been waiting some time, as a small queue of people had formed behind her.

As she sat down opposite him, he asked how he could help her.

'In all sorts of ways, I should imagine, but taking some dictation will do for now,' she said, with a smile that to his mind was a little too arch for a first meeting.

She wanted a letter written to her brother in Kent. He was a few years older than her, and she had not seen him for ten years, nor heard word of him for nearly that long. He was a terrible waster, she told Monsarrat, and she had always been concerned for his future. 'If you had asked our mother which one of us would be transported, she would instantly have pointed to Charles,' said Sophia.

He asked her what she would like to say to him, and she dictated a mundane letter, telling him of the guest house she owned, the difficulty in securing curtains which were heavy enough to speak of quality at a cheap enough price, and how she pretended there was a husband upstairs should any of her guests give trouble.

Doing his best with the information she gave him, Monsarrat crafted as fine a letter as had ever left the colony, and found himself asking her to let him know if she ever received a response. She thanked and paid him, and left.

The next day she was back, but deliberately stayed at the rear of the line, stepping aside to let later arrivals pass her. Monsarrat stole occasional glances at her, but knew that his customers would become peevish if he seemed to be paying attention to anything other than transcribing then translating their thoughts into fine and edifying language.

When the line finally drew her towards him, she took a seat in front of his desk and smiled.

'I am presuming you have not yet had a response from your brother,' said Monsarrat.

She chuckled. 'You hear the navy boys boasting about how fast the ships are now, as though they were solely responsible for it. But no, there is no ship that fast.' Her face clouded slightly. 'I don't expect a response, not really. There's been none for ten years, and I don't expect that will change. But perhaps he's getting the letters, you see, and reading them, and knowing that he still has a sister, although at an impossible remove. Or, if the letters do not reach him, they may at least reach someone who knows what has become of him, who may one day be kind enough to enlighten me on that score. I will continue to write until I receive word that he has died, or I die myself.'

Monsarrat found himself uncharacteristically lost for words. The small frown that had rippled over her face made him want to sail for England and find this poor correspondent of a brother, sit him down, and make him dictate a letter back to her.

'Regardless,' she continued, 'that's not why I'm here. I came to ask you a question. A little indelicate perhaps, but I'd appreciate your honest answer. How much do you rely on the coins you get paid drafting these letters?'

From anyone else, Monsarrat would have found the question rude. But he didn't hesitate a moment before answering her. 'His Majesty very kindly feeds and lodges me, so I have no need of the money for the present. I am seeking to put it by for the happy day when my ticket of leave arrives.'

'In that case, do you feel you could tear yourself away one afternoon during your free time? You see, belief in my fictional husband is wearing thin amongst some of the more amorous of my guests, and I would be greatly indebted to you if you would give him form – for an afternoon.'

Monsarrat had already entertained very vague thoughts of playing the role of Sophia's man for more than an afternoon. And he felt honour-bound to help prevent the molestation of a lady. It was agreed that the following afternoon he would make his way to the guest house, the Prancing Stag.

The place, like its owner, was small, neat, and did its best to look respectable on limited funds. It was mostly patronised by visiting merchants and the occasional officer, but sometimes some rough trade came through the door. Sophia didn't discriminate as long as she had proof that they could pay for their board, but she was thinking of changing this practice, given the looks a few of them sent in her direction.

It was for the benefit of these men that Monsarrat, on entering the parlour, addressed Sophia as 'my dear' and moved assuredly around the room, having been briefed as to its dimensions and contents on the short walk to the place. And to maintain the deceit, it was only natural that he should retire upstairs with her as evening began to draw in.

They did not become lovers that day. Shortly after being admitted to Sophia's bedchamber, Monsarrat had to sneak downstairs again and out the back entrance to return to his hut by curfew.

But the following day, the correspondents of Parramatta were disappointed to find their accustomed scribe missing from his perch at the Caledonia Inn. A few of them muttered, and made other arrangements, but most decided to give the man a few days' benefit of the doubt, in the hopes that he would return shortly.

The man himself was at that time not in a fit condition to polish the sentiments of the town's people. He was in a rare state of neither thinking about nor needing words, closeted with Sophia in her bedchamber, his cravat on the floor slowly soaking up the contents of a cup of tea which had been accidentally spilled in his eagerness to discard it.

❧

In London, Sophia had been a chambermaid in a hotel far grander than the establishment of which she was now proprietress.

While Sophia was a diligent worker, her brother was in and out of employment, here a labourer, there a streetsweeper. No job lasting long, as his raging thirst inevitably made him late, and not a little violent.

Sophia, who lived in a small room in the hotel's subdivided attic, made barely enough money to keep herself alive. She feared daily for her brother, whom she still thought of as the strapping lad who had thrown her over his shoulder, tickled her, played hide-and-seek with her, and told her stories when she was tiny. She worried that one day, not so far in the future, she would hear of him being found facedown in a puddle, or in the Thames.

The patrons of the hotel, meanwhile, clearly had enough funds to feed an army – why else would they give scraps from their plates to the owners' mastiff? She reasoned that if you could afford to feed a dog as well as yourself, you could certainly do without that pocket watch, or that brooch. Such items did go astray during travel, after all.

But coming from a background where treasures were few, and jealously hoarded, Sophia failed to recognise the fact that for some fortunate people, treasures were tossed aside as casually as trinkets. So the brooch she mistook for a minor piece, of little value to its owner, turned out to be an heirloom passed down through the family for several generations, and it was missed instantly on its owner's return.

Later that day, Sophia was arrested after being caught trying to pawn the brooch. Within the year she had stepped ashore at Sydney Cove.

Sophia still hoped to make a marriage one day, and live in respectability, or what passed for it here. But a great many of the men she met seemed to mirror her brother's liking for alcohol followed by violence. She might be fortunate enough to snag some nice merchant who would turn a blind eye to her past, but if she waited too long her looks would be gone, and she would be left with men who resembled her brother, but without the humanity.

To guard against this eventuality, Sophia decided to make sure she was always able to provide for herself. She saved the money she made as a seamstress, and on getting her ticket of leave was able to afford a short lease on a well-made but slightly shabby building near the centre of town. She wasted no time in turning it into a cosy if uninspiring guesthouse, setting her rates in the narrow band which enabled a handsome profit without putting the customers off. As she became more profitable, the rooms were dressed in themed colours, and the cream teas were widely acknowledged to be amongst the best in Parramatta. By the time she met the brooding convict, she had been able to buy the building outright, and felt secure for the first time in her life.

She had had her eye out for some time now for a marital prospect, and felt this young Welsh–French hybrid could make a suitable candidate. He was industrious, and his skill with a pen meant that he would never be out of employment. He did not seem to be overly taken with drink, plying his trade surrounded by the stuff at the Caledonia Inn, but never visibly intoxicated. And she genuinely came to care for him, despite needing to hide her boredom when he recited some of Catullus's more saucy work.

For his part, Monsarrat was also indulging in indistinct dreams of respectable domesticity. He saw himself, a respected clerk or perhaps more, maybe a government functionary, maybe even a lawyer if such a profession was allowed to a former convict, returning to the guesthouse each evening, to drink tea on the porch with his wife or discuss the latest political news with some of the more educated guests. He came close on several occasions to broaching the subject of marriage, but wanted to wait until he was able to do so from a position of freedom.

There were those, however, who would have preferred Monsarrat to get on with it without waiting for his ticket. Churchmen in the colony often turned a blind eye to relationships between men and women which weren't sanctified by God. They performed colonial marriages between men and women who already had spouses in England or Ireland, reasoning that such a great distance was tanta-mount to death, and treating the nuptials as those between widows and widowers. And as long as things didn't get too lascivious or lewd, they also chose to ignore the sin of fornication – making an effort to stamp it out would have consumed every waking hour, and most of the sleeping ones besides.

The Reverend Horace Bulmer was not amongst these pragmatic clergymen.

As a convict, Monsarrat was required to attend church on a Sunday. Visibility in the pews was also a prerequisite for respectability, so Sophia likewise submitted herself each week to one of Bulmer's rambling yet emphatic sermons. His favourite topic was fornication and licentiousness, of which he saw evidence every day. Even if his homilies started out on a different tangent, they inevitably snaked their way back to sins of the flesh.

Monsarrat continued writing letters, but on fewer days than he had previously – he tried to keep two or three afternoons open to visit Sophia. On Sunday afternoons, of course, he wasn't permitted to work or hang around at an inn, so he tried to squeeze the same amount of business into three afternoons. Rumours began to circulate that the clerk was losing his touch, as the letters became less well formed and the sentiments less elegant.

His customers did not need to wonder at the reason for his absences. Parramatta, with its connections between each office, workplace, home and farm, enabled gossip to spread rapidly. So word of Monsarrat and Sophia's arrangement had started to trickle out almost before it was consummated.

During Bulmer's rants, Monsarrat would look at the back of Sophia's dark head and imagine his own beside it. He saw them generously donating to the poor box, and being greeted by other local worthies outside after the service. Perhaps one or two might be invited to the Prancing Stag for luncheon afterwards.

Along with the rest of the town, the Reverend Bulmer had heard of the guesthouse owner and the convict's relationship, and he redoubled his efforts to warn the general population of the dangers of fornication. He emphasised the irredeemable moral decay to be seen in those who committed this sin, and seemed to Monsarrat to stare pointedly at Sophia, and then at him.

Bulmer was a purist. A sin was a sin in his view, and a crime a crime. There were no shadings, no matters of degree. One of the few criteria which he used to distinguish between felons was education. Those who had been exposed to knowledge, whatever their crime, should know better. They clearly must be so deeply mired in sin that their souls were lost and therefore of no concern to him. One of his most emphatic views centred around the treatment of these convicts – the education which should have prevented their offences should not be allowed to afford them a comfortable assignment in government offices. They should be breaking rocks, and their backs in the process.

It was hardly surprising, then, that Monsarrat was quickly becoming one of Bulmer's chief obsessions. Unfortunately, the man held some sway in the upper echelons of Parramatta society, so his influence may well have contributed to the only word on Monsarrat's ticket of leave, which made him despondent when he finally achieved it a few months later: Windsor.

Not so far from Parramatta. One could travel between the two twice in a day, and still have several hours to spare. But he might as well have been restricted to the moon. Being caught out of his area would be a secondary offence. Monsarrat was unable to see Sophia again without risking his freedom.

Chapter 20

Mrs Mulrooney whitened as Monsarrat described the contents of Diamond's letters.

'No wonder she seemed so frightened that day in that dreadful water contraption. But surely this seals it, Mr Monsarrat. Diamond has taken her away, all for ignoring his advances.'

'We are fortunate,' said Monsarrat, 'that Dr Gonville shares a similar view. The word of a convict and, with great respect to you, a housekeeper might not stand against that of a loyal officer, but adding the voice of a surgeon might make our case.'

'We've not only to make a case against him,' said Mrs Mulrooney. 'We've to dismantle the one against me, though no one has yet put it.'

'Anyone with eyes to see can tell that you're not capable of such a thing, and especially when such an obvious villain can be constructed out of the papers in my pocket.'

No hiding place had presented itself to Monsarrat the previous night in his hut. He had very few personal effects and was unwilling to deposit the precious documents underneath his bedroll, where rats and damp might see them destroyed. But neither did he want to leave them in the major's office, as the man would have a funeral to organise and attend and might not be spending much time there, leaving the way free for Diamond to search there – Monsarrat had little doubt, now, that these letters were the subject of his recent efforts in the study.

In the end, he had decided the safest place for them was in his capacious pocket, where he could not stop himself fingering them occasionally to ensure they hadn't evaporated.

'You mustn't worry, really,' he assured Mrs Mulrooney, as she salved her anxiety by making a pot of tea, despite the fact that the two cups in the kitchen were full, and the second ones of the morning.

'Ah, it's not only me,' she said. 'I fret for Fergal too. This business with Dory must've brought his own sorry past back on him.'

Slattery had never discussed his past with Monsarrat in any great detail. It was an unwritten rule of the place: if anyone was unwilling to share details of their past – and there were many who were reticent – they were not pushed.

The extent of Monsarrat's knowledge was that Fergal had grown up in a small village in County Wicklow, the son of a farmer, with innumerable brothers and sisters, before being apprenticed to a plasterer. He found the work unsteady, though, and some of his workmates had fallen to lung complaints of one form or another, so he'd thrown it over and joined the army, where, he said, he could get a decent income, free food, and half a chance of seeing the world outside the village. He'd had no idea at the time, he said wryly, how far outside the village that decision would take him. 'I have the King himself feeding me now, and giving me a tour of the world besides,' he had told Monsarrat over one cup of tea or another.

So Monsarrat had a line-drawing view of Slattery's background, without any daubs of paint to give it colour or texture. This suited Monsarrat, who had no interest in returning the confidence with tales of London, Exeter and so forth. His friendship with Slattery was based on genuine liking, but was superficial in its way, rooted in their shared predicament of being relegated to this place, their love of banter and tea, and their regard for Mrs Mulrooney. Monsarrat had always appreciated Slattery's generally happy and playful disposition as an antidote to the grim and dour reality of life in the settlement. If there were dark rabbit holes in the Irishman's past which he occasionally ventured down in moments of melancholy, Monsarrat would prefer not to know of them.

'I was under the impression,' he said, 'that Slattery had left his past behind him too, together with whatever horrors it may hold.'

'And so he has, most of the time at any rate. He's told me often, Mr Monsarrat, that he tries to exist here and here only. But it's still there, you know, waiting to jump up and entangle him. And there's nothing surer to make that happen than having to flog a young man whose story is so similar.'

'I knew they both came from farming families,' said Monsarrat. 'But surely that's where the resemblance ends.'

'Not a bit of it,' said Mrs Mulrooney. 'You know the reason he was so fond of Dory?'

'I always thought it was because he had a little spark to him,' said Monsarrat. 'He didn't look at the world out of dead eyes, the way some of them do.'

'His eyes are dead enough now,' said Mrs Mulrooney, crossing herself. 'You're right: that was part of it. But they also both knew what it was like to be dispossessed.'

'Dispossessed? I thought Slattery decided farming wasn't for him and took an apprenticeship as a plasterer.'

'Ah, no, that decision was made for him. He plays his cards close to his chest, does Fergal, with information as well as with kings and aces. I thought he had told you all of this.'

'No, he hasn't. You are Mother Confessor to us both, but we don't compare notes. We don't have much occasion to interact, apart from under your protective gaze in this kitchen.'

Monsarrat hadn't yet mentioned his visit to Slattery's still. He could feel the weight of unshared information building up behind his eyes, but now was most certainly not the time to further burden his friend.

'Well, I wouldn't have started, had I known that. I'm not one for breaking confidences. But you should probably know, in case I'm not around . . . I suppose it would be good to know that there was somebody else who understood the young tearaway.'

So Mrs Mulrooney told Monsarrat how Slattery's family had been forced off their land and into a Dublin tenement by a classically greedy lord. His gambling debts had prompted him to ratchet up the rent to levels which were unrealistic, and certainly impossible for Slattery's family. The man had done himself a disservice in the end, losing all his tenants and unable to find others to replace them at such high rates. The ennobled family had slid towards bankruptcy, until some of the daughters were old enough to be sold off to families who wanted aristocratic wives for their sons, families who themselves had wealth but no nobility.

By that time, however, it had been too late for Slattery's mother, who had contracted a disease from the constant exposure to human excrement which was a feature of life in the new dwelling, and died. His father had become a ruinous drunk, and followed her when he became incapable of work, or speech for that matter.

Slattery himself had been at a loss. He was a reasonably bright boy, and had done well enough with learning his letters and numbers. But the only trade his parents had been able to teach him was farming, thinking it was the only one he would ever need. So he went from business to business, offering cheap labour, hoping that if the proprietor liked his work they might consider him for an apprenticeship.

A local plasterer, whose family had been on the land as well but had to leave due to insufficient yields, took pity on the boy. The man was a Catholic, but did fine enough work to be admitted to the grand houses of Dublin in order to smooth the walls and put up the papers that were in fashion at that time. He had seen Slattery in church, and thinking him devout (erroneously, as Slattery went to church for the express purpose of being seen to do so by prospective employers), decided to teach him the rudiments of the plasterer's trade.

Within a short time Slattery was able to plaster a wall as smoothly as any of the man's apprentices, and showed great attention to detail. Slattery was taken on as his apprentice, and the man did his best to teach him his craft.

Slattery had enjoyed the work, and had no problem with his master. But as he saw more of the grand way in which some lived – not his co-religionists, of course, but those who bore more of a resemblance to his family's former landlord – he became impatient. He would overhear tales of their travels to Europe, and wonder whether his village and Dublin were the only two places he would ever see.

There was no way, as an apprentice plasterer, that he would ever go beyond Ireland's shores. And no matter how smoothly he put up the paper, he would never earn the life which these people had been given at birth. He had also heard some speak of young soldiers who had distinguished themselves in the military and thereby been invited into the finest homes, in the hopes, probably, that their valour would rub off on some of those families' sons.

The solution seemed clear, then, to Slattery – travel, and the opportunity to return a hero and be invited as a guest through the doors at the front of the house, rather than entering at the rear as a tradesman. So, like many before him, and dimly aware that he would be serving the monarch of a nation responsible for setting up the system which had robbed his family of their livelihood, he joined the army and donned the red and buff coat which put him on the same level on the parade ground as the sons of wealthy Protestants.

'He once told me,' said Mrs Mulrooney now, 'that he might have done the same thing as Dory – had considered it on a few occasions – but an opportunity had not presented itself. He would have seen stealing for the sake of his mother as only a fraction of what his family was owed. He could have as easily been here wearing broad arrows as a red coat and that ridiculous hat.' Mrs Mulrooney did not approve of the dress hats the Buffs wore – tall and cylindrical, with a small brim and a plume sticking out the top. She saw no point to them, and had occasionally threatened to use Slattery's as a duster.

Monsarrat listened to Mrs Mulrooney's tale with astonishment. Slattery had always been light, with enough of the rogue about him to make him interesting, but not enough to make him seem untrustworthy. He had none of the darkness which Monsarrat would have associated with such a history. He said as much to Mrs Mulrooney.

'Oh, but he does,' she said. 'He's uncommonly good at hiding it – I'll give you that. But on one occasion, he got a hold of some sly grog – a terrible thing for those who aren't used to it – and he came hammering on the wall of my room in the small hours. Heaven alone knows how everyone else stayed asleep, or perhaps they didn't, they're just so used to hearing drunkards late at night, but I bundled him into the kitchen, got a slurred promise from him to stay there until I went and dressed. By the time I got back, his head was on the table and he was drooling into those little grooves in the wood. So naturally I had to hit him in the back of the head to wake him up.'

Monsarrat glanced down at the table briefly, then asked, 'What did he want from you?'

'I don't know, and I doubt he did. Perhaps he had some vague idea of having me grant him absolution for being taken with drink. I asked him what had got him into this state, and he said he'd remembered that morning it was his sister's birthday. She's dead now, he said. He said an evil man blighted her, and then moved on to the rest of the family. He was cursing the man – he used one of my favourites, actually, wished the fellow's cat would eat him and then the devil eat the cat. He was wailing about it so much that I readied a pail of water to dump over him, just to shut him up – I was greatly concerned he would wake the major and Mrs Shelborne. This was a couple of months ago, you see, before the major left and herself got ill.'

In spite of everything, Monsarrat found himself smiling at the image of a dripping-wet Slattery. 'And did you carry through on your threats?'

'As it turned out, I didn't need to. I was well prepared to' – Monsarrat didn't doubt this – 'but all of a sudden he went deadly calm, and he said he'd come by some information which might help make amends, to allow his mother's soul to lie quietly in her grave, and his sister's too.'

'What information?'

'I'm not entirely sure. But he said he'd been helping unload a ship and had found himself holding a packet of letters. He said the address on one of the letters – the place that it was from – showed that while the tree was still standing and rotten to its core, some of the branches might at least be pruned.'

'Well, that's rather cryptic of him.'

'Would you ever stop using words like that, Mr Monsarrat? Be a plain-speaking fellow – people will appreciate it.'

'I do apologise. What I meant was, it's puzzling.'

'That it is. I pressed him for more information, but he just rambled. He was becoming very difficult to understand then. Kept saying names – I assume the names of his brothers and sisters – and wailing for them to come out and join him here, where there was good farmland to be had. He was really getting most irritating. And then put his head down on the table again, and that was it. Snoring within seconds. I took off his neckerchief and put it under his mouth – if something had to soak up the drool, better that than my table. I went to bed then, and resolved to return to the kitchen a little early so I could send him on his way before he was missed.

'When I came back a few hours later, he was already gone. He showed up for his usual morning cup of tea, looking a little bit bleary, and begged me to say nothing. He said that men misspeak after strong drink, particularly if they're not used to it. You arrived a short time later, actually. You seemed too absorbed in your own matters to really notice the state of him, although how you could have missed the smell coming off him, I'm not sure.'

'I probably didn't miss it, as such. I imagine I would have just ignored it – I'm used to Slattery and the rest of the soldiery smelling rather ripe.'

'Ah, you must never miss things like that, Mr Monsarrat. Even if you just tuck them away at the back of your head, and don't mention them to anyone. Like I've tucked away the fact that you asked me about wallpaper a little while ago, and then stalked off without telling me where your line of questioning was going.'

Monsarrat sighed. 'I was going to tell you, but you've enough on your mind at the moment, and I didn't want you to worry. It's probably nothing, one of those random connections that seem like they might be significant and turn out to be meaningless.'

'I don't believe there is any such thing as a random connection, Mr Monsarrat. There's a pattern everywhere, you just need to keep your eyes open enough to spot it. Your own eyes have been cast downward too much of late, who knows what's passed you by. Now, the price of the continuation of your tea supply is to let me know what you were getting at that morning.'

So Monsarrat told her about the article, about the connection between green pigment and illness. 'But it was Diamond, and he used the arsenic that he sent the private to requisition from the stores, pretending it was for rats,' he said. 'It's an interesting wrinkle but I don't think it can really be anything more than that.'

Mrs Mulrooney sat down heavily. 'And yet with green wallpaper being put up just in the next room, and some of the plastering crew sickening from it,' she said, 'do you not find that just a little too wrinkly altogether?'

'I don't, as a matter of fact. She can't have been exposed directly, because she was never in the parlour while the paper was being put up, and while some children have died from licking it, I can't imagine Mrs Shelborne doing so! And how would Diamond somehow synthesise the pigment into something he could give to her without himself being affected by the stuff? For that matter, how would he give it? You or Dr Gonville were always with her.'

'Some interesting questions you raise, Mr Monsarrat,' she said. 'And I've not a hope of answering them. But there may be answers. Just have a care you don't miss them when they show themselves, or mistake them for some more, as you put it, wrinkles.'

⸺⁓⸺

Monsarrat hated leaving Mrs Mulrooney that morning. She had no one to cook for or fuss over, and it was telling on her, for all that she tried to hide it. Her pinafore bore a grease stain – the first which had been allowed to mar it since Monsarrat had known her.

And she was rearranging the teacups on the shelves, over and over, as though trying to parade them like soldiers.

But he would be of no use to her if he was on bread and water for neglecting his duties. So in the absence of any word to the contrary from Lieutenant Carleton, he made for the hospital.

Gonville was not there, and neither was Edward Donald. Nor, unusually, were any of the beds occupied. He found the doctor in the dispensary, being assisted by Donald in mixing a draught.

Gonville looked up. 'Good morning, Monsarrat. I'm taking a precaution here – I'm not a betting man but I'd suggest Major Shelborne may be in need of a little soothing on his return. And I hope that return is sooner rather than later. There is no fitting place for the lady to rest in the hospital, so she remains in her bed, washed by Mrs Mulrooney and her tears. Thank God it's winter. But if the major is gone for much longer, he will unfortunately have to return to a gravestone.'

'Shall I go back to the major's office, then, and wait until you have need of me?'

'Before you do, I have a message for you to deliver to Lieutenant Carleton for me,' said Gonville. He moved away from the bench he was working on towards a small table, on which papers and ink rested. He scratched out a hasty note, not bothering to blot it, leaving it to the fibres of the paper to soak up the excess ink. He folded it and handed it to Monsarrat.

When Monsarrat reached the parade ground, the soldiers were going through their third parade that week. While the major had intended regular parades to prevent boredom, the looks on the faces of many of the soldiers indicated that their frequency was making them counterproductive.

He handed the note to Lieutenant Carleton, who read it before putting it in his pocket. 'Dr Gonville suggests that I post a sentry on the other side of Shoal Arm Creek, to alert us to the major's approach. So we may ride out and deliver the sad news to the man. A terrible circumstance in which to hear of an even more terrible circumstance, but I can see the doctor's logic – better this than that he race up to the bedroom to check on his wife and find none there.'

Or the shell of one, thought Monsarrat.

Carleton called over a private – Cooper, Monsarrat saw, he who had requisitioned the arsenic.

'You, Mr Monsarrat, may return to your workroom and complete such work as the major left for you. Remain there until called for – do not go to dinner. We do not know when he may be returning; however, I would like his office to be staffed until nightfall, in readiness.'

Chapter 21

Monsarrat had, of course, long finished all the work that the major had left for him. He wished some functionary would come and load him up with a week's worth of reports to transcribe. The process was soothing and distracting, and he desperately needed to be soothed and distracted.

For want of anything else to do, he started work on a letter to Sophia – a process which was well and truly distracting, and anything but soothing.

He tried to comfort himself with the knowledge that Catullus, all those centuries ago, had felt as he did. The Roman seemed to believe no feeling was valid until it was expressed in verse, and had written: *Sad Catullus, stop playing the fool, and let what you know leads you to ruin, end.*

If he was honest, Monsarrat suspected Catullus felt more keenly than he himself did. But he still clung to the connection between them.

The letter to Sophia had been through several dozen drafts, and had never been sent. It was a follow-up to the note he had sent her on the eve of leaving Sydney, more than two years ago. He did not know, now, whether the Prancing Stag still stood, and whether she was still its proprietress. Worse, he did not know whether she still had to fabricate a husband, or whether an actual one had taken the place of the illusion. He couldn't help but fear the latter.

Monsarrat's ticket of leave was by far the most precious document he had ever held in his hand. Previously, it had been his call to the bar, although the ticket of leave had a significant advantage over its predecessor, being genuine.

But of course, the document came with its own drawback – in the one word which sat innocently on it, Windsor.

Before he left Parramatta, he visited Sophia one last time, letting her know why he could no longer come to her, asking her whether she would be willing to wait until such a time as he had managed to set the situation to rights. To his amazement, she did not seem at all concerned.

'You're a resourceful man, Hugh, as resourceful as any I ever met. What does it matter if we can't be together openly for the present? It's not a long ride to Windsor; you can, I am sure, find appropriate times to come to me when you won't be missed, and have the sense to get off the road if you hear hoof beats. At least you're no longer subject to a curfew – you can stay the night here, and be back at the breakfast table as though nothing has happened.'

Monsarrat's first reaction was to immediately dismiss the suggestion. The freedom his ticket of leave conferred on him had been his lodestar for so long, spurring him on to be a conscientious clerk.

But there was that within him, too, which latched onto risk, a Monsarrat who thought an actual reward was worth the prospect – the probability – of punishment. This shadow Monsarrat had not been in evidence since Exeter, when it had convinced him he could pass himself off as a lawyer indefinitely. Whenever the rational part of him asserted itself and forced him to examine the likely repercussions, the shadow Monsarrat squinted, so that the picture blurred around the edges and therefore became less realistic, less likely.

After a long slumber, shadow Monsarrat suddenly arose in fine voice. What was the good of freedom, he asked, if you weren't actually free? Should one not be able to live where one wanted, work as one chose, and bed and marry regardless of location? Surely his diligent service entitled him to that, regardless of one word on a piece of paper. Already, the prospect of losing the freedom he had just gained was seeming a little fuzzy.

But shadow Monsarrat was not entirely without caution. And under his auspices Monsarrat made a big show of putting down roots in Windsor, and only in Windsor. He applied for and won a position teaching the sons of a local landowner and magistrate, a reasonable man called Cruden.

'Just drill what you can into them, Mr Monsarrat,' he said. 'If they come out the other end learning to appreciate art and literature, and able to parrot a few phrases in Latin, I will be well pleased.'

Monsarrat intended to do a whole lot better than that. That was, however, before he met his students. The only school Monsarrat had known was the quiet of Mr Collins's grammar school, while his university was the old man's study. It had never occurred to him that not all classrooms were places of silent application.

Mr Cruden's boys, while not bad, would certainly have been birched by Mr Collins.

He taught the boys Latin grammar, algebra, proper handwriting and the history of the ancient world, but the young Crudens were nearly wild children, raised indulgently by their father because, like their new teacher, they had lost their mother, and much adored by a convict housekeeper who – it became apparent – was Mr Cruden's mistress. The boys were good-natured, hard-riding, cursing and jovial young men of thirteen and fourteen and their father hoped one day that they would hold a commission in the army. Monsarrat could imagine them thundering around some colony subduing the natives.

Their father was grateful that Monsarrat seemed at least to be making some inroads into their education. He was careful to teach material that would interest them – so the history of the ancient world focused on great battles and great generals, while he had them practise their handwriting by making up stories which cast themselves in the role of knight or redcoat. It was not possible, sadly, to make algebra and grammar similarly appealing; however, he made a bargain with the boys that if he had their full attention for three-quarters of the lesson, they could take the last quarter off, and race outside to wrestle with each other or gallop around on the horses.

Cruden's gratitude, and his domestic arrangements, encouraged shadow Monsarrat all the more. This man, the shadow whispered, is unlikely to care what you do in your own time, nor is he likely to report you even if he should become aware of the situation.

With Mr Cruden's leave, Monsarrat set up a scribing business at a local inn during the evenings, as he had at the Caledonia Inn. With the money from this, and his pay from Cruden, he was able to afford a horse – a nag, to be honest, but one capable of easily making the journey between Windsor and Parramatta.

One of the many things he enjoyed about being free was that he was not required to account for every movement. So if the tutor was absent from his cottage when not on duty, no one called him on it.

Thus he visited Sophia once a week – far less than he had when a convict, but he assured her he would write to the Colonial Secretary and beg to be assigned to Parramatta. He might even ask the man for a job as a free clerk at the court – surely the Colonial Secretary would see a benefit in having a clerk there who already knew how the place operated, and who could serve as a model of emancipated respectability to those still bonded.

But he received no reply from the Colonial Secretary. And as his weekly visits came close to fifty-two in number, Sophia's discontent was becoming more apparent.

'Why must you only come to me on Saturdays?' she said. 'Surely you are at liberty to come on Sundays as well?'

'You well know that I'm not at liberty to come at all. But a Sunday, that would necessitate my absence from church. It would be noticed. There would be talk.'

'What of it?' she said. 'I, of course, must be seen at church on Sunday morning. I have a full pardon and I own a business in this community, which makes my appearance essential. But you've been going faithfully to the church in Windsor every Sunday for nearly a year. Is it not out of the question that you might find yourself with a sore throat, or a cough, which would prevent your attendance? You could then travel up while I am attending church, and I can meet you back at the Stag. After all, the only reputation which will matter is our reputation together here.'

Monsarrat, however, pointed out to her that Bulmer was likely well aware of the condition on his ticket of leave – in fact, he suspected the man of engineering it. The possibility of encountering the Reverend on a Sunday, when he was abroad after service, daunted him even against the urgings of shadow Monsarrat.

'And how will you meet him, my love, when you're cloistered with me at the inn?' Sophia laughed. 'I assure you, Reverend Bulmer is not in the habit of coming here.'

So Monsarrat allowed himself to be persuaded, and made several Sunday visits to his unofficial fiancée, to augment the Saturday ones they had been enjoying for a year.

This success emboldened shadow Monsarrat, so that he left his departure on a Sunday later and later, having to force his poor horse to feats of speed it had never been called upon for in the past in order to return to Windsor at a respectable hour, to prepare his lessons for the rowdy Cruden brood the next day.

Cruden, though, was not oblivious to the wanderings of his children's educator, having called at Monsarrat's cottage a few times on a Sunday on the way back from church. Monsarrat's absence there, too, had been noted. Cruden wished that all of the staff associated with him be above reproach – at least in the eyes of his neighbours – and so had visited the man's cottage in order to drag him to church, even if he was spraying catarrh onto the whole congregation, an eventuality the magistrate considered unlikely, as none was in evidence during his children's lessons. But his hammering on the door, of course, produced no reply.

As a magistrate, Cruden travelled, and was in the habit of dining in the inns between Windsor and Parramatta. Both the colony and the guesthouse business were small ponds, and he soon heard the rumours of Monsarrat's visits to Sophia – a great many of her guests had noticed the tall man making his way up the stairs to her bedchamber, and remembered him from his time scribing at the Caledonia Inn.

Some of them, too, after Monsarrat had first received his ticket of leave, had heard Sophia rail against the unfairness of his restriction to Windsor. This they gleefully reported to Mr Cruden, always happy to exchange the currency of information for possible leniency later, should it be needed.

One Monday, Cruden came to the room set aside for classes and asked Monsarrat to come outside into the hallway. He did not lose much time in getting to the point.

'I have heard of your awkward situation, Monsarrat,' said Cruden. 'You're not the first convict on whom Bulmer has had a geographical restriction placed in order to prevent moral turpitude. Don't look so surprised, man – of course it was Bulmer. He's an impossibly inflexible man. He has an eye on a spot on the bench, you know, and I understand he brought some influence to bear to make sure you didn't keep your position there. Clerks as good as you, I understand, are not lightly disposed of.'

'With the greatest respect, sir, what precisely do you mean by my awkward situation?' asked Monsarrat, careful to lather his words with the appropriate tone of subservience.

'Now, Monsarrat, despite your nefarious background and convict past, I have never treated you other than as a man of intellect. I would appreciate the same consideration in return.'

Monsarrat bowed his head. 'Of course, sir.'

'I will only say it to you, Monsarrat, and will deny it if you repeat it, but it seems improper to impose a legal sanction for a supposed moral failure, if it be just that, a moral failure, but not a murder, or a robbery. I am no friend of the Reverend Bulmer either, as you might have inferred. His brand of morality is wholly unsuited to life here, and serves only to cause a great deal of anger and worry amongst his parishioners.'

Cruden was silent for a moment, staring at the former convict thoughtfully.

'I understand what you are sometimes doing with your long rides. The letter-writing, yes, that is quite licit and appropriate, but . . . the visits to other places . . . Let us just say, I shall not take any action unless forced to, but I must warn you, if you are brought before me for a technical breach, I will be required to apply the appropriate ordinance, and will thus lose a very good tutor to my wild children. So be careful. I don't expect a man to be inhuman, but I expect him to be wise. And as for frailty, be frail as infrequently as you can manage.'

Monsarrat felt he was already doing this – his frailty needed expression at least twice a week. And though he was newly awake to the dangers after Cruden's warning, shadow Monsarrat chose to interpret it as a permission as well as an admonition.

In the failing light of a winter Sunday, Monsarrat left the Prancing Stag and set out for Windsor. Shadow Monsarrat was unfurling and quickly occupying all available space, having not held this much sway since Exeter.

His recent dusk departures came at the expense of speed – the roads were rutted enough, in places, to lame a horse. He lacked the funds for another, and would never be able to make the journey to Parramatta by foot in time. Nevertheless, Monsarrat made considerable haste, weaving his way across the gouged surface at a trot, rather than the canter he would have employed in full daylight. He always felt safer when he reached the Windsor police district.

On hearing the wheels of a carriage behind him, quarrelling with the rough road surface, he rode into the fringes of the eucalyptus forest and watched the vehicle go by containing a well-dressed male and female and a driver. When it had clattered past, he emerged onto the road again, but the sound he had thought was the departing carriage was a second one bearing down on him. There was a curse from the driver of the second carriage, Monsarrat spurred his horse out of the way, came to a standstill on the verge of the road, and saw, staring at him in the last of the light, the Reverend Bulmer and his wife.

Monsarrat felt an impulse to gallop off then, but he resisted it, from gallantry but more accurately from a sudden desire to defy this minor consecrated bully who nonetheless had the authority to destroy him.

Bulmer's nasty smile crept over his face. 'Out of your district, I see, Mr Monsarrat,' he squealed. 'And are you coming to your concubine, or going from? Do you think you are free to be? Out of your district, I mean?'

'By a technicality,' said Monsarrat, 'no, sir.'

Then shadow Monsarrat gave a final flex, and wholly consumed his host. 'But by the laws of natural justice, I am where I should be.'

Bulmer's smile transformed itself into a thin red line, a sword slash. 'I have my own views about where you should be, according to the laws of divine justice,' he said. 'Return to your district at once. And do not think for a second this will go unreported.'

Again, Monsarrat felt the compounding anger. 'May I ask, sir, if marriage be the most desirable state – the only morally possible one – between a man and a woman, why you go to such lengths to prevent the development of the amity which leads to it?'

'Amity, is that what you're calling it now?' Bulmer sneered. 'Marriage has one purpose and one only, Monsarrat: the production of children, for which amity is not required. As for any marriage you might make, I'll do anything I can to prevent you breeding. Intelligence and criminality in the one form is a dangerous thing, and those who carry both within them should not expect mercy.'

He gave a little nod, then, as though agreeing with himself. Well done, he was likely thinking. That was very elegantly phrased. I might use it in a sermon.

The gesture, though small, irritated Monsarrat beyond words. 'I would not expect mercy from your pulpit, sir,' he said, thinking that he never would have expected to miss Exeter's reverends, or London's, who put off their moral strictures at the end of the workday. They served a god of nods and winks. The antipodean god seemed to be a much harsher deity, if His representatives here were anything to go by.

The Reverend Bulmer reached forward and pulled a coach whip from its holder beside his convict driver. He slashed it in Monsarrat's direction but it merely grazed the shoulder of

Monsarrat's horse. 'Get going, sir,' said Bulmer, in a tight voice, 'lest I forget that I am a man of peace.'

A sudden dispassion descended on Monsarrat. He skirted the glorified dray in which the Reverend and his wife were travelling and cantered up the road to Windsor. But when he had gone perhaps a mile he waited until he was certain that Bulmer's carriage had passed.

Monsarrat was still in a sufficiently defiant state not to realise the full weight of what he had done. He had not only been found out of his district, but he had also been guilty of insolence, and magistrates – even sometimes the progressive Cruden – loved to have the insolent flogged, since they knew that without servility they might face some sort of white-slave uprising.

So Monsarrat doubled back to Parramatta to warn Sophia what was to happen.

He had expected a more emotional reaction. True, one perfect tear from each eye strolled down her cheek – anything more would have been overdoing it.

She walked up to him, and he thought she was going to kiss him. Then she drew back her hand and struck him, hard, across the face, opening a small gash in his cheek with her ring. It was a fake engagement ring she wore, together with a gold band, as a silent warning to amorous boarders. Monsarrat had hoped to replace it with a real one, but knew that would never happen now.

'You foolish man,' she said. 'What an awful, awful waste. We could have been amongst this place's first citizens.'

He did not point out that it was she who had encouraged him to extend his visits. He touched an index finger to his face, examined the blood on it, and looked at her pointedly.

She did kiss him then, and started crying in earnest.

It was a great honour for a man in New South Wales to be wept for, because few in the place were in a position to utter promises of deathless love. Congress between men and women was either headlong and reckless or a matter of convenience, of sensible choice, of the person possessing the resources to keep a man or woman out of want and out of trouble.

There were no New South Wales Eloise and Abelard, no Dante and Beatrice, no Romeo and Juliet. He could not expect the comely Sophia to wait for him – he had not asked for such a thing, nor had she offered. She would not remain a nun to honour his misfortune, a banal one by New South Wales standards. She would see how things turned out – he knew it and she knew it, and though neither of them said it, they both understood that was the way a sane person should proceed. In any case, Sophia would be unlikely to remain alone for long, especially in a place where men so emphatically outnumbered women.

He rode home undetected later that night, taught the Cruden boys on Monday morning, and was visited by a constable with a warrant on Monday afternoon. He would have been held in gaol pending the Wednesday morning magistrates' court, but Cruden insisted to the constable that Monsarrat could safely stay there, on his property.

Taken to court by Mr Cruden in his own surrey, Monsarrat faced his employer in Cruden's persona as magistrate, and was stripped of his ticket of leave and given into the care of two constables who were to escort him to Parramatta and then by river down to Sydney, where he was to be detained in the prison at Hyde Park awaiting the discretion of His Excellency.

Monsarrat had feared that he would be flogged, but Mr Cruden and his fellow magistrate were not willing to accommodate the Reverend Bulmer to that extent. But by the judgement of the magistrates, subject to approval by His Excellency, three years were added to his sentence.

Monsarrat knew he would not be staying in Sydney – the administrative centre had no place for those who had offended twice. They had, in the past, been sent to Norfolk Island, a place of terrible repute before it was abandoned. It was said that groups of men would draw straws, with the winner to be killed quickly by the man with the second longest straw, who would hang after the loser testified against him, all the while envying him and his victim. This, it seemed, was the most reliable manner of escape. Or they had been sent to Newcastle, but that was now the preserve of free settlers, as the place had proved too easy to escape from.

For a few years now there had been whispers of a new place of banishment, a new slag heap of second offenders, remote enough to prevent easy access to Sydney. A place, it was rumoured, of cruel overseers, threatening mountains and even more threatening natives. And it was here that Monsarrat was sent.

He wrote Sophia a note – apologising, letting her know she had had a genuine place in his affections – before he boarded the *Sally*, bound for Port Macquarie. She did not write back.

He missed Sophia Stark, but after a time he realised he did not ache for her. He ached for a conditional pardon. Not even Bulmer could undermine him then.

Chapter 22

Monsarrat laid aside the unfinished – and destined to remain forever so – letter to Sophia. He expected to be called on to write other letters soon enough. Letters to Honora Shelborne's family. He started polishing some of the phrases which he might incorporate in them, anticipating that the major would be overcome with the dual imperatives of making the necessary arrangements for his wife's burial, and bringing her killer to justice.

While Monsarrat was used to being still, he was most definitely not used to being idle. His mind rambled in all sorts of directions he would rather it not go. Chief amongst these was what – or whether – to tell the major about Diamond's secret commission. He could ill afford a third offence against his name. But none of them could afford a killer – particularly one of Diamond's supreme viciousness – to go unpunished.

He hoped that the letters together with Gonville's testimony regarding the incident with the convict's daughter would form enough of the picture for Major Shelborne to at least question his second-in-command.

But Monsarrat was not in any way certain of being able to shake the major's faith in the captain. Distasteful necessities could crop up, even here; subordinates without qualms could prove useful. And a shared history of battlefield blood could bridge gaps between those who might not have tolerated each other in civilian life.

Monsarrat fully intended to lay out the facts, such as they were, pointing to Diamond's culpability, but he would not relish it. He recognised that in doing so, he would be robbing the major of one of his few certainties in the uncertain world, where healthy wives could sicken and die over the course of weeks, and vipers sat in chairs intended for allies.

As he turned all this over in his mind, he scratched crosshatches onto the page in front of him – the cheaper government-issue paper, but still a crime to waste it. His hands, however, refused to be still, and if they were given no words to write, then by God they would at least make marks.

The paper was looking rather scarred by the time Monsarrat heard a tread outside the door. It most definitely didn't belong to a soldier. It was sedate and employed only as much force as was needed to carry its owner along, rather than overdoing it the way most soldiers did, ramming the soles of their feet down as though they hoped to crack the ground beneath them.

Spring, he thought, or Donald. One or the other. No one else.

The door opened and indeed Edward Donald stood in the doorframe, staring at Monsarrat silently.

Monsarrat was usually careful to talk in a measured tone to the other convicts, particularly his fellow Specials. One never knew when goodwill might be crucial. But recent events had shredded his nerves, so that they were in no state to enable him to hold back his irritation. 'Good God, man, what is it? You're not an ornament to that doorway, you know.'

Donald moved his head back slightly as though he had received the tiniest of slaps. He didn't respond in kind, as to do so would have wasted his precious store of words. 'The major is approaching Shoal Arm Creek,' he said simply. 'The doctor bids me notify you, so you can be standing out front to give him such a welcome as is possible under the circumstances. He also requests the house-keeper do likewise.'

'Thank you, Donald. I apologise for misspeaking. It is a trying time for us all.'

Donald inclined his head. It may have been the acceptance or rejection of the apology. Monsarrat had no idea which, and was beyond caring. He made his way to the kitchen, finding Mrs Mulrooney darning a gash in her apron.

'I'm getting clumsy these days, Mr Monsarrat. It must be my advancing age. But I seem not to be able to move as well as I did previously, and that blasted table has prodded a nail at me, at just the right angle to catch an unwary apron.'

'It looks well enough, and will have to do for now in any case,' said Monsarrat. 'You and I are required at the front of Government House to greet the major. By the time he reaches us, I am presuming that Gonville will have given him the news.'

Mrs Mulrooney pushed herself up, her palms flat on the scrubbed table. 'How on earth am I going to face him?'

'How are any of us, knowing the burden he now carries? But face him you must. There are those whom we both know, who would not hesitate to implicate you in his wife's death, and your bearing on greeting him today must be finely calibrated. Sliding your eyes away will only make you look culpable. Despite the fact that you and I are both well aware of your innocence, ours may not be the prevailing view.'

So the pair made their way across the courtyard and around the side of the house, coming to a stop at the front steps which led down from the shaded verandah. From that vantage point, they could see that the major and his party had already crossed Shoal Arm Creek and were beginning to wind their way up the hill. A lad from the stables joined them, presumably to take away and care for the horses, no doubt dispatched by Donald after he had left Monsarrat.

'She loved that verandah, you know,' said Mrs Mulrooney. 'She once told me she felt as though she was looking at all of creation from it. You know, I first became aware that all was not right with her just up there, where her chair still sits. She got sick there, as you know. But before she worsened too much, God help me I was smiling. I thought it was a baby, you see. I rather fancied myself in the role of nursemaid to a young one. Lord forgive me, but that first sign of her illness made me excited.'

Mrs Mulrooney's eyes were shining now. Good, thought Monsarrat, surprising himself by his dispassion, it will do no harm for her to be visibly moved at her mistress's death.

The party was close now, and Monsarrat recognised Slattery's large frame as he and many of the others split off from the group to head for the barracks. Only Major Shelborne, Captain Diamond and Dr Gonville continued to progress to Government House.

The major wasn't the tallest man in the settlement, but his horse was the largest and finest to be had here, and he bore himself with an authority which suited his mount. Despite his days in the bush, Monsarrat noticed that his red coat and its buff facing were spotless. The major shared his clerk's fastidiousness when it came to personal appearance, and he had clearly thought to take a razor with him, as his face was smooth while other faces showed signs of forestation.

He dismounted and handed his reins to the stablehand, the captain and the doctor following suit. Monsarrat saw there was a pallor to the man's face, but if one didn't know the grievous news he had just received, one might have attributed it to hard riding and lack of sleep. His even features were strangely immobile, but this would only be significant to those who knew of their usual mobility, and their owner's ability to transmit an ocean of meaning with a look. It's costing him to keep them so still, thought Monsarrat.

The doctor and the captain had also both taken care in how they arranged their faces. Gonville's was a sombre mask, so artful that Monsarrat could have believed he had studied a diagram on how precisely to quirk down the edges of the mouth and the lids of the eyes to convey respectful and appropriate sorrow.

The captain's face was neutral, and if you saw it from the nose down you might assume he was asleep. But the eyes were anything but sleepy. They were moving over every object in his field of view, assessing it for its utility or threat. Those objects included Monsarrat and Mrs Mulrooney, and the captain's gaze fell for a significant period of time on each of them.

As Shelborne approached the steps, Monsarrat stepped forward and bowed. 'I would like to tender my most sincere condolences on your loss, sir,' he said.

Mrs Mulrooney did not step forward, but her drawn face and shining eyes conveyed a similar message.

'Thank you, Monsarrat. You will await me in the office; there is much we need to take care of. Mrs Mulrooney, tea to my study, if you please. I'll be there shortly.'

And he faced the entrace to the house, drew himself up to full height as though about to face the fiercest enemy, and entered.

Gonville started forward to accompany the major to his study; however, Diamond inserted himself between the two men. 'We are grateful to you for taking the trouble to bring us this news on the road,' he said. 'It is to be regretted that you did not recommend sending a party sooner. I will ensure the major is appraised of all the relevant facts with regard to his wife's illness. I am sure you have patients to attend to.'

With a slight eyebrow raise to Monsarrat, the doctor turned and made his way back to the hospital.

'Come along then, Monsarrat,' said Diamond. 'You have work to do.' He turned, with Monsarrat trailing after him.

They sat in silence for perhaps half an hour. The major, when he entered, didn't acknowledge either of them, walking slowly to his desk and sitting down, then forcing his eyes to focus, with visible effort. He picked up the sheaves of paper which Monsarrat had left for him. On the top of the pile in his hand lay Gonville's official report on Mrs Shelborne's death.

'Is there any correspondence which can't wait, Monsarrat?'

How would I know? Monsarrat was tempted to say. Someone was making himself at home here while you were gone, and could well have pocketed any important letters while he was rifling through your effects.

But the someone was, of course, standing right next to him, so close he could hear the man's breathing – smooth and calm, as befitting someone with nothing to fear and nothing to hide. I really hope I never have to face you across a card table, thought Monsarrat.

He said, 'Nothing which requires your immediate reply, sir. Only acknowledgements of your latest reports to the Colonial Secretary. The gist seems to be that they wish you to proceed as you are; there are no new orders.'

'Very well,' said the major, setting down the papers. Then, looking up: 'Now, Monsarrat, you will tell me what you know of the death of my wife.' Monsarrat thought he heard a judder sneak into the last word the major uttered.

'The surgeon has dictated to me a full report, sir, which is there at your elbow.'

'That is not,' said the major slowly, 'what I asked. What do you, personally, know of the death of my wife?'

Someone has lost no time pouring poison into the well, thought Monsarrat. He needed to answer quickly but carefully. Any misstep, or any suspiciously long pause, would be pounced on by Diamond as evidence of complicity in the crime. The man himself had taken a seat opposite the major.

'May I have your permission to speak plainly, sir?' Monsarrat asked.

'By all means. I have no patience for any other type of speech at the moment.'

'Sir, I know that your wife was improving, and that Dr Gonville held hopes that she might recover, despite taking the precaution to send the captain after you. However, shortly after the captain's departure, the lady regrettably took a turn for the worse, and died soon after. Dr Gonville believes the cause was arsenic poisoning, and that the poison was deliberately administered. This is the entirety of my knowledge on the matter, save for the fact that Mrs Mulrooney has barely left your wife's side during the course of her illness, and has been a most dedicated nurse.'

Diamond looked up at this last statement. 'Barely left her side – as I told you, sir. If Mrs Shelborne was indeed victim to poison, who would be better placed to administer it than the person who has been constantly in her presence, and bringing her tea?'

Monsarrat inwardly cursed himself for giving Diamond such an easy entree into the idea of Mrs Mulrooney's guilt. However, he knew Diamond was looking for a path to that destination regardless.

'Sir,' he said in as steady a voice as he could muster, 'the surgeon dictated his report to me, in which he said any poisoner would be loath to get near their poison, as there was a possibility of it leaching in through the skin. And as you've given me permission to speak plainly, I would like to express the opinion that Mrs Mulrooney is amongst the finest of women; she had a genuine regard for your wife and would never have harmed her.'

'Of course,' said the captain, 'that is what we would expect from her accomplice.'

Here, Monsarrat thought, was a crossroads. It demanded skilful handling. He remembered his interaction with Reverend Bulmer in the Parramatta police district a couple of years ago. He must be more adroit now than he had been then.

If there was one thing military men appreciated, he thought, it was a show of strength under fire. He drew himself up and said in polite but clipped tones, 'Sir, if the captain is implying that I may have had a hand in the death of your wife, I would like the opportunity to defend myself under all the rigours imposed by a court of law. If this was not his intention, I would appreciate a clarification on the matter. In either case, I must assure you that I played no part in the tragedy.'

The major's tightness began to tell then. He massaged the bridge of his nose with his thumb and forefinger. 'Of course, Monsarrat, nobody believes that you are in any way responsible. And I tend to share your assessment of Mrs Mulrooney's character. There will, nevertheless, need to be a full investigation, in which you and Mrs Mulrooney will be called on to provide information. That, however, can wait until I have seen Honora buried as she deserves. As I have some arrangements to make on that score, I would appreciate some solitude.'

Monsarrat gave a bow and withdrew to his workroom. As he did so, he heard the major say, 'You too, Michael. I apologise, you've been a constant friend, but in the next few hours I would be grateful for some privacy. In any case, I'd like you to review the regiment, ensure young Carleton hasn't been so distracted as to let discipline lapse.'

'Of course, sir,' said Diamond. As he left the office, he paused by Monsarrat's desk. He laid his hand on one corner, drummed his fingers, and stared directly at the clerk, who met his gaze because he didn't know what else to do. Then he turned and left.

All was silent then, save for the shuffling of papers as the major sorted through his correspondence. After a few minutes though, he called out to Monsarrat, 'I know you have been working very hard in my absence. I would like to make a gift to you of an afternoon off. Please return here after dinner for further instructions. Until then you may use yourself in whatever lawful way seems best to you.'

Monsarrat stood up, said a brief 'Thank you, sir', and left, closing the door carefully behind him and pretending not to hear the start of the major's sobs as he did so.

Chapter 23

Monsarrat was, for once, at a loss for what to do, not used to being in charge of so much of his own time. He took a walk past the parade ground, where Diamond had already taken it upon himself to address the non-existent lapse in order. Most of the soldiers were being marched up and down at double time. Slattery, as one of the returned expeditioners, must have been given leave to tidy himself up: he was heading to the barracks, and winked when he saw his friend. A touch too cheerful for the circumstances, Monsarrat thought. But then Slattery winked like a dog barked, heedless of convention.

A short time later, Monsarrat found himself making his way around a headland from Lady Nelson Beach, scrambling along the native tracks. The wind was angry and fans of spray forced themselves up onto the cliffs, reaching out for Monsarrat with fingers of white foam until the sea drew them back in and gathered them for a fresh assault. He rubbed the shiny, hard leaf of one of the shrubs as he passed, a small packet of moisture which the plant could draw on during the merciless summers. These shrubs, swept back like pomaded hair from years standing against the winds, looked odd to him on calm days, bowing to an absent gale. Today, though, their cowering stance was appropriate for the circumstances.

From the native track, he could see the black rocks on each of the beaches he passed. The beach he secretly thought of as Smugglers Cove – being narrow and well covered by headlands on either side – would nevertheless not have been fit for purpose, due to the fact that almost its entire front was fringed by jagged black teeth which looked as though they would like nothing more than to hole a boat or smash a skull.

He pushed himself on, though. Walking helped him think, and his hours of liberty were so constricted as to make it an uncommon treat to be able to stray this far.

After a time, he reached the rise from which he'd seen the smoke of Slattery's still. There was no smoke now, of course. And certainly no one was there. But Monsarrat decided he wouldn't mind a look at the thing. Just to satisfy his idle interest. He made his way down to the stand of paperbark trees, and there on the ring of stones which had encircled the fire on his last visit stood the copper. All innocence, it looked, despite its role in making contraband.

A surprisingly neat stack of paperbark lay on one of the stones, obviously ready for use as kindling. It must be a difficult business in winter, for the only quartered logs Monsarrat could see were soaked through. The next time one of Slattery's customers fancied a tipple, they might have to wait for dry weather.

Any liquor that was still left in the copper would no doubt be contaminated by now – days' worth of dead insects and rain were unlikely to add to the flavour, even though flavour wasn't the substance's main selling point. Monsarrat decided to check anyway. He thought if he was able to smell it, he might be able to gauge its strength.

But when he looked in the copper, he did not see clear liquid, or liquid made murky by rain. What he saw instead was a sludge of mostly evaporated water, with some flecks of an unknown substance floating in it.

The flecks, and to a lesser extent the water in which they floated, were green.

On his way back, Monsarrat cursed himself for his curiosity. A disturbing idea was beginning to form itself.

Why couldn't he be satisfied, he thought, with the clerk's wage and lifestyle, or with just enough knowledge to get him into his dotage? He strode back to the settlement with considerably more speed. There was only one person he could trust with this information, and only one who he knew could help him interpret it.

But as he was making his way around the side of Government House, he saw Diamond emerging from the major's study. His mind flew to the documents in his pocket, as did his hand.

Diamond, who had already noticed him, noticed also the gesture. He marched over. 'Turn your pockets out, Mr Monsarrat.'

Shadow Monsarrat came surging in with a vengeance, pushing aside all caution as he always did, like a drunk sweeping cutlery off a table. 'Why, sir? Are you looking for your conscience?'

'Have a care, Monsarrat,' said the captain with a nasty smile. 'I am running the investigation into Mrs Shelborne's death. And I have a very keen idea of who was responsible, and who aided her.'

'You cannot find proof where there is none to find, not unless you intend to manufacture it.'

'Oh, no manufacturing is needed. The circumstances point quite clearly to the guilty parties. Although you had a wasted trip to the store recently – you'll find all of the rat poison you procured for Mrs Mulrooney has vanished. And furthermore, Monsarrat, I'll ensure you get a nice short rope. Even a man as gangly as you might prove a good dancer.'

Monsarrat's bone marrow liquefied. The noose, mercifully snatched away in Exeter, might yet make its way to these shores for him, he realised. But as he had already been staring Diamond down, he remained paralysed in that act, more out of happenstance than any force of will.

'What possible reason would an old housekeeper have for killing Mrs Shelborne?' he asked.

'Old, yes indeed she is. Must be difficult to live daily beside someone who is so much brighter than you. And richer. The crone has a son who she hopes to set up in a public house, does she not? So, I ask you again, Monsarrat – turn out your pockets.'

Monsarrat remained paralysed.

The captain darted forward then, ripping Monsarrat's hand out of his pocket and delving into it, to extract the packet of his own correspondence, and Gonville's unsigned report on his conduct with Mercer's daughter.

He smiled in recognition as he turned over the letters, and quickly scanned the other document. 'I must thank you, Monsarrat, for recovering these for me. Although it seems you have ill-used them. I couldn't think where they had got to; they certainly weren't anywhere in the major's study. I am very grateful,' he said, giving a mock bow.

'I intend to acquaint the major with their contents, whether I have them or not,' said Monsarrat. 'Together with the details of the arrangement into which you forced me.'

Diamond laughed. 'Oh, please do,' he said. 'I will simply say it's all a fabrication, concocted by you or the Irishwoman to put blame on an officer who has, unlike you two, never been guilty of any crime. As for the doctor's report on my adventures, well, perhaps I may find that he also had a hand in this.'

'You can't honestly believe that.'

'It doesn't matter one jot what I believe, Monsarrat. It only matters what I can make a case for. Go off to work now, while you still can. Or I might find a place has opened up for you on the lime-burners' gang.'

❧

As Diamond stalked away, Monsarrat smoothed down his waistcoat. He did not know how to protect Mrs Mulrooney now. But he knew he needed to try. And information was the only weapon he, and she, had.

She was absent from the kitchen, but the hearth was lit and a flatiron lay on the stove, a glow coming from within it. As he stood regarding the iron, Mrs Mulrooney entered from the outer door. Like the first-class convicts – those whose original offences were not so severe and who had demonstrated good behaviour – she had a separate set of good clothes for Sunday. These were over her arm now, a black skirt and plain white shirt with a red jacket.

'It's Thursday,' he said, sitting down.

'And I know that very well myself without any help from you, Mr Monsarrat.' She shoved him aside with her hip and laid the clothes on the table – which looked as if it had lost yet another quarter inch – and cursed at them for developing creases as she ironed. 'Mrs Shelborne's funeral is tomorrow, Mr Monsarrat. The very least I can do is go with pressed clothes. You'll have to do without tea for today.'

'For once, I didn't come for the tea,' said Monsarrat. 'Diamond is making a very good show of being convinced that you took Mrs Shelborne's life. He realises that we suspect the truth of the situation, and he is quite happy to see you take his punishment.'

'Mr Monsarrat, next time make sure your news is current. Diamond had me into the major's office after you left. The major just sat there and stared at me, while the captain asked me why I killed her. I said I did no such thing, that I tried to prevent her death by every limited means at my disposal. Then Diamond asked me whether I had been jealous of Mrs Shelborne. Or whether I bore any grudges – he said it was well known that I had not wanted to go into the bathing machine with her, but had felt obliged to do so. He wondered whether what I saw as her high-handedness was behind it.'

'You denied it, surely?' said Monsarrat.

'Of course I did, eejit of a man. I feel I acquitted myself well, actually. No tears, I just faced them down the way they were facing me.'

'Under the circumstances, a few tears may have been wise,' said Monsarrat.

'I'm not a crier, Mr Monsarrat. Not usually. You can't ask a cat to bark.'

'I fear that's precisely how Diamond sees us,' said Monsarrat.

'As animals. Of a sacrificial nature.'

'But I can't believe the major would lay such a thing at my door. In fact, Diamond made much of the fact that Mrs Shelborne hadn't been wearing her ring when she was taken off this morning. He suggested that I might have stolen it, and much more besides. Well, at least I was able to enlighten him on that point. I told the major where it was, said it kept falling off her finger as she wasted, said I wanted to keep it safe so that he could decide what to do with it. The poor man, he looked stricken just then, only for a moment but I noticed. I wanted to rattle Diamond, too. It would do the blackguard no end of good to get a dose of his own treatment. So I said that it was amazing what one could find in the drawers of the dressing table like the one which held Mrs Shelborne's ring.'

'Ah,' said Monsarrat. 'I fear we may have had something of a setback there.' He described his meeting with Diamond.

'Why on earth did you not hide them?' said Mrs Mulrooney. It was the closest he had ever heard her get to yelling.

And he felt a small amount of irritation rise. 'And where exactly would you want me to hide them? Behind that blasted wallpaper?'

'Well, even without the letters, surely we can make the major see who is really responsible.'

'I fear that may be difficult,' said Monsarrat. 'He judges others by his own standards. And Diamond has sunk to a level the major does not believe a brother officer is capable of, so he simply doesn't see it.'

'Well, for the moment he doesn't see my guilt either,' said Mrs Mulrooney. 'Diamond wanted me locked in the gaol. But the major overruled him. He even drank the tea I made him – not the act of a man who believes I'm the poisoner.'

Monsarrat was silent for a while, watching Mrs Mulrooney iron her clothes into submission, enjoying the way the iron passed over hillocks of fabric and turned them into plains. Order imposed, on whatever scale, was a comfort.

He knew Diamond was guilty. Everything fitted so neatly. But he hadn't yet told Mrs Mulrooney about his walk, and the green tinge at the bottom of the copper that had troubled him. It could be that there was an entirely innocuous explanation – something to do with the brewing process. He was most certainly not willing to sample the stuff himself to find out. But perhaps Mrs Mulrooney knew more than he did about these things, so he told her what he had seen.

When he'd finished, she sat down heavily. She looked, he realised, as shocked as he had ever seen her. The way he imagined he had looked when he realised that the long-feared prospect of his discovery in Exeter had become a reality. It seemed, to Monsarrat, a disproportionate response, but perhaps she was more prone to shock at present, given recent events.

'That stupid boy,' she said. 'For a smart lad he's an imbecile.'

'Well, he might get a reprimand for it, but that doesn't make him an imbecile. I'm sure I'm being fanciful linking the green to the wallpaper – I thought it might be part of the brewing process. Do you know, yourself?'

'Oh yes, all of the Irish are well versed in the art of making grog,' said Mrs Mulrooney. Shouting and now sarcasm, Monsarrat thought. She must be terrified.

'You don't think . . . I can't see why he would, but you don't think it's possible?'

She pulled up her fist and thumped the table. 'Mr Monsarrat, if you say one word against Fergal, give one sideways look which implies you might think he had something to do with this, our friendship will end in that moment, and you'll be ashes to me.'

Monsarrat knew that she meant it. 'Of course. Please don't trouble yourself. I was a little surprised to be reading an article about poisonous green wallpaper when a similar paper was being laid in the sitting room next door. My imagination is being uncharacteristically overactive. I do beg your pardon.'

Mrs Mulrooney sighed. 'And I beg yours, Mr Monsarrat. I don't know what I would have done without you, these last years but most especially these last two weeks. Forgive a woman. I'm letting the situation upset me too much.'

'I would doubt your sanity if you weren't,' said Monsarrat.

'Anyway,' said Mrs Mulrooney, 'it's Diamond. We agreed. It has to be him. If it isn't, we are lost.'

⌒∾⌒

Monsarrat ate a silent meal in the mess. When Edward Donald entered, not the most gregarious of men at the best of times, Monsarrat slid onto a bench next to him.

'I have always taken you, Donald, to be a man of discretion,' Monsarrat said.

Donald pursed his lips slightly. Monsarrat chose to interpret it as a gesture of thanks, but he could equally have been saying 'More fool you'.

'I hope I may rely on that discretion now, and on your assistance in a matter which I know to be of importance to the surgeon.'

A slight nod from Donald.

'If you would be kind enough to relay a message to Dr Gonville for me, I would be in your debt.'

Monsarrat often wondered why, when Donald did speak, his voice didn't come out as a rasp, rusted from the lack of use.

'Well, Monsarrat, having such an elevated person as you in my debt may be handy in the long run.'

Monsarrat ignored the jibe. He couldn't afford to take offence, and was thankful Donald did not know quite how low his own stocks were. 'Thank you. Would you kindly tell the doctor that a document of interest to him is now with its subject?'

Donald nodded again, and Monsarrat was grateful for the man's taciturn nature – others might have asked what the document was and who it was about. He wouldn't have answered the questions, of course, but preferred not to be in a position to be seen denying knowledge to others.

After the meal, as directed, he returned to his workroom. Major Shelborne was sitting at his desk, this morning's tea half-drunk and cold. He was scratching out a letter, but judging by his constant crossings-out and muttering, its composition was not flowing as smoothly as usual.

Monsarrat knocked discreetly on the study door, and the man

245

looked up. Monsarrat noticed some lines of rough skin where the collar of the major's red coat had rubbed his neck raw, probably not helped by the damp conditions he had been sleeping in during his search for the river. It surprised Monsarrat that he had not thought, until now, to wonder whether the river had turned out to be other than a figment of Kiernan's imagination.

'Ah, Monsarrat. Please, come in. Shut the door behind you.' The major put down his pen. 'I wonder if I might impose on you to assist me in framing correspondence to my wife's family, letting them know of her passing. I'm afraid my hand is not as fine as yours, nor are my sentiments easily expressed.'

Monsarrat indicated that of course he would do as the major asked, silently grateful that he had thought to draft such letters in the dead time while he was waiting for the major's return.

'In the meantime, I'll have need of your hand on official business. I must report the discovery of the river and pasture land to the Colonial Secretary.'

Monsarrat did his best to hide his surprise. You old dog, Kiernan, he thought. How on earth did you find such a place?

'Your expedition was successful, then, sir.'

'Yes. At too high a cost, as it turns out. You know, if Oxley had continued just a little further north, he would have found this area. A wide, strong river with fertile ground on either side. I must say, I was quite delighted with it, until I returned here.'

The major stood up, and walked to the window. 'I've read, by the way, the doctor's reports on my wife. I've also heard what Diamond has to say. And he says a lot. He is perhaps not the most tactful of officers, but an excellent bloodhound to put on the scent of the guilty.'

He turned to Monsarrat. 'I want you to know, Monsarrat, that I do not believe that you were in any way party to my wife's death. I fancy myself a judge of character, and while I know you can sail close to the wind at times, murder is not in your nature.'

'Thank you, sir. Neither is it in your housekeeper's.'

'I would like to agree with you, and find it hard not to,' said the major. 'But Diamond makes a compelling case, circumstantial though it may be. There is simply no way for the poison to have entered her system save through the tea which Mrs Mulrooney served her each day. She herself claims innocence, as one might expect. It is my fervent hope that some information will arise to exonerate her. However, Monsarrat, I must prepare you – and myself for that matter – for the eventuality of her arrest, should Diamond be able to build a strong enough case.'

Monsarrat did not know how to respond. The major was a fair man, but a grieving one.

'My wife will be laid to rest tomorrow, in the grounds of the church where I had thought to baptise our children,' said the major. 'The following day, you and I will start work on the reports to Sydney. In the meantime though, I do have a service to ask of you.'

'Of course, sir.'

'That wallpaper, the stuff she was so keen on festooning the sitting room with. I never cared for it, to be honest. Now that she's gone – well, I would prefer not to have to stare at it. I know the papering is not yet quite complete, and I wish it taken down. You'll appreciate, this doesn't require the same touches as putting it up, so the private who was overseeing it will go back to his normal duties. I will give you a crew of two men, and I wish it to be gone within the next few days.'

On directions from the major, Monsarrat took these instructions to the superintendent of convicts, a stern man named Crow. The superintendent nodded his assent when he read the note containing the request. 'Take the two who are left from the crew who put it up; hopefully they'll have the wit to do the same thing backwards,' he said.

So Monsarrat procured the services of Frogett and Daines. They would report to the kitchen first thing the following morning, as they had under Slattery. Their erstwhile overseer was being kept busy, as part of a contingent of men sent to guard a group of cedar-cutters working a little further up the river. Spears made from the stalks of grass trees had, in the past, occasionally whistled through the air and found their mark, as a result of which all wood-cutting parties were now well guarded.

Monsarrat did not, in fact, see Slattery until the following morning, when he had a welcome cup of tea in front of him and was awaiting the crew's arrival. They would work on the room until midday, at which point practically the whole settlement would attend the funeral of the commandant's wife.

Mrs Mulrooney was busy making a large breakfast for Major Shelborne. 'There's a lot less of the man than there was when he set off. Hard bush living, and then a shock.'

The man may hang you, thought Monsarrat, and you're making eggs for him.

For a moment, Slattery's entrance restored a sense of normality. He slammed the door against the wall as he always did, exhorted God to bless all there as he always did, and took his seat at the table as he always did, with a wink and a smile. But the twinkling which marked him out as a capricious, slightly naughty but basically good young man was not in evidence.

'God love you, Mrs Mulrooney,' he said as she placed a cup of tea in front of him. 'There's been precious little of this marvellous stuff recently, first in the bush and now guarding those cedar-cutters. A rough lot they are, too. None of the pleasures of the conversations we share.'

'And I understand that you met your objective, that the land around the new river was just as fine as Kiernan had promised,' said Monsarrat.

'So I'm told. We came upon the major on his way home, so I didn't get to see the wondrous sight for myself. But I'll tell you this: I've had enough of rivers. Our own one is in a very bad temper at the moment – it keeps complaining at me over the sound of the woodcutters' axes.'

'It probably wishes you to button your coat properly and brush your hair once in a while,' said Mrs Mulrooney.

'Actually, Slattery,' said Monsarrat, 'you may do me a service, if you would be kind enough. It turns out I am to undo the work which you did, with your two remaining plasterers under my supervision. Perhaps you could accompany me to the sitting room, show me how it's done.'

'How could I refuse when you use such pretty language, Monsarrat? A shame that you can count the convict women here on one hand, and that you're reduced to practising your silver tongue on me.'

Monsarrat and Mrs Mulrooney shared a look, like indulgent parents of a wayward but mysteriously endearing child.

So after Mrs Mulrooney had let them into the house proper, muttering inducements at the key as she did so, they stepped into the sitting room.

Monsarrat had not spent any amount of time there, but now that he looked at the paper – which currently took up about half the wall space of the whole room – he had to admit that Slattery and his crew had done a remarkable job. The joins where one strip of paper met another were barely visible, and where these joins bisected the image of a flower, they were lined up perfectly.

'It's a fairly simple matter, Monsarrat, even for a shiny-arsed clerk such as yourself. You simply hold a damp cloth over the stubborn parts to loosen the glue, and make sure you take it off slow. We don't want patches of greenery on a sea of white plaster.'

'And should I breathe while I do so, private?'

Slattery looked surprised. 'I'd have thought so, Monsarrat. Otherwise you'd fall over dead, wouldn't you? Didn't they teach you anything at that grammar school of yours? We don't want anybody else going and dying on us, now do we?'

'No, we don't. And there's one person in particular who I'd as soon see continue breathing. Have you heard that Mrs Mulrooney is being suspected in Mrs Shelburne's death?'

Slattery's surprise quickly gave way to shock. 'I'd heard that she had been done away with, or so they thought, yes. But no one said anything about who the guilty party might be. A few of the less kind lads are laying bets. Then there is the curse, of course. Stranger things have happened than that one of our kind might be done away with in that way.'

'I don't believe in curses, private. Neither, I suspect, do you. But if I did, I would say they were embodied in the person of Captain Diamond. He is determined she should hang.'

'I wouldn't worry too much, Mr Monsarrat. Everyone knows she adored the major's wife, though God alone knows what they found to talk about – Mrs Shelborne being raised with a silver spoon, and Mrs Mulrooney being lucky if she saw one from a distance.'

Monsarrat wondered whether to mention the article on the deadly nature of green wallpaper, or the green sludge at the bottom of Slattery's copper. But he felt it might be better, for now, to keep the knowledge to himself.

'Fergal, I have to ask you straight out, and please don't take offence – do you know of any information which might exonerate our friend?'

'If I did, Mr Monsarrat, I assure you I would be shouting it from the Government House verandah.'

And such was Slattery's sincerity that Monsarrat chose, then, to believe him.

Chapter 24

Monsarrat went and sat with Mrs Mulrooney while he was waiting for his two charges to appear, and when they did he retraced his steps back into the sitting room. They needed little supervision, having done this work before, and had the paper coming off in great sheets.

Monsarrat stood by the door, watching, or at least appearing to. He had a sense that Slattery was not being entirely honest with him, but then he often had that sense about the young soldier – it was, perhaps, part of his charm. Of one thing he was certain – Slattery would not allow Mrs Mulrooney to hang.

He made sure to run his eyes up and down the paper from time to time as it was being stripped away, so that Frogett and Daines knew they were under strict observation. But when half of the first wall was denuded, something snagged his eye.

'What's that over there, Daines?' he asked, moving next to the convict.

Daines gave a silent shrug. If the location of the Holy Grail had been inscribed in the plaster, he couldn't have cared less.

As Monsarrat moved closer, he saw that it was writing. Small, not much larger than he himself would employ in the major's service. And in a language he didn't recognise: *Tioc-faidh ár lá.*

Monsarrat had no idea what the words meant. The 'ar la' suggested poorly spelled French, but the first word seemed Celtic to him. He knew the Irish language occasionally employed accents, but there were very few Irish speakers here. Though he had heard Irish convicts speaking in their native language, an English gentleman's expertise was in Latin and Greek, not in barbarous tongues from across oceans or borders. People like Mrs Mulrooney and Slattery knew a smattering of phrases, but their language had been outlawed for so long that many Irish had forgotten it.

Whoever had put the words there had done so with a narrow piece of wood or a fingernail. The way the plaster was grooved told him that much.

He was tempted, for a moment, to call Slattery back and ask what the words meant, see if there was any reaction. But the young man was no doubt well on his way by now, and in any case, Monsarrat would rather know the significance of the words before he started sharing them.

A short while later, he instructed Frogett and Daines to return to their barracks and ready themselves to attend Honora Shelborne's funeral. He himself retired to his own hut to wash his face and adjust his cravat.

Monsarrat felt that appearances always mattered, but never more so than at major church events – weddings, funerals, beginnings and ends. And he didn't want Mrs Mulrooney to trudge up the hill alone, a pariah. He called at the kitchen for her on his way, and they walked there together.

'I was in two minds about whether I should attend, Mr Monsarrat. If I'm suspected of putting her in that grave, surely there would be people who resent it.'

'Well, would you attend were there no shadow of suspicion over you?'

Mrs Mulrooney gave him a look which suggested she felt he might have had a recent head injury, to ask such an idiotic question.

'Well, there you are,' he said. 'You should do exactly as you would do in the normal run of things. Doing anything else would only attract more suspicion, and you little deserve that which is on you at the moment.'

Honora Shelborne was to be buried in the grounds of what would become St Thomas's, the church to be built around her. The foundations had already been set, and layers of convict-made bricks were beginning to inch upwards, but the church was for the moment not much more than a footprint. The earth had the advantage, though, of being consecrated.

She was laid to rest that afternoon in a place which would ultimately be covered by one of the church's front box pews. She lay opposite Major Shelborne's predecessor, who had been buried there in expectation of the eventual church after he had succumbed to heat exhaustion.

As the church would be erected over her, Honora Shelborne's headstone was flat, and was set at one end of the hole into which she would be lowered, to be slid into place afterwards. It had been hastily carved by one of the settlement's stonemasons, on instructions from the major, and even Monsarrat had to admire the script. It bore no decoration – as she had needed none in life – and said simply:

Sacred to the memory of Honora Belgrave Shelborne
Beloved wife of Major Angus Shelborne, commandant of
this settlement
Departed this life 29 June 1825, aged 26

The Reverend Ainslie, recently returned from Sydney, conducted the service, with a great number of the settlement's inhabitants, both free and bonded, looking on. There were those, of course, who were cutting timber upriver, or tending the farms or the sugarcane fields, or engaged in work on chained or unchained gangs, and their attendance was not expected. But those convicts who worked at the heart of the settlement, as Specials, overseers, constables and so forth, were all in attendance, as was every member of the regiment who could be spared, and their wives.

Monsarrat noticed, too, some strong Birpai men, Bangar amongst them, standing some distance off towards the edge of the hill, close to Dr Gonville's house. He was not the only one to do so. Diamond glared at them, and whispered something in the major's ear. The major shook his head, looked at the Birpai and nodded.

The Reverend sought to give the ceremony as much gravitas as could be managed on a building site. Monsarrat was impressed that he included some examples of Honora's focus on educating the convicts – the man had obviously done some research, which was no less than Honora Shelborne deserved.

The major stood stiffly throughout the burial, eyes straight ahead. He bent only to shovel a small amount of earth onto his wife's coffin, a box which looked barely big enough for a child.

After it was over, the major asked Diamond to supervise the garrison for the rest of the day. He himself retired to his study.

Monsarrat followed the commandant at a respectful distance, drawing near only when they got close to the study door. 'Major, can I be of any assistance today?'

The major paused at the threshold, as though wondering whether Monsarrat or anyone could help him at the moment. 'No, thank you, Monsarrat. You may return to the sitting room to supervise the wallpaper. I imagine the light will fail by four or so, to the point where you won't be able to continue. When that happens, have the rest of the afternoon to yourself. I have some important decisions to make.'

Monsarrat hoped those decisions did not concern the guilt or otherwise of his friend. As he turned to leave, the major called him back. 'Monsarrat, I know I can rely on your discretion in regard to the manner of my wife's death.'

'Of course, sir. I have no value without discretion.'

The major gave a small smile. 'I was not sure whether it had been made clear to you that the suspicion of foul play is not common knowledge. I wish it to remain so. Only Captain Diamond, Dr Gonville and a very few others are party to the investigation into her likely murder. I know I can trust you to make sure that this number does not increase.'

Monsarrat was surprised – Slattery had, after all, told him there had been talk, a plausible eventuality in a small settlement. But he'd heard no whispers from other sources.

Shadow Monsarrat, meanwhile, was urging his host on to an irredeemable act of indiscretion. The letters, the secret spying, the lot: shadow Monsarrat wanted to spew it out, gouts of information that would wash away all thoughts of Mrs Mulrooney's culpability.

But Monsarrat had just enough control of himself to realise that such rashness would diminish his utility and credibility in the eyes of the major, and thus his ability to argue for Mrs Mulrooney, should such an argument become necessary. However, he would not waste the opportunity to begin framing his case.

'Sir, you may depend on me to hold this information to myself. However, I seek your forgiveness, but Mrs Mulrooney is not capable of the act for which Diamond is investigating her. I do not know who is responsible, and I wish to see them fully and comprehensively punished in this life and the next, but it is not her.'

The major rolled his lips in on each other, his eyelids descending to half-mast as he weighed what he was about to say. 'I also find it hard to believe it of her. She doted on my wife from the moment Honora arrived. To be honest, it's thanks to that woman that my wife's time in this settlement was as happy as it was. Her disposition is not that of a murderer. I know what makes a murderer, Monsarrat – I have seen enough of them. And she fails what I like to think of as the Cicero test. I'm sure I don't need to tell you what that is.'

Monsarrat had indeed read about the Roman lawyer (whom Catullus had called the most fluent of Romulus's descendants). He had formulated the central question at the heart of every crime. '*Cui bono.* Who benefits. Yes, sir, you're right, certainly not her.'

'Nevertheless, Monsarrat, my instincts have been wrong before. I am not convinced of her guilt, but neither am I convinced of her innocence. And unless somebody can come to me with a compelling means through which the poison was administered, which does not involve Mrs Mulrooney, I believe her future is at best uncertain.'

Monsarrat could think of no safe response to this. He bowed and withdrew to the sitting room, where he had nothing to distract him from his anxiety save the gnarled hands of Frogett and Daines as they scraped the paper off the walls.

As the sun began to dip, Monsarrat sent the two convicts back to their barracks. He was on his way back to his hut, via the kitchen, when he heard the sound of raised voices coming from the commandant's office. He decided to hang back, then, in the shadows. Eavesdropping had become second nature to him, as from his privileged perch outside the commandant's office he had been able to hear much of what transpired within over the past two years. He wondered, for the first time, whether his supervision of wallpaper stripping had more to do with preventing him overhearing things he oughtn't than with needing a steady person to supervise the labour.

The door to the office opened then, and Dr Gonville stepped out into the dwindling light. Monsarrat made after him, falling into step beside the surgeon as he headed for the church construction site where Honora lay, and the hospital, dispensary and his quarters beyond.

'Monsarrat,' said the doctor as Monsarrat drew level with him. 'Thank you for your message via Donald. I fear we may be paying for my decision not to report the captain at the time.'

'The major cannot be taking Diamond's word over yours, surely,' said Monsarrat.

'You've never been in a battle, Monsarrat. But the major and the captain have, in places the likes of which you and I will never see. It has linked them, as these things tend to do. And the captain, over the years, has taken full advantage of that link, pouring his own brand of misinformation into the major's ear. The end result is that the major, who is an honourable man, nevertheless sees the captain as the shortest and straightest path to the truth. There was a time when he would hear other views. But I fear his wife's death has robbed him of equilibrium, so that he clings to Diamond as though the captain was one of those black rocks in the middle of the ocean. Everyone else is a potential obfuscator, and is to be treated thus until proved otherwise.'

Monsarrat walked in silence for a moment, his fingers unconsciously interlacing behind his back. 'I presume, then, that he did not fully accept your view that any poisoner would be keen to avoid direct contact with their weapon,' he said.

'Sadly, no. Diamond, God rot him, pointed out myriad historical examples of poisoners who were only too intimately involved with their victims. You know they sometimes call arsenic inheritance powder and, for God's sake, the powder of divorce. Used, so it goes, to help nudge along an obstinately breathing relative who happens to be sitting on a large pile of money, or an inconvenient husband. Diamond said it was a woman's weapon. He said if poisoners were loath to touch the substance, a great many matriarchs and patriarchs would have graced the earth for a few years longer than they did.'

'Surely the major can't have approved of his conduct with Mercer's daughter, though,' said Monsarrat.

'I'm sure he wouldn't, if he fully believed it. But he asked – very reasonably, too – why I hadn't come forward with it sooner. My credibility with him has been dented, perhaps fatally so. And of course Diamond denied it. May I ask, did you leave him a report on the flogging of young Dory?'

'Absolutely. It was close to the top of the pile I had left for him, just underneath your report on Mrs Shelborne's death.'

'He most definitely would not approve.'

'I shall make sure it receives his attention first thing in the morning,' said Monsarrat.

'You'll have to rewrite it. Diamond has taken all of the papers. He says he wishes to remove some of the burden from the major's shoulders. It will be with him now, if it's not already in a fire.'

As they reached the hospital, Gonville turned and put his hand on Monsarrat's arm. 'I've done everything I can, Monsarrat, and I very much fear it may not be enough. I know you're a man of intellect, and I also know I don't need to urge you to bend that intellect exclusively towards finding a means to exonerate Mrs Mulrooney. In the absence of anything startling, a confession from the guilty party would be nice, but maybe enough evidence to throw doubt on Mrs Mulrooney's culpability might do. Otherwise I very much fear she will ultimately hang.'

Monsarrat hadn't reckoned on the major's increasing reliance on Captain Diamond. You think yourself very clever, he chided himself, but a mere inflection, a slight change in the boundaries of trust, is all it takes to trip you up. And one of the best people you have ever known may pay for that dearly.

He walked back towards the kitchen, thinking to share the information from Dr Gonville with Mrs Mulrooney. But the kitchen was dark, and ominously a guard had been posted, standing between the kitchen and Mrs Mulrooney's room.

The guard – one of the young privates whom Monsarrat didn't know very well – was in the process of receiving orders from the captain. But when Diamond saw Monsarrat, he couldn't resist stalking over to one of his favourite playthings. 'Any more stolen documents in your pocket that I need to confiscate, Monsarrat?'

Shadow Monsarrat had well and truly had enough. He let it be known that he was taking command. 'No, sir. I understand they're all in yours.'

'I saw you with the doctor earlier, quite a cabal. I'm sure he told you he was unable to provide any convincing medical proof that Mrs Mulrooney would have been poisoned herself in the process of poisoning Mrs Shelborne. And given that somebody did indeed poison the lady – Gonville's own report says as much – I think we may safely say we have identified the culprit. I am simply awaiting the major's official approval to arrest her. The man is too trusting; he doesn't want to believe it. I am quite sure he will come around, though.'

'But you know Mrs Mulrooney to be innocent! And me, and the doctor. But especially her – how could you think it? Even a snake like you can recognise decency when he sees it, it is to be hoped. And in any case, you well know who the real killer is.'

'And who might that be, my educated friend?'

'It takes a particular kind of evil to obliterate a person one can't have, to ensure no one more deserving can enjoy her society,' said Monsarrat.

Diamond's smile, which had taken on a dangerous tinge, faded now. 'You think I did this?'

'You might as well admit it to me, sir. As you say, you can later deny it, claim I made it up to exonerate myself.'

Diamond slowly, very slowly, lowered one shoulder, so that Monsarrat wondered what he could be trying to accomplish. He found out an instant later, when the officer charged him, knocking the air out of his lungs, until Monsarrat was pinned up against the side of the main building. In his fury, Diamond had nevertheless taken care to push him towards a corner where they could not be readily observed from the study or the house.

The soldier's face was red now. It could not have been from exertion: pinning Monsarrat had been the work of an instant, and the latter was not making any attempt to struggle.

'I would never – never do anything to hurt her. The devil take you for suggesting otherwise. She was the only scrap of beauty in this damned settlement. Why on earth would I have taken her away? And why on earth would I let those who did go unpunished?'

Diamond's spittle was showering Monsarrat's face, where he hoped there were no nicks or cuts to enable access to his blood-stream. He would have spoken but for the hand at his throat, and for a moment he thought Diamond intended to finish him there and then.

Instead, Diamond let go, forcing Monsarrat to the side as he did so. The clerk stumbled and sprawled on the flagstones, the red earth oozing through them making an indelible stain on his white waistcoat.

'I would arrest you now, but due process must be followed to satisfy the major. In any case, where would you flee? A soft one like you would not survive in the forest for long. So I have time, while yours is running out. Enjoy yourself this evening, Monsar-rat, with that tart Daisy or whoever else you fancy. You may expect a visit shortly.'

Chapter 25

Monsarrat spent an uncomfortable and largely sleepless night. The river stones became cold in winter, transferring the chill from the river itself up through Monsarrat's bedroll and onto his skin. He doubted, however, if he could have slept in even the most opulent featherbed. He was shocked by Diamond's vehement denial. He had thought the man was secure enough in his position with the major so as not to need to pretend in front of the likes of Monsarrat, who would never be believed. But Diamond's outrage did not seem like an act, designed as a set piece in which he could state his innocence for the record. And a new possibility was occurring to him, a picture emerging from the green sludge in the bottom of Slattery's copper, and his knowledge of all things related to wall decoration.

Monsarrat berated himself again – he had spent a significant portion of the night doing this, but felt that there were still plenty of transgressions, lapses in judgement and general idiocy on his part, the instances lining up and waiting patiently for him to use them, one by one, as a means of self-flagellation.

The current focus of his self-blame was the flimsiness of the evidence against Slattery. You have the fellow condemned, he thought, on even thinner grounds than those which may be the instrument of Mrs Mulrooney's death. And why are you so quick to admit the possibility that Diamond did not do this? The man must be a consummate actor to have won the trust of the major. He was, no doubt, acting still.

And another detail was hoving into view now, one which he did not want to see, one which he thoroughly wanted to ignore, wished would go away.

He had once asked Slattery what part of Ireland he came from, but it was a pleasantry, and he hadn't really listened to the answer. The other day, though, when Mrs Mulrooney was telling him about Slattery's background, he remembered her mentioning that Slattery was from Wicklow.

Monsarrat had been in the major's office for nearly two years now. He had seen every piece of correspondence which had come through the place, including those addressed to Mrs Shelborne. The back of the envelope always bore a handsome seal, under which were inscribed the words 'Castle Henry, Wicklow'.

<hr/>

Monsarrat walked with little enthusiasm to the commissariat stores to get his rations the following morning. He felt muted, a curtain of tiredness standing between him and the daily life of the settlement.

As he approached, he saw Spring finishing a conversation with Bangar, in his unmarked canvas clothes, before the Birpai man moved off towards the river.

'They are mourning Mrs Shelborne too,' said Spring while he was weighing out Monsarrat's rations. 'Particularly the women. She made gifts for them, you see. Knitted rugs for their babes, or necklaces of seashells for the tribe's little girls, who love a trinket as much as any little girl in England.'

'It was decent of them to attend yesterday,' said Monsarrat. 'I fear not everyone shares my view, however.'

'Yes, I suspect you're right, Monsarrat. They're particularly worried about the curse. They have heard the rumour – God knows where it came from – that some people in the settlement believe she was a victim of one of their curses.'

'There are probably more here who believe in curses than don't,' said Monsarrat.

'That might not be far off the mark,' said Spring. 'They know who and what Diamond is. They fear that with the major immersed in his grief, Diamond may choose to take revenge. It would not be the first time Birpai blood has been spilled, as you well know. And they find it particularly puzzling because, well, they don't really go in for curses. Not as much as the Scots or Irish even.'

'Mr Spring, I wonder whether you would be good enough to share this opinion with the major? If Diamond really is forming a plan to make an example of them – and it wouldn't surprise me – this may help stay his hand.'

'I will do what I can, Mr Monsarrat. But I haven't seen him, you know, apart from at the funeral from a distance. I'm told Diamond is pacing around the perimeter of his study like a caged guard dog. But I can assure you I will speak to him.'

Monsarrat took his rations then, and went back to his hut. He did not have the stomach for breakfast, so he placed them on the small shelf alongside the eucalyptus twig that he used to clean his teeth. Then he set out in hopes of finding Mrs Mulrooney in the kitchen, preferably without a guard.

He was disappointed in this last hope. The private from yesterday had transferred his attentions to the kitchen, which was emitting an encouraging curl of smoke.

He nodded to the young man, who nodded back. Thankfully the fellow did not share Diamond's view of Monsarrat, and of convicts in general. Monsarrat was generally liked, or at least tolerated. He kept quiet and didn't trouble the soldiery too much, which was all they could ask of any convict. He was allowed to pass into the kitchen without hindrance, and he was grateful it was winter – open windows would have made frank conversation impossible.

While a Protestant cleric had conducted the funeral, Father Declan Hanley had also attended the service. To be in the settlement at the time of the burial and not to pay respects would have been an insult. Monsarrat found him in the kitchen, perhaps intending to provide comfort to Mrs Mulrooney and relieve her of some porridge. He was being fussed over by her, his large hands completely obscuring the teacup they held.

'A very sad day yesterday, Mr Monsarrat,' said the priest when Monsarrat greeted him. 'That such a person should be taken so young. You know, we tell people God moves in mysterious ways. That's what the priest told me when my sister died. She was like a mother to me, that girl. She was twelve, carried off by consumption. And our priest told me the usual thing – that God moved in mysterious ways. A little less mystery, together with a little less tragedy, would be welcome.' The priest crossed himself, as if to counteract the heresy of his words. Monsarrat found himself liking the man more.

Monsarrat uncharacteristically declined the offer of tea, despite the fact that Mrs Mulrooney's tea was one of the few bright spots in the current situation. He hoped his access to it wouldn't be curtailed in the near future.

'I just wanted to ask if you would be kind enough to let the crew and me back into the sitting room, to finish the removal of the paper.'

Mrs Mulrooney fished the key out of her pocket, and made for the door.

'Actually,' said Monsarrat, 'before we go, I have a question to ask of both of you. I saw some writing scratched into a wall yesterday. It may or may not be Irish – it used accents in the way I've seen in some Irish script – but I've no idea what it means. It said, as far as I can make out, "ti-oc-fade a la" – at least that's my assumption on the pronunciation; the spelling was rather opaque, to be honest.'

'Ah, the spelling of our Irish words specialises in opacity,' said Father Hanley. '"Ti-oc-fade a la" – no, can't say I've heard it. Might have been put there a time ago. We've all sorts through here, as you know, Mr Monsarrat, even the Welsh. Could it be Welsh, or maybe Cornish? It could mean anything, or nothing.'

'Well, as to the timing, I can say with certainty that it has only been there for a couple of weeks, a month at the most. It's inscribed in the plaster which was recently placed on the sitting room walls.

Quite low down, too, as though whoever put it there wanted it to escape attention.'

'I for one could use something of a distraction today,' said the priest. 'The supply of poteen has completely dried up now, and I make no secret it is a solace to me. So a small mystery will have to stand in its place as a means of soothing my troubled mind.' He rose, and the three of them trooped across the courtyard to the house.

'Good morning there, young Frogett,' said the priest as they approached. 'You have done those Hail Marys, now, of course. Completely absolved, in a state of grace, are you? Unclean thoughts can be the very devil, and plague all minds. You have to keep up with the penance now.'

Frogett smiled, surprisingly shyly for a man twice convicted of violent offences. Typical, Monsarrat thought, the unclean thoughts must've been the only sins he confessed to Father Hanley. Monsarrat knew the man had been involved in a brawl in the convict barracks quite recently, but he had grown up surrounded by casual violence and would not have seen a dust-up as a sin.

Mrs Mulrooney admitted them. As she was turning to leave, he pulled her aside. 'I don't wish to burden you; however, I am afraid I have alarming news. Dr Gonville's views are not being taken as seriously as they might. Please, I beg you to be careful. And rest assured I'm doing everything possible to ensure this situation doesn't keep heading down its current path.'

'I know you are, Mr Monsarrat, and I'm grateful. We shall see what comes. I almost hope they arrest me today – it would put an end to this awful waiting.'

'I have lately come across some information which may exonerate you, but I shan't say more for now. As soon as I know more – enough to draw realistic conclusions – I will come to you.'

Mrs Mulrooney frowned, then, not the response he'd expected to the ray of hope, albeit weak, he was offering. She patted him on the arm, turned and left.

In the sitting room, he drew Father Hanley over to the writing, that patch of wall now having been entirely stripped of its decoration. The priest unceremoniously dropped down onto his haunches to examine the words, and gave a soft chuckle. 'Mr Monsarrat,' he said, smiling, 'I must say, your Irish pronunciation is absolutely atrocious.'

'I would call that a fair comment, Father. I assume, then, that you recognise the words?'

'Indeed. The proper pronunciation is "*chuckie-ar-lah*".'

How one could get 'chuckie' from *tiocfaidh* escaped Monsarrat entirely. 'I've heard that phrase used quite recently,' he said, thinking back to Slattery's departure a few short days ago. 'I was told it was a phrase to bring good luck.'

'Well, now, that all depends entirely on your perspective,' said the priest. 'I suppose some may view it as lucky. Depending on what side of the argument you're on, it could even be viewed as hopeful.'

'Which argument is that?'

'Now, you'll forgive me, Mr Monsarrat, you being an Englishman and all, but the argument to which I'm referring is one of the oldest. It's the argument of the people of Ireland against British rule.'

'I see,' said Monsarrat. 'So it's an exhortation to hope, then.'

'As I said, it depends on your perspective. If you're Irish, certainly. But if you're English, it could be seen as something quite different. A threat, perhaps. Even a curse.'

'And its meaning?' said Monsarrat.

The priest smiled. 'Mr Monsarrat, those words there before you, they mean "Our day will come".'

❧

By mid-morning, Frogett and Daines had finished stripping the last of the diabolical stuff from the walls. They asked Monsarrat if they should burn it. He had no idea whether, if the paper really was toxic, the act of burning it would send the toxin flying through the air. He told them to leave it with the other refuse.

Monsarrat had spent the morning pretending to watch the two convicts while chewing on this latest piece of information. He did not want Diamond to be innocent, and he most certainly did not want Slattery to be guilty, but he was becoming more convinced that the young soldier had had a hand in Mrs Shelborne's death.

He returned to the workroom then, and awaited instructions from the major.

They weren't slow in coming. The major called him in, asking him to bring his writing implements. 'It's past time I sent word to Sydney of our discoveries in the north,' he said. He began to dictate.

Dear sir,
I have the honour to inform you of the outcome of our expedition to the north of Port Macquarie, of which I wrote to you on the third instant. As you may recall, an absconded convict who now dwells with the natives had claimed to have found a river surrounded by excellent farming land a little to the north of the route travelled by John Oxley.

I set out to discover the truth of his statements, accompanied by Lieutenant Frederick Craddock, two privates, a cook, two convict woodsmen, and a native tracker.

We were indeed fortunate enough to find this river, which is wide enough to take a sloop or a cutter and has upriver pastures and limitless stands of native cedar. This may well be the upper reaches of the river recorded from the sea as debouching into the Pacific Ocean near Trial Bay.

As I thought it unwise to be absent from the settlement for too long a period, my objective was to confirm the river's existence and location and return immediately. With your permission, I will dispatch a party to survey the location in more detail.

In recognition of their service, I would like to recommend for a ticket of leave the convicts James Callan, Adam Wright and John Armitage. I also recommend a conditional pardon for Hugh Kiernan, the convict who brought the river to my attention and secured the cooperation of a native tracker in its discovery.

We returned to Port Macquarie two days ago; however, I was delayed in communicating with you due to the untimely death of my wife, who was interred yesterday in the grounds of the church which is currently being built here.

I remain, sir, your most obedient servant,
Angus Shelborne, Commandant

'At least someone will be happy, Monsarrat,' said the major.

'Yes, sir,' said Monsarrat neutrally. He stood to return to his workroom, to make a fair copy of the major's dispatch.

He botched the first go, though, when the door was slammed open, admitting a chilly breeze and Captain Diamond.

The captain didn't acknowledge Monsarrat, but went straight into the major's study. He did not knock – a fact which Monsarrat found alarming. Clearly he was certain enough of his place in the major's esteem to dispense with the usual formalities.

He closed the door behind him, probably to prevent Monsarrat from overhearing. Of course, he didn't know exactly how large the gaps around the door were, and that Monsarrat had trained his hearing to pick up every word from the inner room.

'Sir, I know you don't want to believe it. But who else would have been able to administer the poison? Dr Gonville, perhaps. But I know you won't entertain any notion of a charge against him, nor does he have a criminal past. She does. Maybe she thought to make away with some of your wife's possessions after she had died. Maybe she resented her for some imagined slight. Who could begin to guess at the reason? But the fact is, there is not anybody else who it could be. Any delay in her arrest heightens the risk of her escape. Word of the situation has begun to leak out, and she has many friends in the settlement, some of whom may contrive to requisition a longboat on her behalf.'

There was silence from the major. Then: 'I know. I know, it needs to be done now, or not at all. You are right. Very well, then. See it done.'

'And shall I give orders for the erection of a gallows?'

'No, you shall not, not without my express approval. She will have the benefit of a trial in Sydney. We will hold her here until she is sent for.'

'In that case,' said Diamond in a tone which suggested some disappointment, 'I will see that she goes to the gaol.'

'Michael, I want to make one thing very clear – she is to be treated well. Should she require visitors, she shall have them. She shall receive the same food as she would have done were she free. If I hear she has been mistreated, I will lay the blame directly at your door.'

'Of course, sir,' said Diamond. He shot Monsarrat a look as he stalked past, but Monsarrat barely noticed. He was having difficulty breathing, but that didn't stop his body propelling itself across the workroom. For the first time since he had met the major, he entered the man's study without knocking.

'Sir, you can't do this! She has done nothing wrong. For nights she slept in a chair next to your wife while she was ill. You could never imagine a more devoted nurse. She is guilty of nothing but being a murderer's unwitting tool. I beg you to reconsider.'

The major sighed. 'Believe me, Monsarrat, I wish it were different. But there is simply no other way in which my wife could have been poisoned. You spend enough time in that damned kitchen; have you ever seen anybody come in and fiddle with the tea things?'

Monsarrat knew the major intended the question to be rhetorical. But the fact was, he had seen someone fiddling with the tea things. Recently, too. Under the guise of helping Mrs Mulrooney.

'What possible motive could the woman have for wanting to murder your wife? It beggars belief. Even the ring, she put it by safely – do you know why? She wanted you to be able to decide whether it should be buried with your wife!'

The major's eyes began to harden. 'Please do not talk about my wife's burial, it is no concern of yours,' he said.

Then he sighed again. 'I don't know why she would have done it, Monsarrat. No doubt her trial will bring that to the surface. She will go to Sydney. Nothing can prevent that. You know, Diamond wanted me to arrest you, too. He was convinced you must've been her accomplice. I can't believe it of you, Monsarrat, but then I couldn't have believed it of her, either. So please, be careful how you speak to me, for I am beginning to accept that people will act wildly out of character.'

'There is nothing, then, that I can do to convince you? Forgive me, but I know you are not the sort of man who would want to be a party to the hanging of an innocent woman.'

'If she is innocent, a trial will bring that to the surface too, I have no doubt.'

Monsarrat wished he could share the commandant's faith in the legal system.

'No, Monsarrat, there is nothing that you can do to convince me. Short of bringing me another perpetrator willing to confess to the crime and hang for it.'

Then that, thought Monsarrat, is what I will do.

Chapter 26

For the rest of the day, the major and his clerk spoke only when necessary. The various reports demanded by the paper-hungry administration in Sydney had been laid aside during the major's expedition, and now needed to be dealt with. So the major dictated and Monsarrat wrote. The major also asked him to inform Mr Spring and Dr Gonville that the audits requested by Captain Diamond were no longer required.

Several times, Monsarrat had to drag his gaze back to the page. It kept drifting towards the door. He had heard no scuffle, no commotion, nor did he really expect one – he did not think Mrs Mulrooney would be the type to resist arrest, nor did he think most of the soldiers were of a disposition to treat an ageing woman roughly. But he couldn't help wondering whether she still stood behind the walls of the kitchen, or whether she was now behind the far thicker walls of the gaol.

By the end of the day, Monsarrat thought, Well, the deed must be done by now.

He went into the major's office – knocking politely this time, and waiting to be asked to come in. 'Major, I come to you with a request.'

'I'll not free her, Monsarrat.'

'No, and nor do I expect you to. I'm aware that your mind is quite made up. However, for someone like Mrs Mulrooney – remember, since her first offence in Ireland all those years ago, she has committed no crime – I imagine the gaol will be quite a frightening place. I would like to ask your permission to sit with her for a while this evening. Just to ease her into it, if such a thing is possible.'

The major looked up. 'Fine, Monsarrat,' he said with some resignation. 'Please write yourself a note to that effect and I will sign it. It's important that we follow the appropriate process in this matter.'

But as Monsarrat started for the door, the major called him back.

'I remind you, Monsarrat, and hope I don't need to, that you are obliged to report any conversation which has a bearing on this crime.'

Monsarrat gave his assurance, and made his way down to the gaol. He nodded to the guard on duty, a young fellow called Meehan, and showed him the note.

'It'll be good for her to have a bit of company,' the guard said. His accent told Monsarrat that he was a compatriot of Mrs Mulrooney's. 'This is no place for a poor lady such as herself.'

Monsarrat could not have agreed more. The man admitted him to the cell, and left him to it.

Mrs Mulrooney was sitting staring at the wall. She looked as neat as she had on the first day Monsarrat had met her in the Government House kitchen. She seemed perfectly composed, and only someone who knew her well would notice that she was blinking more quickly than usual, which in her was a sign of distress.

She turned to face him. 'Thank you for trying, Mr Monsarrat. If you have not been able to manage it, then it can't be managed. I wonder, before I go to Sydney, would you ever help me with a letter to Padraig? I'd like to let him know what has happened. Assure him his mother is not a murderer, no matter what the courts say.'

The guard clearly did not consider Mrs Mulrooney a likely prisoner to disappear into the bushes, seeking shelter with the

Birpai. He had left the cell door unlocked, so that Monsarrat was able to enter and sit on the wooden bench, next to her. He stared, as she did, at the cell walls. Not the damp, oozing stone of his Exeter cell, but a patchwork of convict-made bricks, as individual as their makers, different colours and sizes, and with flecks of oyster shell in the mortar holding them together.

She didn't speak, or look at him then, but he noticed the occasional catch in her breath, the occasional inflation of her lungs to their capacity, as though she was trying to get the next fifteen years' worth of breathing done before her execution.

And he had no doubt that if she was sent to Sydney to face trial, execution would be the eventual outcome. If the progressive major was unwilling to spare her, a court in Sydney would not be likely to do so, particularly with the plausible Captain Diamond to give evidence against a former criminal.

Finally, he said, 'I very much hope you'll be able to tell him yourself.'

'It's a cruel thing, Mr Monsarrat, to give hope when none is possible. And you're not a cruel man.'

'But there is hope. And the only reason I did not blurt it out immediately on entering this cell is because this hope will break your heart, as well as save your life.'

She exhaled slowly. 'You're going to tell me it was Fergal.'

In a life which had been full of surprises – mostly unwelcome – Monsarrat had to rank this one chief amongst them.

'How on earth can you know? I'm not completely certain myself – it's just that, much as I hate to say it, the compass needle is beginning to point in his direction. Away from the execrable captain, whom I'd far prefer to be guilty.'

'I've known for a while. His story – dispossession, loss – it's a fairly common one in Ireland. And it tends to change people. Most of the time they slide into drink or despair, or else become open rebels. One path leads to the grave, and the other leads here. Our Slattery, now he's a smart boy, I always thought so. But there's a seam of darkness in him. He took the hurt into himself, in the way his father took gallons of the crater. And then he closed himself around it, that lad, and smothered it with winks and smiles and banter and sometimes his God-awful jokes.'

'But darkness, well, it's there in all of us. Here, anyway. I've often thought you're the only one here untouched by it. You and Mrs Shelborne, perhaps. It doesn't make a murderer, not necessarily.' Monsarrat was surprised to hear himself arguing in Slattery's favour. He still retained some affection for the young soldier, and would have wished Mrs Mulrooney to talk him out of his suspicions, were it not for the fact that in doing so she would be talking herself to death.

'Yes, for a long time I thought that was as far as it went, a stone within him which would always be there but around which he'd made accommodations. And most of the time, he seemed cheerful enough. Occasionally, as I told you, I'd need to put him back together when it had got a bit much and he'd gone and swum in a pool of sly grog. But I can count the number of times that happened on one hand.'

'But you've decided, obviously, that his was no harmless personal demon. It was the vengeful sort. Why?'

'I've told you the story of his background. What he's told me, at any rate. And I knew where he was from. And I also knew where Mrs Shelborne was from. A village in Ireland is not like London, Mr Monsarrat. If you live there, you know the local landowner. And his daughter.'

'So you guessed a connection? And felt it was strong enough to drive him to something like this?'

'Not at first. I've told you, Mr Monsarrat, how delighted I was when she first got ill. It was my first sign with Padraig, you see. We got little enough food, so it was a terrible pity to see it all re-emerge like that, in the early months. And that's what I thought was happening to her. Right up until the end, really, I had a stupid hope of it. But then I spooned that tea into her mouth, and she died so quickly that it was impossible not to link the two. Then I started thinking about how Slattery insisted on helping me with the tray, how he fiddled with the tea chest from time to time. Then you told me about that article.'

'The wallpaper,' said Monsarrat. 'That's right, you mentioned it had been scraped.'

'It had. And I'll tell you what else I noticed – the mousey smell. Or at least I'd got so used to it I'd stopped noticing it. But you said that article had pointed out that wallpaper with the poison in it made a room smell mousey. I'd been wondering why, actually, it was only that room. I was a bit concerned, lest anyone lay the blame for the infestation at my door. I wish that were the worst of my worries now.'

'So you don't think it was scraped in carelessness. You think it was Slattery?'

Mrs Mulrooney reached into her pocket and pulled out a small stick, which had had the bark scraped away from one end.

'He was fiddling with this in the kitchen one day. In a foul mood, too, he was. I wanted to box his ears – in fact, I think I might have, I can't remember. But he was whittling away at this stick, and I noticed that his blade had a few specks of green on it. At the time I assumed it was some corrosion in the metal, but then I saw the green flecks on the stick, as well. There are a few of them still there, you see?' She handed the twig to Monsarrat. He saw that she was right. There, nestling between the crevices made by the remaining bark, were two or three bright green specks.

'When I told you about the copper . . . you seemed to take it very hard,' said Monsarrat.

'Well, until then I'd been telling myself not to be stupid. It couldn't be him – I'd have noticed green flecks in the tea leaves, he had no means of making it into a liquid. But it turned out he did.'

'There's something else, as well,' said Monsarrat. 'Those words I told you about, the ones we thought might be Irish. Father Hanley told me how they were pronounced. They say *chuckie-ar-lah*.'

'Now those words I have heard, and I know what they mean, besides,' said Mrs Mulrooney. 'Those who speak them tend to finish at the end of a British rope.'

'Father Hanley said depending on your perspective they could be viewed as an exhortation to hope, or as a curse.'

'Probably more like a promise, in Slattery's mind,' said

Mrs Mulrooney. Monsarrat noticed the rate of her blinking had increased further. She said, almost in a whisper, 'This is what they do to us. They make us feel unnatural hatreds, without expecting that one day somebody will act on them.'

Our day will come.

Of course! thought Monsarrat. It was exactly what Slattery would do, write a message of subversion and cover it, make a secret boast, celebrate some balance he had asserted both by doing physical harm and making a gesture of defiance of which only he knew. He was howling into the gale, but the point was, he was howling.

Mrs Mulrooney began to cry, quietly. The expression on her face did not change, but tears began to race down her cheeks. 'I loved that boy, Monsarrat. I still do. I'm ashamed of myself for giving him some of the love that rightly belongs to Padraig, but my son wasn't there to receive it. Young Slattery is of an age with him, and a similar temperament; it was very easy almost to imagine he was mine, too.'

'But surely you don't condone what he's done,' said Monsarrat.

'Of course not. Mrs Shelborne was a rarity. Sweet, kind and with a sensible mind – you don't normally get the first two in the same bracket as the third. She should not have died. He should not have done what he did. Her father may have evicted his family, but she can have been no more than a child when it happened, and certainly had no part in it.'

'Slattery clearly believes she did – or at least that the sins of the father should be visited on the child,' said Monsarrat.

He braced his elbows on his knees and put his head in his hands for a moment – pushing the heels of his hands into his eyes until he saw brightly coloured pinpricks in the darkness. The tickle behind his eyeballs, the threat of the onset of tears, subsided somewhat.

Mrs Mulrooney was openly weeping now. 'That stupid boy,' she said, as she had the other day, Monsarrat realised, when he had told her about the copper. Her voice was thickening, emanating from further down her throat than usual. 'The care I lavished on him, the worry. And he turns out to be as indiscriminately vengeful as any of them. That last morning – he knew he'd be away but didn't know how long for. Suppose he decided to give her a nudge along before he left? I would throttle him myself were he here. What good did he think it would do to pick such a flower? I'll venture the darkness is still there. It's probably grown. So what will he do now? Keep killing people?'

'No,' said Monsarrat gently, putting his hand over hers, 'he won't. We will see to it. I would greatly appreciate your advice on how to raise it with the major – you've always been so much better at nuances than I. There is a cutter expected in a few weeks; it will probably take you to Sydney, so we have until then. I'll write a brief of evidence – I have some experience in that sort of thing, as you are aware – and put it before the major. I'll have to be very careful with the tone, though – it must not have any whiff of a fabricated allegation concocted by an accused woman and her friend. I'll read it through to you when it's done, and you can let me know if I have it right.'

Mrs Mulrooney's tears stopped, and she looked at him with a trace of her usual fire. Had she had a cleaning cloth, Monsarrat would have been truly fearful.

'Mr Monsarrat,' she said, 'you'll do no such thing.'

'But how else are we to obtain your release? Not to mention visiting justice on a man who killed an innocent woman. I know you love him, Mrs Mulrooney, and I have a good deal of affection for him myself. But remember how good he is at bluffing. We love what he chose to show us – a version of him which might have existed under different circumstances, but doesn't now.'

'We are not going to obtain my release,' she said. 'Nor are we going to bring Fergal to justice. Once in Sydney, I intend to confess to the murder. I would do it here, but I want the place to have a good memory of me, and I don't want Fergal to do something stupid like stepping forward himself. Then I shall hang. My only wish is that Padraig know the truth of it – you must promise me you'll let him know what I did, and why I did it. He has no need of a mother now anyway, big lummox like him, well able to look after himself. One other request – would you hold my money, Mr Monsarrat? Make sure it reaches him? I've nearly enough saved for him to set himself

276

up in a public house somewhere – he can hopefully provide the rest. I could go calmly to my grave knowing he had a chance of becoming a proper gentleman.'

'My dear woman, have you completely lost your senses? Why on earth would you do this? The man is a killer – you can't settle this debt for him as though it were a grocery bill.'

'As to why,' said Mrs Mulrooney, 'it may have escaped your attention but I am no longer in the first blush of youth. I have seen far more in my life than my sisters back in Ireland could ever have imagined. And I've reared someone who I truly believe to be a good man. But Slattery, now, he is younger than I was when I bore Padraig, and certainly than I was when I was transported. If collecting on this stupid blood debt has exorcised his demon, even slightly, there may yet be hope for him to make a decent life. I want you to let him know, when this is all done, that that was my wish. Tell him to make sure he behaves – he wouldn't want me to haunt him. I fancy I'd make a reasonably terrifying ghost; I certainly mean to be.'

Monsarrat rarely yelled, and had never done so in the presence of Mrs Mulrooney – the threat of her disapproval was far more frightening to him than the prospect of a stint on the lime-burners' gang. But he felt that of all the provocations in his life, this was the sorest.

'I will not allow this! This is every bit as wrong as an innocent being fitted up for a crime they didn't commit. I will make sure the truth of the situation is known, and you will be exonerated whether you want to be or not!'

'No, Mr Monsarrat, I will not. They will have a confession from me, together with Diamond's testimony. Against that, anything you may write will seem like a feeble attempt to save my life, and perhaps even your own – they may conclude that you had assisted me in the business, and were trying to remove the risk of blame. Be careful, or you may earn your own rope necklace. In any case, I'm going to have to leave at some point; what better way to do it than by saving a life? And it'll be over quickly, and then I will be judged and rewarded by the only judge who matters.'

Monsarrat had never used Mrs Mulrooney's first name – she was big on the proprieties, and he had quickly learned to do everything possible to avoid offending her. But now they were as close to the edge of the cliff as they had ever been, and the weight of propriety, he felt, might cause the unstable ground to fall out from beneath them.

'Hannah, you are not going to sacrifice yourself. I will see to it. You may confess to every killing that has ever occurred in this place, and I will still see to it that you walk out of here a free woman. Depend on it.'

If he was concerned about giving offence, he needn't have been, as Mrs Mulrooney followed his lead. 'Hugh, I know how dependable you are. But if the price of my freedom is Fergal's life, then I'm not interested. I'm not overjoyed at the prospect of hanging, but hang I will, and any protestations from you will make no difference except to make my agony a little keener. Please, accept my decision. It's mine to make.'

Chapter 27

Monsarrat had no intention of accepting Mrs Mulrooney's decision.

They had sat together a while longer, after the outburst. He had held her hand. She had drawn her rosary beads from her pocket, where they must've rubbed up against Slattery's stick, and asked him to pray with her. He didn't have the first clue how to say a Hail Mary, but he bowed his head and said amen at the right point, and that seemed to bring her some comfort.

He left with the promise to return the next day, if allowed by the major.

'Only come back if you are willing to let me follow the course of action I've determined on, Mr Monsarrat,' said Mrs Mulrooney, now clearly back on a more formal footing. 'Otherwise you'll just sadden me.'

So he would pretend, if he had to, that he was going to allow her to go through with this act of martyrdom. But he would also work to undermine her, something he had never thought he would deliberately do with this woman.

He faced a problem, though – Mrs Mulrooney, as usual, was right. If the murderer had confessed, any alternative theory of the crime would be seen as wishful thinking at best, and an attempt to divert suspicion at worst. He realised, then, that nothing would save Mrs Mulrooney but a full confession from Fergal Slattery.

He had no idea, however, how to go about obtaining that confession. If it was only uttered in Monsarrat's presence, it would be useless. Slattery could always deny it, and who would disbelieve him when such a convenient criminal was so helpfully offering herself to the gallows?

For a second night, he didn't sleep well, and again it had very little to do with the cold radiating from the river stones. He tested out a number of strategies in his mind – from attempting to lead Slattery obliquely into a confession, to a full confrontation.

By morning, he had resolved that the best course of action was to calmly confront the lad. True, preferably in front of witnesses. Once Fergal realised that Monsarrat knew the truth, he might flee; he might even turn against Monsarrat. Who knew what the boy was capable of, when a month ago Monsarrat would have not believed him capable of slow poison?

But any attempt to lead Slattery into a confession, without him realising the nature of the path he was following Monsarrat down, would probably fail – Slattery was intelligent, and a consummate bluffer. Rattling the bluff out of him with a bald accusation was the only hope.

Monsarrat spent the day quietly in his workroom, as he had the day before, occasionally entering the major's office on request to take dictation. He was a paragon of silence and industry. It was his hope that in giving the major a break from his arguments in favour of Mrs Mulrooney, the man might be more receptive later.

In the meantime, the backlog of paperwork needed to be cleared. He shuttled between the major's study and his own, taking dictation on the output from the sugarcane and tobacco planta-tions, the quantity of cedar and rosewood felled and sawed at the port that month, the amount of grain produced, those convicts who had been punished by working the treadmill to grind it, and the progress of the maize crop.

There were also reports on convict discipline for the month. Monsarrat tried not to show, by the merest flicker, any reaction when the major dictated the words: 'William Dory, aged eighteen, absconded. Thirty lashes. Perished two days later from an infection.'

So Diamond had taken the papers, as Dr Gonville had suspected, and given the major incorrect information. No one had as yet stepped forward to contradict him, because no one would at this stage know of the deception. Monsarrat considered it. But, he realised, his could not be the lone voice. He, as much as any of them, was a recidivist, proven twice untrustworthy. He would need to find a sponsor with more authority and less criminality than he, and reporting Diamond would not help Dory. As well, there were other more pressing considerations.

The administrative niceties complete, the major leaned back in his chair and sighed. 'Well, Monsarrat. Let's not delay the evil necessity any longer. You know, I suspect, the nature of the letter I am now going to dictate.'

Monsarrat said nothing, but nodded grimly and readied a fresh sheet of paper.

'"Sir",' said the major,

I have the honour to acquaint you with information which has come to light regarding the circumstances of my wife's death.

On advice from this settlement's doctor, Richard Gonville, it has become apparent that my wife's passing was caused by the deliberate administration of arsenic over a period of some weeks.

The doctor informs me that the substance may be absorbed through the skin, and speculates that it is possible any murderer might try to avoid contact with it, to avoid poisoning him or herself.

However, the greater likelihood is that the poison was administered through food and drink, by a person in a position to do so on a regular basis without arousing suspicion. The only person who meets this description is our housekeeper and cook, Mrs Hannah Mulrooney, a ticket-of-leave woman who has been of good character since her initial crime. The doctor informs me that the poison must have been administered through the tea Mrs Mulrooney brewed daily for my wife, making her culpability in this matter likely. A motive is at this stage unclear, as Mrs Mulrooney has made no statement regarding the crime.

I have confined Mrs Mulrooney to the gaol for now, pending your instructions on conveying her to Sydney for trial. In the meantime, I intend to depose her and those close to her, and send this information to you for the perusal of the Attorney-General and Crown Solicitor.

'"I remain, sir, your obedient servant" – Monsarrat, I know you will not relish making a fair copy of this; however, I wish it to go at the earliest possibility to Sydney. Please transcribe it immediately and place it on my desk for signature.'

As always, Monsarrat did as he was told, reassuring himself that the letter would be irrelevant once he obtained Slattery's confession. Nevertheless, a number of ink blotches, of the type Monsarrat would never have countenanced in the normal run of things, found their way onto the paper which the major eventually signed.

❧

The major dismissed Monsarrat in the late afternoon. Leaving the office, he saw smoke coming from the kitchen chimney. He knocked on the door, received a croaky 'yes', and entered.

At the hob was Peg McGreevy, her gout obviously much recovered. Having been transported for theft, she was housekeeper to Thomas Carleton's wife, and was then sent here for drunkenness and neglecting work. She was of an age with Mrs Mulrooney, but the pair had never really got along. Mrs Mulrooney thought Peg was a bit slapdash in the way she went about things – she certainly lacked the precision which Mrs Mulrooney thought was essential. And she probably, Mrs Mulrooney had confided, would let the kitchen things get into all sorts of states.

Monsarrat had no idea how Mrs McGreevy felt about Mrs Mulrooney – possibly that her countrywoman was too big for her boots, having been a convict, after all.

On taking in the kitchen, though, Monsarrat felt Mrs Mulrooney might have a point. Water from a bubbling pot on the stove had splashed onto the floor, and breadcrumbs littered the table. Monsarrat could not remember seeing so much as the ghost of a breadcrumb during Mrs Mulrooney's tenure.

'Good afternoon, Mrs McGreevy,' he said.

'Mr Monsarrat. Have you permission to be in here? I don't want to be punished for something I didn't do, letting you in when I shouldn't.'

'Please don't trouble yourself – I will only stay a moment. I just wanted to ask whether you've seen Private Fergal Slattery; he's been in the habit in the past of coming here, but he hasn't done so for a few days now.'

'I don't socialise with the soldiers, Mr Monsarrat. The only one I've seen today was young Cooper, when he came and fetched me up here. He wouldn't tell me where Mulrooney's gone, but there are rumours all about the camp. She's been arrested, they say. Young Meehan, now, he's a guard at the gaol. He says she's been sitting in there staring at the wall for a day. So I suppose she was no more virtuous than the rest of us after all, though God alone knows what she did to get in there.'

While saying this, she had been spooning tea leaves into a teapot (without warming it first), and pouring boiling water directly onto them, making Monsarrat feel unaccountably annoyed. She looked at Monsarrat expectantly now, hoping he would tell her what had landed the housekeeper behind bars. She could then take this information back to the other women, considerably increasing her status by doing so. Monsarrat disappointed her, thanking her, bowing and leaving.

In any case, he thought, Slattery would probably still be involved in regimental duties – no longer exempt by virtue of his plastering job.

He decided to walk past the barracks and parade ground on the way down to the beach, on the off-chance of catching a glimpse of the young soldier. There was no parade in progress. In fact, there were very few soldiers around at all; possibly they were overseeing the overseers on the chain gangs or the lime-burners' gang.

As he often did when he was at a loss, Monsarrat went down to Lady Nelson Beach. He sat at the root of a large fang which pointed out into the water. He occasionally imagined he was looking towards home, but knew this wasn't the case. He didn't know what lay to the east of here, but it wasn't England.

As the dark set in, he stood. He had received permission from the major to visit Mrs Mulrooney again, and he had hoped to have some news for her when he did so. It seemed he would have to arrive empty-handed.

The tide was going out – that much was obvious as he rounded the corner at the mouth of the Hastings River. The river here could eject its contents into the sea at quite an alarming rate, so that anyone foolish enough to swim during this time (and few could) would quickly find themselves looking helplessly at the settlement as it receded into the distance.

Monsarrat plucked a small leaf from a fallen branch lying on the bank, and threw it onto the river surface. It was a game he played with himself sometimes – counting the number of seconds it would take for such an object to travel from this point to the river mouth. The speed with which the leaf bounded over the surface convinced him that the tide was a strong one. He had noticed vaguely, last night, that the moon had been full, and remembered the coxswain telling him that at such a time, more water made its way into and out of the river.

He silently farewelled the leaf on its journey to unknown countries. But as he turned to make his way back to the settlement, he saw another object racing down the river towards him, this one much larger, and with a dull sheen to it.

Planting his feet, he pivoted and grabbed the branch that lay behind him on the bank, turning and reaching out with it to arrest the progress of the object which was now nearly beyond his reach.

He was able to hook the branch under its lip – for its mouth was narrower than its body. Lifting the branch above his head, he saw that what he had fished out of the river was a copper, much like the one that Slattery had been using at his still.

And now, finally, stomping and cursing, came the man himself.

Monsarrat noticed that Slattery walked with a barely perceptible limp, disguised by his long stride and lolloping gait. It occurred to Monsarrat that he had rarely seen the young soldier out of the confines of the kitchen, so his opportunities to assess the way he walked had been limited.

As Slattery got closer in the gloom, he recognised Monsarrat, and smiled. 'Ah, the gentleman fooking convict. Always there when not expected. Good evening to you, Mr Monsarrat. I believe you have something of mine there.'

Monsarrat lowered the branch so that its tip, off which the copper was dangling, was pointed at Slattery. He doubted there were any traces left of the green substance in the bottom of it – probably the purpose for Slattery having it down by the river. 'Doing a spot of sailing, were we? An interesting object to substitute for a toy boat.'

'Just some housekeeping, you might say,' said Slattery. 'I wasn't concentrating, and I lost a grip of the thing, and off it went sailing, and sailing it might still be if you hadn't got a hold of it.'

Monsarrat didn't know whether he was imagining that edge to Slattery's voice as he made this last statement.

'I haven't seen you in the kitchen for a while, Slattery,' he said as Slattery retrieved the copper.

'No, well, now that there's no need of me for plastering purposes, I'm back to my regular soldierly duties. And unfortunately they don't include visits to Mother Mulrooney, much to my disappointment. I have to say, I'm feeling the lack of tea.'

'You'll be feeling the lack of it for the rest of your life, one way or another. Either she'll be dead, or you will, and which way the balance tips is very much in your power.'

Slattery drew his brows together, looking at Monsarrat as though trying to discern whether he was being lied to, whether Monsarrat had developed a bluffing face as effective as his own. Monsarrat stood there, weathering the scrutiny. Slattery had a good, long look, drinking in as much information from Monsarrat's features as he could. What he saw must've satisfied him as to Monsarrat's honesty, for he sat down heavily on the riverbank.

'I'd heard she had been arrested. It's a common topic of conversation in the camp right now. But I thought the major would see through it; I thought maybe she might spend a night in gaol and then be released. Surely that's what's going to happen? They can't try her – my blind father could see she is not capable of it.'

'Capable of what, Fergal? The rumour may have spread that she has been arrested, but not even the gossip in chief, Peg McGreevy, knows what for.'

Slattery stared at Monsarrat but didn't speak, perhaps fearing that in trying to extricate himself from the web he was now beginning to sense, he would only make its strands cling to him more tightly.

'And anyway, it seems your blind father can see more than the major. Diamond has him almost convinced. And why wouldn't he? Who else had the opportunity to poison Mrs Shelborne?'

Slattery kept staring, but showed no surprise at the revelation.

'Very convenient to lay it at the door of the person who was responsible for feeding his wife before she died,' Monsarrat continued. 'And a former convict, too. I know a great many judges who would see this as a case with no need of a trial, who would want to move straight to sentencing, and of course we know that the sentence would be death. So it seems you and I, Fergal, are amongst the few who know of the crime she will be tried for, and the only ones who believe in her innocence.'

Slattery opened his mouth then closed it. He sat for a moment, then spoke again. 'You know, Monsarrat, I was about to ask you who you thought did kill the woman, if not Mrs Mulrooney. But we've shared too much tea to dance around each other, you and I. You know the identity of the person responsible, I'm almost certain.'

Monsarrat didn't answer, staring out at the river, and then looked at the copper which was now sitting between him and Slattery.

'I presumed it was you who came to the clearing while I was away. I didn't have a chance to dismantle it before I was confined to the guardhouse. And then we were off in search of the major, and there's been no opportunity until tonight to get there.'

'I thought you were making poteen,' said Monsarrat.

'Poteen!' Slattery laughed. 'Of course, because I'm Irish, that must be what I was doing. Never mind the lack of a proper still, I can conjure it out of thin air! Magpie, I envy you a life so soft that you've never had to find out how spirits are distilled, or taste the results.'

'I assume that foul green sludge is wafting out on the current as we speak,' said Monsarrat.

Slattery didn't reply, but looked in the direction of its likely travel.

'How did you know?' asked Monsarrat. 'About the properties of the wallpaper pigment, I mean.'

'Ah, well, my years watching, I suppose. Everyone in Dublin, everyone everywhere, seemed to want that colour. We were constantly dealing with it. And some people in our crew would sicken, and some wouldn't, but I didn't really think much of it, for it's the way of things, isn't it, Monsarrat, that some fall and others stand? But that paper cost me a week's wages. One time in Dublin, I had some laid out, all ready to put up, when a dog that belonged to the house wandered in. I didn't notice him at first; I was concentrating on joining the two sheets I was working with – they have to be exact, Monsarrat, you can't have any misshapen patterns. Anyway, this dog, behind my back, walks up to the paper and starts sniffing it, and then licking it and chewing at it a bit, the way they do.'

'So you were docked a week's wages for the loss of the paper?'

'Yes, and the foreman was threatening to do awful things to the dog as well. But it turned out he didn't need to. Later on I found the dog outside in the yard, dead. That's when I first began to wonder – I like patterns, you see. Patterns on wallpaper. And others. And one pattern was that those who fell ill of the plastering crew, it was always the same kind of illness. They would start coughing, then get dizzy, perhaps throw up, but if they had to go home sick or take a few days off, they'd come back right as rain. Then it would start again, on the very same day they returned. I wondered, then, whether something in the wallpaper was at fault.'

'For the love of God, Slattery, tell me you didn't conduct any experiments.'

'I'm not a monster, Monsarrat. No, I'm not. But we started hearing stories. Young children who licked the stuff – God knows why they would, but they did; I'm told young children can do foolish things – well, they died. And then there was talk of banning it. It all came out of England, so if it was banned there we wouldn't get any in Dublin, either. The foreman was very worried, because everyone was demanding that green. If it were suddenly unavailable, well, he wasn't sure he'd be able to sell them on other colours. He needn't have worried, I fancy you can still get that paper in Dublin today. But not from me, of course. I hated being in those places, knowing the paper I hung was likely paid for by the labour of people like my parents. That's why I joined the army. That, and I also thought the system which sponsored the monster who destroyed my family might as well feed me. And I might be able to get up to some mischief while I was in the way of it. No one would know, of course. But I would. The balance would shift just ever so slightly, and it might be enough.'

Monsarrat sighed. 'You know, Diamond has tipped out all of the poison Mrs Mulrooney keeps in the kitchen, to make it seem as though she had used it on Mrs Shelborne. To that point, why didn't you? Use it, I mean?'

'Hard enough to douse the tea without anyone noticing,' said Slattery. 'Getting the white powder out of its jar would have been impossible, not with herself in the kitchen all the time. And you know what she's like – she'd have noticed if a mere grain was missing.'

'Either way, poisoning a young woman who'd done nothing to harm you is a little more than mischief, wouldn't you say?'

Slattery looked at Monsarrat, and rising up to meet him was the hatred he had seen in the young man's face when he was forced to flog Dory.

'Oh, she did nothing to harm me? She was the agent of my sister's deformity; it was thanks to her that Mary was marked forever, that the split cheek which hadn't grown together properly forced her to do unspeakable things to feed me. His lordship may as well have killed her there and then. And then his little girl grew

288

up, fed and clothed by the labour of my family and others. And later, she was fed and clothed by the rents, which just kept going up – every six months or so one of her father's men would show up and let us know that next week it would be twice as much, or three times. And where do you think all that money was going? It was going, Monsarrat, into supporting her lifestyle, into keeping her in pretty dresses and trips into Dublin. So you may think she's an innocent, but she benefited from my loss. She's as guilty as her bastard father.'

'Don't be ridiculous, man. What did you expect her to do? As a child? She wouldn't even have known what was going on.'

'She knew – she must've done. She was always trailing around after Mary. Mary used to call her Honny, and for a long time I thought that was a real name. But the day her father brutalised my sister, he called her by her real name, Honora. There aren't many of those around now, Monsarrat, are there? Not many women on these shores with overblown names like that. And even fewer who come from Castle Henry, which is the pit that demon slunk out of to disfigure my sister and destroy my family. I don't mind telling you, Monsarrat, I nearly choked when I saw that name on the back of a letter. She'd only been here a month, maybe two, so the letter was probably written when she was still at sea. Castle Henry. Addressed on the front to Honora Belgrave Shelborne. I have been in torment since then and yet the ease with which she lived here, the way she played with her mercy when her father had none on us, her show of goodness that cost her nothing ... How could I remember my dead ones and not punish her? Why do you think the Blessed Virgin sent her all this way to the other side of the world, if not for me to balance the scales?'

'Don't call on your faith now as a justification, Fergal. I've heard you rail against it enough, and its priests. Don't pretend that some divine power lifted her across the seas for you to dispatch.'

'But it's hard to believe otherwise, Monsarrat. Especially when she was followed by a shipment of that green. It's a most distinctive colour; I think you'll agree. Very bright. And only achievable through the use of copper arsenic, you know. My family paid for that wallpaper, Monsarrat. Or they might as well have. Why shouldn't I use it?'

'How did you even know what to do?'

'I didn't. I did a number of experiments, there amongst the paperbarks. A little bit of tea might have gone missing from Mrs Mulrooney's tea chest, because I wanted to mix it in to disguise the flavour. I just got a few flakes from the paper here and there. Brewed it up in the copper and diluted it until it didn't look like some sort of witch's potion.'

'But how could you possibly have known there would be no taste?'

'Oh, I made what you might call an educated guess. There were one or two dogs, chickens, pademelons and the like who helped me with my experiments. That man, he was no more than an animal himself, so I thought if other animals would stomach it, so would his daughter.'

Slattery drew a small stone jar from his coat. He opened the cork stopper and showed Monsarrat the contents – a mostly clear liquid with a greenish cast, from which Monsarrat thought he might be able to detect the faintest whiff of almonds.

'And here it is, Monsarrat. The ticket to heaven. A little each day sprinkled over the leaves in the tea chest, the one which holds the good tea, the only kind Mrs Shelborne drank. Not much left now. Before Diamond dragged me off into the bush I had to make sure Mrs Shelborne had enough of this stuff to help her along. She was taking her time about dying – it was making me nervous, to be honest. Pouring this into the tea itself that last morning, rather than over the leaves, was a risk. I hoped Mrs Mulrooney wouldn't be able to smell it. As for tasting it – well, by the time Mrs Shelborne got a spoonful into her it would be too late, even if it did taste a bit odd.'

It was nearly completely dark now, but Monsarrat could see Slattery's teeth and the whites of his eyes very clearly. The young soldier gave him a contorted version of a grin. 'Would you like to try some, Monsarrat? Surely if you're going to investigate this matter fully, you should leave no stone unturned.'

Monsarrat wanted to swat the jar from Slattery's hands, but decided against it – it might be useful as evidence, if he could get anyone to listen to him. Now he said, 'If you were going to kill me, Fergal, I imagine I would have found this in my tea long before now.'

'I would never have polluted Mrs Mulrooney's wonderful stuff with this. It was only those pretentious fragrant infusions that herself liked that deserved it.'

'Did it not occur to you, Fergal, that if Mrs Mulrooney smelled something amiss with the tea, she might have tasted it? You could have killed her!'

'Well, Monsarrat, the thing about Mother Mulrooney is that she is a good girl. She would never have dreamed of tasting her ladyship's tea, because good servants don't do that, now, do they?'

'You can't know that, Fergal. You might have been the cause of her death, and if there's anyone more innocent than Mrs Shelborne, it's Mrs Mulrooney. You might yet kill her.'

'Kill her? I love the woman, Monsarrat. She is the closest thing to a mother I've had since my own passed away. It would be a far darker place here without her.'

'Well, adjust your eyes to the dark, Fergal. She intends to confess to murder.'

Slattery looked genuinely shocked. Such a course of action clearly had not occurred to him. 'Why on earth is the silly woman going to do that?'

'To save you. She will be sent to Sydney for trial, she will plead guilty, and she will be hanged. And there's nothing I can do to prevent it. Even if I went to the major with this story, you could easily say I was making it up, and I'm sure Diamond would back you, for once. In the face of her confession, anything I might say will carry no weight.'

'There must be something you can do, Monsarrat. You're an educated man, you know the law – there must be a way around this. Please! She can't be hanged!'

'If she confesses, it's over. My arguments will be seen as an attempt to save a friend, or even an accomplice. Nothing anyone says will stand if she claims she is guilty. So no, there's nothing I can do. But Fergal, you must realise there's something *you* can do.'

The soldier sat on the riverbank, looking across the wide mouth of the Hastings. Fires were beginning to spring up on the other side and further upriver, lit by natives or cedar-cutting crews.

'I can't hang, Monsarrat,' he whispered. 'I can't. You mustn't ask it of me.'

'Then she will die in your place, take your punishment. And what will that do to the balance you seem so keen on maintaining?'

Slattery did not answer. He looked out over the water, his mouth slightly open, crying now and shaking his head.

This is what was under that card game face, thought Monsarrat. Hatred, a warped sense of justice, and cowardice.

He opened his mouth to ask Slattery one more time to confess, but closed it again. If the soldier would not do so now, he never would. He stood, turned and walked away. He moved more slowly than usual. Maybe there was some legal recourse, some clever trick that could save her. If he thought hard enough, he might just be able to discover it. While his legal training did not make him a legitimate lawyer, his knowledge was nonetheless genuine, and he was Mrs Mulrooney's only advocate. In the meantime, he would certainly tell the commandant what he knew, and take whatever consequences that brought.

He was reluctant to reach his hut and go to sleep. Losing consciousness would make the morning come more quickly, dragging them all one day closer to the event he very much feared was inevitable. Pausing, he tried to pick out which of the few lights still burning belonged to which building. He fancied he saw a light from the major's study, and another from the hospital. Further down, a few of the overseers' cottages were dimly illuminated. But the rest of the lights had already been snuffed out.

As he stood, he became aware of a footfall on the sand behind him. A long, loping stride. And then a large hand, clamped firmly on his shoulder.

He's going to kill me, thought Monsarrat. He will do away with me and let Mrs Mulrooney take his place at the gallows, and no one will be any the wiser.

He turned and looked at Slattery, and was astonished to see the twinkle had returned to the young soldier's eyes.

'Mr Monsarrat,' he said with his odd half-smile, bowing slightly. 'I'd be honoured if you would accompany me to the commandant's office, where I believe we have some business to discuss. There's not much point in redressing the balance, only to have it thrown off again by another unjust death. If Mrs Mulrooney hangs, the bastards have won.'

Monsarrat stared. 'That's brave of you, Fergal.'

The young man shrugged. 'It's to be hoped the fact of my coming forward will convince them to give me a long rope, and I'm a heavy article, so I imagine it will all be over quite quickly. If I can convince some of the lads to come and play cards with me while I wait in the cell, so much the better. Taking some of their money from them before I go would, I think, be fitting.'

BOOK THREE

Chapter 28

Monsarrat suspected the major liked Slattery. He seemed to find the young soldier's impishness endearing, and enjoyed the opportunity to roll his eyes at Slattery's goings-on. If anyone complained of a lack of funds, he would ask them if they'd been playing cards with 'that lightsome Irishman'.

He had also, after his wife's funeral, taken pains to thank those who had come to fetch him, including Slattery, to whom he had said, 'You are not to be blamed that your intervention came too late.'

So he looked surprised, but not annoyed, to see his clerk standing at the door of his study with the tall young man at his shoulder. 'I was about to retire, Monsarrat. Can this wait until morning?'

'I fear not, sir. I have brought the private here on a matter of the most significant gravity. Forgive me for disturbing you so late; however, I believe once you have heard him out, you will forgive the disturbance, if not the news we bring.'

Monsarrat turned and looked expectantly at Slattery, who had been looking at the major and now dropped his eyes.

'Sir,' the soldier said, 'I fear I have done you the most grievous wrong. I don't ask for your forgiveness, as I know there will be none forthcoming. But I do ask for the release of your house-keeper, so that I can take her place.'

Slattery's opening words sounded almost rehearsed to Monsarrat, who wondered whether the young man had foreseen this possibility, and prepared for it, all the while hoping it would not eventuate.

The major smiled sadly. 'It's very brave of you to offer yourself in her stead, Fergal. I do admire you for it. But punishments should be reserved for the guilty. No one benefits when the wrong person hangs.'

'I agree with you, sir,' said Slattery.

The major frowned. He sat down, and gestured both Monsarrat and Slattery to a seat. Monsarrat took one; Slattery decided to remain standing.

'I'm glad to have your agreement, private. So why come to me?'

Slattery inhaled for what seemed like minutes. Then he told his commanding officer the story of his background, and Honora's family's part in it. And he described the means by which he had brought about her death.

Monsarrat had often thought that, had he been inclined to it, the major could have made as good a card player as Slattery. He had clearly put significant effort, over the years, into training his face not to betray his emotions. Now he sat and listened to the tale with so little expression that Monsarrat feared he was concluding Slattery was indeed attempting to be noble, concocting a story which would free Mrs Mulrooney.

When Slattery had finished, the major rose slowly from his desk. He walked around to face the young man, and stood staring at him for several moments. Then he drew back his hand, and cracked Slattery across the face, splitting his lip so that the blood ran down over his chin and disguised itself on the red of his coat.

He turned Slattery by the shoulders, then, and marched him out of the door towards the gaol. He did not appear concerned that Slattery might try to escape, nor did the young soldier seem inclined to do so.

Meehan was on duty again that night. Monsarrat knew he had

been treating Mrs Mulrooney well. When Slattery was marched up to him by the commandant, he seemed surprised and did not immediately comprehend what was happening.

'Get some irons, man!' barked the commandant. 'And release Mrs Mulrooney.'

Meehan had lost money to Slattery in several card games, but clearly had not taken the loss personally – he apologised to Slattery as he applied the irons to his ankles, taking a great deal more care than he usually would. He then clapped a hand on Slattery's shoulder as though congratulating him for a particularly quick win at cards, and moved him gently towards the cell.

Mrs Mulrooney appeared not to have moved since the previous night. She was still immaculate, still sitting on the bench staring at the walls. But when Slattery came into view, cuffed and bleeding from the lip, she sprang up so quickly that a splinter of wood from the bench tore her skirt.

'There's no one to make my tea, Mother Mulrooney, so I thought I'd come and see where you'd got to, and here I find you lazing around in a private room. What's a man to do without you to look after him?'

Mrs Mulrooney took in the state of him, and began to cry. 'Fergal, you haven't done this. Tell me you haven't. There's no need. Everything was in place; there is no need.'

Meehan was unlocking the door of the cell now, gesturing to Mrs Mulrooney to exit before Slattery entered.

Mrs Mulrooney refused to leave. 'Another young life, major. Your wife was an angel from heaven; I was desperate when she passed away. But sending another young soul to join her, now that will do no one any good, will it? I'm getting old – I've limited use to anyone now – let me stay in here.'

'I would do almost anything for you, to compensate you for the injustice which nearly befell you, and to thank you for your care of my wife. But this I will not do, Mrs Mulrooney. This man separated my wife's soul from her body, and the King's justice will come down on him. Nothing you say will change that. Please leave the cell, now.'

Monsarrat stepped past Slattery, put his arm gently around Mrs Mulrooney's shoulder, and started easing her towards the door. As she passed the soldier, she threw herself at him, slapping his face, catching him across the cheek. 'You foolish boy! Why did you do this? Why would you go against me like this?' Then she reached up so that her arms were around his neck – she nearly had to straighten them to do so, as her head only came up to his chest – and her tears were added to the blood on his coat.

Slattery's hands were manacled by now, so he couldn't return her embrace. Instead, he rested his cheek against the top of her head. 'I owe you a lot, Mother Mulrooney. Gallons of tea, and oceans of care. You've made my time here bearable, sometimes even more than that, enjoyable, despite the fact that you wouldn't play cards with me – yes, I know it's the devil's work. Now it seems I've been doing his work even more assiduously than you would have believed. But even someone as diabolical as myself is not going to let you put your head into the noose where mine should be.'

The commandant had stood back, but now clearly decided it was time for Slattery to be contained behind bars. He nodded to Meehan, who nudged the soldier into the cell as Monsarrat eased Mrs Mulrooney out. Meehan closed the door and locked it, frowning at Slattery as though he had suddenly turned into a different kind of beast.

'I'd be grateful for some more tea from your dear old hands, before I dance for the audience,' Slattery called out after her.

Mrs Mulrooney turned as Monsarrat was leading her away. 'Fergal, you will get the best cup of tea I have ever made.'

❧

The three of them walked in silence back towards Government House, the major slightly ahead, not inviting conversation.

By the time they returned, it was closing in on nine o'clock.

'Sir,' said Monsarrat, 'may I have your permission to give Mrs Mulrooney some sustenance in the kitchen before retiring?'

The commandant turned sharply, as though he had forgotten they were there. 'By all means.'

He walked up to Mrs Mulrooney and took her hand. 'I will not pretend to understand the affection you seem to feel for my wife's murderer. But I know it was matched by your affection for my wife herself. I apologise for all that you've had to go through since her death, and I hope I may rely on you in the difficult weeks ahead.'

'Of course, major. And please don't mistake my love for Fergal as approval of what he did. He is like a son to me, and I'm bound to love him regardless of the evil he's done.'

The commandant nodded. 'Goodnight to you, then, and to you, Monsarrat. Please ensure you are in your workroom no later than seven tomorrow morning. You and I have a lot to do.'

Monsarrat thanked the major and said goodnight, before walking with Mrs Mulrooney across the courtyard to the kitchen. The fire had died, and it took Monsarrat a while to get it going again, while fending off Mrs Mulrooney's attempts to assist him. 'Haven't I done enough sitting for the past few days?' she protested. 'This is my fire. I know its moods.'

Nevertheless, he was eventually able to persuade her to sit while he kindled the flames. It was only when the fire was fully established, and the lamps lit, that a look of horror crossed her face.

'Who has been let in here?' she demanded, in a tone which suggested Monsarrat bore full responsibility. She licked a finger and ran it along the table, dislodging crumbs from its grooves. The kettle had been left on the hob, not put back on its hook. And the teapot and cups were absent from barracks, having been placed on shelves where they had no business being.

Once she had noticed all this, Monsarrat did not have the scarcest hope of keeping her in her seat. She flitted from one shelf to the next, looking accusingly at the cups as she put them back in their places, muttering as she moved the kettle to its hook, and imposing a thorough scrubbing on the table.

This done, Monsarrat was able to persuade her to sit again, but only for as long as it took her to realise that he was going to attempt to make tea.

'Now, I've had enough of an imposition here. No one but me will be brewing tea in this kitchen,' she said.

'God save me from intractable women,' said Monsarrat with no real conviction. 'Well, I suppose I can understand if you don't want me to make tea. You clearly feel you did not do a good enough job of teaching me how.'

Mrs Mulrooney jumped back down on the chair, folding her arms. 'Well then, Mr Monsarrat, let's see how well you learn.'

In defiance of the impending evil, Monsarrat made a great show of going through the steps precisely as Mrs Mulrooney had taught them to him, warming the teapot with boiling water, waiting until it cooled enough to be introduced to the leaves, and straining the tea so only black liquid remained. With more flourish than necessary, he presented a cup to Mrs Mulrooney. She picked it up and tasted it, held it in her mouth for several seconds, and swallowed.

'Well, for a man, you appear to have made a decent job of it.'

Monsarrat smiled. He knew this was as much praise as he could expect from Mrs Mulrooney on the subject of tea.

With his own cup, he sat down opposite her. 'Not a patch on yours, of course.'

'Of course it's not,' she said, astonished that he felt it necessary to make such an obvious comment.

They drank in silence for a while. Then Mrs Mulrooney said, 'Was it you who talked Fergal into it?'

Monsarrat wasn't sure how she would feel about the answer. He knew she had, after all, intended to go meekly onto the ship sailing for Sydney, and not return. 'Yes, it was. He didn't realise, or at least I hope he didn't, what mortal peril you were in. He assumed there would be a trial at which you would be acquitted, and everybody would just throw up their hands, say the murder couldn't be solved, and leave him, me and you to go about our normal business.'

'Fool of a boy,' said Mrs Mulrooney. 'A fool on so many levels. I am going to miss him greatly.'

'You and I are going to miss what he showed us of himself,' said Monsarrat. 'That's all. We will be missing an illusion, a smart piece of acting.'

'No, for all his card playing, I don't think you're right, Mr Monsarrat. The mask never slipped, because it wasn't a mask. Certainly he was deceitful, but it was his crime that he tried to hide, not his true nature. I will never forgive him, and I will never forget him.'

'You know, he might be in that gaol for a while. I don't know when the major intends to send him for trial. I imagine he'll seek guidance from the Colonial Secretary. And by the time his letter works its way to Sydney, into the secretary's hands, and back out again through a series of clerks, it may be a month or more before . . . Anyway, hopefully I can secure the major's permission for us to visit him.'

'I'm not sure I want to, Mr Monsarrat.'

'Yet I had trouble persuading you to leave the gaol, to leave him in the place where you were.'

'Now that it's done, though . . . It might be better to leave him where he is, on the doorstep of the next world.'

'But it seemed to me as though you wanted to forgive him.'

'Forgive him? Not a bit of it. I curse him for Honora's death. And I am angry at him for laying claim to some of the love that should have gone to Padraig. Still, that doesn't mean that I take any delight in what's about to happen to him. I desperately wanted to save him. But he is close enough to dead now that any communion with the living might make his passing harder.'

She got up then, taking her empty cup and his, putting them back on the shelf without rinsing them. ('God alone knows whether this water has been kept fresh enough.')

'Well, Mr Monsarrat. I don't know how much convincing it took to get him to come forward, and I don't want to know, but it seems that I owe you my life. For now, though, I'm bone weary and shall go to my bed, if somebody hasn't left that in a mess as well. I'll be back early, though, long before you. I know the major wants you by seven. See that you come by here first. I have reason to think that tea might be the only thing which will carry you through the days ahead.'

Chapter 29

Mrs Mulrooney was indeed in the kitchen and well into breakfast preparations by the time Monsarrat arrived.

She rarely gave him food, and he never asked. They both knew there might be a punishment attached to her doing so, as Monsarrat's food was supposed to come solely from the commissariat, together with whatever he was able to convince to grow in his garden. This morning, though, she placed a bowl of porridge in front of him, with a dollop of honey slowly burrowing into its surface.

'I won't hear no from you, Mr Monsarrat. The commandant owes me a favour, he said as much himself last night. You are far too thin, and I know you can't have eaten – the cookhouse would have been well closed by the time you made your way to your hut. So get this into you, and shut up about it.'

Monsarrat, not having opened his mouth to begin with, was more than happy to follow orders.

He had never understood it when people said, after a meal, that they felt like themselves again. He would have been quite delighted with a holiday from feeling like himself. But with the porridge warming him, he had a sense of what they meant. He knew he was far more able, now, for the duties of the day than he would have been without it.

Before he left the kitchen to head to his workroom, he said, 'Would you like me to seek permission for us to visit Slattery? Or are you still resolved not to?'

'I don't know, Mr Monsarrat. I really don't. But why don't you go ahead and seek permission? And we'll see.'

While he had been eating, Mrs Mulrooney had been putting together a tray of breakfast things for the major. 'He was up almost as early as I was,' she said. 'He will breakfast in his study, he says. He has no desire to do so in the dining room.'

As she was making the preparations, Monsarrat allowed himself to believe, for an instant, that she was doing so for a young woman who was about to go hunting, or to drag her husband off for wild rides along the river. And that soon she would be getting down an extra cup in expectation of a visit from a young soldier.

When she bent to pick up the tray, however, he gently nudged her aside and lifted it himself. She rolled her eyes at him, but didn't seem to have sufficient energy to protest – a fact which worried him. Instead she went to the door, and opened it for him. 'You and I are going to the same place, this morning, Mr Monsarrat,' she said. 'So you'd best be quick. And careful. If you spill one drop of tea, I'll take it out of your hide.'

They made their way across the courtyard together and around the side of the house, Mrs Mulrooney opening the outer door and then the major's study door, Monsarrat gingerly placing the tray in front of the man himself, who looked as though he had slept poorly.

'Thank you, Mrs Mulrooney,' the major said. She dipped slightly, turned and left.

'Now, Monsarrat,' he said. 'Please come and sit. We have a lot to do.'

Monsarrat did as he was told, fetching his writing things. When he returned, the major was allowing his tea and his breakfast to go cold. Monsarrat decided he would not inform on the man to Mrs Mulrooney.

'Let's get it out of the way, shall we?' said the major, and Monsarrat was in no doubt about the task to which he was referring. He began to dictate:

Sir,

Since my letter regarding the culpable party in the death of my wife, new information has come to me with which I have the honour to acquaint you, and I seek instruction on how to proceed.

As I had previously written, it seemed likely that the perpetrator was the ticket-of-leave woman who serves as housekeeper at Government House, as she was the only one with clear opportunity to administer the poison which took my wife's life.

Now, however, Private Fergal Slattery of my own Third Regiment has come forward, claiming he was responsible for the murder, prompted by my wife's family's involvement in the destitution of his own family. On current indications, judging by what he has already confessed, there seems little doubt that his confession is genuine.

I will of course be seeking to verify the statements he has made to me, and in my capacity as justice of the peace and magistrate I intend to convene a coroner's inquest of seven free persons of good character to obtain depositions from all of those whose information has bearing on the matter, together with a written confession from Private Slattery. I will forward these at the earliest opportunity.

The major had been staring at the ceiling as he dictated. Now he lowered his head and looked at his clerk. 'I must ask you, Monsarrat, to steel yourself for what I am about to dictate. You will not like it, though I believe it justified and necessary.' He raised his head again.

Given the most unusual and appalling nature of the crime, it is my belief that for the King's justice to be served, as well as natural justice, Private Slattery should be executed here, at Port Macquarie, where his crime was committed, and I commit this course of action for the consideration of His Excellency the Governor. The murder wronged not only my wife and myself but the entirety of this settlement, which my wife dedicated her time to improving. I further believe Private Slattery's execution here, in public, will serve as a salutary lesson both to the refractory prisoners and to the regiment, illustrating as it does that the King's justice falls equally on the free and the bonded.

In addition, should Private Slattery plead not guilty – an event which I consider close to impossible – I would have difficulty in sparing either myself or others who would be required to testify at a trial for such a period of time as would be necessary for him to be tried in Sydney.

To that end, may I request the attendance of a judge here at Port Macquarie, to hear the private's plea and pass sentence upon him. In the unlikely event he pleads not guilty, such witnesses as the court requires can be immediately called without disrupting the management of this settlement.

I am holding Private Slattery in the gaol while I await the honour of your instructions, and in the meantime will proceed with all haste in regard to the coroner's inquiry.

I remain, sir, your obedient servant . . .

'Monsarrat, you know the rest.'

Monsarrat did indeed, although he had never thought he would be appending those words to such a document.

The major seemed relieved to have got this particular missive out of the way. He turned, then, to the more mundane business of the colony – the receipts and returns which demonstrated to the government in Sydney that all was in good order, or as good an order as one could possibly have when the majority of the population had transgressed not once but twice.

Given the recent complaints by the Reverend Ainslie to the Colonial Secretary, he was particularly insistent that all the formalities and administrative necessities be observed – which, on Monsarrat's watch, they always were, anyway. He also asked Monsarrat to arrange for a sample of sugar and rum from the plantation to be sent, to demonstrate the quality of the produce, together with a few sawn planks of cedar and rosewood, and a letter outlining how these could be used, given their quality, to add to the settlement's coffers.

Finally, though, he ran out of letters and reports to dictate. The shift in his momentum seemed to cost him. Monsarrat noted the change.

'Perhaps I should ask Diamond to take on the administrative duties for a few days,' Major Shelborne mused.

This alarmed Monsarrat. He hadn't seen the captain since their confrontation, but while Mrs Mulrooney was no longer in danger, Monsarrat did not want to remind the captain of his own existence, much less the accusation of murder which had turned out to be unfounded. But he restricted himself to saying, 'As you wish, sir, of course. I must say, though, that the settlement has missed you. But given the heaviness of your loss, no one would quibble should you need some quiet reflection.'

The major sighed. 'You're right, Monsarrat. I have been away too long.'

'I will make a fair copy of everything you've dictated to me, sir. I wonder, though, whether I might ask you a great favour.'

The major sounded weary when he responded. 'Yes, Monsarrat, what is it?'

'I fear Mrs Mulrooney may have suffered somewhat from her incarceration, possibly more than she is admitting to. Would it meet with your approval if I asked Dr Gonville to see her? Simply to look at her and make sure nothing is amiss.'

'Very well then, Monsarrat. Probably a good idea. And before you ask – you and she may visit Slattery, if it is your wish. Do not tell me what you decide to do on the matter, though. I do not want to think less of you.'

෧෨

With the letters and reports transcribed in the fairest copperplate ever to have graced Port Macquarie, Monsarrat asked the major if there was further need of his services. Receiving an answer in the negative, he set off on the familiar walk to the hospital.

Monsarrat's concern for Mrs Mulrooney's health was genuine, but he had another reason for seeking the doctor out. Diamond could not be allowed to administer cruel floggings with impunity, nor to have disturbed the peace of what had turned out to be the last months of Honora's life with his unwanted attentions. If the King's justice was to break Slattery's neck, the least it could do was to also transfer Diamond as far away from Monsarrat as possible.

So Monsarrat went to find Gonville. He came upon the surgeon and Donald engaged in their normal activities – a sawyer had been a little careless with the tool of his trade, and was biting down on a stick while Gonville stitched together a gash in his arm. Another man lay in a bed nearby, his foot a swollen, purple monstrosity. Monsarrat had seen the like before – probably the man had been unwise enough to have his foot in a place where a horse had wanted to step, or a wheel to run.

Gonville looked up from his stitching. 'Wait for me, Monsarrat, if you please,' he said, in a tone which suggested he had been expecting the visit.

When the sawyer's arm had been stitched up with as much finesse as possible, the doctor gestured Monsarrat towards his desk behind its partition. 'Well, a lot has come to pass since you and I last spoke, Monsarrat.'

'You've heard about Slattery, I take it, doctor.'

'Yes, and I dare say by now so has everyone else. How is Mrs Mulrooney taking it?'

'It is a double loss for her, you know. And she had to suffer the ignominy, for a few days, of being thought responsible for the death of a woman she held in high esteem. In fact, it is on her behalf I have come. I fear she may soon work herself into a state of exhaustion, and I doubt she ate much during her stay in prison. I have asked the major for permission to request that you examine her – whether she will stand for it or not – just to ensure she is in full health, or as full as possible under the circumstances.'

'Very well then. And you and I have some other business to discuss, Monsarrat. Let's save it for the walk, though, shall we? A partition does not provide sufficient privacy.'

As they set out, Gonville said, 'We are making a habit of this, Monsarrat. Conferences on foot.'

'Necessary, I suppose, while the captain's around.'

'Yes, the very man I wanted to discuss. Why has there been no discipline, no chastisement for his behaviour with Dory?'

'It seems hard to believe in a place like this, where gossip flows like water, but nobody has told the major,' said Monsarrat. 'Certainly not Diamond – as you suspected, he removed the report on the event. I have been on the brink of it, several times, but have not wanted to broach it with someone so recently bereaved. I suppose, if I am honest, I also did not want to create problems when Mrs Mulrooney's fate was so uncertain. But she is safe now, and the settlement appears to be returning to some variety of normal. That being said, I do believe it's time that we acquaint the major with Diamond's behaviour.'

'Yes, I agree. I must confess, though, Monsarrat, I had been hoping that you would take care of it. Cowardly though that is.'

'I don't think you a coward, doctor. And I would have been delighted to deal with it. The problem is that I am tainted, I fear, by my friendship with, first, a suspected murderer, and now a confessed one. And I am myself a felon. I believe the major will hear me out. But I also believe it will be far easier for him to act if the information is backed by a voice of authority. Such as yours.'

The doctor sighed. 'Yes, you're probably right. Don't ascribe too much authority to my voice, though, Monsarrat. Diamond still has the major's ear, and the captain has no love for me.'

Monsarrat thought of Diamond's letters to Mrs Shelborne, presumably now ash. He had told no one of them except Mrs Mulrooney. And a lot of his intellectual capacity had been spent, over the past few days, on wondering whether the major would thank him for the revelation.

He was decided, pretty much, on keeping the letters and the contents to himself. Despite his stoicism, the major was no doubt devastated by his wife's death. Monsarrat did not wish to add to his grief by forcing him to imagine her, in her last months, secretly fearful of the attentions of a man he himself had imposed on her.

In any case, Monsarrat didn't think the letters were needed to ensure that Diamond got what he deserved. His flouting of the directive that floggings be limited to fifty lashes, and of the major's precedent of thirty or thirty-five, would be enough to offend both the major's humanity and his sense of administrative propriety, especially when combined with Diamond's falsification of the records.

They reached the kitchen, and with difficulty were able to convince Mrs Mulrooney to submit to a check by the doctor. 'Major's orders,' Gonville said briskly, while Monsarrat fixed Mrs Mulrooney with a look which told her he would most certainly be reporting any breach.

Mrs Mulrooney, proclaimed the doctor, was in reasonable enough health given her recent trials, although a little thinner than he would like. The doctor also remarked on the pallor Monsarrat had noticed in recent weeks. Gonville recommended that she be given additional rations of beef until her health was fully restored. 'And see that you eat it, too, dear lady,' he said. 'I will be checking with Monsarrat, and I may also interview the settlement rats to see whether their pickings have improved, so don't think of casting it aside.'

Mrs Mulrooney fixed an expression of subservient attention on her face, and nodded. I will most certainly have to keep an eye on her, thought Monsarrat, even if I have to tip the food down her gullet myself.

Their business in the kitchen having been concluded with a cup of tea, Monsarrat and the doctor stood outside in the paved courtyard at the back of the house.

'I wonder,' said Gonville, 'whether we should produce another version of that document which Diamond confiscated from you. It might add weight to what might seem to the major outlandish accusations.'

Monsarrat knew he could not allow the doctor to delay, to lose heart. He understood the man's aversion to bearing such news, but he knew also that falsehoods which were allowed to stand gradually took on the patina of truth.

'I would be more than happy to write another report, without troubling you for dictation,' said Monsarrat. 'I well remember the contents of the old one. But I urge you, let us get this business with the major done first; we may then take care of the administrative details at our leisure.'

The doctor pressed his lips together and nodded his assent.

~~~~~

Monsarrat's request for an audience with the commandant was granted immediately, and he stood in the corner of the study while Gonville sat opposite Shelborne and described Dory's flogging, together with the flogging which had been averted after Diamond had bent his amorous attentions on the daughter of a convict.

The major scratched notes as he listened, betraying neither surprise nor anger. He thanked the doctor for bringing the information to him, 'although I would have been grateful had you done so sooner,' and dismissed him.

He looked up at Monsarrat. 'Presumably you were there, Monsarrat.'

'Yes, major. The business unfolded as the doctor has described.'

'And when I was dictating the report to the Colonial Secretary, in which I said William Dory had received thirty lashes, you knew this to be false.'

'Forgive me, major. I did not wish to add to your troubles.'

'So you chose instead to allow me to make a fool's report to the Colonial Secretary. Let me assure you, Monsarrat, my stocks in Sydney are not as high as you might suppose, especially given recent activities by our chaplain. As any mitigation of your sentence would come on recommendation from me, this fact should concern you.'

This did indeed concern Monsarrat. To stay for too long in this place, and with Mrs Mulrooney so diminished by her grief over Mrs Shelborne and young Slattery, was a prospect he dreaded.

'Why did the man not try to stop him? Why did he not step in at thirty lashes, let alone a hundred?'

'You may not wish to hear the name spoken, major, but it was Slattery who ultimately stopped him, and paid with a stint in the guardhouse.'

The major stood, and went to the window. 'Well, Monsarrat. As you clearly know far more about this business than me, I will leave you to draft an appropriate letter to the Colonial Secretary. Perhaps you can succeed where I would most certainly fail, in putting a decent light on the news that while one murderer has been exchanged for another, ninety lashes have been retrospectively added to a dead man's sentence. I wish you luck with it. What I do not wish is to see you again for the rest of the day.'

Monsarrat nodded and withdrew to his workroom, feeling suddenly leaden. If his hopes of a ticket of leave rested on a man with little influence, and even less liking for Monsarrat at the moment, he would very possibly be drafting dispatches to Sydney until he was so old he no longer had any use for freedom.

∽∾

The major's attitude to Monsarrat remained cool over the following fortnight. The clerk produced a report for the Colonial Secretary on the flogging of Dory, in which he put the discrepancy in the previous report down to 'an administrative oversight during my absence'. The major requested that Diamond be transferred to another regiment, his rank reduced to lieutenant, and that he be 'given no position of absolute authority in the colony, due to his clear disregard for established precedent'.

Monsarrat wasn't privy to any conversations the pair might have had, but he would not have been surprised to see Diamond walking around the colony with a split lip to match Slattery's. He only saw the captain – now the lieutenant – once more, as Diamond was boarding the *Sally*. Officially, it was put about that he was accompanying a shipment of rum and wood to Sydney, but no one expected him to return.

Monsarrat was standing in the shadow of the boatshed as Diamond approached the ship. He wanted to be entirely sure the captain had left.

When Diamond noticed him, he grinned. 'Goodbye, Monsarrat,' he called. 'I do hope we meet again.'

Monsarrat knew the grin would haunt him far more than any scowl would have, and hoped from now on to see it only in his nightmares.

Chapter 30

Monsarrat still made his way to the kitchen early each day to drink tea with Mrs Mulrooney, both of them pretending not to notice how much quieter their mornings had become.

One morning, he was waylaid by a voice from the direction of the river. 'You!' it said.

If Monsarrat had not been alone, he would have wondered if the voice had been addressing him. But when he saw the speaker, he realised that the man had not been saying 'you' but his name, Hugh. It was a name he shared with the man who had hailed him.

Kiernan, the discoverer of the river to the north (or at least the first one to tell the major about it), stood near a canoe which Monsarrat assumed was of his own making, a long panel of stiff bark tied at the sides to form a boat. Monsarrat had seen much finer handiwork from the Birpai – Kiernan must still have much to learn of their ways.

'Good morning,' he said, feeling surprisingly little rancour, for all of the fretting he had done over Kiernan's impending conditional pardon. 'I haven't seen you here since you absconded.'

Kiernan smiled, displaying more missing teeth than Monsarrat had remembered. Although he was roughly of an age with Monsarrat, his face was leathery and brown, with deep gouges and black spots, and a particularly large and nasty-looking brown mole on his neck. His straggling russet beard, in which flecks of white were starting to appear, bore no evidence of scissors and trailed off like a vine when it reached the middle of his chest. He wore slop clothing – without the broad arrow, so presumably he had been given it by a native who in turn had received it from the major – which, despite its toughness, was beginning to wear thin in places.

'No, Hugh, well, you wouldn't have, would you? I'm hardly going to wander in here and offer myself up to the likes of Diamond for recapture, much as he would enjoy it.'

'Well, Kiernan, you'll be pleased to know that Diamond is no longer amongst us. Don't look shocked – he's still on this side of the grave, but not on this side of the river. He's off to Sydney, as a lieutenant, and not expected to return. He administered a rather vicious flogging, you see. Robbed the settlement of a strong young pair of shoulders.'

'Bastard. I never understood why our major put up with him. And in fact, it is to see the major, or rather you, that I've come. I understand that he wrote to the Colonial Secretary recommending a conditional pardon for me?'

'He did indeed. We've not had a reply yet, but I'm sure nobody is going to arrest you.' He decided not to let Kiernan know that the major felt his recommendations might not carry much weight in Sydney.

Instead, he said, 'I imagine you'll be off to Sydney, then. You won't want to be around here when you're free, surely?' 'And why on earth would I not want to hang around here, Monsarrat? I grew up in Cheapside sleeping ten to a room. Here I have more land to roam across than the King himself. What could I hope to do in Sydney – labouring? Might bring me enough to get a bedroll in some flophouse.'

'You're staying, then? With the natives?'

'Why wouldn't I? They are a fair people, Monsarrat, fairer than us by a long shot. Their justice is consistent, and it's quick – once it's been administered, the debt is considered paid. They

don't force each other to work their youth away in chains. And –
now this will sound fanciful, and as you know I'm not a fanciful
man – I'd never seen the land as something which is alive, not
until I absconded. But living with them these years, it's hard not
to. There's also a matter of a few native babes with redder hair
and paler skin than most.' He grinned broadly, so that the black-
ening roots of his remaining teeth were clearly visible, as though
expecting Monsarrat to congratulate him on attaining the status
of father.

Monsarrat found himself envying the man on so many levels –
a man of the type he would never have envied at home, in England.
Kiernan had found himself a family, an expansive home and a way
of being which suited him well, and he didn't particularly mind
what European society thought of it, if they thought anything
at all. And most importantly, he was about to be granted unlimited freedom in which to live out his days in the enticing bush
that marched up to the riverbank. The only aspect of Monsarrat's life which was unlimited was the number of letters, reports
and dispatches he had to transcribe.

He found himself, unaccountably, shaking Kiernan's hand,
mildly astonished by the contrast between Kiernan's brown and
callused palm and his own white and soft one. 'Well, good luck
to you,' he said. 'I must confess, I thought the river to the north
was a fabrication, and I was quite looking forward to seeing how
you got yourself out of it once it was discovered to be so. But
I'm glad it wasn't. Someone living here, instead of dying here,
makes a nice change.'

Kiernan gave another gap-toothed smile. 'I wish you the best,
Monsarrat,' he said, 'whatever best means to you. Most of all,
I wish you the freedom to chase after it. Be a good fellow, and
send a message with Bangar or Spring when the paperwork from
Sydney comes through, if you'd be so kind.'

His manner of speaking was not that of someone born in
a tenement, so Monsarrat wondered for a moment if Kiernan
was mocking him. But there seemed to be no mocking in his
eyes. Kiernan was a verbal chameleon, able to match not only

his language but also his accent and mannerisms to whatever audience he wanted to win over.

Monsarrat assured him he would send word, and the man somehow gracefully folded himself into the little canoe, paddling away with the roughly hewn oar, again far less fine in workmanship than the Birpai versions. Monsarrat noticed, as Kiernan was getting in, a few fresh bream lying at the bottom of the boat. Probably being taken back to feed the man's children.

He continued his march to the kitchen. He had never thought to find himself inferior to the likes of Kiernan, and nor had he ever expected to be happy about it.

～～

The building which had, for a time, housed the settlement's few females, and had then been put to the work of containing bushrangers, now had another new use. The bushrangers had been transferred to the gaol, to make room for a panel of inquisitors into Honora Shelborne's murder.

There was the commandant, of course. He was joined by Lieutenant Carleton and a few other Buffs, two sergeants and a corporal. The civil officers were also well represented – the chief engineer, the superintendent of convicts, Simon Spring and the harbourmaster. This brought the number of inquisitors to nine, beyond the seven the major had initially envisaged – Monsarrat supposed he felt that the more men of good standing condemned Slattery, the better.

As each witness swore on a Bible to tell the truth, told their stories, and was questioned, Monsarrat wrote everything down and put their words into depositions for them to sign. He recorded the words of Dr Gonville, Mrs Mulrooney, Edward Donald, and the former plasterers Frogett and Daines. No one recorded Monsarrat's testimony. The major said he trusted him to transcribe a true account for his own signature.

And then before the panel came Fergal Slattery, manacled and in irons. The major would not look at Slattery as he made his statement, nor did he put any questions to the young man, leaving this to the other inquisitors. But Monsarrat knew that getting Slattery's signature at the bottom of the piece of paper confessing his guilt was of paramount importance to the major. This was confirmed when, as soon as Slattery had finished speaking, the major nodded to the soldiers who were guarding him to take him back to the cell, and called an adjournment.

'Monsarrat, please transcribe the evidence of the last witness immediately. I would then like you to return here and read the deposition to us, before taking yourself and three inquisitors to the gaol to obtain the private's signature on the document.'

So Monsarrat went back to his workroom, and in a final service to the young soldier, wrote his confession in the best hand he could apply.

Private Fergal Slattery, being duly sworn.

I am a private in the Third Regiment 'Buffs', under the command of Major Angus Shelborne, Commandant of Port Macquarie, where I have served these past two years.

Since the arrival of the major's wife, I have been aware that members of her family had a hand in the ruin of my own, and a great resentment of the fact quickly settled upon me and blighted my mind.

In May 1825, I was appointed to oversee a plastering crew charged with smoothing the interior walls of the Government House sitting room, and hanging wallpaper thereon.

In my previous employment as a plasterer in Dublin, I had learned that certain shades of green could be deadly poison, and recognised that same green in the paper to be used to decorate the sitting room.

At this time, Major Angus Shelborne departed the settlement, with some others of our regiment, convicts, and a tracker, to search for a river he had been told of.

Knowing he would likely be absent for some weeks, and knowing that Mrs Shelborne drank a type of tea the leaves of which were reserved for her alone, I resolved to use the opportunity to sprinkle on the tea leaves an infusion made of the poisonous pigment in the wallpaper. It was a course of action I had been considering for some time. I had brewed the infusion at a still in the woods, in a valley a few headlands to the south, and tried it on various animals to ensure it was sufficiently palatable and had the required effect.

I have since dismantled this still, cleansed the copper, and sent it out to sea on a strong tide.

To avoid detection, I made sure to apply only a little of the substance at a time to the leaves. However, on being commanded to accompany Captain Michael Diamond on an expedition to inform the major of his wife's failing health, I became concerned that the lady in question might recover in my absence.

To prevent this eventuality, I poured a significant quantity of the infusion into tea I knew was destined for Mrs Shelborne, in the hopes it would hasten her end. These hopes were realised, and the lady died that same day.

In confessing my crime, I wish to state that I was not assisted in its commission by any other person, and was solely responsible for the death of Mrs Shelborne.

As instructed, Monsarrat returned to the inquisitors, read them the note, and trooped with Spring, Carleton and the superintendent of convicts to the gaol, to read it to Fergal Slattery. He heard it calmly, and signed it without complaint.

Monsarrat was also responsible for drafting the other statements and having them signed. In the case of Mrs Mulrooney, who could not read, the major insisted she hear her statement in the presence of the inquisitors, and place an X on the paper beside the words 'Hannah Mulrooney – her mark'.

His final task in regard to the inquest was to take dictation from the major, in the presence of the other inquisitors, on its findings.

The said jurors, being charged to inquire on the part of our Lord the King into when, where and by what manner Honora Belgrave Shelborne came by her death, do swear on their oaths that Private Fergal Slattery of the Third Regiment did wilfully murder the aforementioned, through the administration of poison between the dates of 14 and 29 June 1825, against the peace of our Lord the King, his Crown and Dignity, in witness of which we have herewith appended our hands and seals.

Each of the inquisitors read the document and depositions, and each one signed it, paving as they did so another mile of Fergal Slattery's road to the gallows.

～～～

By happenstance, the *Amity* was backloading with lime at the time the documents were ready for departure. The winter winds, which came from the north-west and were therefore less brutal and more obliging than their south-easterly summer cousins, would probably ensure the depositions reached the Colonial Secretary and Attorney-General well within a week of their departure, Monsarrat thought.

Mrs Mulrooney was now two women – one who loved Fergal like a son, and one who would never forgive Private Slattery. For Fergal, she carried a pot of tea wrapped in a cloth to keep it warm, a few tin mugs – of which she did not approve, but she was unwilling to risk china – clanking in her pockets so that she, Slattery and Meehan, who was usually on duty, might share the tea together.

On more than one occasion, she told Monsarrat, she'd interrupted a game of Three Card Brag. Slattery still always won, and Meehan genially paid the money. As Mrs Mulrooney was leaving one day, he had taken her aside and quietly told her that Slattery was stashing the money, to be given to her on his execution.

It was after this revelation that Monsarrat found her in the kitchen, sitting and staring, a state which he had learned did not bode well.

She related the conversation to Monsarrat, then said, 'I had almost convinced myself, Mr Monsarrat, that this would continue. That this time next year I would still be bringing pots of tea and those awful tin mugs down to the gaol, would still be interrupting card games, would still be hearing young Slattery refer to that cell as his private room. Then that Meehan had to go and mention the execution. And I'd done such a good job of convincing myself, that I had to feel the shock of it all over again.'

She had tried to rise, but Monsarrat stopped her. 'Let's see if I can improve on my last efforts,' he said, pouring boiling water from the kettle into the teapot to warm it. The tea made and pronounced drinkable by Mrs Mulrooney, Monsarrat sat down opposite her.

'I'm not used to having room to sit in this kitchen,' she said. 'There's usually a lummox with his boots on the table. For all my scolding I'd love to see those boots there, and I'd love to be putting together a breakfast tray for a lively young girl. But one's gone, and one's going, and most of what held interest for me here has drained away.'

'You talk as though you're considering leaving the settlement,' said Monsarrat, feeling rising panic. Mrs Mulrooney had an unconditional ticket of leave – she could travel anywhere in New South Wales – so leaving the settlement, which for him was a fantasy, to her was merely a matter of planning.

'Perhaps,' she said. 'Would you be good enough to help me with a letter to Padraig? It might be that the station he is attached to has need of a housekeeper, or a cook or some such. It would be good to be with him again.'

Monsarrat knew that their friendship could not keep her here if the prospect of living again with her son was calling her away. But he felt desperately bereft at the thought of her departure, as unplanned as it yet was. Mrs Mulrooney was able to make things move very quickly when she set her mind to them.

He hid his depression, though, in solicitousness. 'Of course, dear lady. You let me know what you would like to say, and I'll work something up and read it to you.'

'Thank you, Mr Monsarrat. You're a good man.' She paused. 'How much longer, do you think?'

Monsarrat did not need to ask what she was referring to. Barring foul weather, of which there had been none, the *Amity* would have reached Sydney by now. If the Colonial Secretary was disposed to deal with the matter quickly, it was not inconceivable that a reply was sailing up the coast towards them.

But her question echoed one he had been asking himself increasingly of late. How much longer before the ticket of leave which so effortlessly settled itself into the pockets of other men would do him the same honour?

He had the same answer to both.

'I don't know,' he said. 'I just don't know.'

⁓ ᴄ⃥ᴐ ⁓

The major's attitude towards Monsarrat had softened a little. His was a nature which couldn't share close quarters with someone he didn't like, and he was too honest a man to conceal that liking, even if he was still very annoyed with his clerk.

He had taken, though, to asking Monsarrat to visit Spring at the commissariat stores at the end of each day, with a request for Spring to unlock the back room, where the spirits and wines were kept. Monsarrat would have instructions to bring this wine or that, or sometimes rum, back to the study and leave it with the major.

Monsarrat did not know whether the major was in the habit of drinking on a regular basis – he was not in a position to observe him at all times, and didn't know what went on in the officers' mess. But he had certainly never seen the man drink in his study, which he viewed as a place of work and therefore sacrosanct.

To his even greater surprise, one night the major invited Monsarrat to join him, pouring him a small measure of rum in a tin cup. Had it not been for that drunken night ten years ago, Monsarrat might yet have got away from Exeter before he was arrested. He might now be living out his days, as a schoolmaster perhaps, under an assumed name in some picturesque corner of England, with a pretty wife and intelligent, well-behaved children. Or his flight might have influenced the judge at his assizes, tipping the balance against the commutation of his sentence from death to life.

Either way, Monsarrat wasn't much of a drinker. But refusing the major's offer, particularly in the man's present unstable state, might be seen as an insult, so he accepted the cup with thanks, and took the seat the major gestured him to.

'I am sorry if I was a little harsh, Monsarrat, over the matter of Diamond,' he said.

Well, this is a day of surprises, thought Monsarrat. He wondered if this was the first instance in the colony's history of an apology from a commandant to a convict.

Nevertheless, he said, 'There is no apology necessary, sir. You were right. I should have acquainted you with the facts as soon as I knew you were not in possession of them.'

'Perhaps,' said the major, 'but there were others in positions of greater authority who could also have done that, and failed to.'

The major took a long draught of rum and put down his cup. 'It is my hope that we have an answer shortly from the Colonial Secretary regarding the fate of the Irishman, as well as the confirmation of the tickets of leave and pardons I recommended. Busy day tomorrow, Monsarrat. Returns due soon. But there is one piece of business I would rather not wait until morning. If you are not yet addled by rum,' this said with a small smile, as the major had noted the tiny sips Monsarrat was taking, 'I would appreciate your assistance in the formulation of a dispatch I would like to send to Sydney at the earliest opportunity.'

'Of course, sir,' said Monsarrat, moving into his workroom to collect his writing implements. Returning, he surreptitiously moved his cup out of the way – accidentally spilling it on the admittedly less than fine parchment would do nothing to help the major's mood, particularly when he arrived at his study with a sore head the next morning to find the place still smelling of rum.

The major leaned back in his chair – another first as far as Monsarrat was concerned, who was used to seeing him sitting equally erect in a saddle and at a desk, his red coat immaculate.

'Sir,' he began. 'In addition to the recommendations I have made of late regarding tickets of leave and conditional pardons for those who assisted me in locating the new river, I have the honour to make another recommendation.'

Who's the lucky bastard this time? thought Monsarrat.

'What's your middle name again, Hugh?' said the major, who had never before addressed Monsarrat by his first name.

'Llewellyn, sir,' said Monsarrat, wondering if this was a harbinger of hope, or whether he was writing his own recommendation for an extended sentence.

'And your date of birth?'

'Twenty-sixth of January 1790,' said Monsarrat.

The major grinned, in a somewhat lopsided fashion. 'I always suspected I was younger than you. You beat me into the world by a full year and a half, Monsarrat. Make sure all of your personal details accompany this letter on the next ship. Now . . . ah, yes.'

The major resumed the voice he customarily used for dictation, clear but expressionless.

I have previously had the honour to acquaint you with the circumstances surrounding the arrest of Private Fergal Slattery for the murder of my wife, and the previous suspicion which had fallen on my housekeeper. To my regret, great injustice was very nearly done to the aforementioned housekeeper, who attained her ticket of leave some eighteen years ago, and who has been of good character since.

The wrongful conviction of this woman was only avoided through the application of considerable skill, intellect and character on the part of my clerk, Hugh Llewellyn Monsarrat, who was able to deduce the identity of the real perpetrator, and convince him to turn himself in to me.

The aforementioned clerk has himself been of good character during his time at Port Macquarie, and has applied himself to his duties industriously.

In recognition of this, and of the most significant service he performed in ensuring Private Slattery confessed to his crime, it gives me pleasure to recommend him for a ticket of leave.

Monsarrat's astonishment fought his eagerness to capture every word Major Shelborne said before the relaxing effect of the rum wore off.

The major leaned back. 'I rarely get to make people happy, you know,' he said. 'I expect His Majesty generally wishes me to do quite the reverse. So I'm delighted to be able to do this for you, Monsarrat, despite the fact that I'll be robbing myself of an excellent clerk. Maybe you could train up one of the boys from Rolland's Plains.'

And when Monsarrat still didn't reply, he went on, 'This is a course of action I have been considering for some days. Do not fear that I will deny all knowledge of it tomorrow.'

Monsarrat recovered his voice. 'I . . . Thank you, sir, I cannot tell you how overjoyed I am at this prospect. And you can be assured I will transcribe it with alacrity.'

The major smiled at this. 'I've always appreciated your sense of humour, Monsarrat, however infrequently you let it off its leash. What passes for humour amongst some of my officers would make a whore blush.'

Monsarrat had little doubt of it.

'Now, this rum is urging me to my bed – I'm not used to it, you see; I have no idea how some of them stay up all night pouring it down their throats. Goodnight to you, Monsarrat, and if the secretary accepts my recommendation I look forward to the day when you walk into this office a free man.'

'Thank you, sir. I am forever in your debt.'

'Don't mention it,' said the major.

As he stood, a little shakily, Monsarrat asked, 'Sir, may I know what police district my ticket of leave will restrict me to?'

'Is there a particular district you'd like to be restricted to?'

Monsarrat didn't know how to respond to this.

'Obviously my own sense of humour doesn't benefit from rum. What I intended to say, Monsarrat, is that you will not be restricted to any region. Your ticket of leave will be unconditional. Now take that thought to bed with you, and sleep well.'

Chapter 31

Monsarrat told no one about the major's letter. Speaking about it without it being official felt somehow wrong, as though he would be tempting a reversal of fortune. He kept the news even from Mrs Mulrooney – seeing her excitement at his impending freedom, and then seeing it dashed should the request not be approved, would be too much to bear.

Nevertheless, he personally escorted the letter – after he had made a fair copy and had it signed by a somewhat bleary major the next day – on to the *Sally* when she arrived three days later, having disgorged Captain Diamond, the rum, cedar and rosewood, and the commandant's earlier letters.

Given that one of those letters contained a less than complimentary account of Captain Diamond's behaviour, Monsarrat had wondered how conscientious he had been in delivering them to Sydney. But a soldier is a soldier, and Diamond had done what his commanding officer had asked of him. He must've handed the letters personally to the Colonial Secretary's office, for the *Sally* bore back with her his reply.

Monsarrat knew the mate of the *Sally*, a man called Tyrell who had also been mate on Monsarrat's original journey to Port Macquarie. During the three days at sea, Monsarrat had helped

Tyrell write a letter to his wife, and when the two had subsequently met at the docks, they had greeted each other amicably enough. He now entrusted the crucial letter to Tyrell's hands.

'I will be forever in your debt, Mr Tyrell, if you could see this one delivered safely into the hands of one of the Colonial Secretary's clerks.'

'Well then, I may have a few more letters that need writing, if you are able to assist me while we're backloading,' said Tyrell, smiling.

So as the mate was supervising the backloading of the vessel, he gave Monsarrat a few sentiments which he hoped to convey to his wife, who was a convict in Van Diemen's Land, and a few more for his brother back in Portsmouth. He also gave Monsarrat the respective addresses. 'I trust you to put this into pretty words, Mr Monsarrat. Old *Sally* won't be by again for a little while, but I believe there is a brig coming in a few weeks – if I could impose on you to put them with the other mail on that, I'd be most grateful.'

Monsarrat assured him it would be done, and Tyrell gave equal assurance that the major's recommendation for the ticket of leave – though he didn't know that was what it was – would reach Sydney with all due speed.

Monsarrat watched the letter as it disappeared into Tyrell's pocket. He was surprised no one else could see it glowing and feel the heat emanating from it. Tyrell handed Monsarrat the packet from the Colonial Secretary, and left to bed down for the night, hoping to catch a favourable tide early the next morning.

Monsarrat considered breaking the seals and reading the reply from the Colonial Secretary to the letter asking for instructions on Slattery's fate. But he quickly talked himself out of it – he was not so impulsive as to risk incurring the major's wrath at this point, and recent events had shocked shadow Monsarrat into silence. In any case, he would know their contents soon enough.

He walked through his workroom and knocked on the major's door, receiving a muffled instruction to enter.

Major Shelborne gestured to a seat as he opened the packet. It would seem, Monsarrat thought, that the major already viewed him as a free man, as previously he was expected to stand silently while the major read.

The major's mouth slowly expanded into a smile. 'Well, Monsarrat. It seems my standing may be better than I had thought. The Colonial Secretary is delighted at the discovery of New River, as we are currently calling it – I think he would like the honour of naming it himself – and will send a surveying team. We will of course provide them all assistance. I will, anyway. You may not be here.'

He shuffled through the other correspondence. 'Ah, it seems my recommendations for the tickets of leave and conditional pardons for those who accompanied me on the expedition have been approved. Monsarrat, can you make the necessary administrative arrangements? I wonder how we let Kiernan know.'

'Allow me to take care of that for you, major. I have a shrewd idea as to how he can be reached.'

'Very good.'

But on the last page, the major's smile vanished. 'As Slattery has confessed, and given the nature of his crime, the Colonial Secretary has acceded to my request to send a judge to hear his plea and pass sentence, assuming the documents from the inquest are in order, which they are.'

The major set down the bundle. Looking up, he said to Monsarrat, 'Do you still bear any affection for Slattery?'

'Not for the man who committed the crime, sir. But for the boy he was, yes, I confess I do.'

'It is with regret, then, that I have to ask you to carry out a task for me, one that I fear you may find distressing,' said the major. 'I would like you please to ask the chief engineer to procure sufficient wood for the building of a gallows.'

⁓

Everything must indeed have been in order, as a few weeks later the brig *Fame* brought with it Justice Curtis, together with his clerk.

Monsarrat saw little of the judge, who stayed at Government House during his few nights there, the major having retired to the barracks – he did not wish to ask the judge to sleep in the room of the person whose murderer he was to sentence, and of course the major had no wish to sleep there himself, so ceded his room to the judge.

The Female Factory was again pressed into service as a courtroom, with Monsarrat given the task of arranging the necessities under the direction of the judge's clerk, a fellow named Turner.

The long table at which the inquisitors had sat, scene of numerous convict meals, would serve as a bench, with Turner to be installed at one end. If the man felt the lack of the wood panelling and coat of arms he was used to in Sydney's new Supreme Court, he gave no indication, instead thanking Monsarrat for his efforts in procuring a large quantity of paper and more than enough ink.

Other long benches were placed against the wall in the long main room of the factory. Here the major and other inquisitors would sit, present should the judge have any need of them. Monsarrat stood at the back corner of the room, ready on a nod from the major or Turner to fetch anything which needed fetching.

If the judge and Turner had to live without wood panelling, they also had to do without a dock. Instead Slattery, when brought in, stood in the centre of the room, in front of the makeshift bench, his eyes fixed on a point somewhere over the judge's right shoulder.

Turner placed a Bible under Slattery's bound hands, on which he swore. The judge, without looking up from his notes, informed Slattery he was hereby charged with the wilful murder of Honora Belgrave Shelborne, and asked him to plead.

'I plead guilty, Your Honour,' Slattery said. His eyes were still unfocused, his voice reedier than Monsarrat had ever heard it. He seemed already a little incorporeal, as though the sentence which would shortly be pronounced was already taking effect.

At his plea, the judge did look up. 'I caution you against entertaining any hopes of mercy should you maintain your guilt. Given the nature of your crime, no mercy is possible. You may retire your plea and withdraw your confession, and face a trial.'

'No, thank you, Your Honour,' said Slattery in the small voice of a chastened child. 'My plea stands. I am guilty in the eyes of the British law, and perhaps even in the eyes of God, but I am confident that he understands things more broadly than a British court might.'

The judge nodded. He withdrew from a box on the table a square of black cloth, which he rested on top of his wig. 'Fergal Slattery, you will be taken hence to the prison in which you were last confined and from there to a place of execution at a time to be determined, where you will be hanged by the neck until you are dead, and may the Lord have mercy upon your soul.'

Slattery was escorted back to his cell, and the judge retired to Government House to dine with the major before the *Fame* sailed back with him to Sydney the following morning. It fell to Mrs Mulrooney to prepare the joint of beef with vegetables which the two men, and a handful of senior military and civil officers, ate in a house devoid of any female presence.

~~~~~

The genial Meehan had become used to dealing with the private's visitors, and waved Monsarrat through the next morning as though he were entering a shop in Sydney. He found Slattery sitting with Father Hanley, engaged in quiet conversation. The two looked up at Monsarrat. The priest stood.

'Ah, Mr Monsarrat, a delight as usual,' he said with the same flourish he had used in the kitchen weeks ago. 'Fergal and I were just discussing some of the practicalities now.'

Monsarrat wondered what practicalities they could possibly have to discuss. The only action Slattery was required to take was to sit quietly and count his heartbeats until they ran out.

'The Father is just ensuring my paperwork's in order for my next journey,' said Slattery. 'I understand the bureaucracy up there is difficult, far more so than any penal colony. I suppose they need it, to administer all those saints. Nevertheless, I want to make sure I have all the appropriate documents. I can't pop back and get anything I may have forgotten.'

The priest smiled, a little sadly. 'Well, Fergal, that's not exactly how I would have put it, but I suppose the intent is basically the

331

same. You will be giving me an extra decade of the rosary for that blasphemy, by the way, won't you, my boy?'

The young man nodded and held up a set of wooden beads. Monsarrat recognised them – they belonged to Mrs Mulrooney.

Father Hanley, Monsarrat knew, would be given unfettered access to Slattery in the lead-up to his execution. The fact that he was here now indicated that he, and Slattery, had some idea that the time was approaching.

'I heard they're sending a hangman, make sure the job's done right,' said Slattery calmly. 'When do you think he'll be here?'

An executioner, the major had told Monsarrat, would be sent from Sydney as soon as word was received that a sentence of death had been passed.

'I'm not sure, but I'm under the impression that he'll be coming at the earliest opportunity. The *Mermaid*'s back in a few weeks; he may be on that.'

'And you'll make sure they build that gallows properly, won't you, Monsarrat? I don't want to slip before I'm supposed to.' Slattery sounded slightly nervous. 'And for the love of God, make sure that the noose is capable of tightening. I saw a hanging once in Ireland where the noose hadn't been made properly, and the poor bastard took a long time to die, slowly choking as he twisted there. I'd as soon avoid that, if you don't mind.'

Monsarrat's throat tightened in sympathy. No one who had spent time in the colony could have failed to witness an execution, and Monsarrat had seen a few: as a convict he was required to watch others receive their punishment. None of them had been botched – but even the most expertly managed hanging still ended with a dead man at the end of a rope.

He assured Slattery he would do everything in his power to make sure things were quick. He had no wish to see the laughing boy strangled alongside the murderous man. He also gave the news to Mrs Mulrooney, as she bustled about the kitchen the next morning with breakfast for the judge, who would leave that day. When she had served the men last night, they had not mentioned the outcome of the day's events, and she hadn't inquired, fearful of the answer.

She paused in her preparations for a moment. She had her back to him, so he could not see whether the news had called forth any tears. But her voice was calm when she said, 'Thank you for letting me know, Mr Monsarrat.'

He knew, though, that she visited the gaol every day with the pot of tea. She, Slattery and the Father often sat together, and she had taken to adding another tin cup to the collection she brought to the gaol with her.

She had also, through Monsarrat, asked the major if she could prepare Slattery's final meal, whenever that was to occur, and the major had agreed with a brief nod.

❧

Despite the fact that he was bonded – still – Monsarrat had always seen his workroom as his own personal kingdom. Things were where they were for a reason. He would have taken it very unkindly had anybody tried to rearrange them. Until this day, nobody had.

But now one of the convict clerks from the agricultural station at Rolland's Plains was here. He had been waiting when Monsarrat arrived at the workroom early one morning. The door to the study was closed, the major out on some business or other. The fellow, a thin young man with a receding chin which seemed to be on the same longitude as his Adam's apple, stood to attention when he saw Monsarrat.

'Good morning, Mr Monsarrat,' he said.

'Good morning, Ellis,' said Monsarrat, remembering just in time that this was the man's name. He probably could have identified Ellis's handwriting out of a thousand documents, but had rarely met him face to face.

He pointedly moved around the man, and unlocked the door.

Following him, Ellis seemed a little uncomfortable. 'I take it the major didn't inform you I would be here, then,' he said.

Monsarrat very deliberately got a sheet of paper and laid it on the blotter, taking great pains to ensure it was completely straight. He then slowly retrieved one of his pens and dipped it

333

in the inkwell, before forming words of exquisite neatness. He intended to give Ellis the impression that he was extremely busy, but in truth he had no transcribing awaiting him, so he wrote the opening greeting of a letter to the Colonial Secretary – he would no doubt have to do one at some point soon, so he might as well get a start.

After he'd written a few words, he said, without looking up, 'No, Ellis, he did not.'

'Oh. You're to train me, you see.'

'Train you?'

'Yes,' said Ellis, shifting from foot to foot. Monsarrat was dimly aware that he held a somewhat legendary status amongst the other clerks in the settlement, scattered as they were. His close relationship with the major, his reputation for intellectual rigour and his copperplate script saw to it.

Monsarrat was not finding toying with Ellis as satisfying as he had hoped. There was only one seat in his workroom, so he couldn't offer another. Instead he stood, and leaned against his desk, so that they were on a more equal footing. 'Train you for what exactly, Ellis? You seem to me to be a perfectly competent clerk as it is.'

Ellis, a small-time counterfeiter from Essex who had been caught out after curfew while in Sydney, smiled at the compliment. 'Yes, I flatter myself that I am. But there's a difference between clerking somewhere like Rolland's Plains and here in the centre of it all, in the commandant's office.'

Monsarrat was slightly amused by Ellis's description of Port Macquarie as 'the centre of it all'. He had trouble imagining somewhere less central. Nevertheless, he smiled at the boy. 'Indeed there is.'

'So I was told you are to be leaving soon, and the major wished me to have sufficient time with you to get to know his preferences, how to organise matters, that sort of thing.'

Further evidence, thought Monsarrat, that the major expected his recommendation for a ticket of leave for Monsarrat to be granted. And also evidence that it was now becoming common knowledge.

He'd better let Mrs Mulrooney know before she found out elsewhere – he would be deprived of tea for a long time otherwise.

'Very well then, Ellis. We will have to find you a chair somewhere, seat you at my elbow. Now, let me start by showing you how to do the returns . . .'

∽◦∾

If there was any relief at all in seeing the gallows built, it was that they appeared to be doing it properly. The structure slowly rising on the parade ground seemed to consist of a proper platform, with a lever-operated trapdoor, such as Monsarrat had seen in Sydney. As Slattery was aware, there were horror stories around hangings gone wrong. Monsarrat had been spared the spectacle the private had seen, of somebody whose neck didn't break immediately, condemning them to a slow death by choking. He was also eternally grateful never to have seen the more grisly type of hanging – where the rope had not tightened properly, and the drop had torn the head from the body.

He was confident that the major would at least try to make it quick. For starters, Slattery was still well liked amongst his peers. Every one of them understood why what was happening needed to happen. But they didn't have to like it. Many of the men seemed to have a relationship with two separate Slatterys, railing against the one who was capable of killing the major's wife, while missing the banter of the other, the twinkling rogue.

Monsarrat knew he would not be able to escape viewing the hanging. This kind of punishment would never be carried out in secret – part of its value, in addition to ridding the world of the guilty party, was to demonstrate to others the necessity of good behaviour if they wanted to avoid a similar fate, so everyone was required to attend.

∽◦∾

Mrs Mulrooney was delighted for Monsarrat when he mentioned his ticket of leave. Despite the fact that he told her not to get her hopes up – it was a recommendation at this point, nothing more

– she had clasped his hand and done a little dance, twirling him around with as much abandon as the confines of the cramped kitchen would allow.

Then she said, 'Well, if you're going now, Monsarrat, I am definitely leaving. There really will be nothing for me here.'

Monsarrat had, in fact, started to wonder how much he could expect to make as a free man, whether he might be able to resume his employment with Mr Cruden or someone similar, and whether this would give him sufficient funds to employ a housekeeper. He had no doubt, though, that if Mrs Mulrooney became his servant, she would be the most intractable and disobedient one ever to bear that name.

But all of this was a consideration for another time, on the other side of the wall which divided a world with Slattery in it from one without. Still, as the days passed with no executioner, Monsarrat and Mrs Mulrooney were almost able to pretend their young friend would be with them for some time, and that they would simply have to go to a few more lengths to visit him than they previously had.

But that, of course, was a fantasy. After a few weeks of working with Monsarrat, Ellis had come into the workroom early one morning with his cravat slightly askew (Monsarrat would have to talk to him about the importance of precision in one's personal appearance as well as in one's handwriting), with the news that the *Mermaid* was even now attempting a crossing of Port Macquarie's treacherous bar.

Chapter 32

The *Mermaid* disgorged a fellow who was referred to as Jack Ketch. Monsarrat never found out his real name – his given one was common amongst executioners, a nod to a notorious hangman of decades past.

Ketch, or whoever he was, inspected the gallows – the sound of the construction of which could not have escaped Slattery's hearing – and found them to be adequate. He suggested the addition of a small wooden barrier at the front for the sake of the dignity of the prisoner and the sensibilities of the onlookers, protecting them from the sight of the lower half of Slattery's body. He spent about an hour closeted with the major, discussing how the business was to proceed, and showing him some nooses he had brought with him from Sydney. The tying of a noose was a delicate art, he said, as it needed to tighten just the right amount to ensure a merciful end. Despite his profession – or perhaps because of it – Ketch did not relish witnessing the outcome of a botched hanging.

He also sought information on Slattery's weight, and did his best to ensure the length of rope selected would break the connection between his brain and his body with the greatest possible efficiency.

That day, Monsarrat knew, the major visited Slattery for the first time, to inform him that the hanging would take place in the morning of the day after next. He told him he could request any visitor, any meal, and any amount of time with Father Hanley until he was taken from the cells to be hanged.

So that night Slattery, having put in a request for a quantity of rum from the stores – which Monsarrat had fetched via Spring – hosted a game of Three Card Brag with Meehan and some other old gambling mates of his, all of them uproariously drunk before an hour had passed.

The next morning, when Monsarrat looked in on him, Slattery said, 'If it was this morning instead of tomorrow morning, I'd not complain – hanging is preferable to the head I have at the moment.'

He then pressed some coins into Monsarrat's hand. 'Rum or not, I still did well at cards, although I expect some of them would have let me win even had I not been capable of doing it on my own. Would you do me a great service and give these to Mother Mulrooney after . . . Well, after.'

Monsarrat promised he would. And that night he saw Slattery again. For the soldier's last meal Mrs Mulrooney had requested some fresh pork – 'so much better than that salt beef stuff from the cask' – and roasted it together with some vegetables she herself had grown. Monsarrat contributed the meagre return from his own small garden, and with the major's approval requested a bottle of the better wine to be had here, which Spring again provided, grumbling that the stores of wine and spirits would soon be dry.

Monsarrat helped Mrs Mulrooney carry the food down to the gaol, together with proper china plates – 'I doubt he's eaten off anything except tin these past years,' she said. Once there, they spread a blanket over the river pebbles which made up the floor, and watched Slattery eat – Mrs Mulrooney had brought a setting for three, but neither she nor Monsarrat had much of a stomach. And unlike Slattery, they had at least a chance of a similar meal at some point in the future.

'I never asked you,' said Monsarrat as he watched Slattery eat, 'about that message on the plaster.'

Slattery smiled. 'Our day will come,' he said. 'My father used to mutter it sometimes, after his lordship had been by with a request for more money. His day never came. Nor will mine, now. Maybe your boy, Mother Mulrooney, will see his day come.'

'I like to think he has no need of a day, so to speak,' said Mrs Mulrooney. 'Everything to do with Ireland is a story to him, things I used to tell him when he was little. He hasn't been infected by the old hatreds, the ones that put you here, young man. And I hope he never will be.'

'They can kill you whether you're infected or not,' said Slattery. 'Dory, now . . . no hatred for anyone, that boy, not really. His day will never come, despite my promise to him just before the flogging – turned out to be the last promise anyone ever made to him.'

The dinner done, Mrs Mulrooney began to pack up the things. She was taking her time about it though. Slattery bent down and gently helped her, before putting his arm around her. 'Will you be there, tomorrow?' he asked. He didn't need to ask the same question of Monsarrat – he knew Monsarrat would be amongst those required to attend.

Mrs Mulrooney looked, suddenly, terribly anguished and tired. 'Do you want me to be, Fergal?'

'If you've a choice, now, I'd as soon you didn't. I want you to remember me with all my considerable charm. It's hard to be charming when you're in the process of dying, or so I've been told.'

Mrs Mulrooney nodded. 'I think that's best.'

And then the awareness settled on both of them – that this would be their final moment together.

'I would never have done it, you know, had I thought you would suffer for it, even for a moment,' said Slattery. 'You're as good a woman as I've ever met, for all your crankiness, and I could never have borne it here without you and your tea.'

'You take care, Fergal,' said Mrs Mulrooney, before catching herself. An exhortation to take care implied a man had a future. 'You concentrate on what Father Hanley tells you. Make sure you say all the prayers he asks for, go tomorrow in a state of grace, and then you and I might have a chance of seeing each other again.'

She started to cry then, and he folded her into a hug which nearly obscured her from Monsarrat's view. He patted her head, somewhat awkwardly. 'Don't you go putting tears and viler substances on my shirt. I need to look my best for tomorrow,' he said, his twinkle a little dimmed, matching her tears with his own.

She looked up at him. 'I love you, young eejit,' she said. She stood on her toes to kiss him on the cheek and then abruptly turned and left the room, leaving the dinner things behind her.

Monsarrat, who had been watching from the corner, cleared them up.

'You will be there of course, Monsarrat.'

'Yes, though I don't relish the prospect.'

'Even less do I,' said Slattery with that odd half-smile.

Monsarrat stood, setting the plates and other things aside on the wooden bench. 'Fergal, I am going to miss you. I wish with all my heart you had never done this, whatever your grievance. Life will be colder without you; there's no question. I need somebody occasionally to shake me out of my constraints. Without you, I remain in them forever.'

'Ah, you won't, Monsarrat. You've a bit more imagination than you give yourself credit for, even for a fooking Englishman.'

Monsarrat, because he knew it was expected of him, gave a courtly mock bow.

'You know,' said Slattery, 'I was allowed a visit from Bangar last week. He says they'll sing for me. To send me off, make a path for me to follow, when I no longer have eyes to see it or feet to tread it. It will help, I think, knowing that. I wonder, though, whether I could also ask you a great favour.'

'Of course, assuming it's not taking your place.'

Slattery smiled. 'I'd like something to fix on in the crowd tomorrow . . . something I can watch until – well, I'm going to ask if they will dispense with the hood, but I don't know whether they will. So I want somebody to watch, someone I know, until either the hood descends over my eyes or I drop.'

Slattery's voice began to crack at this point, but he recovered himself. 'I asked many a more handsome man than you, but they were all busy,' he said. 'Would you position yourself as close to the front of the crowd as you can? I'd be grateful to see you there.'

Monsarrat bowed again, and this time there was no levity in it. 'I'd be honoured,' he said.

⁓

The next day was cold and crisp, but with a beautiful blue sky, the kind this place seemed to churn out regardless of the season. Monsarrat was nearly at his workroom before he remembered that he would not be required there today. He had a different duty to perform.

He turned and headed for the parade ground. But on the way, he looked into the kitchen. It was empty. It was clear that breakfast had been prepared there, and recently too. The kettle was still warm from having been boiled, and hopefully it had behaved itself in the process or it would be the worse for it.

Monsarrat hoped Mrs Mulrooney had taken herself off for a walk, so as not to hear the shouts from the crowd that would accompany Fergal's execution. She was not the maudlin type, not the kind to go and dash herself on the black rocks, but nonetheless Monsarrat was uneasy. He would go and search her out as soon as possible after the business was done with, let her know that she didn't need to close her eyes anymore.

Slowly, then, he turned towards the parade ground. There was a considerable crush of people, far more than had been required to attend Dory's flogging – floggings had happened before and would again, after all, but this was the penal settlement's first hanging and deserved a decent showing.

Monsarrat had heard tales of notorious hangings at Tyburn near London, which had been a place of execution until shortly before his birth. The executions had been the focal point for a large amount of public merriment, with apprentices given the day off to go and look at the spectacle, and anyone who had something to sell fronting up to do business with anyone willing to buy.

The mood here, though, was not that of a carnival. Grim-faced Buffs lined the parade ground with shouldered muskets. Each man seemed perfectly and identically turned out, as if to demonstrate their rectitude and therefore unsuitability for the gallows. No one was chatting; there was no buzz of anticipation. Slattery had been well liked, even by those who had regularly lost money to him. And a great many of the convicts who had been there during the flogging of Dory, who had seen his intervention when Diamond seemed bent on flaying the young man to death, felt that there were others who deserved to be up there on the gallows in his place.

The major stood near the base of the gallows steps; Monsarrat too, shifting periodically to make sure he would be in Slattery's sightline. On the platform was the hangman, like a burned tree in his executioner's black.

The mass of people parted to form an avenue leading from the direction of the gaol. And now down it came Fergal Slattery, his hands tied, dressed in a white shirt and plain canvas trousers, with Father Hanley walking beside him. Monsarrat assumed that Slattery had used Hanley's services that morning to get himself into a state as close to grace as possible.

A few arms, both in red sleeves and slop canvas, reached out and a volley of hands patted Slattery's shoulders as he passed. He turned his head from side to side, smiling and winking, as though about to take the stage to perform a play.

When he reached the base of the steps, he nodded to Monsarrat and gave him a grateful smile. Then he turned to Father Hanley, who sliced the air with the edge of his hand in the shape of a cross, and intoned an absolution in a surprisingly deep and sonorous voice. '*Ego te absolvo ab omnibus peccatis tuis in nomine Patris, et Filii, et Spiritus Sancti*,' he said.

Monsarrat was amongst the few Protestants there who could have translated, if asked: 'I absolve you of all your sins in the name of the Father, the Son and the Holy Spirit.'

Slattery said his final amen, and mounted the steps of the gallows. At the top, he turned to face the crowd. 'I ask God, the major, and all here present to forgive me for my crime in taking the life of Mrs Shelborne. I have come to realise she was innocent of any wrong against me – not, though, her family. But as long as a nation of innocents labour under a yoke unfairly imposed on them, more of those without blame on both sides will find their graves too early. May God have mercy on my soul, such as it is.'

The assembled convicts had never, when in a group, been as silent as they were now; however, the occasional mouth tweaked slightly upwards at Slattery's last remark.

He walked over to the hangman, and nodded. The major had granted his request to dispense with the hood.

The hangman positioned Slattery under the arm of the gallows, tested the noose for the umpteenth time to ensure it would slide close around the man's neck at the appropriate moment, and placed it over his head. He then stepped back, and looked at the major, awaiting direction.

Slattery's eyes, meanwhile, were fixed on Monsarrat, who returned his gaze. He felt a huge weight of responsibility, realising that this was the last human connection Slattery would ever experience.

For a few seconds, the major did nothing, and Monsarrat with his eyes on Slattery entertained the impossible hope that there might be a last-minute reprieve. But then the major nodded to the hangman, who pulled the wooden lever on the platform. The door underneath Slattery's feet sprang open, and he dropped far enough so that only his upper body was visible behind the barrier.

Monsarrat kept his eyes fixed on the young soldier all the while, steeling himself for a seemingly endless series of twitches, jerks and convulsions. But the hangman had done his job well – Slattery did bounce slightly and convulse, and his mouth spread further than it ever had, into a gaping, rugged hole from which a gurgle emerged.

The stench which always accompanied a hanging began to waft in Monsarrat's direction, and he was grateful on Slattery's behalf for the barrier Jack Ketch had insisted on, so that the final products of Slattery's last meal could not be seen staining his trousers.

But now, Slattery was beyond caring. That awful gape remained in the centre of his face, but his eyes were no longer fixed on Monsarrat, or on anything.

In keeping with standard procedure, the thing that used to be Slattery was to be left dangling there for half an hour, to make absolutely certain that no traces of soul had stuck to his body.

The crowds began to be dispersed, being nudged by the Buffs back to their duties. Monsarrat turned to the major, whose face was as stiff as he'd ever seen it.

'Sir,' he said, 'may I beg leave to stay with him? Until he is cut down?'

The major nodded, without looking in Monsarrat's direction, and stalked off towards Government House.

So Monsarrat sat on the edge of the platform, close to the hole through which Slattery had fallen, and which resembled a similar hole back in Exeter which might have consumed him had the judge not commuted his sentence. He heard, from a distance, the sounds of a strange keening starting up, and wondered if it was Bangar's song, leading Slattery away. He did not look at what was now hanging from the rope. But he spoke, in his mind, to the boy who had been there until a few short minutes ago.

I hope the Lord accepted your apology, and that the priest's words worked their magic. I hope the hatred which destroyed you is no longer with you.

He tried to gather the words he would say to Mrs Mulrooney. It was good that she hadn't been there, but she would still want to know the truth of it.

And then, when the hangman cut down the body, he followed the major to Government House, his hands behind his back and his head tilted upwards, glaring at a sky which had no business being that blue.

Chapter 33

Monsarrat tried to numb himself with administrative detail, being curter than was perhaps warranted with the young and hapless Ellis, and then making up for it by praising the boy's handwriting, or his eye for detail.

The major spent most of the day absent from the study. Monsarrat and Ellis passed the time pulling together accounts of maize production, rum, cedar and rosewood, wheat, and the much-vaunted sugar cane. Monsarrat showed Ellis how to put these into a form which would please the Colonial Secretary, and impressed on him the importance of transcribing an appropriately obsequious signature – 'your obedient servant'.

At the dinner hour, he looked into the kitchen. Mrs Mulroony had returned, and looked up when he entered.

'Did he make a good end, do you think?' she said.

'He made the best of ends. You'd have been proud of him, although perhaps you might not have approved of some of the sentiments he expressed in his last moments,' said Monsarrat, and told her about Slattery's gallows statement.

She smiled, a little. 'He died as he lived, then. A fierce, bright and misguided boy.' Then her smile faded. 'You don't think,

Monsarrat, that I could have done more? Should I not have spotted the darkness in him, tried to drive it out?'

'To be honest, I think you did more than anyone to bring some light to him. But the damage was done a long time ago. I doubt there is anything you could have done, even had you realised what his true state of mind was. You should hold to yourself those words he spoke – you made his last time here bearable.'

He kissed her cheek and took his leave, back to the office to plunge into the emotionless pool of detail on the settlement's production.

He had thought the major might stay away the whole day, but as evening closed in, the man returned. Shelborne looked over Ellis's shoulder and nodded his approval at their efforts. He then dismissed Ellis and asked Monsarrat to come into his study.

Monsarrat still felt slightly uncomfortable sitting in the major's presence, but nevertheless was grateful for the chair which the major gestured him to. He began to perceive in himself a weariness which went far deeper than mere fatigue.

'Ellis seems to be picking up the necessary details?' asked the major.

'Yes, sir. If he had been trained in London he'd have made a first-rate clerk, but even so he has exceeded my expectations, and his script is improving daily.'

'Well, that is excellent news,' said the major.

'Sir, may I ask you – if the application for my ticket is rejected, do you intend to deploy me elsewhere?'

'Well, had you said that Ellis would not make a half-decent clerk, I would have kept this information from you,' said the major, smiling, 'but the ship which brought the executioner also brought a letter from the Colonial Secretary. The governor has approved your ticket, which I have here. Congratulations, Monsarrat. And thank you, truly, for your service.'

It was the news for which Monsarrat had been hoping, but now that it had come he could only gape in amazement, fearful that it was a mirage which would disappear when he tried to reach out for it.

But the ticket was real enough, as he saw when the major passed it over to him. And he was overjoyed to see no district inscribed on the section of the document where the word Windsor had once stood.

His mind raced ahead, galloping over the seas which harried the coast, and up the river to Parramatta. He would find Sophia Stark, and hope that she might throw over whichever man was currently enjoying her company. He supposed he would take up again at the Caledonia Inn to start with, until he was able to get a steady position. Poor souls were being disgorged from boats by the day, and most of them had at least one person to whom they wished to express love, regret, desperation, or just awe at the new surroundings.

He wondered if he could convince Mrs Mulrooney to come with him. Perhaps he might call on Magistrate Cruden. He held out few hopes of being able to resume his former position, and the boys would be too old to have need of a tutor now, anyway. But who knew whether the magistrate's Irish housekeeper was still in place, or whether he might have room for somebody to perform the official parts of her duties. At the very least he might know of somebody around Parramatta, and he resolved to ask the major for a reference as to Mrs Mulrooney's good character.

'I must warn you, though, Monsarrat, that this ticket comes with conditions,' the major said.

Shadow Monsarrat began to stir again, then. Whispering rebellious thoughts. Saying, Here they go again, giving you freedom and then proscribing it so that it's not worthy of the name.

But all he said was, 'Conditions, sir?'

'Yes,' smiled the major, though Monsarrat could not think for a moment what was prompting such glee. 'Your story, it seems, has rather captured the imagination of some in Parramatta. There is a degree of admiration for your part in identifying Private Slattery as my wife's killer, and in prompting him to come forward.'

Monsarrat had, in the past, taken credit for insights which had really emanated from Mrs Mulrooney. He urged himself, now, to explain her part in identifying Slattery, to praise her perspicacity. But he remained silent.

'So, it seems your thoroughness impressed a certain member of the governor's Parramatta staff. A Mr Ralph Eveleigh, the governor's secretary there, is in need of a clerk. One with legal understanding – however acquired – who can be called on to manage more delicate matters as they arise.'

Monsarrat knew he was gaping, but the muscles in his face seemed to have stopped working. And even as life returned to them, they were struck numb again when the Major mentioned the handsome figure Monsarrat was to be paid for performing this service. His first thought was, It's more than enough to employ a housekeeper.

The major stood and extended his hand. 'May I be the first to shake your hand as a free man,' he said, still smiling. 'You're to report to Parramatta by the end of next month. I hope I may rely on your services until then.'

Monsarrat shook the proffered hand. 'Thank you, sir. I can't begin to thank you enough, especially as I'm about to ask you yet another indulgence.'

The major raised an eyebrow and waited.

'As you know, Mrs Mulrooney has been severely distressed both by the death of your wife, and by the execution of Private Slattery. I fear for her should she remain here, particularly without me. I will understand if you do not feel this is appropriate, but may I beg you to release her from your service, so that I may employ her?'

'I was actually going to suggest something similar,' said the major. 'I don't think there's anything left for her here, and to be honest seeing her reminds me of everything that's gone by these past months. I would be grateful if you were able to offer her a position.'

And then the major sat again, the smile well and truly gone, and reached into a drawer of his desk. He pulled out a piece of paper sealed with wax; thick and luxurious paper of the type Monsarrat had rarely seen since leaving Sydney.

'And here is another reminder of what I've lost,' said the major. 'I found this in Honora's papers recently. You'll note that it's addressed to you, and you'll also note the seal is broken – I make no apology for reading it.'

'Nor would I expect one,' said Monsarrat. He was astonished that Honora would have written to him, for any purpose. But as he opened the paper, with a date which showed it had been written as Honora's illness was worsening, he began to understand.

My dear Mr Monsarrat,

I hope you'll forgive my hand, which is not as steady as it once was, although I do expect it will recover its strength in due course.

I know that you understand the value that I place on education, and that you share my interest in seeing that this blessing is spread as widely as possible.

There is a request I have been meaning to make of you. I find myself unable to do so in person at present, and I'm unsure how long I will be in this condition. But as I would very much like you to act on this request with all speed, I wanted to ensure you were aware of it as soon as possible.

You and I share an admiration of Hannah Mulrooney, and I know that I do not need to tell you that I believe she has an uncommon intelligence. It is shameful that she has not been able to use this intelligence to its full extent, being without letters.

But while education is of crucial importance to the young, I believe the old can benefit from it as well. To that end, I would like to beseech you to teach Mrs Mulrooney her letters. I believe the world can only benefit from the addition of a literate woman.

I trust you are continuing to work on the talk on Sisyphus and Icarus, which I hope to be in a condition to give before too long. May I request that you hold a draft in readiness for my perusal on my recovery.

Yours sincerely,

Honora Belgrave Shelborne

Monsarrat did not know whether this was the last letter Mrs Shelborne wrote, and whether her husband had found a message for himself amongst her papers. It was a question he would never ask. But if not the last, it was certainly close to it – the letter's date told him that it had been written days before she slipped into a state of semiconsciousness. And he intended to honour her wishes to the fullest extent – knowing all the while that Mrs Mulrooney was unlikely to take his tutelage quietly.

The major had obviously had a similar thought. 'Well, Monsarrat, I wish you the very best of luck in convincing your housekeeper to submit to your teachings,' he said.

He looked directly at Monsarrat. 'I would like you to do me this favour. I speak of my bemusement at and fascination with your condition. Perhaps I am in the minority, but I don't believe in a criminal class, in people born with deformed characters which incline them to offend. But some, like you, have offended. Often to survive, but that was not the case in your instance. I wish to know what drove you here, Monsarrat. I have a notion that understanding that might help me understand a great deal else.'

A decade of penal servitude had taught Monsarrat the dangers of answering before framing measured sentences in his head. After a few moments, he said, 'One cannot argue with a sentence. It must be endured in the hope of redemption.'

'Please, don't hedge with me, Monsarrat. I asked the question because I have never known quite so closely, and yet at the same time not known, a man in your position. In your mind, did you deserve your sentence of transportation? And similarly, what of your second sentence?' The man's eyes were still on him, frank and lacking in artifice or malice.

'I fear that if I began to speak, I might offend you, sir.'

'I fear that if you do not begin to speak, I will know less than I should about the world, and particularly about this netherworld here. Do you feel, tell me, that there is something essentially criminal in you?'

'Very well,' said Monsarrat, returning the commandant's gaze. 'You must understand that the greatest criminals do not know that they are criminals and will not admit it. If I were to explain my founding crime, impersonating an officer of the court, I could say that there was as much yearning as any intent to do harm in it. For it is a terrible thing to have a mind for a particular profession and, despite one's best intentions, to be thwarted in the study and pursuit of it. It would be a wonderful world if all who had the talent, and I dare say I did have the talent, were given the means to pursue the desired destiny – the honour of a profession. That was what I yearned for, a licence to practise my own intelligence. And what a day it would be if everyone were able to pursue their talents to whatever limits society permitted them.'

'Alas,' said the commandant, 'you speak of utopia.'

'I fear I do, sir. In any case I shall not see the day. There is a price to be paid under the present system. It is a harsh price, and it has embittered me. But it is the way of the world and must be borne.'

'Indeed, my dear fellow,' said the commandant. 'I am sad nonetheless that you must bear it to the limits. With a commuted death sentence, you will never be allowed to leave New South Wales for Britain or Ireland. I am sorry.'

'I feel an equal sorrow for you, sir. For the loss of your angel.'

'Indeed, indeed. But now, what of your colonial sentence? Again, speak freely.'

A second, and then Monsarrat did. 'When I first acquired a ticket of leave, the malice of a particular man ensured that it would be restricted to a district, unlike the tickets of many other convicts which allow them to move freely about the colony. I was stupid enough to leave my district, and a second sentence was imposed. And that was purely technical, I thought – and think to this day. That a man should be punished for leaving his district, if he is unlucky enough to be limited to one, is just, but that he should be sentenced to three more years of servitude is far too severe and does not encourage the reformation of our characters.'

Monsarrat was now alarmed at himself.

'I am pleased that you were here, of course,' said the commandant. 'But I understand fully that it was not a joyful eventuality for you. I will try to take a personal interest to save you from magistrates narrow and punitive in their views. It is good to hear the honest feelings of a transportee. In New South Wales convicts dare not tell the truth to those above them. I feel that is part of the colonial malaise. Thank you, Monsarrat. But do be careful.'

Then he stood again and said, 'I think that's all for today. You may let Ellis take greater responsibility, day by day, over the next few weeks. In the meantime, you're relieved of your duties until tomorrow morning. I believe you have a situation to offer.'

Chapter 34

Monsarrat went back to the kitchen. In his exhilaration, he pushed the door open with all the force that had once been applied to it by Private Slattery, and immediately regretted it. The sound of the door banging so violently made Mrs Mulrooney look up hopefully for a second, before she registered the identity of the person in the doorway.

Nevertheless, she managed to smile. 'The fact that you're charging around like some sort of demented young colt leads me to deduce that a certain ticket of leave has arrived,' she said.

'Indeed it has. And a situation of employment with it. I am to report to Parramatta, to the Governor's office, by next month.'

He must've been grinning like a loon, he realised, because Mrs Mulrooney was looking at him as though the last threads holding his sanity together had snapped – and perhaps they had.

Then the despondency reasserted itself. 'I am delighted for you,' she said. 'This is richly deserved. But I will miss you, and I make no secret of it. I doubt I'll be here long anyway, one way or the other.'

Monsarrat did not like the sound of that last statement. 'Well, you may be right. It turns out I'll be able to rent a reasonable house when I return to Parramatta. And of course, I'll need a housekeeper. But I would absolutely understand if you didn't feel able to work for a former felon such as myself . . .'

Mrs Mulrooney was suddenly grinning. She got up, and he thought that she was about to embrace him. Then she stopped. 'Quality servants cost money, you know,' she said, and named the salary she expected.

Monsarrat knew it was more than she was earning here, and did not begrudge her one penny of it. 'There is one condition on your employment, however,' he said. 'Two, actually. One is that you continue to make the tea you've been making for me all these years.'

Mrs Mulrooney snorted, offended at the suggestion that she would do otherwise. 'And?' she said.

'And, I am to be not only your employer but also your tutor. I am to teach you to read.'

Mrs Mulrooney came towards him again, but this time it was with the tread of a hunter stalking a deer. She moved around behind him, gestured him to a chair, and when he sat, took her cleaning cloth from the waistband of her skirt and flicked him with a surprising degree of force in the temple.

❧

September could still occasionally be a little chilly in the settlement, but the worst of it was over, and the rains had receded, lurking beyond the horizon to return at the height of summer, as they had a habit of doing.

But, Monsarrat thought, they would have to find someone else to fall on. He had swept out and cleaned his little hut as best he could, knowing it would become Ellis's home. He had even convinced Spring to give him some tar, with which he tried to stop up the holes through which the chilly draughts gained access.

Mrs Mulrooney had been making similar preparations in the kitchen, making sure everything was in place, impressing on Margaret McGreevy the importance of proper tea-making procedure, telling her that this skillet or that kettle needed to be watched at all times, and warning her about the misbehaviour of the fire.

She had put her meagre possessions in a small crate some days earlier. Monsarrat took with him only his spare waistcoat (which had been his main waistcoat, until it acquired a permanent red smear thanks to his run-in with Diamond), his sleeping shirt, and his ticket of leave, which never left his person. In one of the voluminous pockets of his black coat, however, nestled a volume of Catullus in the original Latin, a parting gift from the major, who also allowed him to take his ink pot and pens. 'I would as soon allow you to leave without your arms and legs, as to leave without these,' he'd said.

The major was, in fact, at the riverside now, chatting to the harbourmaster, as the *Sally* made ready to depart at the high tide, giving her the best chance of travelling safely over the lurking bar.

Monsarrat was delighted when he learned that it would be the *Sally* which would convey him to Sydney, the same vessel which had brought him here, and he would have its genial mate Mr Tyrell to while away the time with on the voyage. The winds were still favourable, Tyrell had told him the night before, so if they continued to cooperate, the journey to Sydney should be an easy one.

Mrs Mulrooney curtseyed to the major before she got on the ship, and he clasped her hand and thanked her for her care of his wife. He apologised, again, for her incarceration.

'Ah, enough of that now,' she said. 'Had I not known I was innocent, I would have thought me guilty too.'

Then it was Monsarrat's turn to board, which he expected to do with a great deal more ease than Mrs Mulrooney, having far longer legs with which to accomplish the task.

The major again shook his hand. 'I wish you the very best in Parramatta, Monsarrat, I really do. I have been well served by you in the past two years, and I know you'll apply the same industry to your work with the Governor's secretary.'

'I would not be making this journey if not for you, sir,' said Monsarrat. 'And I will not forget it. If I am ever in a position to do you any service at all, rest assured it will be done.'

The major nodded, and gestured Monsarrat onto the ship. They crossed the bar without incident, and were soon sliding past Lady

Nelson Beach and her cousins, with their sands pierced by black dragon's teeth. The three brothers seemed to be watching the small boat, and Monsarrat wondered whether they wanted to ensure it bore him away, or were plotting to prevent him from leaving.

Mrs Mulrooney didn't like the ocean – of all untrustworthy things, it was top in her view – so she had immediately made her way below decks in an attempt to pretend that she was anywhere but on a boat.

Monsarrat sought her out. 'Shall we get started?' he said.

'Started on what, you great streak of a man?' she said. Her mood was not being helped by the motion of the boat.

'Well, you are to learn to read. The sooner the better, I feel.'

'Well, I happen to feel differently,' she said. 'As if a soul could concentrate on anything with this infernal rocking. I refuse to even consider it until we are well away from the ocean, with no prospect of returning to it in the foreseeable future.'

'Mrs Mulrooney, really, that is certainly not an appropriate way to address your employer,' said Monsarrat.

'Don't think that just because you're paying me a pittance for my considerable services, I'm going to suddenly start bobbing and curtseying. Nothing will change, Mr Monsarrat – I give you my word.'

'No, I believe it won't,' said Monsarrat, ducking out of range of the cloth which she reached for now, having forgotten to remove it from her waistband before boarding the ship. 'And that, I can assure you, is what I'm relying on.'

Authors' Note

The Soldier's Curse is a work of fiction. Its main characters never existed, and only three minor characters – William Branch (junior), Margaret McGreevy and Richard Neave – bear the names of people who actually resided in Port Macquarie at the time this book is set. Apart from these, only governors Lachlan Macquarie and Thomas Brisbane, referred to briefly, existed in the real world.

Having said that, many aspects of our story draw on historical fact. For those who are interested, we'd like to describe the people, places and events rooted in actual history, those which have been wholly invented, and those which inhabit the blurred border between fact and fiction.

Port Macquarie Penal Settlement

The site which became Port Macquarie was discovered in 1818 (from a European perspective – the Birpai had discovered it many generations earlier).

In September 1818 Surveyor General John Oxley, on an expedition to the unexplored north, came upon the valley through which flowed the river that he would name the Hastings, in honour of the man he believed was still the governor of India (he had actually died some months previously).

Had Oxley gone a little further north, by the way, he would have discovered the Macleay River, the inspiration for the river Major Shelborne searches for in the book. The combination of fine farmland and a landscape that could keep people hemmed in made the site – the future Port Macquarie – ideal, in Oxley's view, for a penal settlement. Governor Lachlan Macquarie agreed, and a penal station for second offenders was founded there in 1821. At the time this book is set, the place housed 1500 people – convicts, soldiers and civil officers – only a handful of whom were women.

The layout for Port Macquarie used in this book is based on an 1826 map. The buildings mentioned are shown on this map or drawn from other sources. The footings of the overseers' cottages (where William Branch and his son, William Junior, lived) are still visible beneath the Port Macquarie Glasshouse. The skeleton of a dog, found during excavation, can also be seen.

The description and layout of Government House comes from the 'Port Macquarie Former Government House Ruins Conservation Management Plan'. There is now an apartment building where Government House once stood, on modern-day Clarence Street, and visitors can enter its foyer and look at the building's footings (discovered during construction) through a glass panel in the floor.

Near Government House, St Thomas's church was indeed being built in 1825, of convict-made bricks bound together by mortar in which you can still see flecks of oyster shell, extracted by the lime-burners at such a great price. It stands near the dispensary and the site on which the hospital once rested.

Port Macquarie is now a thriving seaside town and holiday destination, a few hours' drive north of Sydney. Lady Nelson Beach now goes by the name of Town Beach, and Shoal Arm Creek is now Kooloonbung Creek.

Fact and fiction
Hugh Llewellyn Monsarrat and Hannah Mulrooney, of course, exist only in these pages. The inspiration for Monsarrat came, however, from a real gentleman convict, James Tucker, a clerk

sentenced to transportation for sending a threatening letter. He arrived in Sydney in 1827 (per *Midas*). He lost his first and second tickets of leave for drunkenness (of which Monsarrat would not have approved) and forgery, and spent some time in Port Macquarie, where he is believed to have written one of Australia's first novels, *Ralph Rashleigh*, chronicling the misadventures of a fictional convict.

While researching this book we encountered another man, Charles Desroches, who bore a passing resemblance to Monsarrat. Sentenced to Port Macquarie for 'running away and committing various forgeries', his work as a clerk between 1824 and 1828 won him admiration from various commandants, with Commandant F. C. Crotty writing to Governor Ralph Darling of 'the great utility of prisoner Charles Desroches'.

Desroches shared Monsarrat's yearning for freedom. In 1828 he, too, wrote to Governor Darling: 'I am apprehensive ... that when returning to headquarters I shall never obtain the object for which I have so long toiled – a Ticket of Leave. Having been allowed to live separate from the rest of the prisoners, I cannot conceal the dread I feel at being herded with them at the Hulk and the Barracks.'

Hannah Mulrooney is a complete fabrication (as are Fergal Slattery, Honora Shelborne, Michael Diamond, Father Hanley and a great many others). Those who did her work at Government House in real life would have been convicts, as the only free women at the settlement were wives and daughters of officials, or of men serving sentences.

The spot which would have been Honora's burial place is across the aisle from a real grave at St Thomas's, that of Commandant John Rolland (after whom Rolland's Plains is named), who died in December 1824. He was buried on the building site, and the church was constructed over him.

Honora's husband, Major Angus Shelborne, owes his character to two progressive and humane (for the period) Port Macquarie commandants, Captain Francis Allman and Major Archibald Clunes Innes. The major's real-life chronological counterpart,

Captain Henry Gillman, may have been a somewhat darker individual. Michael Diamond's advances towards the daughter of a convict were based on actions attributed to Gillman. Shelborne and Gillman do share one aspect, though – Shelborne's dispute with Reverend Ainslie is based on a similar disagreement between Gillman and Reverend Thomas Hassall.

There was never a hanging in Port Macquarie (capital crimes were dealt with in Sydney), but there would have been had Gillman had his way. In April 1825, he wrote to the Colonial Secretary for permission to execute a convict, Patrick Malone, who had struck prisoner William Elliott on the head with an axe when Elliott claimed he had none of the tobacco Malone wanted. Malone had also made an escape attempt, and cut off the fingers of a fellow escapee.

In a hand which might have made Monsarrat jealous, Gillman's clerk transcribed the following words for the commandant's signature: 'Patrick Malone, a Respite on this Settlement, by his Conduct has rendered himself so notorious that as a warning, particularly to the refractory and ill-disposed part of the Prisoners here, I find myself under the disagreeable necessity of suggesting for the Consideration of His Excellency The Governor, that he may suffer immediate Execution.' His request was ultimately denied, and Malone was sent to Sydney, where he was tried, convicted and hanged.

The Port Macquarie Female Factory was closed, as described in this book, because of concerns for the health of the few women confined there, and a desire to make more efficient use of the building. In this book, however, the factory is closed earlier than it actually was, in October 1825.

All the vessels in the novel bear the names of ships that actually visited Port Macquarie during the period (although the *Sally*, a frequent visitor, was wrecked in April 1825). The escape of eight convicts on the *Isabella* actually occurred (in October 1824), and the commandant of the day, John Rolland, ordered the vessel fired on, without success. Rolland told the soldiers they had done their best, as Major Shelborne does in the book.

The Birpai

The relationship between the Birpai and those who invaded their territory was complex. There is a strong oral tradition surrounding a massacre of 300 Birpai at Blackman's Point in 1841. Prior to this, it seems there was also tension between cedar-cutting parties and the Birpai. In his book *Baal Belbora: The End of the Dancing*, Geoffrey Blomfield notes: '. . . conflict followed the arrival of the cedar cutter . . . it seems likely . . . that the cause of hostility was due to a breach of good conduct by the cedar cutters'.

But the Birpai were a peaceable people, and of considerable help to the interlopers. As described in this story, they provided assistance in returning escapees, and also saved convicts from drowning when boats overturned.

Major Archibald Innes wrote of the Birpai: 'I consider the natives to be very friendly. Numerous tribes for sixty miles round constantly visit us and, in my opinion, security and prevention of desertion of the prisoners is greatly to be attributed to the natives who generally apprehend them a short time after they are at large.'

Geoffrey Blomfield reports that the Birpai also befriended commissariat clerk George Macdonald, who resembled a dead tribesman called Bangar (whose name has been used in this book).

The story of the three brothers, as related here, comes from Uncle Bill O'Brien of the Birpai Local Aboriginal Land Council, who attributes it to the oral testimony of Aunty Marion Hampton.

Arsenic

There are no cases, as far as we are aware, of Scheele's Green, the copper arsenic pigment in Honora Shelborne's wallpaper, being used in a murder. But other substances impregnated with arsenic certainly were. In 1911, insurance company administrator Frederick Seddon poisoned his boarder, Eliza Barrow, with arsenic derived from soaking flypaper in water. Like Honora, she took some weeks to die.

But while it may not have been used to murder, Scheele's Green certainly killed people, although concerns about it were not raised until the 1830s, so its dangers would have been unknown at the time this book is set.

There was a popular theory that Napoleon died of arsenic poisoning due to the green paper in his bedroom in exile on St Helena. This theory has since been discounted.

By 1830, one million rolls of wallpaper were printed annually in the UK, with later tests finding four out of five samples contained arsenic. The article 'Deadly Décor: A Short History of Arsenic Poisoning in the Nineteenth Century' by Jessica Charlotte Haslam in *Res Medica* provides a fascinating insight into the discovery of the toxic properties of the pigment.

German chemist Leopold Gmelin raised concerns about the pigment, noting that damp walls covered in green paper gave off a mouse-like smell, and suggesting the vapour could be an arsenic compound. Gmelin was the first, in 1839, to warn against applying papers containing Scheele's Green.

Four children in London's Limehouse district died in a room papered with Scheele's Green. And in the mid-1850s, physician William Hinds noted that he suffered nausea, abdominal pains and light-headedness in his green-walled study. He had samples of the paper tested and found they contained arsenic. The paper was removed and the symptoms vanished. Haslam reports Hinds wrote that 'a great deal of slow poisoning is going on in Great Britain'.

The article Monsarrat reads draws on these and other cases reported by Haslam.

Acknowledgements

We're indebted to the following people, who made this book possible: Judy, our beloved and insightful first reader; Craig, for his love and support; Rory and Alex, for being so patient and understanding when their mother was appropriated by Monsarrat and Mulrooney. 'Mum's gone to 1825 again,' was a frequent comment during the writing of this book. Fiona Inglis and all at Curtis Brown Australia, for their passionate commitment to the project. Meredith Curnow and the team at Random House Australia, for their belief in this book. Stephanie Henzlik, for her friendship and for taking the time to read the draft.

We're also very grateful to those who generously shared their expertise: Debbie Sommers and the volunteers of the Port Macquarie Historical Society; Mitch McKay of Port Macquarie Hastings Heritage; Janet Cohen of the Sea Acres Rainforest Centre.

Select Bibliography

For those interested, we found the following references extremely helpful in the writing of this book:

Baal Belbora: The End of the Dancing, Geoffrey Blomfield, APCOL

Dancing with Strangers, Inga Clendinnen, Text Publishing

'Deadly Décor: A Short History of Arsenic Poisoning in the Nineteenth Century', Jessica Charlotte Haslam, *Res Medica: Journal of the Royal Medical Society*, Volume 21, Issue 1

Female Skeletons in the Cupboard: Stories of Convict Women at Port Macquarie, Gwen Griffin, Port Macquarie Historical Society

Place of Banishment: Port Macquarie 1818–1832, Iaen McLachlan, Hale & Iremonger

Port Macquarie: A History to 1850, Frank Rogers (ed.), Port Macquarie Historical Society

'Port Macquarie: Former Government House Ruins Conservation Management Plan', Rosemary Annable, Margaret Betteridge, Christopher Marks and Colleen Morris, prepared for the New South Wales Heritage Office, March 2003

Port Macquarie, the Windingsheet, Gwendoline Griffin and Ronald Howell, Port Macquarie Historical Society

The Colony, Grace Karskens, Allen & Unwin

The Inheritor's Powder, Sandra Hempel, W. W. Norton